Praise for the Alex Craft Novels

Grave Visions

"*Grave Visions* has been a long-waited-for read and it certainly delivers."   —A Great Read

"If you love urban fantasy, DO NOT miss out on this series."   —Kings River Life Magazine

Grave Memory

"I hope there will be many more books to follow."   —Fresh Fiction

"A truly original and compelling urban fantasy series."   —*RT Book Reviews*

"An incredible urban fantasy . . . This is a series I love."   —Nocturne Romance Reads

"An action-packed roller-coaster ride . . . An absolute must-read!"   —A Book Obsession

Grave Dance

"A dense and vibrant tour de force."   —All Things Urban Fantasy

"An enticing mix of humor and paranormal thrills."   —Fresh Fiction

continued . . .

The Alex Craft Novels

Grave Witch
Grave Dance
Grave Memory
Grave Visions

Grave Ransom

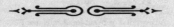

AN ALEX CRAFT NOVEL

KALAYNA PRICE

ACE
New York

ACE
Published by Berkley
An imprint of Penguin Random House LLC
375 Hudson Street, New York, New York 10014

Copyright © 2017 by Kalayna Smithwick
Penguin Random House supports copyright. Copyright fuels creativity, encourages
diverse voices, promotes free speech, and creates a vibrant culture. Thank you for buying
an authorized edition of this book and for complying with copyright laws by not
reproducing, scanning, or distributing any part of it in any form without permission.
You are supporting writers and allowing Penguin Random House to continue to
publish books for every reader.

ACE is a registered trademark and the A colophon is a trademark
of Penguin Random House LLC.

ISBN: 9780451416582

First Edition: July 2017

Printed in the United States of America
1 3 5 7 9 10 8 6 4 2

Cover art by Aleta Rafton

To Dad,
who sparked my love of fantasy fiction
at a young age and who read all my books.
I miss you.

Grave Ransom

Chapter 1

The first time I realized I could feel corpses, I had nightmares for a week. I was a child at the time, so that was understandable. These days I was accustomed to the clammy reach of the grave that lifted from dead bodies. To the eerie feeling of my own innate magic responding and filling me with the unrequested knowledge of how recently the person died, their gender, and the approximate age they were at death. When I anticipated encountering a corpse, I tightened my mental shields and worked at keeping my magic at bay. Usually that was only necessary at places like graveyards, the morgue, and funeral homes—places one might expect to find a body.

I never expected to feel a corpse walking across the street in the middle of the Magic Quarter.

"Alex? I've lost you, haven't I?" Tamara, one of my best friends and my current lunchmate, asked. She sighed, twisting in her seat to scan the sidewalk beyond the small outdoor sitting area of the café where we were eating. "Huh. Which one is he? I may be married and knocked up, but I know a good-looking man when I see one, and, and, girl, I *don't* see one. Who are you staring at?"

"That guy," I said, nodding my head at a man in a brown suit crossing the street.

Tamara glanced at the squat, middle-aged man who was more than a little soft in the middle and then cocked an eyebrow at me. "I've seen what you have at home, so I take it this is business. Did you bring one of your cases to our lunch?"

I ignored the "at home" comment, as that situation was more than a little complicated, and shook my head. "My case docket is clear," I said absently, and let my senses stretch. When I concentrated, I could feel grave essence reaching from corpses in my vicinity. All corpses. There were decades of dead and decaying rats in the sewer below the streets, and smaller creatures like insects that barely made a blip on my radar, but like called to like, and my magic zeroed in on the man.

"He's dead," I said, and even to me my voice sounded unsure.

Tamara blinked at me, likely waiting for me to reveal the joke. Instead I pushed out of my seat as the man turned up the street. Tamara grabbed my arm.

"I'm the lead medical examiner for Nekros City, and I can tell you with ninety-nine point nine percent certainty that the man *walking* down the street is very much alive." She put extra emphasis on the word "walking," and on any other day, I would have agreed with her.

My own eyes agreed with her. But my magic, the part of me that touched the grave, that could piece together shades from the memories left in every cell of a body, disagreed. That man, walking or not, was a corpse. Granted, he was a fresh one—the way he felt to my magic told me he couldn't have been dead more than an hour. But he was dead.

So how the hell had he just walked into the Museum of Magic and the Arcane?

I dropped enough crumpled dollars on the table to cover my portion of the bill and tip before weaving around tables and out of the café seating. Behind me, Tamara grumbled under her breath, but after a moment I heard her chair slide back as she pushed away from the table. I didn't wait for her to follow me out as I all but sprinted across the street to catch up with the walking corpse.

The museum's wards tingled along my skin as I stepped through the threshold. I'd been inside the museum a few times, and the collection of rare and unusual artifacts from both pre- and post-awakening was impressive, but I was a sensitive, capable of sensing magic, and between all the security wards and the artifacts themselves, the museum tended to be overwhelming. Definitely migraine-inducing in large doses. I noted that the magic in the air was particularly biting today, like one of the security wards had recently been triggered. I sucked in an almost pained breath, trying to adjust to the sudden crush of magic all around me. The extra sting of the deployed ward didn't help.

I should have walked the extra few steps to clear the entrance wards.

I'd entered only minutes behind the man, but he almost barreled into me as the door swung closed behind me. His shoulder brushed me at the same moment he hit the antitheft wards, and several things happened

at once. The wards snapped to life, blaring a warning
to the museum staff to let them know something was
being stolen. Simultaneously, a theft-deterring paralytic
spell sparked across the would-be thief, locking his
body—and the artifact—in place.

Unfortunately, while the wards were powerful,
they weren't terribly specific. Where his shoulder
touched mine, the spell jumped from him to me, im-
mobilizing me as well. Under normal circumstances,
that would majorly suck. Under these circumstances?
It was so much worse.

My magic still identified him as a corpse. I could feel
the grave essence lifting off him, clawing at me. My
mental shields, while strong, were already overwhelmed,
and my magic *liked* dead things. A lot. I hadn't raised
a shade in nearly a week, so the magic was looking for
release. Typically I made a point not to touch the dead.
Now I couldn't get away.

My magic battered against the inside of my shields,
looking for chinks in my mental walls that it could jump
through. Fighting the spell holding me was a waste of
energy—I was well and truly caught—so I focused all
of my attention on holding back my own magic. But I
could feel the chilled fingers of the grave sliding under
my skin, worming their way into me and making paths
for my magic to leach into the animated corpse frozen
against me.

I wanted to open my shields and *See* what the thing
in front of me was truly made of. But if I cracked my
shields to gaze across the planes of reality and get a
good look at the body, more of my magic would escape.
And too much was already whispering through my
shields, making fissures where more could follow. Sweat

broke out on my paralyzed brow as I poured my focus into holding my magic at bay.

But I was touching a corpse.

The grave essence leaking from the body clawed at the fissures my magic was chewing through my shields, and it was too much. If I could have stepped back . . . But I couldn't.

All at once a chunk of my mental wall caved, and the magic rushed out of me. Color washed over the world as the Aetheric plane snapped into focus around me. A wind lifted from the land of the dead, stirring my curls and chilling my clammy skin. I could now see the network of magic holding me in place, as well as the knot of magic in the sprung ward, but more importantly, I could see the corpse in front of me. And it was a corpse, no doubt about it, the dead skin sagging, bloating.

But under the dead flesh, a yellow glimmer of a soul glowed.

Which meant the body was both dead and alive. Considering it was up and walking around, it was a heck of a lot more alive than a dead body should have been.

The soul inside was the color I associated with humans, so this wasn't a corpse being worn and walked around by something from Faerie or one of the other planes. I still couldn't see spellwork shimmering across the dead flesh, but it had to be there, binding the soul inside the corpse. But whatever kind of half-life the man existed in wasn't going to last much longer if I couldn't get hold of my magic.

The hole in my shields wasn't huge, but I could feel my magic filling the body. And the grave and souls didn't get along. I couldn't stop the hemorrhage of magic, but I managed to slow it to a trickle.

I'd barely noticed the crowd gathering around us until one of the museum guards began releasing the spell holding us. If the antitheft paralyzing spell was dropped, I'd be able to get my distance from the corpse.

But either he wasn't a very good witch, or he was stalling—likely to wait for the cops—because he was taking his sweet time as more and more of my magic flowed out.

I'd ejected souls from dead bodies before. While souls didn't like the touch of the grave, they tended to cling to their flesh pretty hard and it took directed magic to pry them free. I was actively fighting expelling the soul, and only a small portion of my magic had filled the corpse, but the soul's connection to the body felt weak, tentative.

I couldn't shift my gaze to the museum worker, but I could see him out of the corner of my eye. *Oh please, release the damn immobility spell.*

Too late.

In a burst of light, the soul popped free of the corpse.

Nothing about the body changed. It had already been dead and it was still held immobile by the spell, but the soul stood free. For a long moment it was almost too bright to look at, a shimmering, crystalline yellow. But souls can't exist without a body, and in a heartbeat the glow dimmed, the form solidifying as the soul transitioned to the purgatory landscape of the land of the dead.

If I could have stumbled back in shock, I would have, but I couldn't even blink in surprise. Not because the soul transitioned—that I expected—but because the ghost now standing in front of me was that of a young woman.

My focus shifted from the balding, middle-aged man to the woman who might not have been old enough to drink. Ghosts weren't like shades. While shades were always an exact representation of the person at the moment of death, ghosts tended to reflect how a person perceived himself. Appearing a little younger or more attractive was common. I supposed it was even possible that if someone identified across gender lines, their ghost might reflect that discrepancy. But this ghost was a drastically different age as well as being a different gender and ethnicity. And that was unheard of.

The ghost-girl looked around, no longer inhibited by the spell holding the body she'd been inside. Her dark eyes rounded as her eyebrows flew upward and her motions took on the frantic quickness of panic.

A panic that didn't last long as a figure appeared beside her. He was dressed from head to toe in gray and carrying a silver skull-topped cane. The Gray Man. A soul collector.

I wanted to scream *No*. To run between him and the girl who clearly hadn't belonged in the dead body. Things didn't add up here, and I wanted to talk to the ghost.

But I still couldn't move.

I stood silently frozen in place as the Gray Man reached out, grabbed the soul, and sent her on to wherever souls went next. Then he turned and looked at the body she'd vacated. His expression gave away nothing as his gaze moved on to me. He gave me one stern shake of his head, which could have meant he didn't know what was going on or that he knew but it wasn't any business of mine.

Then he vanished.

Of course, that was the moment the guard released the spell. I stumbled back as the now truly dead body collapsed.

I barely registered the gasps and screams. I only half noted the gun that clattered across the marble as the lifeless body hit the floor. I was far too busy staring at the spot where the Gray Man and the ghost had been. She hadn't belonged in the wrongly animated body. So how the hell had she gotten into someone else's body? And why?

Chapter 2

"You're saying the man was dead *before* he *ran* into the security system?" The cop interviewing me looked up from his notepad, one skeptical eyebrow raised. "And what makes you think that?"

"I'm a grave witch. I sensed him when he walked by on the street," I said, not paying as much attention to the questions as I probably should have been. Most of my attention was focused on the body that someone had draped a black tablecloth over just a few yards away, still where it had collapsed near the door. When I'd first sensed the body—when it was still up and walking around—it had felt like the very recently dead. Now my magic told me it was older, days, maybe even a week, deceased.

I squinted, as if the action could reveal more about the body. It didn't, of course. I could have reached out with my ability to sense the dead, thinned my shields so I gazed across the planes and spanned the chasm between the living and dead, but there was a lot of magic—both latent and active—in the museum, and my shields were already rather worse for the wear after getting caught in the antitheft spell with the corpse.

The cop's eyes narrowed. "So you're saying you noticed the deceased before he entered, and you followed him in?"

"I, uh . . ." Crap. Yeah, I definitely should have been paying more attention to the questions at hand. One look at the cop's expression told me that I'd just gone from "unlucky witness" to "potential suspect."

The door to the museum swung open and my gaze flicked over the cop's head. Tamara stepped inside. She held out her laminated medical examiner ID as she assessed the scene, clearly trying to identify who was in charge.

"That was fast," the other officer—the one interviewing the museum curator—said with a look of relief on his face. He wasn't a homicide detective and he'd responded to a robbery call only to discover a dead body. He likely wanted to hand over his notes and be done with this mess.

Tamara shook her head. "I was across the street. At lunch." The last words held the barest edge, no doubt aimed at me. "I let my office know I was at the scene. The rest of my team should be here soon." She made her way toward the prone figure. Her baby bump was just barely showing, but her gait had changed slightly. Nothing major, but I'd known her long enough to notice. "Did anyone try to resuscitate the victim?"

The cop who'd been questioning me held up one hand, two fingers raised, clearly indicating I shouldn't go anywhere. He half turned toward Tamara, never letting me out of his sight. Yup, I was officially in his suspect category, and I hadn't even told him I'd been responsible for driving out the soul who'd hitched a ride in the man's body.

"He was clearly dead when we arrived, ma'am. I checked for vitals, but he was gone."

Tamara nodded absently and reached down to pull the makeshift shroud from the corpse. "What the—?" She jumped backward, dropping the cloth. "Get a magical hazmat team here now. This body needs to be sealed and contained behind a circle. Now."

The cop in front of me radioed in Tamara's order as his partner began drawing a circle around the corpse. Tamara kept backing away, never turning from the body.

I took advantage of the sudden chaos and slipped around the officer so I could get a better look at the body. The shriveled lips had pulled away from the corpse's teeth, giving him an eerie death grin as his skin had slipped down his face. This wasn't decay that happened in less than half an hour—this was days of rot. Which corresponded with how long my magical senses claimed the man to have been dead.

Tamara's backward stride—steady and slow as if she were afraid that if she turned and ran, the corpse would jump up and give chase—had finally brought her to my side. I knew it wasn't the decay that had her on edge— I'd seen her happily autopsy bodies in much worse states. No, it was a recent experience she'd had that had nearly killed her and her unborn child. An attack by a body that had transformed after death.

She turned to me, her dark eyes wide. "What have

you gotten me into now? And why do I hang out with you?" She hissed the question, her voice too fast, too breathy with fear. "You don't think he is . . . ?"

"A ghoul?" I shook my head. "Trust me, I'll never forget what they feel like. No, this is something different. I don't know what's going on, but I definitely don't like it."

I sat in an uncomfortable folding chair at Central Precinct in a room that, if I were being generous, I'd call a waiting area. A more accurate description of the space was that it was a tucked-away closet where the cops could shuffle off someone they didn't want to deal with but whom they couldn't arrest. Yet.

The Anti–Black Magic Unit had arrived at the scene before the homicide detectives. To secure the scene and better assess the situation, they'd decided to clear the civilians out. Which included me. I'd been asked to come down to Central Precinct to give a formal statement. Which was fine—I needed to explain what I'd seen and felt. Quick-rotting corpses walking around piloted by the wrong soul were *not* normal. In fact, I'd never heard of any other reported case. I was hoping the NCPD would put our prior differences behind us and resurrect our retainer agreement so I could raise the shade and get some answers about the whole thing. But sitting in a dingy room between two empty folding chairs for over an hour was not leaving me optimistic on that front.

Standing, I paced around the small room, but there wasn't enough room to make that a satisfying endeavor, and it left me more irritated instead. I could at least check and see if the detectives in charge were back from the scene. And if they weren't, well, I had my own business to run. They could set up an appointment for me to come back. I was done waiting. With a decisive nod, I pulled open the door and walked down the short hall to the lobby of Central Precinct.

The front lobby buzzed with activity. Tensions had been high in the city of late, and that translated into an increase of both petty and serious crime. Some of the detectives and supervisors had private offices deeper in the building, but the bulk of the officers had desks scattered mazelike in the front. Blue-clad cops sat at these desks typing up reports, talking to witnesses, informants, or concerned citizens, or working on cases. An officer I vaguely recognized pushed a handcuffed man past me, toward fingerprinting, the man blathering about how this was all a big misunderstanding. As he passed, the assortment of spells the well-dressed suspect carried tingled along my senses. Most were commonplace enough, but then my ability to sense magic zeroed in on something he should definitely not have been carrying.

"You might want to check his right forearm," I called after the officer. "He's carrying at least a dozen primed knockout spells."

The officer glanced at me and frowned, but I saw the spark of recognition in his eye. He turned back to the man and pulled up the tailored suit sleeve. A pouch no larger than a small coin purse was secured to the man's arm with a strap.

"That's not . . . Uh," the man started, sweat pouring down his face. "Who the hell is she? I want my lawyer."

"You're going to need one," the cop muttered, pushing the suspect forward. He gave me half a nod of acknowledgment before I turned and resumed my trek to the front.

"Why am I not surprised to see you here?" an eerily familiar, and not completely welcomed, voice asked from off to my right.

I spun, my gaze darting around the busy front lobby of Central Precinct. I didn't see the dark-haired woman, who had always been clad in black leather during my short experience with her a few months back and who should have stood out in the precinct. Of course, I didn't fully expect to spot her with my eyes—she wore so many charms meant to make the gaze slide over her that, even knowing who and what you were looking for, it was often hard to focus on her. But I expected to sense the magical armory she carried. Any other time I'd encountered her, my ability to sense magic had zeroed in on the massive amount of weaponized magic she carried like a spotlight.

At least half the people in the lobby carried a spell or two. Most were mundane, a couple were less so, but no one carried so many as to stand out in a crowd. Maybe I'd been wrong. Maybe I hadn't heard—

Briar Darque stepped directly in front of me.

I jumped, stumbling back before catching myself.

"I take it from your expression, this spell was worth every penny I paid," Briar said, smiling a wolfish grin. I only frowned at her. It had annoyed her that she couldn't sneak up on me during our previous acquaintance. Apparently she'd found a way around a sensitive's abilities.

Letting my ability to sense magic stretch, I mentally reached for Briar. At first all I could pick up was a single spell surrounding her like a haze. It was large, but not terribly interesting or threatening, which was why my magic had skimmed over it initially. Under that, though, when I focused on piercing that veil, I could sense her magical smorgasbord. I'd never encountered a spell that camouflaged magic before, at least not without it shining a huge blinking light on the thing it meant to hide.

"Damn," I whispered, my voice breathy both from being startled and from respect for the piece of magical craftsmanship in front of me. "Who crafted that spell? And how?"

Briar's grin only widened. Then her gaze moved past me and she held up her badge, flashing it at the officer approaching us. "I need to talk to someone who can brief me on your current open cases, in particular your more bizarre or unexplained ones." She paused and then jerked a thumb at me. "Probably anything she's involved with."

The officer, who looked young and likely fresh out of academy, didn't say anything. He scrutinized Briar's badge for a moment, and then he turned on his heels and walked back the way he'd just come. I assumed he was going to retrieve someone with more authority.

"So what's been happening, Craft?" Briar asked, walking over to lean on an empty desk. Her big biker boots and leather made no sound as she moved, as if she were more mirage than flesh-and-blood woman. "Keeping your magical nose clean, I hope? I see you're still glowing."

I cringed. "Can we not talk about that here?" Most people couldn't see the telltale glow that emanated from under my skin, betraying my true heritage. The fae chameleon charm I wore let people see what they expected to see—which for most people was just a human witch. But once someone saw the truth of my fae nature, the charm didn't work on them anymore. Briar was now immune to that particular visual deception. "How are you here already, Darque? The weird shit only started about an hour ago."

She lifted one leather-clad shoulder. "The MCIB has a robust staff of precogs. Sometimes I get sent places a little early. Works out better that way. So define 'weird shit.'"

I glanced around. No one was paying particular attention to us, and the officer Briar had sent scurrying for someone higher in rank hadn't returned yet. Briar was an inspector with the Magical Crimes Investigation Bureau. When we'd first met, she'd told me she was the one they sent to clean up magical messes—and those who'd made them. A corpse trying to steal priceless artifacts sounded to me like a "magical mess," so I told her how I'd sensed the walking corpse before it had entered the museum, about the soul I saw, and about the body's quick decay after the soul's departure. I left out the part about my magic being instrumental in the body and soul's separation because Briar was . . . unpredictable.

Briar sat with her arms crossed over her chest as I spoke, attentive but unmoving, her expression unreadable. The situation made me twitchy, my fingers searching for something to fidget with as if to compensate for her uncanny stillness with excessive movement. I half expected her to pull out a file of neatly written facts about the case, like the one she'd shoved under my nose the first time we met, but when I finished, she only nodded.

"And you're sure the corpse wasn't a vehicle for a ghoul to enter this realm?"

"Yes, I'm sure. The ghouls we fought back in September had a tie back to the land of the dead. Once the soul left this body, it was just a corpse."

She pursed her lips, but I thought that there was a look of relief in her dark eyes. No one liked ghouls. "Did you sense any spells on the body?"

"My best look at him was when we were both tied in a paralyzing spell, after he'd already successfully snatched an artifact from behind even more wards and we were inside a museum of magic—there was a lot of magic everywhere. I didn't feel anything I would think would make a corpse walk, but I didn't really have time to parse it out."

"Hmmm. Interesting." She pushed off the desk, her gaze going over my shoulder.

I turned. A visit from an MCIB investigator was clearly a big deal because the chief of police was headed straight for us, flanked on either side by a homicide detective.

"Well, if I have any more questions, I know where to find you," Briar said, as she stepped around me.

"I'd like to talk to the man's shade," I called after her.

She only half turned. "Like I said, I know where to find you." Then she held out her hand, greeting the chief.

I'd been dismissed.

Chapter 3

"You're late," Ms. B chided as I walked into the Tongues for the Dead office the next morning.

I glanced at the large clock looming in the back of the small lobby as I set my dog, PC, down by my feet. I was only five minutes late, but punctuality was second only to neatness in the brownie's personal priority list. Since she'd appointed herself as office manager for the firm, she'd held Rianna and me to her standards. I failed regularly.

"I had some commute issues." Which was true enough. Since the Faerie castle I'd inherited had forced itself into the mortal realm a month ago, my daily commute had gotten interesting, to say the least.

Ms. B just looked at me with her large, dark eyes, and I forced myself not to cringe because, yeah, she and Rianna both lived in that castle as well, and they were both on time. Regardless of what she thought, Ms. B didn't say anything, but dug into the top drawer of her desk, pulled out a bone-shaped dog biscuit, and threw it to PC. The small dog wagged his tail and gobbled it down happily. Then he pranced around, making the white plumes on his head and feet—the only places beside the tip of his tail where he had hair—flop around. Ms. B chuckled in her deep, gruff way and tossed him a second treat. She actually wasn't that much taller than the small Chinese Crested, but she liked my silly dog. Which was good. That wasn't the case with every brownie I'd encountered. Dogs were messy, and as a whole, brownies were fastidious.

"My clients didn't beat me here, did they?" I asked, as I noticed my office door was open—I always closed it at night.

"No, I've started scheduling around your repeated tardiness," Ms. B said, the reprimand in her voice again. "You have a visitor who doesn't seem to think I noticed she entered." Now the little brownie sounded insulted.

I frowned but nodded, heading for my office. PC tried to entice another treat from the brownie, but when she shooed him away, he trotted after me.

I felt the varied and deadly collection of Briar's arsenal of spells before I even reached the door. She wasn't wearing that impressive magic-cloaking spell, though she did have a look-away spell active, as well as a sound-dampening charm. She was hiding, just not from me. Or maybe she kept those charms active by habit.

Briar was sitting at my desk when I entered, her dark braid falling over one shoulder as she rummaged through the contents of my desk drawer. I frowned at her.

"Do you have a search warrant?"

She smiled as she looked up, a big, predatory smile, like a hunting cat. "Just looking for a pen while I waited for you."

I stepped up to the desk and pushed the small cylinder holding both pens and pencils toward her. She made an *ah* sound, as if she hadn't noticed them before. I wasn't fooled.

"What are you doing here, Briar? You insulted my office manager by trying to sneak in."

"The little creature in the front lobby?"

"Her name is Ms. B, and she's a brownie." Which most humans had never seen before. She scared some clients with her diminutive stature and noseless features, but she was good folk and my friend, and I didn't take kindly to people calling her a creature.

The thoughts must have been clear on my face because Briar's false smile faded, her expression becoming serious. "'Ms. B.' I'll remember that. I'd apologize, but . . ." She held out her hands, palms up, and I knew what she meant. Ms. B was fae, and you don't apologize to fae unless you want to end up in their debt. "I didn't actually come here to harass you."

"Good, because I have a client interview scheduled for this morning, so if you could . . ." I motioned to the door.

Briar leaned back in my chair, tucking her hands behind her head. "I said I wasn't here to harass you, not that I was leaving."

The chime of the bells on the main door sounded. My clients, no doubt.

"Out," I said, keeping my voice low.

"I apparently showed up to town too early," she said,

not only not leaving, but kicking her motorcycle-boot-clad feet onto the surface of my desk. "Fast-rotting corpses are interesting, but a relic thief who died while the crime was in progress isn't exactly the kind of case I tend to get called in on. The precogs have no more clues for me yet, so I just have to cool my heels. I'm not good at that. But you seem to attract the scary and strange like it's a hobby, so I figure I'll stick close to you, at least until something more interesting arises."

Outside my open office door, I could hear Ms. B talking to someone. "Out," I said again. "My clients have a right to privacy."

"You're a magic-eye, not a doctor." "Magic-eye" was an insulting term for a private investigator who used magic and no real investigative work to solve cases, and based on the way her eyes twinkled as she said it, she meant it as the insult it was. "No one will even know I'm here, unless you make a big fuss."

That at least was true. Unless my client was a sensitive.

Footsteps sounded in the hall. Since the door was open, Ms. B knocked on the frame.

"Your scheduled appointment is here," she said, her tone making it clear that Briar was not on her schedule.

Briar dutifully dropped her legs and vacated my chair, but she didn't leave the room. Instead she moved to the corner and leaned against the far wall. There wasn't much I could do. Even if I called the cops, she outranked most of the locals in her role as an investigator for the Magical Crimes Investigation Bureau—I'd learned that the last time she'd been in town.

So I chose to ignore her presence and hoped she'd keep her word about my clients not knowing she was present. Walking around my desk, I sat down and pulled my laptop out of my bag, setting it up before turning and nodding at Ms. B.

"Show them in."

I pushed the box of tissues across my desk, closer to the clients sitting in the chairs in front of me. Rachael Saunders immediately grabbed two, dabbing them at her nose. Her husband, Rue Saunders, stared down at his hands. He'd done that since he'd sat down, letting his wife tell their sob-broken story of loss.

"Katie was only six," she said, grabbing a third tissue. "She was planned. Wished for. We were older already when she was born."

I nodded in what I hoped was a sympathetic manner. This story had been convoluted at best, and all I'd gathered so far was that they'd lost their daughter to a blood illness. Some days I wished I had time to take a couple of courses on grief counseling because while I was excellent when it came to speaking to the dead, I found it a lot harder to handle the bereaved families. Shades were just memories animated with magic. With the living I had to worry about offending, and I had to navigate a business contract while they were focused on lost loved ones. It didn't help that I couldn't utter the simple words "I'm sorry for your loss." My recently awakened fae nature wouldn't allow me to express even insincere condolences without creating a debt that could be called in.

When Rachael paused for a particularly jagged breath, I seized my chance to interrupt her story.

"Katie was very young," I said. "What are you hoping to learn from speaking to her shade?"

Rue looked up for the first time. His eyes were dry, hard, but bloodshot and tired. "'Her shade'? We have no interest in her shade, Miss Craft. We want you to find her ghost."

"I don't—" I started.

His wife interrupted me. "We saw you on TV, last summer. With the ghost. You can talk to ghosts."

Well. Crap.

"I can speak to ghosts," I said, nodding slowly and trying to keep them focused on my face as I discreetly pressed a button on my office phone. Nothing overt happened, but it would cause a light to flash on the phone at the front desk, and with luck, Ms. B would interrupt in a moment with an excuse to end this consultation early. It was a signal we'd worked out back when the firm had been inundated with unreasonable requests leading up to Halloween. Opening my palms in front of me and offering the grieving couple my most placating smile, I said, "But ghosts are very rare. Most souls move on immediately following death. It is very unlikely your daughter's ghost remained."

"She was a very good girl, Miss Craft. She wouldn't have passed on. She would have waited," Rachael said, her glassy eyes pleading for it to be true.

I glanced at the photo of a pretty young girl with sun-kissed cheeks and ringlets pulled back from her face with blue bows. She looked small for her age, frail from the disease that had claimed her life. I couldn't imagine her putting up the frantic fight that would have caused a soul collector to release her into the purgatory of the land of the dead. And if Rachael's description of her being a good girl was accurate, she probably wouldn't have fought the collector in the first place, going peacefully from here to wherever souls went next. But I couldn't say that. It fell into the category of sharing secrets about the soul collectors, which was rather frowned upon, and since I was sort of dating one, I tried not to do anything that would get him into trouble. You know, more than his forbidden relationship with me would cause.

"I don't think there is anything I can do for you."

"We need to find her," Rue said, pushing to his feet. He pressed both hands flat on my desk, leaning forward.

He was a big man, over forty but still in decent shape based on the muscle tone his suit hinted at. Grief had pulled at the skin around his eyes and his mouth, and his hair was slightly unkempt, like he normally kept it cut short but had forgotten to see a barber in a while. Magic buzzed around him. Nothing active, or even focused. He had some charms in his pocket, too weak while inactive for me to pinpoint what they did. Raw magic filled rings on each of his pointer fingers, and more raw magic waited in what I guessed was a pendant around his neck.

His wife grabbed his arm, trying to pull him back to his seat. "Rue, stop. We need her help."

"I won't lose my daughter again," he said, shrugging off his wife and leaning closer to me, invading my space. For her part, his wife melted back into her chair, collapsing into herself as she sobbed into her hands.

I met Rue Saunders's piercing stare evenly. Grief did strange things to people. Some people broke under their sadness. Others got angry. Rue was clearly the latter. And while I felt for him—losing a child was a horrible thing—that didn't give him a right to try to bully me.

His aggressive posture had apparently gotten Briar's attention as well. Though I couldn't afford to look toward her, I could feel the cluster of spells she wore moving closer. I did not want her getting involved, which meant I needed to defuse this situation fast.

"I can't help you. Mr. and Mrs. Saunders, I think it's time you go."

Rue lifted his palms and slammed them back on my desk, making everything on the surface shake. The picture of my dog toppled.

I gritted my teeth and pushed out of my own chair. Standing switched our positions so I loomed over his hunched form now, and he had to either straighten and move out of my space or crane his head to look up at me.

Briar was so close, I could have reached out and touched her, but she hadn't revealed herself. I hoped she'd hold back. Ms. B should interrupt any minute now.

Rue straightened. We were nearly the same height when both standing, the expanse of my desk separating us. His hands balled into fists at his side. "You can help. You have the magic. You just won't."

On my desk, the phone buzzed, indicating Ms. B wanted to open the intercom line. *About time.* I hit the flashing button.

"Hate to interrupt, but your next appointment is waiting," the brownie said in her gruff voice.

"I'm just finishing up here," I said in response, hitting the button to close the line again. Then I gave the couple in front of me a tight smile. "I hate that I can't help you, but there is nothing I can do. Now, if there is nothing else, I think we're done."

Rue Saunders stared at me a moment longer, his wife still sobbing behind him. Then he grabbed the photograph of his daughter off my desk and turned.

"Come on. There are other grave witches." He stormed out of my office without waiting for his wife. The door slammed behind him and I felt Briar back off, retreating to her corner again.

Rachael moved slower. As if she had to rebuild herself to climb out of the chair. She clutched the soaked tissues in a hand curled against her chest. "I'm so . . . He didn't mean all that. It's hard on him."

I nodded acknowledgment of her not-quite-voiced apology and held out a fresh tissue to her. "I would help if I could."

She made a sound under her sob that might have been anything and accepted the tissue. Then she dragged herself out of my office, moving slow, stiff, as if she'd aged twenty years in the short consultation. Once the door shut behind her, I sagged back into my chair, letting out a long breath.

The door opened before I could even turn toward Briar. I looked up, but the doorway was empty. So I looked down.

Ms. B studied me from where she peeked around the door. She stood no taller than my knee at her full height, her quill-like green hair fanning around her face like a mane.

"I take it we won't be billing them?" she asked, glancing back over her shoulder.

"Not so much."

She nodded, but if she was disappointed or upset

about that fact, I couldn't tell. Though brownies are diminutive in size, their features are fairly similar to a human's except that brownies lack noses. I'd never have guessed a nose was an important feature to allow others to decipher expressions until I had daily dealings with Ms. B. Or maybe the brownie just had a killer poker face and lacked microexpressions.

"Are you ready for me to send in the next client?"

I sat up straighter. "You mean there really is another client?"

She cocked her head, fixing me with her dark eyes. "I'll send him in."

I stared at the door as it shut. She'd said another client was waiting. I'd assumed that was for my rescue, but she was fae. She couldn't lie.

Taking a deep breath, I made a quick assessment of my office. As high as the tensions had been for a moment, there wasn't much evidence. I picked up the fallen picture and moved the tissue box back to its spot, and everything was as good as new. I glanced over at Briar's corner. The spell made my eyes want to skid past her, not seeing her, but the fact that I could feel the spell made it easier to resist its influence. She pantomimed a yawn when my gaze landed on her. I wanted to tell her she could leave if she was bored, but footsteps were approaching in the hall.

The door slid open slowly, admitting a girl who appeared to be about seventeen years old. Inwardly I groaned. I needed *paying* clients. Still, I plastered on my professional face as she stepped inside, but cringed again when she turned and thanked Ms. B for showing her in.

"Don't thank fae," I said, on reflex.

The girl froze, her cupid's bow of a mouth half open. "Did I offend her?" She turned and looked like she was about to say she was sorry to Ms. B's retreating figure. I preemptively cut her off.

"Don't apologize either," I said, trying to keep my smile in place. The girl was jumpy. "But it doesn't offend them. It acknowledges a debt they could cash in. Ms. B is good folk, but it's best to never thank or apologize to anyone whom you suspect might be fae."

"Oh, I didn't know. Thank you."

And back to my internal cringing as the smallest gulf of debt opened between us. But she couldn't have known. I intentionally passed as human, mostly because until a few months ago, I'd thought I was a normal human witch. Well, a wyrd witch, at least.

"I'm Alex Craft," I said, standing and holding out my hand. "What can I do for you, Miss . . . ?"

"Taylor. Taylor Carlson." She took my hand tentatively, but once she made contact, the handshake was good and firm.

I motioned to the client chairs in front of my desk. She took one and I sank into my own chair.

"What can I do for you today?"

Taylor pulled a cell phone from her bag, tapped the screen for a moment, and then pushed it across the desk toward me. "This is my boyfriend, Remy."

I glanced at the displayed photo. In it was a smiling boy not much older than Taylor wearing a football jersey. He had one arm around Taylor's shoulders, pulling her close, and the other disappeared off the edge of the photo at an awkward angle, the telltale sign he was taking the picture. The time stamp of the photo was only a week old.

I glanced at my prospective client. She perched at the edge of her chair, one hand twisting and untwisting the strap of her bag. A small crease had formed over her nose, and her lips compressed as she stared at the picture she'd passed me, but if I had to put money on it, I would have said she was scared, not sad. She certainly wasn't displaying the sorrow I'd expect from someone whose boyfriend had died within the last week.

"Okay," I said, passing the phone back to her. "I'm assuming you're not here to have his shade raised."

"No." She blanched, shaking her head. "No. I mean. I hope not. He's missing."

"A missing person is probably something you should take to the police, not a private investigator."

"I know." Her face scrunched tighter, making her nose crinkle and her mouth purse as if too many emotions were jostling for space on her face and crowding each other into her features. "And I tried them. But he's over eighteen and hasn't been missing long enough for anyone to pay attention. But if I'm paying someone to look for him, you have to take me seriously, right? And this is a magic-based firm, so you can track him with a spell. I brought you some of his things." She opened her bag and pulled out a large T-shirt, a high school ring, and an origami flower before shoving them across my desk.

I glanced at the haul and then back up at Taylor. "How long has Remy been missing?"

She winced. "I'm not sure? Since last night definitely. He was going to pick me up after I got off work at eleven, but he never showed. He's not answering his phone, and I talked to his college roommate, but he says he hasn't seen him since yesterday afternoon. I just know something awful has happened to him."

I glanced at the clock on my computer. It was barely ten in the morning. No wonder the police had sent her away. Her boyfriend had been seen less than twenty-four hours ago.

"And he's never missed a date before?"

She shook her head. "Not without calling. This isn't like him. We've been together since my junior year. I know him. He wouldn't just not contact me."

To me, someone who'd been out of college for a while, being together since junior year of high school sounded like a long time, but I was guessing it wasn't in this case. "He's in college now, and you are . . . ?"

"A senior in high school." She crossed her arms over her chest, sulking that I'd questioned her age, which only made her look younger. "But look, here are the texts he sent me yesterday afternoon." She tapped on her phone again before passing it to me. "I *know* something is wrong. If you will investigate, I want to hire your firm. If you won't, tell me now so I can find someone else and neither of us wastes our time."

I read over the texts she'd pulled up. They were gag-worthily sappy, but it sure sounded like he'd planned to pick her up last night. Of course, he could have been going through the motions of the script they'd made in high school while having outgrown his high school sweetheart now that he was in college. Or maybe I was just cynical about relationships.

Taylor leaned forward, the pink of her lips almost invisible as she pressed them together, waiting for me to answer. She looked earnest, scared but hopeful. I sighed.

"Okay," I said, handing her back her phone. "But before we go any further, let me break down the fees and contract for you." Because this was going to be one very expensive broken heart if it turned out he was fine but dumping her.

"I'm good for the money. I've been saving for a car."

Great, because that didn't make me feel guilty at all. But this was a business, not a charity, so I dug through my desk drawer until I found the boilerplate "search and recovery" contract my partner and I had drafted. Rianna, my business partner, had taken a couple of lost item cases, and even one lost pet, but I'd never used this particular contract, and neither of us had taken a missing-person case before.

The contract was fairly simple, laying out how charges and fees would break down. The retainer covered the initial tracking spell as well as the first five hours spent on the investigation. Taylor's eyes bulged a bit at the number, and I considered knocking it down to a two-hour charge, but it would be better to refund her some of the retainer if Remy turned up quickly rather than bill her for more later if tracking him proved difficult.

After she'd signed the contract and I'd processed her debit card, I once again examined the haul she'd spread on my desk.

"Did he wear the shirt last or did you?" I asked, lifting the crumpled T-shirt that looked like it had been slept in more than once.

"Uh, me. But it is his."

"And the ring?"

"I've been wearing it on a chain around my neck since early summer."

Which left the origami flower. I motioned to it. "Did he make this himself? How long ago?"

Her shoulders lifted in a slight wince. "Our first date?"

Which meant it had been over a year since Remy had touched the paper. Technically, a tracking spell could be worked with nothing more than a name or photo, but the working would be a lot more precise with something to focus the spell. Hair, fingernail clippings, blood, or the like were the preferred focus, but a personal item that the person used often or carried with them would work as well. Unfortunately, all the items on my desk would likely lead back to Taylor.

"It would be helpful to have something a little more personal to him—a toothbrush, a comb, an article of clothing only he's worn, or something of that nature."

Taylor's lips screwed sideways as she thought, and then her eyebrows lifted, her face brightening with a thought. She opened her bag and dug around inside. "He used my brush just this weekend."

She pulled a bright pink, soft-bristled brush from her purse and held it out toward me triumphantly. Clearly the words "personal" and "only he uses" hadn't quite registered. Then again, Taylor had long bottle-blond hair, and even with my bad eyes, I could see short, dark hair mixed in her brush.

"Remy is the only other person who has used this brush? You're sure?" I asked, because I wasn't digging hair out of someone else's brush only to have the spell lead to one of her school friends.

"I'm positive."

She answered a little quickly for my taste, but it was the best possibility we had available. I accepted the brush but then hesitated. An evidence bag, or even just a plastic baggie I could write on, would be useful in a situation like this, but as it had never come up before, I didn't have either in my desk. After a moment's indecision, I placed the brush in my top desk drawer. Then I opened a document on my computer and collected Remy's full name, phone number, and current address. As an afterthought, I jotted down his roommate's name and number as well, as I'd almost certainly have to contact him.

"Well, that should get me started," I said, saving the document.

"You'll start looking immediately, right? Can I wait here while you cast the tracking spell?" Taylor asked, perching on the edge of her seat again.

"My business partner will be the one who casts the spell." Because my traditionally witchy spells were notoriously unreliable. "But I'll follow it, and we don't know yet where it will lead, so there is little point in you staying here, which is one place we know for sure Remy is not located."

"Oh. That makes sense, I guess." She rose to her feet, but she didn't move toward the door.

"Go home in case he tries to contact you. I'll call as soon as I have information."

She nodded and trudged toward the door, as if hoping I'd stop her if she hesitated long enough. I had nothing more to offer, so I didn't stop her. Instead, I escorted her out of my office and across the Tongues for the Dead lobby. At the main door she hesitated again.

"You'll let me know as soon as you find something?"

"That's what you're paying me to do."

"Right." She gave me a weak smile, but she nodded, and then, hiking her bag higher on her shoulder, she marched up the sidewalk.

Once she was gone, I turned and glanced at Rianna's door. It was closed.

"Is she out or—?"

"With a client," Ms. B said in her typical gruff manner.

I nodded, not taking offense at being cut off. That was just the brownie's way. By all accounts, she liked me. I'd hate to think how she'd act if she didn't.

As I reached my office, Rianna's door opened. I turned in time to see a man of about fifty step out of her office. He wore a dark suit, as if he'd just come from a funeral, but he was dry-eyed. In fact, he was smiling. When he saw me, he dipped his head in a friendly nod. He even smiled at Ms. B before heading out to the street, his well-manicured hands clasped behind him.

I watched him stroll past our large picture window before I turned to Rianna, one eyebrow lifted.

"Lawyer," she said with a shrug.

That made sense. He definitely didn't have the look of a bereft loved one.

"Interesting case?" I asked, and Rianna wrinkled her nose as she shook her head.

"Insurance dispute. But it should be a quick case. I'm guessing an hour at the graveside this afternoon. Two at most."

"Fun," I said, and she shot me a dirty look.

Insurance and probate cases were basically the bread and butter of our firm. Someone contesting the validity of a will, second-guessing the deceased's wishes, or an undetermined cause of death suspected of being caused by something that would invalidate an insurance policy. They tended to be high-tension cases for the families, and sometimes rather drama-filled at the graveside, but they weren't particularly demanding on us as investigators. We raised the shade and repeated the questions from the family and lawyers and then put the shade back. Regardless of the outcome, our part was done after that.

Rianna had been taking the brunt of those types of cases recently because while they might not take much from an investigation standpoint, grave magic was hard on the eyes—mine more than hers. As well as being a grave witch, I was a planeweaver, and seeing through the planes seemed to be doing extra damage to my eyes. While Rianna and I both suffered from the poor low-light vision so common to grave witches, she could hold a shade for an hour or two and drive herself home twenty minutes later. I, on the other hand, ended up with severely impaired vision for a few hours, sometimes to the point of complete blindness for a time. So I tried to only raise one shade every week or two, which meant if more cases came in, Ms. B. quietly arranged for them to go to Rianna. It wasn't the most ideal situation, but it worked for our firm.

"Any other clients scheduled before the ritual?" I asked.

Rianna shook her head. "Nah, I'm free until one. Why? What are you working on? Anything interesting?"

"I need a tracking spell. I have a missing-person case."

Rianna's eyes lit up. "Really? I want all the details."

Becoming a private investigator had been Rianna's longtime dream career, not mine. She was the mystery novel buff, and the one who'd talked about her plans for a firm when we were roommates at our wyrd boarding school. She'd already vanished by the time I graduated, and with a little help from a local detective, I'd eventually fallen into starting the firm. She'd joined me after I'd rescued her from Faerie, and while I suspected it wasn't as glamourous as she'd dreamed, anything had to be better than spending hundreds of years as a captive of Faerie while only half a decade passed in the mortal realm.

"Don't get too excited yet. I was hired to find a college freshman by his still-in-high-school sweetheart. This might be a very expensive breakup."

"Oh." She crinkled her nose. "Still, it's a missing-person case. This is the firm's first. We're moving up in the world." She turned toward the lobby. "Ms. B, will you block off the rest of my morning? I've got a tracking spell to cast."

Ms. B nodded from her desk, and Rianna disappeared back into her office. I headed back to mine, dreading the inevitable confrontation that was about to occur.

Sure enough, Briar was sitting in my chair when I got back to my office, her feet kicked up on the surface of the desk and her hands behind her head. "Is this what you do all day? Listen to weeping parents and take cases from lovestruck teenagers too stubborn to know when they're being dumped?"

"Not all day. Now I have to go find said teenager's boyfriend."

Briar snorted. "And what will you tell her when you find him with his new girlfriend?"

"The truth. Hey, we can't all make our living incinerating ghouls and whatever else you do. Now if you're just going to sit there insulting how I run my investigation firm, you can leave." Because I'd worked hard to expand my business beyond just raising shades. My vision couldn't take the damage it would take to raise enough shades to pay my monthly bills.

Briar looked like she was about to say something, but then her expression changed as she fished a phone out of her pocket. She glanced at the display for a moment and then dropped her feet from the desktop.

"Good news, Craft, looks like you get your reprieve. I know you'll miss my company—"

Now it was my turn to give a sarcastic sniff.

"But it appears that someone finished the job your fast-rotting corpse started yesterday and smuggled the exact same artifact out of the museum while the wards were down for inspection. So, maybe there is more to that case than it seems. You have fun with your teen drama. I'm going to go investigate something interesting."

I scowled at her back as she walked out. At the main door, she lifted her hand and cocked it to the side slightly, making the wave look sarcastic.

I shut my office door.

"Come on, PC, we have our own case," I said as I stepped around the small dog on my way to my desk. "I don't care if she is off to look into a case with walking dead people. Which is bizarre and should be impossible."

He lifted his head, ears at half mast, and squinted at me. Even he didn't look convinced.

"With Briar involved, it'll probably turn out dangerous. My case will be a nice, easy car payment." Well, half of my car payment. It was a nice car.

My dog put his head down on his paws, going back

to sleep on the pillow beside my chair. Yeah, okay, my case was probably a dud. And I was curious about the corpse from yesterday. But I had my first missing-person case, and I was going to throw myself into finding Taylor's—probably cheating—boyfriend. Bizarre cases with walking corpses be damned.

Chapter 4

While Rianna created the tracking charm, I made a few phone calls. I started with Remy's phone. I didn't really expect him to answer, but it would definitely shorten my investigation if he did. I left a brief message identifying myself and asking him to return my call. I didn't tell him why. The next call I placed was to Remy's roommate, Colin.

He answered on the first ring. "You've reached the coolest dude on campus. Talk to me."

Riiight. "This is Alex Craft, an investigator for Tongues for the Dead. I'm looking into the possible disappearance of Remy Hollens. Have you—"

A sound somewhere between an exasperated laugh and a sigh cut me off. "Seriously? An investigator? Did Remy's jailbait call you? And who did you say you're with? She thinks Remy's dead? Dude, she's crazy."

"No one thinks he's dead," I said, leaning back in my chair and pressing the palm of my hand over my eyes. "I'm simply trying to locate him. Have you seen or heard from Remy today?"

"No. But, dude, it's Saturday. Hopefully the guy went to a party, got some college tail, and is sleeping off the hangover in some chick's bed."

"Do you think that's likely?" I asked, but was greeted by silence on the other side, as if Colin was indecisive about spilling secrets. "I'm only trying to locate him. I have no obligation to report back his activities to my client. Trust me, I don't want any drama."

He hesitated a moment more, then released a slow, defeated hiss between his teeth before saying, "No. It doesn't sound like him. I mean it's possible, but it would be out of character. He's devoted to that girl." As an afterthought he added, "But I'm not worried. This is the college life."

"Of course. If you hear from him, give me a call, okay?" I rattled off my number, but he didn't repeat it or sound like he was writing it down. I'd never hear from him again, but the call did confirm Remy wasn't likely to be avoiding Taylor because he planned to dump her.

I added a few notes to my document and then glanced over the information Taylor had left me. She had given me Remy's dorm address only, but when I was in college, a lot of the local kids in my dorm headed home regularly, typically with a basket full of dirty laundry. I didn't have Remy's parents' info, but Tongues for the Dead paid for several online database services we used for background checks. Less than ten minutes online earned me the home address as well as cell and work numbers for Remy's parents.

I punched the first four digits of his father's number

but then hesitated. If Remy really was sleeping off a hangover, I didn't need to panic his parents by telling them I was investigating his disappearance. Of course, if Taylor was right and something had happened, early warning would likely be welcome. I dithered a moment and then cleared the number. I'd given Rianna the hair from the brush half an hour ago. She would be done with the tracking spell soon.

As if summoned by the thought, Rianna stepped into the threshold of my doorway. "One tracking spell prepared and ready to track. Want to place bets on where you find him?"

I stood and collected the spell from her. "As long as I don't have to report back to a brokenhearted client that I found him in someone else's bed, I'll probably be happy. It sounds out of character for him, though." I frowned. "Okay, revision. I'm hoping he's not in the hospital either."

"Or the morgue," Rianna added cheerily, and I frowned at her.

"Yeah, I'm really not even holding that out as an option."

She just shrugged and handed the charm to me. The tracking spell was contained in a blue microsuede bag suspended on a nylon cord. The components were nothing fancy, but my ability to sense magic told me the spell inside was strong and good. Rianna had always been an excellent spellcaster. As soon as I touched the cord, I felt a distinct tug from the tracking charm. Remy was north. Somewhere.

"This is great," I said, in lieu of thanking her.

Rianna nodded, silently accepting the words as they were intended. She was a changeling, not a fae, so while she didn't share my particular need to avoid particular phrases, she understood the limitations.

"Well, Desmond and I are going home to do an early lunch, I think." She buried one hand in the black fur of the doglike fae who was her ever-present shadow. He leaned into the touch, his red-pupiled eyes gazing up at her with affection. "Have fun tracking your missing person. I want all the details tonight."

With that, she turned and headed for the front door. I just shook my head as I tied the nylon cord of the charm around my wrist. She had a lot more confidence that this case was going to be interesting than I did. Or maybe I was still distracted thinking about the walking corpses.

I'd just double-checked that I had both Remy's home and dorm addresses in my notes and uploaded to cloud storage when a figure floated into my room and hovered by the door. Well, not literally; ghosts more or less obeyed the laws of physics, their plane of existence just didn't always mirror ours perfectly so they often appeared to float through solid objects.

"You have a case?" asked Roy, ghost and junior detective—hey, no one ever said a guy couldn't have career aspirations after death.

"Missing person. You tagging along?"

He shrugged as if he didn't care one way or another, but not even being slightly translucent hid the excitement that lit up his features. "Yeah, I could do that."

I closed the laptop and returned it to my bag before sliding my cell into my back pocket. "Hey, if you're too busy, I get it," I said as I walked past the ghost and toward the front door.

"Well, I have . . . I mean . . ." His shoulders hunched

and he pushed his glasses farther up his nose. "No one ever hires a ghost detective. You should really add my name to the door."

I pushed open said door, stepping onto the street, and then paused, waiting for my eyes to adjust to the bright, nearly noonday sun. "What would that do besides confuse people who wouldn't be able to see or hear you, and thus still wouldn't hire you?"

This was an old argument, almost a script at this point, and the ghost sulked as he followed me toward my car.

"Maybe if my office was bigger, nicer . . . Maybe Icelynne would . . ."

"Leave the castle?" I offered when he trailed off. He nodded and I patted his slumped shoulder. "She'll leave when she's ready. She's still adjusting to being a ghost."

He only nodded again, but it was a halfhearted movement. One that acknowledged my words but didn't agree with them. I couldn't fault him. He'd fallen hard for the frost fae when we'd been investigating her murder, and she'd seemed interested in him as well, but when I'd finally solved the case and been granted my independent fae status, the castle that had been hanging out in limbo since I'd inherited it had forced itself into mortal reality, unfolding a small pocket of space that was both reality and Faerie perfectly entwined. Icelynne had taken to haunting the castle since it felt the most like the home she could never return to, and she hadn't left since. It wouldn't have mattered how big or nice Roy's office was. She didn't particularly like the mortal world, preferring the castle and its strange meld of mortal and Faerie planes.

I sucked at consoling people, so once patting Roy's

shoulder started to feel awkward, I dropped my hand and climbed into the car. He followed moments later.

"So where are we headed?"

I lifted my hand with the charm secured to my wrist and pointed. "That way."

"Anything more specific?"

"Not yet, but I thought we'd head toward the university unless the charm pulls us in a different direction first."

"Very scientific."

I shrugged and pulled the car away from the curb. "Hey, it's magic, not science."

The college was a bust. The charm kept pulling, indicating we had farther to go. I keyed Remy's home address into my GPS, but it was in the opposite direction of where the charm was leading us. So I just drove, trying my best to follow the pull of the charm despite the fact that streets were not designed to go in one straight line for extended periods. Several times the street we were on would curve and I'd have to consult the map screen of my GPS, searching for the nearest street that would send us in the right direction again.

We'd long ago crossed the river that separated the Magic Quarter from Nekros City proper. Once we'd left downtown the streets had become less organized, with intersections appearing farther and farther apart and side streets that dead-ended into neighborhoods or empty lots, making following the charm that much more difficult. Now even the outlines of the city's skyscrapers had vanished on the horizon, and I hadn't seen another street to turn onto in over a mile.

"Why are we stopping? He can't be here," Roy said, indicating the boarded-up building whose overgrown parking lot I'd pulled into.

I shook my head and frowned at the charm around my wrist. "I think this thing is malfunctioning," I said, giving the charm a shake—as if that would actually change anything. It continued to convey the same confusing information. "It's telling me Remy is in two different directions."

"Huh," Roy said. "Maybe he was murdered and his body is actively being scattered across town."

"Gross. And may I add what a positive outlook you have today?"

The ghost only shrugged.

I shook my head and prodded the spell with my ability to sense magic. It felt exactly as it had when I'd examined it in my office. Unless it had always been flawed, and I didn't think it had, it didn't seem to be a magical issue.

"Maybe it's the focus. I pulled several dark hairs from Taylor's brush for the charm. She might have lied about who she let use it." That was the most likely scenario. Roy's suggestion, though gruesome, was also possible, but I was guessing highly unlikely.

"He could have a twin."

"Only child."

"Separated at birth?"

I frowned at the ghost.

He shrugged again. "Hey, I'm only offering ideas. So which way?"

I didn't answer but returned to trying to decipher the information from the spell. Tracking spells weren't terribly sophisticated magic. Tricky to cast, yes, but they were simple in function. The spell pulled in a straight line toward its subject. As the charm's holder got closer to the spell's subject, the pull grew stronger. This charm had appeared to be functioning perfectly until just a few moments ago. The pull had gradually grown stronger for the nearly two hours we'd been driving. But now the charm seemed confused, trying to pull in two different directions in a tug-of-war-like sensation.

I looked around. We were in the outskirts of the city, past the sprawling suburb, and approaching the wild areas where there were few humans and fewer paved roads. The road we'd just pulled off was one of the few remaining tributaries that eventually fed back into the highway that was the only way in or out of the unfolded space containing the entirety of Nekros City.

"I think he might have passed us," I said, moving my arm back and forth between the two warring directions. They weren't completely opposite directions, more like whatever the second reading was coming from had passed by on a road slightly to the north of us. I'd have put money on the fact that both trails had been in the same area not long ago. But then one source had broken off, heading back to town. That one seemed to still be moving. And it was close—closer than the one pulling either toward the wilds or possibly out of the folded space and into the next state. So who could Taylor have been sharing her brush with who would have been out in the wilds or beyond with Remy? Why? And most importantly, was Remy the one headed back into town, or was that the unknown source?

Roy watched my arm swing slowly back and forth between the opposing points for a moment before saying, "I vote we follow the one heading back toward the city."

"Why is that?" I actually had the same inclination, if for no other reason than it felt closer, but I was curious to hear the ghost's reasoning.

"It's past lunchtime, and there is food in the city. Nothing to eat in the wilds. Things that might eat us, but definitely no fast food."

"You're a ghost. You can't eat."

"No, but I can watch you and remember."

I cut my gaze across at him. "And that's almost as creepy and weird as the scattered-body theory. But I agree about tracking the one in the city. It's closer. Let's just hope it's Remy."

We followed the pull of the charm back through the outskirts and the suburbs, until, when the businesses began outnumbering the houses, the tracking spell began all but jumping on my wrist, we were so close. We weren't in the city proper yet; the skyscrapers and municipal buildings of Nekros were still a distance off. This was more sprawl that had grown around the city since it was founded fifty-odd years ago. Most of the buildings in this area were retail establishments or restaurants, but as if anticipating joining the city, or maybe just to increase foot traffic to the local businesses, all the roads had sidewalks.

I pulled into the lot of an outdoor mall—it was far too gentrified to be called a strip mall—and parked. The charm was dancing on my wrist now. If I kept searching by car, I'd likely pass Remy and have to double back. It was smarter to go on foot and pay attention to the changes in the charm.

Roy followed as I set a brisk pace up the sidewalk. It was early afternoon on a Saturday and the sidewalks weren't exactly packed, but they boasted clumpy crowds of shoppers scattered sporadically between shops. Several young people were gathered in a green space between a bookstore and a coffee shop, and I scanned the faces eagerly, but none belonged to Remy.

The charm at my wrist was no longer pulling—except for the light tug back toward the wilds—but was more like silently buzzing, alerting me its target was here, close. But where?

I pulled up the photo Taylor had sent me of Remy and held it up for Roy. The ghost wasn't the best at identifying the living—being dead it wasn't something most ghosts paid attention to particularly because the chasm between the living and the land of the dead tended to distort things, but he'd been honing the skill since deciding he wanted to be a detective.

"This is who we're looking for," I said, earning me a questioning glance from an elderly couple sitting on a bench not far away. Puzzled looks from bystanders happened sometimes when talking to someone no one else could see. But I didn't have time to worry about people thinking I was crazy. Remy was around here somewhere. Or, at least I hoped that was who the spell had tracked here.

Roy studied the screen, tilting his head this way and that as he tried to see the image through what likely appeared to be a broken phone on the other side of the chasm. After a moment, Roy nodded and dashed into the nearest store to check the patrons. I continued up the sidewalk, searching, the charm vibrating on my wrist.

As I passed a branch of the First Bank of Nekros, the charm at my wrist gave a lurch. *Yes.* I jerked open a door that proclaimed the bank's new extended weekend hours and rushed inside. The bank had soft lighting, and the sudden change from the bright outside sunlight left me blind.

"Lock the door," a deep male voice instructed.

I blinked, willing my magic-damaged eyes to adjust quicker. Shadows resolved around me, slowly bleeding into color. A dark-haired man in a football jersey stood in front of me, still not quite in focus, but with the charm vibrating its excitement at my wrist, I took a guess.

"Remy?"

The man lifted something dark right in front of my face. I squinted. Then I yelped as the hazy shadow revealed itself to be a matte-black gun.

"I said, lock the door," he said, and from farther inside the bank, I heard the distinct sound of a gun cocking.

Behind him were two more figures, both carrying even bigger guns. Patrons were on the ground, their hands behind their heads. I turned and twisted the lock on the door, as instructed.

"Now, on the ground," Remy said, and I did as told, sinking to my knees.

Well, I'd solved my first missing-person case. Yay? Taylor would be relieved to know Remy was alive and well. Now I just had to hope I stayed that way too.

Chapter 5

"Cash in the bag," yelled a woman in her midthir-ties, throwing a dark duffel at the teller's counter. She wore a button-up sweater with pearls, white jeans, and sandals—not at all what I would expect from a bank robber. She held her shotgun clumsily, pointed at the teller, but braced low, near her hip. I didn't know a lot about guns, but I was guessing the lady knew even less because even I knew that if she actually shot from that position, she would end up doubled over in pain from the recoil.

Remy still stood in front of me, but his gun was now pointed at the security guard several yards to my left. The guard was on his stomach, hands tucked behind his head, but Remy hadn't given me any more instruction since he'd told me to get down, and he hadn't instructed me to get down on my belly, so I still knelt, looking around. My eyes were finally clear and able to make out finer details again. Like the fact that while Remy held his Glock with much more confidence than the lady with the shotgun, his grip was all wrong, and if he pulled the trigger, the gun's slide would break his thumb.

The third person in the group was considerably older than the other two. If I had to guess, I'd place her somewhere in her sixties, but life had ridden her hard, so I couldn't be sure. Her skin was dark with accumulated grime, her stringy gray hair greasy and matted, and her layered clothing threadbare. She limped as she walked, but she carried the sleek, deadly-looking assault rifle in her hands with an expertise her companions lacked. She moved among the patrons, forcing them to place wallets, jewelry, charms, and anything of value into another dark duffel bag.

"Taylor is worried about you," I whispered to Remy.

"Stay quiet," he snapped without looking at me.

"When you didn't pick her up last night, she went to the police to file a missing-person report."

Now he looked at me.

"I said shut up," he said, swinging the gun to point at me again.

My teeth snapped together and I shut up. Remy stared at me, his mouth a tight line, but when it was clear I was done speaking, his gun swiveled back to the security guard.

A small clicking sounded behind me, and I probably wouldn't have noticed it if a hand hadn't landed on my shoulder a moment later. I jumped but managed to muffle any sound I might have made when a familiar voice whispered, "I unlocked the door."

Roy. Bless that ghost. Not that I could currently use the door to my advantage, but at least I had an escape route at my back. Of course, that wouldn't help any of the other bank patrons being held hostage.

I gave the briefest nod of thanks, and the ghost stepped to the side, surveying the room.

"Isn't that our missing person? Well, this case took an unexpected turn."

Tell me about it. But I didn't say anything. Instead, my gaze moved between the unlikely trio of bank robbers. A homeless woman, a college student, and a lady who looked like she belonged in a country club—how had they come together to rob a bank? And not one of them wore a mask or gloves. According to any cop show or novel I'd ever seen, that was a really bad sign for those of us who were witnesses.

As if summoned by that thought, three new people appeared in the center of the room. Well, not strictly people, as they were soul collectors, grim reapers, angels of death, or whatever people chose to call those beings whose job description involved ferrying souls from the mortal realm to wherever they went next. Soul collectors only appeared when the likelihood of death was probable—it wasn't always guaranteed, as mortals had free will, and insignificant-seeming choices sometimes had cascading effects that could literally be the difference between life and death. But when collectors appeared, someone dying was highly likely. Which was definitely a bad sign for an unknown number of people in this bank.

I recognized all three collectors. Anyone who expected skeletons in black robes carrying scythes to reap the dead would be sorely disappointed. The dark-skinned woman was a blinding display of neon colors, from her bright orange dreadlocks down to her go-go boots. I'd nicknamed her the Raver, and she was a stark contrast to the man beside her, whom I'd nicknamed the Gray Man because of his monocolored gray suit and gray cane topped with a small silver skull. The third man I just called Death. I'd known him my whole life, and recently, rather intimately. As in intimately enough to know what it felt like to fall asleep with my fingers tangled in his chin-length hair. But I didn't know his name.

Roy gave a curse at their sudden appearance and vanished, withdrawing deeper into the land of the dead. Soul collectors collected souls, and ghosts were just wandering souls, fair game to collect anytime they were caught.

The Raver's eyes landed on me and she shook her head, making her long dreads dance over her shoulders. "Damn, girl, you have a knack for being at the wrong place at the wrong time, don't you?"

I gave her a thin smile and made the smallest waving motion with a single finger to Death.

"What the hell?" the homeless woman yelled, spinning to level her gun at the small band of collectors. "Where the hell did you come from? Get on the ground."

The collectors frowned at the woman in unison, surprise evident on each of their faces. Remy and the shotgun lady also spun, their guns moving to the collectors.

"Well, that was unexpected," the Gray Man said, lifting his cane to push his gray fedora back on his head.

"On the ground," Remy yelled at the same time Country Club said, "On your knees!"

The mortals already on the ground looked around the room, faces showing fear, puzzlement, and panic. They couldn't see the collectors. Only grave witches could see collectors, and only when spanning the chasm between the living and the dead. And planeweavers like me, of course, but to my knowledge, I was the only one of those in this realm. Maybe some other rarely encountered magic users could see collectors, but Remy was theoretically human. The other two? I wasn't sure, but I was guessing human. The only time mortals saw collectors was in the moment before their death, and at that point, the collector typically had their hand wrapped around a soul already.

So what was going on?

A woman pulled her legs to her chest and sobbed into her knees. A man began muttering. A prayer? A spell? To my left, the security guard's hands were slowly dropping, moving toward the gun at his belt. This situation was about to escalate quickly.

I met Death's eyes. I wasn't close enough to see if the colors in his irises were spinning, if all the possible scenarios of different potential futures were playing out before him, but I could guess they were. Soul collectors were forbidden from getting involved, from leading mortals toward one possibility over another, but their sudden appearance had thrown them into the thick of this mess. The question was, who were they here to collect?

Death slowly lifted his hands and nodded to his companions. "It's okay. *See*, we are getting down."

He knelt as he spoke, and the Gray Man followed his lead. The Raver shook her head again.

"This just isn't right," she muttered, but she knelt as well, lifting hands with neon-colored nails.

"*See*," Death said again, putting emphasis on the word. He wasn't looking at the robbers now. He was focused on me. When he'd told me to *See* in the past, he always meant he wanted me to gaze through realities.

I cracked my shields, letting the wall I mentally pictured as a hedge of vines peel apart so that I could gaze across the planes. A cold wind cut across my skin, the world around me changing as different planes of existence overlaid reality. I was only seeing across the planes, not weaving them together, so I saw without actually touching the swirls of raw magic waiting to be gathered and directed. The putrid colors of fear soaked into the floor around the cowering bank patrons. The polished marble of the floor looked dull and cracked. The wood of the teller's booth rotted, becoming pitted, half of it crumbling. All around me, purses and clothing, paper and briefcases weathered, becoming thin and full of holes. But the patrons on the floor remained the same, their life force separating them from the decaying touch of the land of the dead, their souls twinkling bright, merry yellow from beneath healthy flesh.

The three robbers were a different story.

With my shields up, I hadn't caught a hint of death or decay from them, but now that my shields were cracked, my magic reached for them like it would any other corpse. But they weren't like any corpse I'd ever encountered. The last walking corpse I'd seen had felt dead, even if he hadn't looked it until after the soul inside him—not his soul—vacated his body. These bodies were dead, my magic was sure of it, but it was like the moment of death had been paused, drawn out to keep going endlessly. They walked, they talked, but I realized the only time I'd seen any draw a breath was directly before they spoke. Robbing a bank was a tense, adrenaline-pumping kind of activity. At least one should have been sweating with nerves, breathing a little too fast. But no. When they stood still, they were eerily still . . . they were dead.

Remy, my client's boyfriend, the person I was supposed to find, was dead.

His soul was wrong as well. All three robbers' souls were wrong. Souls didn't overlay a person with a duplicate image. They weren't clear and defined the way Roy's ghost appearance was, though he was, in fact, a soul. That level of definition didn't occur until after the soul separated from the body. Inside a body, souls were more like an internal glow that radiated outward, surrounding the person in a warm, auralike glow. All three robbers glowed the faint yellow I associated with a human soul, but the glow didn't encompass their bodies right, like the soul inside didn't quite fit.

Country Club had turned back to the teller, urging him to fill the bag with cash faster. The homeless woman kept her assault rifle trained on the three collectors. To my left, the security guard had his weapon in hand and was pushing off the ground. Remy was just starting to turn. He hadn't seen the guard yet, but when he did . . . Regardless of who shot first, if anyone started shooting, the other two robbers would as well. And people would get hurt. Die.

I could see the possibilities on Death's face as he stared at me. He mouthed my name, inclining his head as if giving me permission, or urging me onward. Because I could stop it.

Remy finished his turn. Saw the guard. His gun lifted, aiming, his mouth opened to yell something. I didn't have time to think, to weigh my options. I let my mental shield fall, let the icy touch of the grave rip through me as I let my own magic stab outward and coil around the robbers. Their dead flesh offered no resistance, letting my magic slide right through to the warm, glowing souls beneath.

The souls tried to recoil from the icy touch of my magic, but they were weak, diminished from being trapped inside dead flesh, and the smallest tug of my magic pulled them free.

Three bodies hit the floor simultaneously. Inanimate. Truly dead.

Three souls stood beside them, looking confused, scared. Not one soul matched a body on the ground.

Chapter 6

❧━◆━◆━❧

My ears were ringing, and it took me a moment to realize the security guard had fired a shot before the robbers' bodies hit the ground. People were screaming, crying. I tried to look around, but I hadn't had time to use any finesse when opening my shields, I'd just thrown them wide, and the cacophony of information barraging my senses was overwhelming. I squeezed my eyes closed, but it barely helped. I managed to keep my new secondary shield in place, though, the one that kept my psyche from reaching out and merging planes until everything I saw became part of mortal reality. So, while the racking wind from the land of the dead was whipping my hair around and had caught a stack of deposit envelopes, at least the building wasn't in danger of decaying around me.

Someone brushed by me on their dash to the door. The heat of the brief contact felt scalding even through the light jacket I wore. I needed to get my shields under control. Taking a deep breath, I drew my magic back and then focused on closing the walls I kept around my psyche. Slowly, piece by piece, the living vines I visualized forming my mental shields slid into place. The wind around me died down, but the chill that had snuggled under my flesh remained.

I shivered, opening my eyes.

The room was dimmer now, my magic having burned out some of my vision, at least temporarily. The collectors were clear, though—it was more than my eyes that I saw them with. The Gray Man had already collected the soul that had been inside the homeless woman. I hadn't even had a chance to look at it. The Raver was approaching the soul standing beside the fallen country club lady, though the soul was that of a man. Death was en route for the soul that had popped free from Remy's body.

I held up a hand. "Wait."

Death didn't meet my eyes now, and I pushed off the ground. I was trembling, both from the cold that had ripped through me and from the adrenaline of the last several minutes. I wobbled as I got my feet under me, but my legs held, and I focused on the soul.

She was female. I couldn't tell her age, but I was guessing not much older than Remy. Ghosts often took a moment to realize they'd lost their bodies, and I'd pulled her all the way across into the purgatory of the land of the dead, which was probably an even bigger adjustment. She stared down at Remy's body, shaking her head.

"Hello," I said, trying to get her attention. Death had almost reached us. "What's your name?"

She looked up, and I was close enough to the land

of the dead to see that she'd had big brown eyes in life. They were brimming with insubstantial tears.

"Put me back," she said, kneeling down over Remy's body and plunging her arms into his chest as if trying to pull him back on like a coat. "Put me back right now."

"It doesn't work that way," Death said, kneeling down beside her. "It's time to go." He held out his hand.

She reeled back. "No. No. He said if I did this, he'd put me back."

"Who did?" I asked her, and shot a pleading gaze at Death. I *needed* to talk to this ghost.

He only shook his head. "It's time to go," he said again, and reached out, catching her arm. Her form shimmered, losing its distinctness and becoming brighter, clearer as she transitioned from the land of the dead to the realm of souls again.

"No!" the girl and I shouted at the same time.

Death flicked his wrist and she was gone. The look he gave me was apologetic, but he didn't apologize—he knew what I was. Without a word, he vanished as well, and I was left in the sea of chaos that was the bank.

Two hours later, I was back in the closetlike waiting room in Central Precinct. I again wasn't under arrest, but I had the sinking suspicion I couldn't walk out as easily as I had the day before.

Remy's body was also in the building—presumably in the morgue in the basement. I knew because the charm was once again alerting me that its target was close. At the same time, it had a thin, distant pull to another location, no doubt toward the wilds where I'd first felt the schism.

I considered that as I sat there in an uncomfortable folding chair. I'd assumed the issue was contamination of the focus because a person can't be in two places at once, but what if it wasn't? Remy's body had been at that bank, but his soul hadn't been. Maybe his soul was somewhere in the wilds? I'd never heard of anyone tracking a soul specifically, but typically there wasn't much of a point. Either it was in the same place as the body, or the person was dead, and almost all souls crossed over immediately.

The door opened, revealing a young officer who looked vaguely familiar but I couldn't name. "Ms. Craft, if you'll come this way," he said, gesturing.

I followed obediently. Any hope I had for a friendly sharing of information evaporated when he turned the opposite direction from the detectives' offices and led me instead into an interrogation room.

"Have a seat," he said, pointing to a sturdier but even more uncomfortable-looking chair.

For a moment I thought he was going to be the one leading the interview, but then, without waiting for me to comply, he turned and walked out of the room, the door shutting behind him.

I considered trying the knob, but I was fairly certain it would be locked, and there was a good chance someone was watching from behind the two-way mirror, so I refrained. Walking up to the chair, I sat with as much dignity as I could scrounge up and attempted to not slouch as I waited.

And waited.

I'd succumbed to boredom and was playing a game on my phone when the door finally opened. John, my once-favorite homicide detective, was the first into the room. He carried a small laptop that looked even smaller against his bearlike bulk. His partner, Jenson, followed him. As the door crept closed, I felt more than saw a third figure enter.

Briar.

She was working hard at not being seen, and the spell that masked her magic was once again in place, but while it felt innocuous unless I explored deeper, it was still a spell, and in a group this small, it highlighted her location. I made a point of not looking at her, focusing on the two detectives instead. I knew she was there, but she didn't have to know I knew.

John sat in the chair across from me and set the computer on the table, closed. Another chair waited for Jenson, but he only leaned against the table, arms crossed over his chest. Briar hovered near the far wall, hidden from sight behind her veil of spells. I looked at John. They all looked at me.

No one spoke.

I waited. If I'd learned anything from the summers I'd spent in my father's house, it was how to keep silent. It was never a good idea to offer explanations to questions that hadn't been asked just because a silence stretched too long.

"So why were you at the bank today?" John finally asked.

"Missing-person case."

John and Jenson exchanged a look I couldn't decipher.

"Did you find the person?" Jenson asked.

"He's in your morgue."

Jenson grunted, and there was silence a moment before John said, "Tell us what you witnessed in the bank."

And that was the tricky question. I took a deep breath, but I didn't hesitate. "I walked into a robbery in progress. I believe Remy Hollens was about to lock the door when I walked inside. He held a gun to me and had me click the lock before getting to my knees. He then turned his attention to the bank guard. There was a woman with a shotgun at the teller's desk. She had the man behind the counter fill a duffel bag. There was also an older woman with an assault rifle robbing the hostages."

John nodded, motioning me to continue. This was the hard part. I was fae, so I couldn't lie, but I also couldn't reveal everything I'd seen. I was still unsure I should reveal exactly what I'd done either. All three robbers had been dead already. The collectors would have ripped the ghosts out of the bodies if I hadn't — I was sure that was what Death had been telling me — but they'd *looked* alive. It might be a tricky distinction for someone who hadn't felt the grave rolling off the bodies.

"Someone caught the older woman's attention and she started yelling. That drew the other two robbers' attention. While they were distracted, the security guard drew his own gun. He fired and all three robbers collapsed, dead. Or maybe they collapsed as he fired. It happened really fast." And I'd been otherwise distracted, so I wasn't sure on that detail, but I was guessing none of the bank witnesses could have given any account other than what I just had.

John and Jenson exchanged a look again, and then John opened the laptop. He pulled up a video file and hit play without saying a word.

The screen filled with a quad screen of crisp black-and-white videos. There was no audio file, but I didn't need one—I'd been in the room where it had been recorded. It was security footage from the bank. In shades of gray I watched myself enter the bank. A chill crawled down my spine as I saw Remy shove his gun in my face while I blinked dumbly.

The events unfolded on the small screens exactly how I remembered.

John hit the pause button, freezing the video version of me yelling a silent but clear no, and reaching a hand forward, toward empty space deeper inside the bank. Which was extra odd, as all the other patrons were running out the door.

"Care to revise your statement?" John asked, looking from the series of frozen images and then back up at me.

"I wanted to question the ghost that popped out of Remy's body, but she moved on before I could."

"She?"

I nodded. "Like the museum thief yesterday, today's souls didn't match the already-dead bodies they were wearing."

Briar stalked toward the table, dropping her invisibility spell as she moved. It probably would have been damn impressive and shocking if I hadn't known she was there, but I'd been expecting her to jump in at any moment, so I simply turned, focusing on her for the first time.

"Here's the thing, Craft," she said, sliding the laptop away from John. "That wasn't the only weird moment."

She used the trackpad to back up the video. John's lips compressed, and Jenson scowled, but neither interrupted her. When it came to magical crimes, she outranked them.

"Here, you jump for no reason, and then nod," she said, hitting play. She couldn't see Roy in the video, but the clip was the moment he'd let me know he'd unlocked the door. "And here, before 'someone caught the older woman's attention' as you put it, you focus right on the spot that is about to be the center of the robbers' attention. And again, you nod." She enlarged one panel on the screen, playing a closeup of me when the collectors first appeared. "And then, of course, there is this, right before everyone drops dead." She cued up one more selection, and no big surprise, it was the moment I'd thrown open my shields.

I grimaced. In the black-and-white images, you couldn't see that my eyes were glowing eerie green, but the change in light spilling onto my cheeks and the way my hair lifted in a sudden violent wind were dead giveaways to anyone who'd ever seen me raise a shade that I'd been using my magic. On the screen, it happened so fast. The guard lifted his gun, the maelstrom started around me, and then all three robbers fell, simultaneously. At least I finally knew that the guard shot after they were already falling, though he couldn't have realized it at the time.

I looked back up at Briar. She hadn't asked a question. Yet. I redirected before she could.

"What did the ME determine was the time of death?"

She frowned. "The field determination was inconclusive."

"Because two of the bodies were already in full rigor mortis when the medical examiner arrived, and the other appeared to be coming out of it," John said. Then he sighed and rubbed one large hand over his expanding bald spot. "Alex, help us out here—help yourself out—we have four bodies downstairs who were walking and talking before they met you. The footage from the museum yesterday is horrible quality, but the bank clearly shows you using your magic when three people suddenly drop dead."

"Technically, they were already dead," I said, which earned me a scowl from all three. "Remy Hollens's girlfriend exchanged several text messages with him at five o'clock yesterday, but we don't know at what point he actually went missing between five and eleven that night, when he missed picking her up from work. That's a window of fourteen to twenty hours between his abduction and the robbery. Rigor releases what? Twenty-four to eighty-four hours after death? I'm guessing Remy must have been one of the bodies in full rigor. Have you identified the other two—"

John slammed his palms down flat on the metal table, and I flinched.

"I know you can accelerate decay," he said, so softly that I doubted Jenson, only a few feet away from John, could hear him. "I've been on crime scenes where you have done it."

I opened my mouth. Closed it. I didn't know what to say. He wasn't wrong. It was the root of the issues that had come between us. Until earlier this year, John and I had been good friends. He'd been the one who'd hooked me up with my retainer job with the police years ago, I used to have dinner at his house with him, his wife, and several other cops from the station nearly every Tuesday, and I'd considered him a father figure. We'd drifted apart in recent months. There were just too many things I hadn't told him about my changing magic, my newfound heritage, and my tenuous relationship with the Faerie courts. The fact that a combination of those things had landed me in the middle of some very weird crime scenes, most of which wound up classified above his pay grade, had chipped away at the trust and friendship until a giant gulf had opened between us. I had no idea how to span it, and it looked like I was about to tumble down into it and probably get buried in a landslide.

"I . . ." I started, but then floundered. I was fae, so I couldn't lie. I couldn't claim that my magic had no part in the bodies aging, because my magic had forced the souls out, and from what I could guess from the little I'd seen of these walking corpses, the souls were what prevented the bodies from decaying. Once the souls were out, it all caught up to them. So, in an indirect way, my magic had done this, but not the way he meant.

"Back up the video," I said, and nodded at the laptop.

Briar dragged the bar back to the exact moment I appeared to startle on the screen.

"That was when the ghost who haunts my business informed me he'd unlocked the door. You'll notice later in the video that the first person who rushes by me doesn't stop, just pushes the door open." I nodded for Briar to forward it to the next questionable spot. "Our friendly neighborhood grim reapers appeared here. Most people can't see them, but the robbers were already dead, so apparently they could."

John frowned, and Jenson raised a skeptical eyebrow, but Briar nodded. Almost nothing was known about soul collectors, and many didn't believe they existed. On forums frequented by grave witches, there were threads reporting sightings occasionally, and there were often entire chat rooms devoted to speculation about collectors, but as far as I was aware, I knew more than any other living person. I was also bound with oaths of secrecy about much of it. Briar did know a little, though, as the case we'd met during had resulted in her meeting Death before a creature from the land of the dead had temporarily taken over his body.

"And here?" she asked, forwarding it to the moment before the three robbers collapsed.

"These bodies were better . . . preserved . . . than the thief at the museum. With the museum thief, I felt the grave essence rolling off him from the sidewalk. These three I didn't realize were dead until after the collectors showed up. Here I've opened my shields so I could see into the land of the dead and get an idea of what we were dealing with." Which was true, just not the whole truth. "They were piloted by ghosts. Once the souls were out of the bodies, they stopped mimicking life and collapsed. But all of these people were murdered before they ever walked into that bank."

Briar glanced from me to something in her palm. She scowled at it. Then she set a small glass charm on the table. A lie-detecting charm. It glowed a cheery green, indicating it hadn't caught any lies being spoken.

With a sigh, Briar stepped around John and sank down into the empty chair beside him. Maybe Jenson had left it open for her the whole time. Nah. Jenson wasn't that polite. Or maybe it was just me he didn't like.

"Initial reports indicate no active spells on any of the bodies," Briar said. "How were these corpses, as you call them, walking around?"

And wasn't that the question of the hour. I'd been asking myself that since yesterday. I still didn't know.

"I didn't sense any spells before they stopped moving either, though I admittedly wasn't looking. I am technically still on retainer for the NCPD. The shades might—"

"You're still a suspect," Jenson said, his eyes widening as if he couldn't believe I'd had the audacity to mention the shades. "You're not going anywhere near those bodies."

John frowned, the motion dragging down his gray and red mustache. "Unfortunately, he's right. And that's coming from the top, Alex."

"So now what?" I asked.

Jenson just scowled at me, but John looked to Briar, who shrugged.

"You remain a person of interest in this case," Briar said, then held up her hand to stop my protest when my mouth opened. "But there are enough questionable circumstances that you are not currently under arrest. Geez, Craft, I leave you alone for a few hours and you take a case that should have concluded with a bad breakup and end up with three bodies at your feet." She shook her head, whether in amazement or disgust wasn't clear. "Go home. And, of course, don't leave town."

Chapter 7

---❦---

I wasn't going home. Not immediately, at least.

It probably would have been smart to head straight home as, by the time I walked out of Central Precinct, dusk was only an hour or so away and I wouldn't be able to drive much longer—legally or in actuality. Years of magic had destroyed my night vision. But there were too many questions boiling in the back of my mind. I needed to talk to Death. He'd snatched that ghost right out from under me. If he'd given me five minutes, maybe I'd have more answers now—something to tell my client at the very least. Hopefully he'd have some idea what was going on, if I could get him to answer. Besides, it had been too long since he'd visited. I didn't like feeling like my boyfriend was avoiding me.

The problem was, as always, how to contact him. He hadn't visited me in over a week, and I had the feeling that after today's brief disagreement about the ghost, he wasn't going to drop in tonight. Which meant I needed to get a message to him. And I knew only one way to do that. I had to pay a visit to the Raver, the only collector whose haunt I knew.

The temperatures were quickly dropping with the drooping sun, and I set a brisk pace for my car, turning the heat up to high as soon as I cranked the engine. A charm worked into the air system and seats made the heat kick in and warm to a nice toasty temperature quickly, and I held my hands in front of the vent, letting the warmth flow over them. This car soaked up a sizable chunk of my income, but times like this made it totally worth it. That, and the fact it was fae-engineered without a trace of iron so it didn't make me sick to sit inside it, of course. Always a plus to not be on the verge of passing out every time you crawl behind the wheel.

On the drive, I made the call I really didn't want to make, but it was better if my client heard it from me than from the news. Telling someone her boyfriend was dead was news you should deliver in person, but there was only so much time before sunset and I couldn't drive after dark. So it was the phone, or risk her hearing about it some other way, which would be even worse.

"Hi, Taylor. This is Alex Cra—"

"Did you find him?"

"I did, but, Taylor, it's not good news." I paused, unsure how to continue.

"What do you mean? He wasn't with another girl. I know he wasn't. Is he okay?"

"No," I said, and then blew out the breath I hadn't realized I was holding. "No, he's not okay. You're probably going to hear a lot of confusing stories about . . . about how Remy died. But, Taylor, I don't want you to jump to any conclusions. No matter what you hear, remember that you knew who he really was."

A jagged sob cut through the line, and I heard a loud clattering crash as she dropped the phone. I didn't think she'd fainted because I could hear her crying on the other side, long, loud cries of pain ripping from her heart to her throat and out. I waited, keeping the line open but staying silent.

It took several minutes, but finally the screams and sobs coming from the other side quieted. A moment later, something scuffed along the microphone of the phone and Taylor returned.

"Ms. Craft, are you still there?" she asked, and at my affirmative said, "How did he . . . ? How did it happen?"

"The police are investigating. My personal belief is that whatever happened, started last night before he was supposed to pick you up. Magic of some sort was almost certainly involved. His body was at the First Bank of Nekros near the East Town Village shopping center."

"Why would he be way out there? Magic? So not an accident. You're still investigating, right?"

I wanted to say that looking into a murder wasn't part of our contract, but that seemed too blunt, too heartless to say to someone who'd just received the news I'd given her. Instead I said, "It is an active police investigation now."

"The police didn't do squat when he was missing," she yelled, and then it sounded like she slapped a hand over her mouth to try to reclaim the frustrated sentence. I heard her take a long, shaky breath before she continued. "Sorry. I didn't . . . No, I did mean that. But I paid you for five hours of investigating already. Surely some are left?"

If I didn't count the time I'd spent at Central Precinct — and I hadn't planned to charge her for that time despite the fact that I'd only been there because of my work searching for Remy — I still had a couple of hours left. I'd planned to issue a refund for those remaining hours, but I could use them following up on the remaining trace from the tracking spell. I was fairly certain it was Remy's soul, and I had the sinking feeling I'd find it in someone else's body. That might answer some of the questions that had been cropping up since I'd spotted the first walking corpse yesterday, but it also sounded more dangerous than it was worth and would probably get me in further trouble with the police.

"I will look over what I have on the case and see if there are any leads I can follow for you," I said, not committing to continuing but not dismissing the possibility. It wasn't the answer she wanted, but it was the best I could offer right now. I'd weigh the options tonight but would probably turn the tracking charm over to the police and let them follow up on it.

I had Taylor promise she'd stay with family or friends tonight before wrapping up the conversation. I hung up as I pulled into a parking lot in front of a large, squat industrial-looking building. It looked like just another warehouse, but it wasn't. The low, rhythmic pulse of a bass beat proved that this was exactly the building I was looking for.

A large man with bulging muscles and two full sleeves of magic-laced tattoos sat on a bar stool just inside the door of the building. His arms were crossed over his chest, his posture announcing that he was imposing, and going for a touch of menacing. Maybe it was just the fog in my eyesight in the dim entry, or the fact that the bar I usually frequented kept trolls as bouncers and this guy was small in comparison, but I just wasn't impressed by his show.

I paid my cover and he let me pass with a disparaging look at my less-than-club-ready attire. I pulled open the second door and passed from the relative calm of the entryway into the chaos of sound and light of the club.

What was mostly bass outside the building became full-bodied synthetic electric music once I entered the club proper. Strobes flashed, black lights glowed, and fog machines filled the air with cloudy water vapor. It was early evening on a Saturday, and the club was already hopping, but not as packed as it would be later in the night. While it was loud, and the lights were disorienting, at least there wasn't a crush of bodies to contend with.

I moved forward slowly, weaving between tables and trying not to trip over chairs, which appeared to all be gathered around the outskirts of the room and the back where the bar was situated, leaving the bulk of the large space open as a dance floor. I could make out several dark shapes moving on the dance floor, as well as a few who glowed fluorescent in the black lights. None were who I was looking for. When I finally spotted my target, it was obvious—she was the only person in this club I could see clearly. Mainly because I saw her with my mind more than my eyes.

She spotted me before I made it halfway across the

dance floor, and she stopped undulating to the beat to glare daggers at me.

"Didn't we discuss this club being off-limits to the likes of you?" the Raver asked, pressing her fists against hips clad in orange pants that glowed even brighter than normal under the black lights.

"I need to talk to him, but I don't know how to reach him. You do."

She huffed, cocking a hip. "He *should* be staying away. You're nothing but trouble."

Neither one of us had to clarify who "he" referred to. Death. Of course, that wasn't his real name, or a name the Raver would recognize him by. I didn't know his real name—or hers, for that matter—and as far as I'd observed, collectors didn't use names at all. It could make things confusing, but we both knew there was only one person I'd track her down for.

"He's my boyfriend."

She rolled her eyes so hard her whole head moved with the action, making her long dreads twitch like snakes curling around her.

"I need to talk to him," I said again. "Can you let him know I'm looking for him?"

The Raver just stared at me a moment, incredulous. I met her gaze, not backing down. After a moment, she made a sound that wasn't dissimilar to a growl before slashing her glowing orange-capped nails through the air in a dismissive gesture. "Sure. I'll tell him. But don't you think he knows? He pops off to see you whenever he can. If that's not enough for your mortal heart, then you should cut him loose. Don't you know how dangerous your forbidden dalliances are?"

I had some idea, but I had the suspicion he hadn't told me the full extent of it. "I'm not trying to endanger him."

"Then let him go."

My hands clenched at my sides. I hadn't come here to have my relationship critiqued. "He could walk away anytime."

"Until you have a case you can't solve without trying to pry the secrets of the universe out of him. Then you'd crawl back, looking for him."

My jaw clenched, but I looked away because she wasn't completely wrong. Wasn't that basically what I was doing here? I wasn't here because I was worried about him, or because I missed him so much I'd burst if he didn't visit soon. I was here because he hadn't visited in a while and I wanted to ask him about a case. If I was completely honest with myself, I was angry with him. Angry he hadn't visited. Angry for him taking the soul at the bank, even though he was just doing his job. Angry about all the things he couldn't tell me. Like his name.

Yeah, she wasn't completely out of line. And that made the words sting a lot worse.

"Just let him know," I said, forcing myself to meet her eyes again.

"I already said I would."

Right. So that was that then. I nodded to her, trying to acknowledge thanks without actually verbalizing it. Then I turned.

Several people were staring at me. In fairness, I'd been standing in the middle of a dance floor, not dancing, and having a conversation with someone no one else could see. Yeah, that likely didn't seem strange at all.

"You're welcome," the Raver called behind me, her voice dripping with sarcasm.

I didn't turn but focused on navigating back to the entrance and the more reliable evening light outside.

It was far too dark for my comfort as I reached my neighborhood, and I found myself squinting into the dimness as I reached the driveway. I hated this time of year. The days were too short. Four cars were already in the drive, so I parked at the curb. We'd been cited for doing it by the homeowners' association already, but they'd be even angrier if someone parked on the lawn, so until we widened the drive, it was what it was.

I took a moment to brace myself before I left the cozy warmth of my car and dashed for the front door of Caleb's house. Until recently, I would have gone around the side of the house to a set of steps that led to the second-floor room I used to rent, and, on paper, it was still listed as my legal residence. But the situation had changed.

I let myself through the front door into the empty house beyond. Despite the nearly half dozen cars out front, the house was dark, silent. No one actually lived in it anymore. Caleb still used his studio on the main floor, and it was kept furnished in case anyone visited, but the house had been used more as a passageway than a residence for nearly a month now.

I started to navigate my way through the darkness

toward the back door, but then hesitated. The house did serve one other purpose. It was the place with power and Wi-Fi. There was one other source where I might be able to find information about walking corpses, or at least if other grave witches had encountered them: the Dead Club Forums.

I detoured, heading through Caleb's living room toward the inner stairs that would lead up to the old apartment I used to rent. A power charger for my laptop and phone waited on the small bar area in the one-room apartment, and I pulled out both and plugged them in, booting up my laptop.

I clicked the desktop shortcut that sent me to the Dead Club Forums, the unofficial Internet home of grave witches all over the world. While the site was geared toward grave witches, other magic users dropped in occasionally as well. Many of the non–grave witches were morbidly curious about magic dealing with the dead, and others were obvious forum trolls, but sometimes more bizarre elements posted.

I turned to the search feature first. It was . . . limited, to say the least. I looked for information on tracking a soul first. A handful of hits popped up. Most were hypothetical, but a few claimed they'd actually managed to track ghosts. In each case, there were no details listed and most of the profiles had been deactivated, making me think they probably weren't legitimate accounts. I then tried every iteration of "walking dead" and "animate corpse" I could think of. Most of the results were unrelated, but two showed promise. Both were infuriatingly vague but seemed to hint at necromancy, which was what I was already leaning toward.

Despite being a witch who worked with the dead

regularly, I knew almost nothing about necromancy. Spells that physically affected dead bodies or used human or fae body parts were illegal in every country in the mortal realm. Practicing necromancy was banned, and even owning books about it was punishable with huge fines and/or jail time. So, even on the Dead Club Forums, necromancy was talked around, not about.

I opened the compose mode on a new thread, but hesitated as I considered the very few details I knew about the case. The ghosts piloted the bodies. The bodies decayed abnormally fast once the ghosts were ejected. What else? I stared at the blinking cursor in the center of the blank box, not sure how I could ask if anyone had dealt with either of those scenarios without the thread getting tagged by an admin.

"Hard day?" asked a masculine voice from across the room.

I startled at the sound, even though the voice was wonderfully familiar. My head shot up, my gaze landing on Death leaning against the wall, watching me.

"You came."

He lifted one shoulder, the movement making the black T-shirt he wore pull tight across a well-muscled chest. "You called," he said, pushing off the wall.

Somehow he managed to cross the room quickly without ever looking hurried, his stride confident but languid as he closed the distance between us before I had time to do anything more than let my eyes drink in his form. He leaned down, his fingers brushing featherlight along my cheek before coming to rest on my neck so he could guide my lips to his.

I went willingly, the kiss starting oh-so-soft and then becoming more as we both answered the need that snapped like electricity between us. My hands moved up Death's chest, feeling the contrast of his soft shirt over hard muscles as I wrapped my arms around his shoulders. He in turn dragged me closer, engulfing me in strong arms.

The kiss spoke of lost time and longing, and while it lasted, it washed away everything else. There was just him and me. His hazel eyes so close. His sweet breath on my skin. This moment. This connection.

Then the kiss broke, and the world crashed down between us again.

He smiled. My answering smile was slow, feeble.

Death brushed a strand of hair from my face. "What's wrong?"

I forced myself not to look away.

"It's been over a week since you visited." I could have added to the list, but while I had once shared every secret I had with Death, I didn't anymore. I couldn't. After all, how do you tell the man you love that when you'd been dosed with a hallucinogenic drug that made nightmares come to life, it had been images of him that had tormented you?

It would hurt him. It hurt me, mostly because it had been manifestations of my own doubts, fears, and the slew of unanswered questions about things I didn't know about him that had given the visions power. Now the secret hung over me.

And I had to wonder how he kept so many secrets himself.

It wasn't something I wanted to dwell on. My time with him was always too short for such things. Instead I lifted onto my toes, bringing my lips up to his again as I said, "I missed you."

"Obviously." He whispered the word against my lips before submitting to the kiss I'd offered.

There was just as much heat in it as our first kiss, but something was different about this one. The desire was still there, but now the time apart wasn't a desperate need to be made up for, it was distance between us.

When the kiss broke, he leaned his forehead against mine. "I'll try to visit more."

"Do that," I said, giving him the smile I knew he needed. But he'd told me that before. Sometimes he was better at following through with it than other times. Like the Raver had said, our relationship was dangerous. I knew that, and it bought him a lot of slack in the boyfriend department.

"So the bank today was crazy, right?" I said, as I straightened.

Death frowned at me. "Alex, did you call me here to exploit me for your case?"

"You'd rather I exploit you for sex?"

The frown vanished, and he lifted his arms, opening them wide. "Yes, please."

I laughed, but cut off abruptly when I looked up and noticed the colors spinning in his hazel irises. He was being called away.

Death lifted his hand to my cheek, his thumb trailing along my jaw, the touch both caress and apology. "Rain check?"

"Please don't go." The words slipped out before I could catch them.

I wished I could call them back as soon as they escaped. Not because of the potential debt that sprang up between us with the words—and it was a lot; my desire for him to stay was immense and would require him to ignore his duty as a soul collector. But that wasn't why I wished I could call the words back. No, I wanted to retract them because of the heartbreak that spread across his face.

He couldn't stay. I knew he couldn't. When the color spun in his irises like that, someone whose soul he was responsible for was at a crucial moment in their life. One likely to lead to death. He needed to be there to send the soul on to wherever it was souls went.

"Go," I whispered.

Death leaned forward and kissed me. It was a soft kiss, tasting of sorrow and secrets and duty.

He broke off and leaned his forehead against mine. "I'll return as soon as I can."

I nodded, closing my eyes.

He kissed me one more time. A mere brush of his lips against mine.

Then he vanished.

After Death left, I packed up my laptop without ever finishing—or starting—my post on the Dead Club Forums. I'd think about the best way to word my questions tonight and write up a thread when I got to the office in the morning.

Heading back downstairs, I didn't even bother turning on the lights as I passed through the living room and kitchen to the back door. I'd walked this path so many times now, I could do it blind. I used my key to unlock the double-cylinder deadbolt and stepped out into a yard very different from the one I'd walked through to the front door when I'd first arrived home.

The air that greeted me here was warm and comfortable without a hint of the crisp November wind that had whispered of coming winter less than half an hour earlier. The sun had almost finished setting, but the oppressive blindness that hung over my damaged vision during most low-light situations was lessened, not gone, but less severe. The shadows were deep, but not all-consuming, and I could clearly make out the castle in the distance.

It was a hike to reach it, and for the last portion, I was walking in starlight. Moon-loving flowers bloomed along the path as I walked, offering their light glow to the stars above. It was beautiful. Magical.

Like literally, magical. If I'd walked around the side of Caleb's house, I would have wound up in the predictable small backyard with two of its sides bordered by the fences of our neighbors. But Caleb's back door now acted as a passageway into a folded space that had opened to hold my land and castle when I'd been granted my independent status by the Winter Queen. The Faerie castle had wedged itself into mortal reality.

It had been shocking to discover the newly unfolded space, but once I'd gotten over the initial disbelief, I'd accepted that it was home. It wasn't exactly Faerie or the mortal realm, but an intricate weave of both. My eyes liked it, my magic liked it, and it felt right.

Everyone else apparently liked it as well.

The current occupancy beyond me included Rianna, Desmond, Ms. B, and a garden gnome, all of whom had lived there before I'd accidentally inherited the castle. The new residents were my former landlord, Caleb, and our other roommate, Holly; two ghosts; an assortment of gargoyles who'd moved in on their own and decided to start guarding the place; and Falin Andrews, the

Winter Queen's knight and my sometimes—but not current—lover. It should have been getting pretty full, but it was a magical Faerie castle, and I was starting to think it conjured more rooms when needed.

I crossed over the moat and under the portcullis, and then into one of the magnificent gardens within the stone walls. I still hadn't gotten a chance to fully explore the gardens, but tonight wasn't going to be the day. Crossing through the garden quickly, I entered the castle proper and followed the sound of people to a dining hall. There was a huge banquet room in the castle somewhere—I'd wandered into it once by accident—but this room was narrower, holding only one long table in the very center of the room. A roaring fire crackled in an enormous fireplace along one wall, directly beside the table, which should have made the room uncomfortably hot and dry since the weather outside the castle was so pleasant, but instead the room remained at a constant ideal. *Magic.* The fire and the half dozen candelabras scattered among the serving platters on the table were the only light in the room. Typically I would have needed a little more light, but here it was enough for me to see by. This place might have been a blend of mortal reality and Faerie, but there was a lot of Faerie magic here.

Holly, Caleb, and Ms. B sat at one end of the table, talking and laughing as they ate. Falin sat at the other end, alone except for the smartphone in his hand. He looked too preoccupied to be interested in joining the cheery gathering at the other end of the table.

And maybe he was.

But I doubted it.

Falin was the Winter Queen's knight, her enforcer,

her bloody hands. He was subject to her commands, and she'd made him do some pretty terrible things in her name in the past. It hadn't made him very popular. Unfortunately, it wasn't a job one could easily resign from.

The queen's nephew had been poisoning her, driving her increasingly insane, possibly since before I'd first had my less-than-comfortable introduction to her. Many of her commands had reflected that growing insanity. I'd been told she was getting better now that she hadn't been exposed to the drug in nearly a month, but she still hadn't reversed one of her last commands to Falin, that he live in my home to keep an eye on me. So he lived in the castle with the rest of us, much to the disapproval of most of my castlemates.

You would think a magic castle would be big enough that everyone could avoid each other if they wanted, but the castle had other plans. It served an enormous feast, family-style, every night. The kitchen and pantry went missing during the evening hours, and even normal, mortal food we brought into the castle and secreted away in our rooms disappeared. If you were in the castle and wanted to eat, you came to the table or went hungry.

Some days Falin came down long enough to fix a plate and carry it back to his room, but mostly he sat at the far end of the table, alone. It always forced me to choose whether I should sit with him or the rest of my friends, like some grade school cafeteria table dilemma. Today I wasn't in the mood to choose. I'd had a long, hard day. I didn't feel like having to think about it.

Walking around the table, I scooped up the plate in front of Falin. I'd intended to keep going, walking away with it, but I didn't make it a full step before he caught my arm. He frowned at me, but I grabbed his wrist with my free hand and gave him a tug. Now, I'm not a small girl—in my boots, I'm easily six feet tall—but Falin was taller, and broader, and all muscle. I couldn't have moved him if my life depended on it, but when I tugged again, he rose to his feet. The look he gave me was skeptical at best, but he followed when I led him around the table. I sat down beside Holly, placing his plate on my other side.

"—which is why I said bikes," Holly was saying as I sat. She turned, offering me a friendly smile while completely ignoring the blond-haired fae standing at my back. "What do you think, Al?"

"About bikes?" I said, leaning forward to fill my plate with some sort of carved bird that had been cooked until the outside was crisp but the pale meat oozed with mouthwatering juices. "What about bikes?"

"To reach the house quicker. A bicycle would cut down the time it took for us to respond to things happening outside the folded space."

"True." I accepted a plate of rolls as Caleb passed them my way. "But you'd get pretty sweaty on a bike. Wouldn't a vehicle of some sort be faster and more convenient? "

Caleb shook his head. "How would you get a vehicle through the door, not to mention my house?"

"An ATV could work," Falin said, finally sitting down. "Though we might have to carry it through the door and put the wheels on once it was on this side."

The others at the table frowned at him, and I wasn't sure if it was because he'd joined their conversation or if they disagreed.

"That could work," I said between mouthfuls of food.

Ms. B shook her head. "Those things are loud and the wheels rip up the ground. You'll give our poor gnome a fit."

The elusive garden gnome. I was starting to think he was a myth. I still hadn't met him.

"Well, I bought a bike," Holly said, setting down her fork and leaning back in her chair. "Maybe it will help me work off all these elaborate feasts."

I laughed and shook my head. "It's Faerie food. I'm pretty sure it magically lacks calories."

"It has to have some calories," Rianna said from the door. "Otherwise we'd all starve while gorging ourselves. But we do seem to be able to indulge rather more than we would in mortal food."

"Well, in that case," Holly said, picking back up her fork, "someone cut me a thick slice of that German chocolate cake."

Caleb and Ms. B chuckled, but I was focused on Rianna. She crossed the room slowly, leaning heavily on Desmond as she moved. She was paler than she'd been when I saw her in the office earlier, her movements labored. When she finally reached the chair across from me, she sank into it gratefully. Desmond fussed at her side a moment longer, as if ensuring she wasn't going to collapse sideways out of her seat, and then he turned and climbed into the chair beside her. I might have commented on the huge black dog sitting at the table, but the barghest wasn't really a dog, he was a fae, and he actually had a man-shaped form, though I'd only seen it twice.

Rianna's movements remained stiff and slow as she served both herself and Desmond, but they smoothed out as she went. By the time her plate was full, they seemed much less laborious.

"You're frowning at me," she said as she filled a mug from a pitcher on the table.

Oops. "I'm just concerned. Maybe you should go to the Eternal Bloom for sunrise and sunset."

She shook her head. "I'm fine. It's a little uncomfortable during the transition, but it wears off fast. Besides, here I don't have to worry about losing time to the stupid doors."

That much was true. The doors at the Bloom sometimes deposited people back into mortal reality hours later than anticipated even when every precaution had been addressed. Still, sunrise and sunset, the times when Faerie's magic was weakest in the mortal realm, were hard on Rianna. As a changeling, she relied on the magic of Faerie to hold off the centuries she'd lost while a captive in Faerie. If she were ever to be caught in the mortal realm during sunset or sunrise, all those years would catch up to her, aging her hundreds of years in a moment. A mortal couldn't survive that. The castle, with its strange blend of planes, prevented those transition moments from being deadly to her, but there was still enough of the mortal world here to make sunset and sunrise draining for her.

"I'm fine," she said again. "Nearly back up to full strength already. Now tell me how the investigation went today?"

I groaned. "Not so hot. I ended up being taken hostage in a bank robbery."

Around me, the chatter at the table went silent, and I could feel all eyes turn on me, particularly the silent fae at my side who was part spy, part protector, and, despite his attempts to distance himself, my friend.

"Obviously I walked away from it okay," I said, though with the rash of recent walking corpses, maybe that wasn't quite so obvious as it should have been.

"Another bank robbery?" Holly asked, breaking the growing tension, for which I was grateful. "That's what, the third in a week? Was it the same three people? Did they catch them this time?"

"Uh . . . sort of?" They certainly wouldn't be robbing any more banks. But Remy had only gone missing last night. While there had been three robbers, he couldn't have been involved with the previous robberies, could he? "What did the people from the other two robberies look like?"

"Haven't you been watching the news?" Holly asked, raising one of her perfect strawberry-blond eyebrows.

I shrugged. "Not so much. No electricity in the castle and I've been busy at work."

She granted me that one with a begrudging nod as Caleb jumped into the conversation. "None of the robbers wore masks, but only one has been identified. Annabelle something or other. Her husband had reported her missing a couple days before the first robbery. The other woman and the man have not been identified yet, but the media has been splashing their pictures around."

Huh. That sounded eerily similar. I made a mental note to look up the coverage as the conversation around me moved on to how we could get electricity and Internet in the castle. I was still deep in thought, mindlessly attacking my food, when I realized Falin was staring at me.

"What?" I asked, turning to face him.

His icy blue gaze swept over me, filled with worry and warmth. "You're okay?"

I waved a hand, gesturing at my still whole and unharmed body. He studied my face, as if he could find the truth to any nonphysical pains I might be hiding.

"I'm fine," I said, and I meant it. I didn't like what I'd done. Seeing those seemingly living bodies drop like marionettes with cut strings would probably join the other nightmares that regularly woke me, but I stood by the fact that I'd done the right thing. They'd already been dead, and my actions meant no one else got hurt.

But it *would* haunt me.

Falin's frown deepened, and I changed the subject before he could pry further. "Do you know any fae who could move a soul between bodies?"

"Like Coleman?"

I thought about it and then shook my head. "No, what he did when he stole a body left a lot of magic and glyphs on the body. And the bodies he stole were still alive. I'm looking for something that could put a ghost in a corpse without leaving a magical trace." I thought about the female ghost I'd pulled out of Remy's body and how she'd begged to be put back inside. "The ghosts may be cooperative, but I think they need someone else's help to inhabit and take control of the stolen body."

"Alex, what's going on?" Rianna asked, her food forgotten in front of her. Her reaction made sense, as Coleman had been the one to hold her captive in Faerie. He'd used her to facilitate his body thieving, so she might know more about moving souls between bodies than any other living person. At least any I had access to. I hadn't wanted to rehash what I'd encountered at the bank again until I got a chance to talk to Death at length, but it seemed I didn't have much choice.

I summarized the story the best I could, focusing most of my details on what little I knew about the walking corpses. Falin listened silently, the scowl on his face darkening. Rianna interrupted to ask questions a few times, but by the end, she was shaking her head.

"That definitely sounds like necromancy," she said, her voice thin, strained.

"So you know something about it?" Did I sound a little too hopeful to hear that one of my best friends had knowledge of forbidden magic?

"Eh, probably not much more than you," she said, an apologetic note to her voice. "Coleman used death magic, true, but not necromancy. He wanted his bodies still alive and functioning."

"Oh." That made sense. I sighed. It had been worth a shot.

I focused back down on my plate, pushing the food around more than actually eating it. When I glanced back up, I noticed the soul collector watching me from beside the fireplace. I hadn't expected Death to return tonight, but there he was, waiting and glaring at where Falin sat beside me. I swallowed the food I was currently eating and excused myself. Rianna started to protest, but I wasn't sure how long Death could stay. When your boyfriend could be called away at any moment, there was no time to dally.

Chapter 8

PC met us at the door to the sitting room in my personal suite of rooms. He barked his greeting, standing on his back legs, front working the air as he begged. I released Death's hand, taking a moment to lean down and rub the crest of white hair on the top of PC's head. Rianna and I had a standing agreement that if I didn't make it back to the office before she left for the night, she'd take PC home and lock him in my room. He would have loved to roam the castle, but we weren't sure if animals could get addicted to Faerie food, so we weren't taking any chances.

Once my dog had calmed, I straightened, turning back to Death. I lifted onto my toes and kissed him. Light and quick. Just a greeting. The "hello" that neither of us had said. I started to step back, but he wrapped his arms around me, drawing me into a hug that tugged me against his chest. He held me like that in silence for a moment, and for the first time in a while, I felt warm, completely safe, and content. I relished the feeling, and I hated it because I knew it wouldn't last.

"I missed you." He said the words into my hair, still holding me close, blocking out the rest of the world.

"You just saw me this afternoon." I meant for it to be a joke. It fell short.

He stepped back, holding me at arm's length so that he could look at me. "I didn't want to go earlier."

"I know." I did. Our relationship was the definition of complicated. He was breaking all the rules to be here. The other collectors kept telling me if I truly cared, I'd send him away. Relationships between soul collectors and mortals were forbidden. Dangerous.

The being in charge of the soul collectors, who I called the Mender, had already stripped Death of some of his abilities because Death had twice exchanged essences with me. The ability to exchange essences was meant to allow soul collectors to pass along their mantle when they grew weary so that they could move on to wherever souls went next. As in, it was meant to be used on another disembodied soul, not a still-living mortal. Under normal circumstances it couldn't have been used on the living, but because I was a planeweaver and touched several planes at once, Death had been able to use it with me. He'd saved my life, and in the process had become mortal himself, at least temporarily. I'd bargained with the Mender and taken a huge debt I'd yet to repay, but the Mender had agreed to return that ability once Death was ready to pass on, ensuring he wasn't doomed to eternity as a soul collector.

That bargain didn't mean the Mender approved of our relationship. What more would he do if he found out we were still together? Relocate Death? Strip all

of his abilities and send him along with all the other
souls? That was one of my greatest fears. Whenever the
time between Death's visits stretched too long, I worried
that Death had moved on, and I'd never get to say good-
bye, or even know what happened. He'd just vanish.

Complicated. That was an understatement.

"No running, remember?" Death said in response
to whatever he saw on my face.

I tried to smile, but my smile felt too far away, out
of reach, buried under all the things we didn't say, didn't
discuss. I barely admitted it to myself, but I was worried
about us. He had never said it, but I could see in his
eyes that he was too. That fact hurt worse than I was
prepared for. He was always the confident one. The one
so sure of his feelings. The one not afraid to say "I love
you."

I couldn't stand there anymore, staring into his
warm eyes and seeing both love and worry. My first
instinct was to pull away, to cross the room and focus
on something—*anything*—else. But he was right. When
we'd first started this, I'd promised not to run. If I broke
that promise, if I pulled away, I'd be giving up on us.
That wasn't an option. So I stepped forward, toward
him, sliding my arms up over his shoulders, pressing
my lips to his.

The kiss started soft and sad, and then grew, becoming needy, full of longing and urgency as our bodies
mirrored the chaotic swirl of emotions tangled between
us. Time was short. He could get called away. But he
was here now. Real and warm and mine for right now.
My hands slid down his chest, tracing muscles still hidden under his shirt. When I reached his waist, I shoved
the hem of the shirt up, anxious to feel more skin under

my palms. To drag my fingers through the fine dark hairs on his tanned chest.

He broke off long enough to pull his shirt over his head. Then his mouth closed on mine again. His hands slid over my ass, and he lifted me. I obliged by wrapping my legs around his hips, drawing my body over a part of him that was now very hard. He groaned and walked us to the nearest wall, pressing my back to it. I was pinned between the cold stone behind my back and Death's warmth seeping into me from the front.

I broke from his mouth, gasping as I said, "I own a bed, you know."

"So you've told me. You own a wall too."

He leaned in, but I pressed a finger to his lips, stopping him only an inch away.

"I own the whole damn castle."

I moved my finger, the distance between us closing so that his reply of "You do" was murmured directly against my lips.

His hands moved to my waist, sliding under my sweater, making my skin tighten and tingle as he moved upward, over my stomach, my ribs, until his thumb hooked under my bra and stroked my breast. I inhaled, squirming against him. Needing more.

"We have too many clothes on." My words came out more as a moan as he unsnapped my bra so he could cup one breast. He seemed to understand anyway, pulling back enough that I could wiggle out of my sweater before attacking the button on his jeans.

We left a trail of discarded clothes from the sitting room to my bedroom until we tumbled completely naked into my bed. I scrambled on top of Death, taking the length of him inside me, my movements slow but rhythmic, enjoying watching him under me, responding to every twitch of my body. The moonlight flooded through the window, bathing both of us in soft light. His fingers dragged at my hips, trying to change my rhythm, but I resisted until he sat up under me.

"You are trying to torture me," he said, sucking my nipple in his mouth and drawing hard.

I moaned, my rhythm faltering, and Death used the opportunity to flip us over. Despite his words, he didn't rush it but let his pace build gradually. I met him thrust for thrust until we both came screaming and panting.

"That was . . . We should definitely do that more often," I said, one hand still tangled in his dark hair. I couldn't feel my legs yet post-orgasm, but they were probably still locked behind his butt.

He laughed, the sound deep and masculine rolling over my sated flesh. Then he kissed me, though we had to break off quick as we were both still gasping.

"I love you," he said, and rolled us over so we were both on our sides.

It took only a little wiggling to find a comfortable position in each other's arms. We'd fit together since the first time we embraced. We lay there, holding each other, until we were breathing normally again. I was exhausted, both in a post-great-sex kind of way and emotionally exhausted after a long day, but I didn't know when I'd see Death again, so I couldn't put off asking him the questions I needed answers to, even if the conversation would kill the contented post-sex buzz we had going on.

"We need to talk."

Death's arms tightened slightly around me. "I'm told it's never a good sign when a woman says that."

I pushed up on one elbow so I could see his face. "Not *that* conversation." Though at some point, we were going to have to talk about our relationship and all the unanswered questions that hung between us. They might not affect our sharing really, really good sex, but if this was a relationship and not just a booty call when he could spare a moment, we had to have that talk. But not tonight. "It's about my case."

Death didn't say anything, but he didn't vanish, so I took that as a positive sign.

"How does a ghost get inside someone else's body?"

"Magic, obviously," he said, and when I glared at him, he shrugged. "Hey, you asked the question. Don't hate me for answering."

"Okay, fine. I didn't feel any trace of magic on the bodies. How were the ghosts staying inside? And how were they moving the bodies? I've seen souls inside bodies after the body has died. They're stuck. They can't make the body walk around."

Death was silent so long, I didn't think he was going to answer. Finally he said, "Most of the magic was on the souls, not the shells. I could see it. As to the rest . . ." He shook his head. "I've never encountered it before. Souls and bodies usually work in harmony, but these . . . The souls fueled the bodies without the bodies returning the favor. It was an unsustainable condition."

I blinked in surprise. That might have been one of the most straightforward and informative things he'd ever said. Typically he was as elusive and obscure as a cat. I considered what he'd said, fitting it in with what I'd seen.

"So they are both driver and a battery for the dead bodies," I said, more thinking aloud than anything. It didn't explain how it was done, but it gave me more than I had. It also eased a knot that had been tightening inside me. Despite knowing the bodies were dead, there was a nagging question of whether I'd killed something alive in a way I couldn't comprehend. But if piloting the bodies depleted the ghosts, it would destroy the soul over time. "Do you know who is making them? Where the ghosts are coming from?"

Death shook his head, a frown pulling on his full lips.

I tried something different. "One of the corpses, Remy, he would have died less than a day before the robbery. Do you know where? Was his soul collected, or is it still out there?"

"I didn't collect him. The others? We don't make a habit of discussing our souls, but . . ."

But this case was an oddity, and he suspected they hadn't either.

"Today, in the bank, did you come for the ghosts or . . . ?" I knew this question bordered on a forbidden topic. Just because I knew about the lines of possibility that collectors could see didn't mean Death was allowed to discuss them with me.

He studied my face for a long time, and I sighed.

"Not exactly the best pillow talk, huh? I can't say I've had a lot of practice." The words were a peace offering, a joke at my own expense as well as a pass for him.

He smiled and brushed a kiss across my nose. "You never cease to be fascinating." Then the smile faded a notch and he said, "No, we weren't there for the ghosts. Once dead, a person has no more possible paths for us to foresee. We were there because almost every other soul in that room had a probability of dying in one possible line of the future or another. The possibility that no one at all would die was almost negligible. But you are always the wild card."

I swallowed. So my actions had saved people. I *had* read him right in those too-fast moments in the bank. But that also meant he had broken even more rules. Soul collectors couldn't interfere with the living, but through me, he had. He'd helped make a negligible possibility come to pass. Because he'd wanted to save the people in the bank? Or because he couldn't see my lines of possibility, so he didn't know if I'd die too?

This was why relationships between collectors and mortals were forbidden. You try to save the person you love.

"A penny for your thoughts," he murmured.

"What's your name?" I hadn't meant to ask the question. It just slipped out.

It was such a simple thing. A name. But I didn't know it, and it was one of the unanswered questions eating away at me. Could I really know him if I didn't even know his name?

"Alex . . ." He was frowning.

I frowned back. "That's my name."

He'd been so candid tonight, I thought it was possible that maybe . . .

But no.

I sighed, changing the subject to let the last pass. "Is there some way for me to contact you? It's hard having no way to reach you, and I think your friend might eventually collect me out of spite if I show up to her favorite club too many times."

He shook his head, the sadness tugging at his eyes deepening. He had a spell tied to my soul that let him find me as well as let him know if I was severely injured. He'd only admitted to it recently, but he'd attached it years ago. But there was no way for me to call him, to let him know I needed to see him. Or that I just wanted to. That sucked.

Death kissed me lightly on the forehead. "You should sleep. It's late."

He was right, and I was exhausted. But . . .

"I'll try to stop in more," he said, his hand stroking gently down my spine.

I should have told him no. I wanted to tell him I cared about him too much for him to take that risk. But all I said was, "That would be nice," as I tucked tighter against his body. "Will you still be here when I wake?"

"Probably not, but I'll stay as long as I can."

Which was about as much as I could hope for. I closed my eyes and breathed in his scent, focused on enjoying the feel of his body against mine while he was still here. Comfortable and safe in his arms, it didn't take long for sleep to find me.

I woke an unknown amount of time later, chill bumps prickling along my bare body. The pillow beside me was still faintly warm. Death must have recently left, the absence of his encircling warmth having woken me. I wished I could hope he'd be back soon, but I knew he wouldn't. I was exhausted and doubted I'd been asleep more than an hour. I considered crawling under the blanket and going right back to sleep, but the bed felt too cold and empty and I really needed a shower.

Dragging myself out of bed, I took a quick but hot shower, not even bothering to brush out the snarls passing for my curls. Either Ms. B or the castle itself took the liberty of laying out pajamas for me each night—I wasn't sure which, or which possibility was odder, but I'd gotten used to it at this point. I pulled on the silky shorts and thin top before sliding under the thick comforter on my bed. I was asleep again almost as soon as I closed my eyes.

Chapter 9

I woke to Jim Morrison proclaiming that people were strange when you're a stranger, and it took me several disoriented moments—and two more lines of the song—to realize the sound was coming from my phone. Roy must have been playing with my ringtones again, which meant I had no idea who the song had been assigned to. I rolled to the edge of the mattress and fumbled blindly across my nightstand. My fingers landed on the hard plastic of my phone and I dragged it to me.

"Hello," I said, my voice heavy with sleep and my eyes gritty as I flopped over onto my back. My hair was still damp from my shower. It was clearly too early for someone to be calling.

"Craft? Why aren't you answering your door?"

Briar's voice sent the clinging remnants of sleep running. I jolted upright, my feet hitting the ground a moment later.

"I'm, uh . . ." Not there? But my car was outside with nearly half a dozen others. *Damn it.* Hadn't Caleb warded the house in such a way that we would get a warning if someone showed up at our door?

I glanced at the small glass orb sitting on my dresser. It glowed a cheery yellow color, indicating that someone had climbed the stairs to my old rented room. Well, so the wards had technically done their job, but it sure as hell hadn't woken me.

"Give me a minute," I said, already rushing out of my rooms.

I didn't wait for an answer but disconnected as I took the castle halls at a run. As I reached the front garden, I spotted the bike Holly had been discussing at dinner the night before. I jumped on it without hesitation, but then took an awkward moment wobbling through the garden as I tried both to remember *how* to ride a bike—it had been years—and to deal with the fact that it was adjusted for Holly, who was at least a head shorter than me.

I stood on the pedals, hunching over the handlebars, and the bike straightened out, picking up speed. The plastic ridges on the pedals bit into my bare feet, but the bike zoomed down the path. The sky above me glowed with the hazy light of predawn, streaks of color becoming visible in the distance. Most other places, it wouldn't have been enough light for my bad eyes, but here it was enough to stay on the path.

I reached the back door to Caleb's house in record time, but it was still taking too long. I jumped off the bike before it stopped rolling and dashed into the kitchen, through the living room, and then up the inner stairs leading to my old apartment. How was I supposed to explain why it had taken me over five minutes to answer the door?

I paused a heartbeat before pulling open my front door, and sucked down a deep breath so I wouldn't be panting when I answered. It barely helped. I opened the door.

"Briar," I said, forcing a smile onto my face, mostly so I could suck down as much air as possible between my teeth.

Briar Darque was leaning against my porch rail, her arms crossed over her chest either in impatience or for extra warmth in the bitter, predawn November wind. That wind rushed through my now-open door, chilling the sweat beading at my hairline and making me wish I'd thought to grab a jacket. Or real clothes.

"Come in," I said, stepping aside.

Briar stared at me, taking in my bare feet, my rather unseasonable camisole-top-and-silk-shorts pj's, and my hair still a mess from yesterday's activities as well as being slept on wet and windswept from my bike ride. My pulse pounded in my ears, and I wondered if she noticed my chest was heaving as I tried to get my breathing under control. Another cutting breeze swept in through the door, and I shivered, gooseflesh breaking out across my exposed skin.

"I'm going to shut the door now, so if you're not coming in . . ."

Briar pushed off the railing and stepped inside. I gratefully shut the door, locking the chilly morning outside. She scanned the small room, not that it had changed much since the last time she was here. I hadn't owned much—or nice—furniture to start with, and the castle was furnished, so I'd left all the big items here.

As long as no one started opening drawers, the place still looked lived in.

Briar's gaze caught on the bed—the still perfectly made, not even creased bed. Her eyebrows rose and she turned back to me, taking in my appearance again.

"What took so long?"

"I . . ." I faltered. She at least guessed I hadn't slept here, but I obviously couldn't claim I'd taken a moment to change or shower before answering the door. I silently cursed the panic that had me rush out of the castle without taking time to get dressed.

My hesitation had trailed a moment too long when the door behind me, the one leading down into the rest of the house, opened.

Briar's posture changed, her weight shifting between her feet as her hand dipped into her coat. I whirled around as Falin stepped into the room.

He smiled, but he didn't close the door behind him and his hand hovered near the Glock holstered on his waist. Which was fairly obvious because aside from the gun and holster, the only other thing he wore was a pair of faded denim jeans. No shoes and no shirt covering his expanse of pale chest. With his long hair loose and slightly mussed, he looked like he'd just rolled out of bed, and as I did as well, I could only guess what Briar thought.

I clenched my teeth to bite back my groan, and tried to make my face communicate for him to get out.

Either he didn't notice, or I seriously needed to work on my expressions because he continued to smile and said, "You left so suddenly. Who is your guest?"

I rolled my eyes but glanced back at Briar. She had eased her hand away from the vials of potent magic stored in the bandolier across her chest, but her stance still indicated that she was prepared to move, and fight, if she had to. Her cocked eyebrow was even higher than it had been when she'd studied my un-slept-in bed, which I hadn't realized was possible.

"Well, he's definitely easy on the eyes, but what happened to the other one?" she asked, her gaze trailing over the taut muscles he'd left on display.

Yep, she thought I was sleeping with Falin. I sighed but didn't correct her. It didn't matter and supplied a plausible reason why it took me so long to get to the door.

"Special investigator Briar Darque of the MCIB, meet Lead Special Agent Falin Andrews of the FIB," I said by way of introduction, waving a hand through the air between them. Then I walked over to my bed and sank down onto it, pulling my legs up to sit cross-legged on the now-not-quite-perfect comforter.

I didn't like the way Briar looked at Falin like she wouldn't mind seeing him with even less on while still holding herself in that slightly aggressive posture. But as I wasn't actually sleeping with him, it wasn't my place to care, so I tried not to notice.

Falin's appraisal of Briar was much more business-like. He couldn't sense magic, so he couldn't know exactly how armed to the teeth she was, but he took in her posture and outfit along with her official title before his hand moved away from his holster and he stepped out of the doorway, finally shutting the door to downstairs behind him and walking farther into the room. They were, theoretically, both working for the good guys. For now, that seemed good enough for him.

He stopped about a foot away from me, at the night-stand beside the bed. I was relieved he didn't plop down on the bed beside me, because that would have been awkward, and considering I planned to let Briar continue to assume we were sleeping together, there would have been no good way to handle it.

"What can I do for you?" I asked, turning my attention back to Briar.

"Did you want to get dressed?" She cut her eyes purposefully to my pajamas.

I glanced down. The camisole was thin, and between the fact that we'd turned the thermostat in the typically empty house way down and that the front door had let in quite a bit of the chilly air, it was obvious I was cold. The problem was, there were no clothes in this apartment anymore.

I hugged my arms across my chest but shrugged. "I could meet you in my office when we open at nine."

"If I wanted to wait that long, I wouldn't have shown up at your door at the ass crack of dawn," she said, scowling at me.

Great.

"Are you arresting me?" Because if that was the case, this was really going to suck as I didn't even have a jacket in the apartment anymore—an issue I probably needed to fix. But if she planned to arrest me, I didn't think she'd be nice enough to offer me a chance to dress first. Besides, this awkward intrusion seemed a little too informal for an arrest.

"Not yet," she said, to my limited relief. "But go get dressed. I can see that you're not wearing anything under that. I really don't need to know that much about you, Craft." She turned to Falin. "And it wouldn't be amiss if you were not standing around like some Greek marble statue."

One edge of his mouth twitched into the smallest amused smile, but he strolled across the room, toward my dresser. Crap, what was he thinking? I started to jump to my feet but then faltered. What was I supposed to do, yell that he couldn't open that drawer? That would draw even more attention. Maybe I could claim all my clothes were in the wash? Except that would be a lie and I wouldn't be able to utter the words.

Falin pulled open the top drawer, appeared to fumble with something, and then dragged out a small stack of clothing. I tried not to gape. Those drawers were empty. I'd emptied them myself.

Which meant the stack of clothes in his hands, which appeared to be a shirt for him and an outfit that looked a hell of a lot like one of mine, had to be pure glamour.

He turned to me, a mischievous smile touching his lips, and held out his hand to help me off the bed. I took it dumbly, not sure what else to do. Falin was good at personal glamours, but he wasn't great at making lasting objects without some similar raw material to work with, and there had been literally *nothing* in that drawer. There was no chance I'd be able to accept that pile of clothes, go to another room, and put them on. Still, I let him pull me to my feet.

He waved a hand toward my small bathroom on the other side of my kitchenette. "After you," he said with another smile.

I frowned at him but headed in that direction, Falin on my heels.

Briar rolled her eyes. "I'm regretting this already. Hurry up, I don't have all morning."

Before the bathroom door fully closed behind us, I channeled raw magic from my ring into a small privacy charm on my bracelet. A soundproof privacy bubble sprang up around me. I'd crafted the charm myself, so the bubble of privacy was small. Really small. As in for both Falin and me to be fully covered by it, we had to be close enough that if I took too large a breath, our chests would touch, but the spell itself inside that small area was solid.

"What are you thinking?" I whispered in a hiss of breath. Whispering wasn't necessary inside the spell, but it seemed prudent.

Falin shrugged. His hands were empty now, the stack of glamoured clothing having vanished as soon as the door had closed. "I was thinking that cooperating over little things would look better for you. Unless you want to explain to the OMIH and MCIB how your own private space unfolded for you with a Faerie castle inside."

Yeah, that wasn't high on my to-do list. I was still attempting to pass for human as much as I could.

"What I forgot to take into account is how close it is to dawn," he said, looking up as if he could see the rising sun through the ceiling.

I followed his gaze, frowning. "Glamours break at dawn, right? But the exact moment has passed. Faerie magic should be flooding back into the world by now."

His brow creased and he studied my face as if searching for some kind of recognition I clearly wasn't giving.

"What?" I hissed.

"You still can't feel the ebb and flow of Faerie magic, can you?"

I didn't answer, and that must have been answer enough, because his lips compressed into a tight line. I'd spent most of my life with my fae nature sealed away by a spell my father had put on me before I was even born. The seal had been crumbling since the Blood Moon months ago, and had theoretically been fully ripped away the night of the Fall Equinox, but there were still several parts of my newly discovered nature that weren't working for me. Glamour for one. And apparently, sensing ambient Faerie magics.

"I wouldn't exactly say it rushes back into the world," Falin said, and shook his head. "If I weave a glamour now, it will be relatively weak. I'll have to reinforce it later."

"Do it. We've been in here too long already."

He nodded and his hands lifted to my waist. An electric zing shot through me that had nothing to do with magic and everything to do with Falin touching me. A tinge of guilt met the response in equal portions. I glanced away, trying not to let it show on my face, but surely the way my skin seemed to tighten gave me away.

If he noticed, he was good enough not to show it. Instead he knelt, trailing his hands over my hips. It was oddly businesslike and intimate at the same time. And it was really, really awkward. As his hands moved, my silk shorts darkened and lengthened. His hands glided down to my knees and then over my calves, and as he moved, buttery soft black leather crawled down my legs until I was wearing a pair of pants nicer than anything I actually owned.

He stood and lifted the bottom hem of my cami,

rubbing the material between his fingers as if testing what it was made of. Then he placed his hands on my shoulders and trailed them slowly down my arms. The thin straps of the camisole seemed to swell, becoming thicker, growing to follow his fingers but also rippling down the shirt until I wasn't wearing a camisole but a purple V-neck sweater. I turned and looked in the mirror. It was similar to a sweater I wore often, but like the pants, it was softer and better-quality than anything I owned. The outfit fit better too, hugging every curve as if it had been painted on, which, in a way, it had.

"Nice," I said, fingering the sleeve of the sweater. It was so soft, it had to be some sort of cashmere blend.

By the time I turned back around, Falin had on what appeared to be his typical oxford button-up. He had shoes too. Which was a very good idea.

"I hate to ask . . . but if she wants me to go somewhere with her . . ." I lifted my bare foot.

Falin shook his head. "It was hard enough stretching what little material you're wearing as far as I did. If I re-created your boots from scratch, they'd never hold." He reached out and lifted the necklace I wore. "Your chameleon charm seems to be helping maintain the clothes, but I don't trust it enough to try boots. And, of course, the standard glamour warnings: Stay away from iron, don't let your planeweaving magic disbelieve it out of existence, and put on real clothes before sunset, or you'll very suddenly find yourself only half dressed again."

I nodded. "Well, we better get back out there."

"One more thing." He reached out and ran a hand through my hair. Curls fell free of the knotted, windswept mess to bounce lightly down my neck.

"Okay, now that's a trick I need to learn," I said, glancing at the mirror. It was just glamour, I knew, but they felt like they were free of tangles. It would have taken me another shower, an hour working out knots, and some styling products to get my curls to look this nice. This was definitely a trick I needed to add to my arsenal.

Except for my bare feet, we looked totally presentable now. I pulled the magic back out of the privacy charm, releasing the soundproof bubble, then led Falin out of the bathroom.

Briar had commandeered the one chair in the small apartment, my bar stool, and had a folder with several sheets of paper spread across the short bar. She looked up as we walked back into the room, then very pointedly glanced at her watch, but she didn't comment. Instead she gathered the papers, shuffling them back into the folder.

"So," I said, sitting down on my bed once again. "Are you going to tell me why you're here so early?"

"No shoes?" she asked, glancing at my feet.

Was she stalling? What was going on? She'd barged in here, but she seemed to keep finding reasons not to tell me whatever she'd come to say.

"They're not up here," I said, which was the truth. They weren't downstairs either, but she didn't have to know that. She frowned, still staring at my bare feet. "Do I need shoes, Briar? Am I going somewhere?"

She sighed and shook her head. Her mouth screwed together hard, like she didn't want to admit what she was about to say, but finally she said, "I have it on good authority that I'm going to need your assistance to solve this case. I'm here to hire you."

Chapter 10

I stared at Briar. All this buildup and . . . "You want to hire me? And not that I'm refusing, but exactly who is the 'good authority' who told you that you would need me to solve the case?"

Briar still looked like she'd swallowed something bitter. "My partner."

"Do I know her?" I hadn't even known she *had* a partner. I'd thought she was a one-woman ass-kicking machine.

"Him. And no, you've never met him. Remember when I said the MCIB has great premonition witches? Well, he's one of the best. And when prophecies plague his dreams, and he wakes up raving about how I'm going to need your help, then I drive my ass over here to wake you up."

Now it was my turn to grimace. It was rarely good when you showed up in a premonition witch's prophecies. The future they saw was typically written in stone.

Many wyrd abilities were considered difficult to live with; the magic used the witch as much as it was used, but prophecy was a particularly potent burden—most premonition witches went mad before they reached adulthood.

"What did this prophecy entail?" I asked, not sure I actually wanted to know.

Briar shrugged. "That's all he told me." The look on my face must have betrayed my skepticism because she continued by saying, "He's thirty-two and still sane. He's found a way to manipulate the best possible outcome out of his prophecies, so I don't question him. He tells me what I need to know, and I don't push him for more. If I'm going to solve this case, I need to work with you, so I will." She pulled a page from the folder in her hands. "Regardless of what cards and certifications you carry from the Organization of Magically Inclined Humans, I think we both know you're not strictly human. So I drew up a hire agreement to ensure that there are no misunderstandings about debt."

I cringed internally but accepted the paper when she passed it to me. Falin stepped closer, reading the document over my shoulder. I didn't stop him. While his loyalties weren't always clear when it came to the Winter Queen, he was a friend who generally had my best interests in mind. He'd point out anything that could leave me compromised, probably.

I read the document carefully, but there was nothing blatantly unusual in it. The contract would hire me at a generous daily rate that would encompass any hours I worked with Briar or on the case independently. If I accepted the job, I would be agreeing to work the case for the listed fee without expecting additional compensation for any magic performed, information shared, or injury sustained during the case. That last bit wasn't exactly reassuring, but overall, the document was simply a way to cover one's ass and avoid incurring debt from a manipulative fae. It was smart—I'd have to keep a copy in case I ever needed it.

There was only one line that was a deal breaker and would prevent me from signing. I turned the page around, holding it up toward Briar. "This line that reads, 'The contractor agrees to disclose any and all information pertaining to the case at the earliest opportune time.' That's not going to work for me."

A muscle above Briar's jaw bulged and she crossed her arms over her chest. "You're flat-out admitting you plan to keep things from me during the case?"

"No." Well, yes. Even if she hired me, I still couldn't tell her everything I saw in the bank, at least not the parts that pertained to the soul collectors. I was oathbound to keep their secrets. "There may be some things I can't tell you. I will share everything I can."

Her glare should have sliced the skin from my bones. I forced myself to meet her gaze, but it took effort. After a moment, she rolled her eyes, but that didn't lessen her glare.

"I probably shouldn't have told you about the premonition before you signed. You know you have me over a barrel." She glided to her feet and snatched the contract from me. She crossed out the words "any and all" and initialed the change before handing it back to me. "Better?"

I read over it one more time and then glanced at

Falin. He gave a small nod, which I took to mean he didn't spot any binding loopholes I'd missed. I initialed the change as well, then signed on the line.

It wasn't a magical oath, but it was still a binding contract, and I was fae enough that I could feel the agreement etching itself into me as I wrote my name. It was disconcerting.

"So does this mean you want me to raise the shades from the robbers at the bank?" I asked, holding out the contract.

"I'm working on it. Unfortunately, you're still the NCPD's main suspect. You can't go anywhere near those bodies until you're cleared or we finagle you special permission." Briar plucked the contract from my stunned fingers and tucked it into her folder. "Now that the paperwork is out of the way, tell me what you left out yesterday at the police station. Derrick said you have a lead already."

I should have seen that coming. Unfortunately, I couldn't tell her more. Everything else I had was guesses or pertained to the soul collectors. So what lead did I have?

The tracking charm.

"Remember when I said I tracked Remy to the bank using a charm, but that the soul navigating his body wasn't actually his?"

Briar nodded.

"There was an . . . irregularity when I was following the spell. At one point the trail split in two different directions. At the time, I thought the focus was contaminated." I took a breath, because I hadn't actually said this next part out loud before. "Now, I wonder if the

other trail might lead to Remy's soul; probably in someone else's body, if the pattern holds."

Briar stared at me a moment. "You can track a soul?"

"Maybe? I don't know. To my knowledge, it's never
been attempted." The research I'd done last night hadn't
turned up any verifiable cases. People tried to summon
ghosts with personal objects all the time, but aside from
some bragging posts with no details on inactive profiles,
I couldn't find a single mention of people trying to track
one. Either it couldn't be done, or no one had ever been
successful. "Or maybe the focus really was contaminated and the charm will lead me to some acquaintance
of my client's." I shrugged. "I'd planned to check it out
today."

"Sounds like a lead." Briar pushed out of her chair.
"Grab your stuff. I'm driving."

"Uh, no," I said, not standing.

She turned, her eyebrow cocking. "What's the issue,
Craft?"

I made a conscious effort not to glance at Falin. *He*
wasn't the issue, and if I looked at him, she'd think he
was. The issue was his glamour, and the fact that underneath it, I was still more or less in glorified under-
wear. Also that I had no idea what she was driving, but
last time it was a Hummer with so much metal in it I
got physically sick. If I stepped into it now, the glamoured outfit didn't stand a chance.

"The problem is that she has other responsibilities,"
Falin said without missing a beat. "You woke her, which
means her dog hasn't been walked or fed. You never
once asked if she had client appointments on the books
this morning. And you never even asked if she has this

tracking charm on her." He glanced at me and I shook my head. It was still at the castle. He turned back to Briar. "This case is probably the only reason you're in town, but it's not Alex's only priority."

I gaped at Falin. Okay, yeah, he had my back.

Briar glared. "There are four bodies in the morgue, and if her theory is correct about Remy's ghost piloting another body, there are more bodies out there."

Now I did stand, holding up my hand to Falin before he answered. I appreciated the knight-in-glamoured-clothing act, but I could fight this particular battle on my own.

"You hired me. I'm working this case, and plan to give it my best, but he's right, I have other responsibilities too. Also, if you're still driving that steel monster of an SUV, I can't ride with you."

That last part clearly caught her off guard, and I saw the momentary confusion flicker through her dark eyes before they flashed with understanding.

"Too much iron?" she asked, and at my nod she made a small *hmmm* sound before saying, "I never considered that. This might take a little adjustment for me. I've never worked with a nonhuman before."

And there was me cringing again.

"I can meet you at my office in about an hour," I said, then thought better of it. "Actually, we should meet at Central Precinct. The tracking charm will pick up Remy's body in the morgue and we don't want to get distracted by that trail. But with that drive, give me an hour and a half."

Though she didn't look happy about it, she nodded, seeing herself out a moment later so that I could focus on getting ready. Which was good; I was going to be pushing it as it was, even with Holly's bike, which I probably needed to return. I was definitely going to need a bike of my own. But first I needed to get back to the castle and put on real clothes.

Nearly two hours later, I was standing in front of Central Precinct. The clothes I was wearing were nowhere near as nice as the glamoured ones I'd had to discard, but at least they wouldn't vanish if I walked too close to a cast-iron gate. Briar had been waiting for me when I arrived, which wasn't surprising, and now we were both staring at the small bag dangling from my clenched fist.

"What do you mean it's not working?" she asked, glaring at both me and the charm in turn.

"Well, it *is* working—it is pulling me toward the body in the morgue—but the other trail it found yesterday is missing." I frowned at the charm and reached out with my ability to sense magic, examining it. I'd had Rianna recharge it before I left the castle this morning, as the original charm hadn't been designed for long-term use, but that shouldn't have changed anything about how it functioned. The spell itself felt exactly the same as it had yesterday, but it was definitely only pulling me in one direction, toward the basement and Remy's body.

I turned a full circle, holding the charm out as if I could dowse a trail better that way. It didn't change anything. I shook my head.

"Either there is no longer anything else to track"—

which would mean the collectors had found and collected Remy's soul already—"or he's behind wards."

"Or it was some weird magical fluke," Briar said.

I nodded, acknowledging the possibility. "Now what?"

"You were supposed to be my lead, Craft," Briar said. She looked up, as if judging the time by the position of the sun crawling over the surrounding buildings. Then she pressed both her palms into her eyes a moment before dragging them down her face. She looked tired, which made sense. She'd shown up at my house right before dawn, and she'd drafted that hire paperwork before that. If her partner "woke" from his premonition as she said, it had probably been the middle of the night.

"You want some coffee?" I asked, nodding at a small coffee shop down the street.

"There's coffee inside the station."

"Central Precinct? I've had it before. Trust me, it's not coffee."

She frowned at me but glanced between the doors of the station and the coffee shop down the street. Finally she shrugged.

"Coffee. Sure, why not?"

We trudged down the sidewalk in silence. At the coffee shop, I ordered my coffee black; she had hers with hazelnut and cream. When I stepped toward one of the round tables at the front of the shop, she shook her head and led me to the very last table in the corner. She took the chair against the far wall, which gave her the best vantage point to watch both the door and the rest of the patrons in the coffee shop. It also put my back to both, which I wasn't completely comfortable with. I turned my chair so my back was to the side wall. Briar gave me an amused smile as I sat sideways at the table, but she didn't comment.

We sat in silence as we sipped our coffee. The coffee shop clientele had been trickling in slowly when we entered, but the morning rush hit soon after we took our seats. The tables around us filled quickly, and disappointed patrons searching for empty seats wandered through the shop, some hovering around people they thought might abandon their table soon. None hovered around us. In fact, everyone seemed to avoid our table. Not in an *I'm trying but failing to not stare at the heavily armed, leather-clad woman in the corner* way, but like their gazes just naturally slid away from Briar and her surrounding area.

"Do you keep those charms active all the time?" I asked, turning to face Briar. I could feel that her look-away charm was active, but I was apparently inside the covered radius, because I had no issue focusing on her.

Briar shrugged. "When I'm in public, typically."

"Don't you ever want to get noticed? To stand out?"

"If I want someone's attention, I put a really big weapon in their face." Briar set down her coffee. "What are we doing, Craft? I'm not interested in girly chitchat or becoming best friends forever."

"I don't think there is any danger of that," I said, taking another sip of my coffee.

She stared at me a moment, and then a smile cracked across her face. "I like you, Craft. Not that I'm about to gossip about shoes or purses or whatever girlfriends talk about."

"I often discuss dead bodies with my best girl-friends."

Briar looked like she might choke on her coffee. I shrugged.

"My best girlfriends include a medical examiner, a prosecutor, and a grave witch." And my best guy friends were a soul collector and an assassin. We sure sounded like a morbid bunch, huh?

Briar laughed and held her coffee cup up in a faux salute. "I knew there was a reason I liked you. Now back to the case. Derrick's making headway in getting you access to the bodies. This is so wrapped up in red tape it might as well be a present, but we need to talk to those shades."

Derrick, the mysterious partner. He apparently did the paperwork while she did the ass kicking.

I watched two women dressed too casually to be part of the morning business crowd scan for a table, their brightly patterned purses hiked up high on their shoulders and the heels they wore with their jeans clicking on the tile floor with their annoyance.

"Have the police found any commonalities between Annabelle McNabb and Remy Hollens?" I asked.

Briar lifted an eyebrow. "You figured out who another of the robbers was. You didn't know that during our interview yesterday."

"Yesterday I also didn't know the bank robbery was part of a spree. One of my housemates mentioned it last night, and I looked up what little I could find online." I set down my now-empty cup of coffee and considered whether it would be worth it to buy a refill. The line was now out the door, so probably not. "Yes or no on any common points of interest between Annabelle and Remy? Or should I spend today digging up what-

ever background I can find on those two, which you
and the police likely have already begun?"

"A soccer mom and a college freshman? No, last I
heard there was nothing to connect them, besides the
obvious of both being dead after robbing a bank together. They didn't live, work, or shop anywhere near
each other. It's possible they had a strangers-on-the-train
kind of relationship, but we can't pin down where they
would have crossed paths."

Which was exactly what I was afraid of.

Briar nodded toward my wrist, where I still wore the
tracking charm. "When it did have a second trail, did
you narrow down what area of the city it wanted you
to head toward?"

"Not in the city at all. It was tugging toward the wilds
to the northeast of Nekros." And since Nekros was
completely inside a folded space, the wilds had never
been fully charted.

"You're sure it wasn't pulling toward someplace outside the folded space?"

I shrugged. "It didn't seem to lead toward the road
out." And as far as anyone knew, there was no consistent way out of the folded space through the wilds besides the two interstates that acted as doors.

Briar started to ask another question, but then her
phone buzzed. She dug it out, glancing at the screen,
and a smile spread across her lips. She stood and tossed
her empty cup a good fifteen feet across the room at
the trash can. It passed through the narrow opening
without even touching the sides.

"Grab your stuff, Craft," she said, marching toward
the door.

"Where are we going?" I called after her as I hurried to the trash can—no way could I make the shot she had, and I didn't want to apologize for beaning someone in the head with an empty cup.

"Looks like the red tape wasn't as bad as I thought. You'll have babysitters, but you're cleared to raise some shades. Let's go talk to dead people."

Chapter 11

Briar had warned me I'd have babysitters at the morgue, but we now had enough people in the room to throw a party. Aside from Briar and me, we had been joined by John and Jenson, as they were the detectives in charge of the case; Tamara, since she had direct custody of the bodies, as well as one of her assistants; and two uniformed officers who stood by the morgue door looking very uncomfortable. It had been decided to pull out all of the bodies so that I wouldn't have to lower my circle or start a new ritual to confirm stories between victims, if we needed to do so. The morgue wasn't small, but it also wasn't built to have four bodies on gurneys with eight living people gathered around them. We'd had to do a little rearranging, and I was still going to have to be very careful when I drew my circle to make sure all the corpses fit without trapping any of the living people in the circle with me.

The most uncomfortable part of the whole situation

was how very quiet the entire group was. I dragged my waxy-chalk on the ground with seven gazes locked on me, the room silent except for the buzz of the lights and the whirl of the air purifiers. I tried to ignore them, but I could all but feel their eyes on my flesh. Tamara was the only one who looked friendly out of the bunch. Not that everyone else was strictly unfriendly. Briar looked impatient. The two uniformed officers looked a little freaked out and maybe a little queasy. I wasn't sure if that was because I was about to raise shades or because the bodies were rather ripe. Jenson, well, he was definitely unfriendly as he scowled at me around a handkerchief he had pressed over his mouth and nose.

John stood off by himself beside one of the two video cameras trained on me for this ritual. He held his case notebook in his hand, pen gripped tight by his side in the other hand. I couldn't see his mouth under a mustache that definitely needed a trim, but I could tell by the way his cheeks were drawn down that he was frowning.

When I finished my circle, I nodded first to Briar and then I turned to John.

"I'm ready. Who should I start with?"

"You'll likely end up raising all," he said, which was a nonanswer.

I chose to believe it was permission to use my best judgment and turned to Remy first. Four shades were a lot for one ritual. I could do it, but it would drain me. He was the one I was most invested in, and he was the one I wanted the most answers from. I wasn't planning to charge Taylor for any more of my time—after all, this ritual was now bought and paid for by Briar—but if I could find more information for her, something to give her closure, I would.

Tapping into the energy stored in the ring on my finger, I activated the circle I'd drawn. A barrier sprang up between me and the rest of the living people. The magical barrier also stopped the flow of the grave essence from the other bodies in the morgue, but with four corpses trapped in the circle with me, that didn't offer much relief.

I removed the charm bracelet, which contained, along with various other utilitarian charms I carried, the external shields that helped dull the grave essence that otherwise relentlessly battered my mental shields. As soon as the external shields went down, the full affront of grave essence from the bodies trapped in the circle hit the mental wall surrounding my psyche. It slammed against the living vines I imagined as the barrier encompassing my mind. I peeled them back, letting the grave essence inside, not resisting as the chill rushed into my body, warring with my own living heat. It hurt, but not in an unexpected way. More like an old wound that acted up.

Wind picked up around me, whipping my hair around my shoulders and stirring the sheets covering the gurneys. I had no need to check toe tags or pull back the sheets to see the bodies. I could feel that two were females and one was an older man, so the last, a young male, had to be Remy. I reached out with my magic and let the heat flow out of me into the sheet-covered body. My magic and living heat flowed through it, connecting all the tiny left-behind memories, forming them into a physical representation of the man he'd been at the moment of his death.

A teenage boy on the cusp of adulthood sat up through the sheet covering his body. While he would have been solid to me, he was as insubstantial as a hologram to anyone else, just a collection of memories held together with my magic. One of the officers by the door muttered something rather unpleasant sounding as Remy appeared, and the door creaked, the officer's shoes scuffing on the linoleum as he rushed through it. I couldn't handle gore; other people couldn't handle shades. But Remy wasn't a bad one. Aside from being a little spectral in color and substance, he looked like he should have been a healthy college-aged kid. I'd certainly raised shades in far worse condition.

Despite the fact that the corpse on the gurney had likely already had a full autopsy and wasn't wearing anything more than a sheet, the image of Remy that appeared was exactly how his last memory had caught him in the moment of death. He wore a hat with the university's icon on it over his dark hair. His football jersey sported his high school colors and looked well loved. I vaguely recognized it as the one he'd been wearing during the bank robbery. The real jersey was likely in an evidence locker somewhere; this one was just a memory of the original. His jeans were worn, a hole beginning to fray in his right knee. There was no obvious cause of death evident on his shade, but then there hadn't been on his body either, so that wasn't too surprising.

"What is your name?" I asked the shade, not because I didn't know, but because this was an official interview being recorded. Shades had a lot of limitations, and I'd worked with the police for years, so I tried to put as much properly on the record as I could.

"Remy Hollens."

I turned to John. He gave a slight nod, indicating the shade was loud enough. I focused on Remy again.

"Can you tell me how you died?"

"I volunteered to be part of a study to earn a little money. I had a few hours before I had to pick up Taylor, so I scheduled to meet the researcher. After filling out some paperwork, he told me he was going to begin and I just had to sit very still in the center of a circle. He chanted for a while, and had me drink something, and then . . ." The shade trailed off.

"And then what?" Briar asked once the shade failed to say anything more.

"And then he died. Or maybe fell unconscious and then died," I said, but I was frowning.

Usually when a shade trailed off like that, it was because a collector had jerked their soul from their body. Once the soul left, the record button on a person's life stopped, even if their bodily functions hadn't quite caught up to realizing they were dead. But Death had told me he hadn't collected Remy's soul, and the way he said it made me think none of the other collectors had either.

A soul doesn't just pop out of a body at death. If a collector doesn't come, the soul tends to cling to the dead flesh, trapped inside the shell, the memories still recording as the body rots away around it. I'd talked to shades who'd experienced such fate. Their stories weren't pretty. So how had Remy's soul gotten out of his body?

"One problem here. We all saw this kid drop dead during a bank robbery. Not sitting in a magic circle," Jenson said around his handkerchief.

"He was already dead." I was starting to feel like a broken record telling people that. "Remy, have you ever been to First Bank of Nekros on Old Dunbar Road?"

The shade didn't hesitate. "No."

There was more than one sputter of dismay behind me, and even Tamara muttered something questioning how a shade could lie. Shades had no egos. They couldn't lie, or even obfuscate the truth. Ask the right question, get a good, honest answer, at least to the best of the shade's recollection. While Remy's soul had been inside his body, he had never been inside that bank. After his soul was evicted . . .

"He's not lying. He was already dead." Yup, definitely a broken record. "Remy, what was the date and time of the last thing you remember?"

"November nineteenth. It must about been about seven forty-five because I arrived at the meeting right after seven."

John glanced back through his notebook. "That would be the night before the bank heist."

"And it would be consistent with the state of rigor during my initial observations at the scene," Tamara said.

Jenson made a sound that was particularly growl-like. "So we are actually saying that the people who were walking, talking, and waving guns around were already dead at the time? Is that what I'm hearing?"

"If the shoe fits," Briar said, and turned back toward me. "You said ghosts were piloting these corpses. Ghosts are just souls, right? How come the body didn't start recording again when the foreign soul was inserted?"

I might have gaped at her for a moment. Not only

because it was a good question, but also because she understood enough about grave magic to ask it. That was high-level grave theory she was using to reach those questions. And I didn't have a good answer.

I probed at the body with my magic, searching for anything unusual. Memories were stored in every cell of the body, so it wasn't like I could search for particular ones, but I tried to let my magic seek around for anything that didn't feel connected to the shade I'd raised. There was nothing. Remy's body and shade felt typical, strong even.

I shook my head, indicating that I didn't know the answers to Briar's questions. She sighed.

"We need more details about the man, the place, and the job," she said.

I turned back to the shade. "What kind of study did you volunteer to join?"

"It focused on human interaction with the spirit world. I was being paid to see if an experimental spell could allow me to see into the other side and talk to ghosts."

Well, he'd certainly gotten to see into the other side.

"Who was running this study?" Briar asked, and I repeated the question for Remy's shade.

"His name is Dr. Marcus Hadisty."

All the detective and investigator types in the room were suddenly busy scribbling in notebooks. The chill of the grave was already seeping deeper into me, making me cold to the bone, and I hadn't even finished the first interview yet. I could guess the next series of questions, so I moved on.

"What did he look like?"

"Older. Graying hair. Very professor-like."

Well, that was generic. I pressed for more details. "How old?"

"I don't know. My parents' age? Maybe older. At least forty."

Remy was only a handful of years younger than me, but he still apparently looked at everyone over thirty as old. That wasn't going to help us much.

"How did you meet Dr. Hadisty?"

"I saw a flyer on campus looking for volunteers for his study. It claimed it would pay two hundred for no more than two hours of time. The last study I joined paid only fifty dollars. I'm saving to buy a ring for Taylor, so I watch out for quick ways to make a little cash."

Something inside me twisted painfully. I always hated when shades said something hopeful for the future. Not that shades hoped for anything anymore. They had no emotions, no feelings. He was saving for a ring. The shade said the sentence as a simple fact, but I imagined the living man would have been a bundle of joy and nerves when discussing the ring and his plans.

"How did he contact Dr. Hadisty?" John asked when I followed my own train of thought a little too long without asking the next question. I repeated his words to the shade.

"The flyer had a quickchat number. I contacted it and he sent me a questionnaire to fill out and the first set of waivers to sign."

Murmurs from the room on that one. Quickchat left no trace of the conversation once the session was logged off.

"You didn't think it was odd this doctor was using quickchat?" That somewhat sarcasm-laced question was Jenson's. We had a . . . strained relationship. I almost didn't repeat it, as it would require the shade to make a judgment call, which he'd only be able to do if he'd considered it while alive, but I didn't want to get accused of prejudice or ignoring a line of questioning.

"Quickchat is common on campus. It was unusual for it to be used for something official, but the questionnaire and waiver weren't dissimilar from other studies I'd participated in, and the offered money was good."

"Did you agree to meet as soon as you answered the questions?" I asked.

"No, he contacted me a few days later, via the quickchat app, and let me know I'd been approved as a candidate for the study. We agreed to meet the following evening."

Which brought us back to the nineteenth. "Where did you meet?"

"An old funeral home. He claimed the place was haunted and it would be an ideal location to find ghosts."

"Name, location?" John asked, looking up from the notebook he was furiously scribbling in.

It wasn't a funeral home I'd heard of before, but then I didn't have much cause to visit them. Cemeteries I would have known, but not funeral homes.

Questions kept coming. I shivered, dutifully repeating them. With five people interjecting lines of inquiry, the interview seemed to drag out. Remy described the ritual proceeding his death in detail—or as many details as he could. He wasn't a witch and had no spellcasting training, so he hadn't been paying much attention to Hadisty's circle. He thought there might have been some sort of markings on the floor but was uncertain what they were. He either couldn't understand or hadn't listened enough to remember what words Hadisty had been saying before handing him something to drink. I was pretty sure Remy was the least observant person I'd ever encountered. That, or he'd shown up to the study to get paid and hadn't cared about anything but the money promised.

Tamara quizzed Remy in great detail about the liquid he drank. She wanted to know any impressions about viscosity, smell, and taste. If he'd felt any immediate change, tingling, or numbness while drinking it. His answers didn't seem particularly helpful. She'd run a toxicity screen on all the bodies since their cause of death was unknown, but the preliminary results had all been negative. She was still waiting on the more in-depth panel.

Finally no one had any more questions.

I released his shade, drawing back my heat and magic. I did not like how little of either were left after only the first shade. My trembling was so strong that my whole arm shook when I lifted it to guide the magic into the next body.

"We have to speed this up," I said.

The next shade I raised was Annabelle McNabb. Her story was not that dissimilar from Remy's. She'd seen a flyer for the study at a coffee shop, and while she didn't need the money, she thought it would be nice to stuff it away as "mad money." Her interaction with the researcher was much the same as Remy's, except he'd claimed his name was Dr. Marcus Vogel. After making plans on quickchat, she'd met him at the funeral parlor with much the same results. If anything, her details were even vaguer than Remy's had been. Thankfully, everyone kept their questions short and efficient and the interview was done in a quarter of the time it had taken with Remy.

The museum thief, Rodger Bartlett, had a story much the same except he'd met with Dr. Marcus Basselet after seeing the study in the classifieds. The location arranged on quickchat for the ritual had been different from the others as well. He'd been met at a dilapidated house that Basselet claimed was haunted.

"What day was that?"

"November fourteenth," the shade said, which made him our earliest victim. Annabelle hadn't died until the eighteenth and Remy on the nineteenth.

Rodger's description of Basselet was more detailed than the others. He described him as a man in his mid-fifties of average build and height with hair more gray than black and dark eyes. There were enough similarities to the descriptions of Hadisty and Vogel—even if both had had hopelessly vague descriptions—that it was a safe assumption that all three were the same man using different names. A few more questions were asked, and then Rodger was returned to his body and I turned to the last corpse.

"What is your name?" I asked after the shade of the homeless woman sat up, and this time it wasn't an obligatory question. We really didn't know.

"Rosie Cranford."

"Rosie, do you remember how you died? Can you describe the circumstances surrounding the event?"

"A nice gentleman was walking through the park early in the morning. I was just waking up, trying to get my old joints moving after a cold night. Dr. Moyer approached as I was rolling up my blanket. He said he was involved with the magical science of ghosts and was currently looking for volunteers for a case study. I wasn't doing anything important, and I could use the fifty dollars he said the job paid, so I agreed to volunteer." The shade related her story without inflection or emotion. The observations she'd made were not a part of her now, just a part of the story. "He drove me to an old funeral home and took me down to the basement where a circle was drawn. There were runes drawn around the circle, so many that some were several layers deep beyond his chalk line. I like runes, so I asked about them, but the more questions I asked, the more agitated he became. I started to get a bad feeling and was thinking about leaving when he handed me a goblet. It was a masterful piece, covered in even more runes. I drained the goblet as instructed and then . . ."

And then, like all the others, her soul had left her body.

"You said you asked him about the runes. Did you recognize any of them?"

"Most of them," the shade said. "But he didn't seem to be using them for their meaning. The way it was laid out, it seemed he was using the runes as an alphabet, writing out words."

Finally, one victim who'd actually paid attention. And she appeared to know a bit about magic, or at least runes.

"Could you read the writing?"

"Not really. Way back in high school I joined a club studying runes. Thought I'd be able to learn magic that way. Never did manage to so much as set a circle, but I did learn a lot of runes. It has been a long time, though. That was why I was so curious."

It was more than we'd had before, but it was less than I'd hoped for when her story began. The predictable round of questions began, and I repeated each one, trying to keep my teeth from chattering. I needed to end this ritual soon.

Rosie had been more observant than any of the other victims, but her information still only gave us small pieces of the puzzle. She claimed the drink in the goblet tasted like wine with frankincense and myrrh in it, which was an interesting detail but didn't help figure out exactly what had happened or how.

Finally everyone ran out of questions and I withdrew my magic and heat from her corpse. It rushed back into me but was immediately consumed by the chill flowing through my veins. I'd been in touch with the dead for hours.

I let the vines that made up my mental shield slither around my psyche once more. The grave essence didn't even fight me as I pushed it out. I had so little magic left that there was nothing to draw the grave to me. Once my mental shield was complete, I dug the charm bracelet out of my pocket. The external shields snapped into place as soon as the clasp closed around my wrist.

As I worked on the shields, the people outside my circle all began talking at once. John and Briar were clearly both on the phone, while Jenson was giving directions to one of the uniformed officers. Tamara, who'd grabbed a chair sometime during the ritual because it had lasted a couple of hours and a pregnant woman shouldn't stand for that long, stood to converse with the lab assistant, telling her which tests and panels they needed to run and how to prepare to take the samples they'd need.

I hadn't fully closed my shields yet, or dissolved my circle. I glanced between the people in the room, memorizing where everyone stood because I knew what was coming. I walked to the edge of the circle and scooped up my purse. Then I closed the last gaps in my mental shield, blocking my psyche from gazing across planes, and the world fell into darkness.

I'd been prepared for it. Even short rituals burned out my vision quickly these days, and this had *not* been a short ritual. But even though I'd anticipated the blindness, a twinge of panic still jetted through me as the world fell dark. There were too many people present that I didn't fully trust for me to be confident while this vulnerable. Not that there was much I could do about it. I could have left my shields open longer, but I was so drained, I wasn't sure I had enough magic left to fight off any questing grave essence once my circle fell.

So I closed my shields, letting darkness surround me, and dissolved the circle.

Then I stood there, unsure what to do. I could feel the dead bodies, and Briar and Tamara wore enough magic that I could sense them, but the others in the room? I just had to listen for them to move.

A door whooshed as someone left the morgue. One of the uniformed officers? A gurney squeaked beside me, and I jumped in surprise. It was probably the morgue assistant, but I hadn't heard her approach.

A hand landed on my elbow, hot and unexpected. I jumped again before I realized that the buzz of Tamara's magic had approached while I was distracted by the gurney.

"Let's find you a spot to recover," she whispered.

I couldn't have been more grateful.

No one stopped us as we walked, her guiding gently, discreetly. I felt the whoosh of air as a door opened. And then we were through it, the door swishing closed behind us and Tamara leading me through the darkness, away from the dead.

Chapter 12

"How bad is it?" Tamara asked after the door closed behind us.

I shrugged. "I've been worse."

"You're shaking like a leaf." She led me to a chair, and I sank into it gratefully. "And I've never seen you this bad. Can you see at all?"

I shrugged again, but the movement might have gotten lost in my trembling. I hadn't lied; I'd been a lot worse in the past. Today I'd only raised shades. Yes, it had been a long ritual, but it had only been plain old grave magic. It wasn't like I'd been shoving around layers of reality. I was blind and cold, but I'd bounce back fairly quick.

"Your office?" A guess, but a good one. We hadn't gone far and the space didn't sound big and hollow enough to be the hallway outside the morgue.

Tamara didn't say anything at first. Maybe she nodded before remembering I couldn't see her. Finally she said, "Yeah. What can I do to help?"

"Have any whiskey hidden around here?"

Tamara snorted a laugh. "Not so much. How about some coffee instead?"

"It would be sacrilege to turn down coffee."

"I'll take that as a yes. Which is good, I wouldn't want these nice dark roast beans to go stale while I incubate this little guy."

I couldn't see her, but I knew she was rubbing her now-noticeable bump. Her footsteps moved away, across the room, and then the sounds of her preparing the coffee drifted through the air. I tucked my hands in my armpits, my arms hugged across my chest, as I tried to generate a little warmth, but the cold was deep inside me still. I seriously needed to look into making or buying one of the spells hospitals used to make blankets nice and toasty.

"Here you go," Tamara said.

I lifted my hand and she pressed the coffee mug into my palm, waiting until I'd wrapped both hands around it before letting go. The ceramic was almost too hot to touch, but I held it anyway. If I put the mug down—if there was even anywhere to put it, I wasn't sure where I was in the room—I'd probably knock the mug over when I tried to find it again. So I clutched the scalding cup, inhaling the steaming heavenly scent of coffee.

"How bad are your eyes?" Tamara asked, her chair creaking as she sat.

"You sure I still have eyes?"

"That bad, huh?"

I shrugged.

"So this case." She paused. To shake her head? To shrug? I *hated* being blind. After a moment she said, "Are we dealing with what it sounded like out there? Is this necromancy?"

"It sounds that way. How else can we explain dead bodies walking around? Hopefully this at least means I'm no longer a person of interest in this case."

"Not my department," Tamara said, but I could hear the smile in her voice as she spoke. I'd been a suspect before. My friends were getting to the point where they had to either laugh at it or walk away.

Her chair creaked again, and I waited, listening for clues indicating whether she'd stood or leaned back.

She made a soft, exasperated sound that issued from more or less the same place as before, so I guessed she'd leaned back in the chair. Then she said, "This case is a scientific nightmare. Dead bodies walking around that don't look dead. Then boom. Plug pulled and all of a sudden they show all the signs of having been dead the whole time? How is that possible? Illusion? It can't happen like it seems. The measurable and inevitable stages of decay are based on very predictable conditions like bacteria growth."

"I don't think it's an illusion." But it also wasn't like the decay of the body paused completely while a ghost was taking the place of the native soul. It was more like all that lost time was counted somewhere, and then hit the body all at once after the ghost left. Time hit change-lings the same way during sunrise and sunset when they were cut off from Faerie's magic. In a matter of seconds they could age rapidly if they'd spent years inside Faerie but came back out without the same time passing in the mortal realm. I'd seen one notable changeling age so much that she turned into dust.

You could cheat time, but not forever.

The door gave a squeak as it opened behind me. Briar's magical signature proceeded her, so at least I knew who it was. I turned, not because it would help me see who entered, but because it would at least give the pretense that I could.

"Hey, Craft, you ready to go?" Briar asked, and it was good I could sense her magic, because I sure couldn't hear her footsteps. The woman moved like a ghost. "Cops are already converging on the two locations where the shades said the different rituals occurred, as well as searching for any flyers still hanging and contact information for whoever ran the classified ad. I think you and I should head to the funeral home. It was used for a ritual only three days ago, so it is our best lead. Why aren't you moving yet?" she said when I just sat there listening, still clutching my coffee.

"I think I'll have to sit this one out."

"What? No, come on."

I shook my head. "I just held four different shades for several hours. I'm out for a while. Right now, I'd slow you down."

"You can't be that tired. Suck it up. I might need a sensitive."

"She can't see, Inspector," Tamara said, her chair creaking as she shoved out of it. Her tone was fierce, and I wished I could have seen her, because she sounded like she was going all mama bear, which I'd never heard from her before.

She'd also just revealed a secret I tried very hard to

conceal as much as possible. I could all but feel Briar's evaluating gaze boring into me. I sat straighter, trying to still my trembling and forcing myself not to cringe as the pounding of my heart in my ears marked the seconds it took for Briar to respond.

"You can't see at all? Like, you're completely blind?"

I nodded, the movement jerkier than I wanted. All grave witches had issues with their eyes. Most had permanently lousy night vision and restricted vision directly following a ritual, but it cleared quickly. Mine had always been on the more severe side of normal, but within the acceptable parameters. Until my planeweaver abilities had emerged. Something about gazing across all the planes, not just into the land of the dead, really abused my vision. I'd created some extra shields that helped, but only so much. A short ritual would have been fine, but I'd straddled the chasm between the living and the dead for at least two hours.

"How long will it be before your vision returns?" Briar asked, and I could tell from how much closer her voice sounded that she'd left the doorway and moved farther into the room.

I shrugged. "Several hours, I would guess. Surely no more than six or so." At least for a partial return of sight. I'd had full blindness last days before, with a very slow return to my normal damaged level, but I'd been doing some very serious, plane-shaping magic at the time. Even a ritual as long as I'd just performed couldn't compare to that kind of magical expenditure.

Briar was silent several moments. Then I heard the door swish open again.

"I can't wait that long. I'll call you if I need you." She

must have said it over her shoulder as she walked out, because the door clicked closed a moment later.

Tamara clucked her tongue in disapproval and then lifted the now-empty mug from my fingers. "More coffee?"

I called Rianna for a ride. I still couldn't see by the time she arrived—no big surprise—so Tamara helped me to the parking lot. I'd have to come back for my car some other time.

"There's a dog in the front seat," Tamara said after Rianna pulled the car to the curb.

"Desmond, can Alex sit shotgun?" Rianna asked in a sweet voice.

The barghest growled.

"That's not very nice," Rianna said. "And wouldn't you be more comfortable stretched out across the backseat?"

The doglike fae made a grumbling noise that was not quite a growl, but I heard the scrambling of his nails and huge paws as he climbed into the backseat.

"Am I good?" I asked Tamara.

"Yeah, but watch your head."

I nodded, too proud to let her guide me any farther into the car. Putting a hand on the roof, I lowered myself into the little car, managing to still bang my knees into the dash because the seat was up farther than I thought. Once I was inside, I said my good-byes to Tamara and we were off.

"Anything interesting at the office today?" I asked as Rianna drove us through the city. Her small sedan was a gently used older model, and the feel of the steel around me made my stomach cramp. Still, it was a better option than taking the bus or waiting for my vision to return enough to drive myself. As far as human-built cars went, Rianna's contained much less iron than the average vehicle while being much cheaper than a fae-built one, but it was still uncomfortable. I had to wonder how Desmond could stomach riding in Rianna's car every day.

Rianna made a noncommittal sound that likely accompanied a shrug before saying, "We got a walk-in client. He asked for you specifically, but it was a missing-artifact case and once I explained you were engaged on a different case for a few days and I'd be the one casting the tracking charm regardless, he finally agreed to let me take the case as long as the paperwork said it was being covered by the firm. It was odd."

"Sounds odd. But on the plus side, at least it wasn't another ritual for an insurance case, right? So what did he hire the firm to find?"

"Family heirloom." The words were flat. I was missing something. She should have been excited. She loved cases that let her be more detective than grave witch.

"Did you locate it already?" I asked, because while it was only early afternoon, I would have expected her to be off tracking it when I'd called for a ride, and not at the office willing to pick me up.

"No." The single word sounded sullen and I wished I could have seen her body language. "Would you look over this charm for me?"

I held out my hand, and she placed something that felt identical in size and texture to the charm I'd used to track Remy onto my palm. I might not have been able to see, but I knew she didn't want me to examine the charm with my eyes. While I couldn't have created the tracking spell myself, my ability to sense magic let me check a spell's strength and purpose, as well as feel out any irregularities. Kind of like running a diagnostic. It was a skill I'd taken full advantage of when Rianna and I were in our wyrd boarding school. While I'd barely passed my remedial spellcasting class, I'd made a fair chunk of change troubleshooting other students' homework and projects. Not exactly approved by the school's code of conduct, but all the practice meant that when I'd gone to get my OMIH certifications, I'd tested into the highest category for a sensitive. I never even bothered trying to get certified for spellcasting.

Like almost every spell I'd seen from Rianna since she returned from Faerie, the magic itself was tight, clean, and very strong. It should have been perfect, but while nothing in the magic of the spell felt wrong or even that different from the one she'd made for my case, the reason for her concern was immediately obvious. The magic was there, ready, but the charm itself was silent. There was no tug in any direction, no pull toward the missing artifact she sought. The charm was lifeless.

I frowned, squinting at the charm in my palm as if that would somehow make it come into focus. It changed nothing. "The magic is flawless. What did you use as a focus?"

"An illustration. I know, I know," she said, clearly having read the skepticism on my face. "But I have successfully traced items with as little before."

"No, it's not that. You said the client claimed it was a family heirloom? Why didn't he have more than an illustration? What exactly is this family heirloom anyway?"

"An ornate, filigreed, and jewel-encrusted bottle. He called it a *buidealanam*. Though I'm probably pronouncing that wrong. It's apparently been in his family for hundreds of years. I have no idea why he didn't have a picture, but it was a very detailed illustration that he provided."

When I continued to frown, Rianna sighed, the car slowing. "You think he never owned it to begin with."

"I think that's a distinct possibility. The charm you made is good, and the focus, while not a great one, should be enough to get at least some feedback from the spell. That means the bottle is either too far away to track, or well warded. If his bottle is warded, that means it wasn't lost."

"No. It was stolen. He was up front about that."

"Did he contact the police?"

She was silent a moment before finally saying, "He said he contacted the authorities but that there had been no movement on the case in weeks. I'm not sure if he contacted the police or the FIB."

That last part surprised me enough I almost dropped the inert charm. "The client is fae?"

"He didn't say, but Desmond thinks so," she said, and from the backseat the barghest chuffed, as if agreeing.

If the client was fae, that put a bit of a different light on things. It explained why he would have walked into our firm looking specifically for me and insisted the firm take the case, not Rianna. There were rules in Faerie about involving mortals, but Tongues for the Dead was technically a fae-owned firm. It would also mean he couldn't lie, so if he said the bottle had been stolen, it was. It might also explain why he'd had an illustration instead of a picture. Photography, being only about two centuries old, was still relatively new and mystifying technology to some of the older residents of Faerie.

Of course, all of that was assuming the client really was fae, which at this point was just that, an assumption.

"Are you supposed to locate the bottle or recover it?"

"Just locate. Do you really think Desmond would let me take a case that might be dangerous?" She laughed as she said it, and the barghest gave another chuff from the backseat.

We drove in silence for a few minutes, and even though I couldn't see the city pass outside the window, I knew as soon as we crossed the river and into the Magic Quarter. The magic in the air was distinct, almost welcoming.

"So if the tracking spell isn't working, will you contact the client and release the case?" I asked as the feel of ambient magic grew around the car.

"Have I ever given up that easy?" she asked, and though I couldn't see her, I could hear her determination. Rianna could be the epitome of a fiery, stubborn redhead. "I thought I'd try some scrying, even though I hate it. And keep monitoring the tracking charm, of course. If the bottle isn't already in a vault somewhere, it might move from behind the ward guarding it at some point."

"Good luck."

"I need it," she said, but she sounded less discouraged than when I first entered the car. Maybe talking over the stumbling blocks in her case had helped, though I didn't see how. "How about you. Is it the necromancy thing you're working on with the MCIB investigator?"

Now it was my turn to give a sour sigh. I filled her in on what our interviews of the shades had revealed. Going back over it, we actually had a lot of leads. It was just that most of them were thin. Our necromancer had been covering his trail using false names and disappearing conversations. It was no wonder a link between victims hadn't been found before.

The car pulled to a stop. In the distance I could feel the wards protecting Tongues for the Dead, so we were parking, not just at another stoplight. The engine cut off, and I climbed from the car, glad to be released from the cage of iron. Orienting myself by the feel of the wards and the now-familiar magics of the shops surrounding our office, I turned toward the alley where our little firm was located. There was no room to park directly in front of our building, so we always used the street parking a block or so away.

Rianna walked up beside me and locked arms with mine. The position was friendly and companionable, and hopefully didn't look like she was leading a blind woman down the street. It was something we'd used before, mostly because of my pride. Rianna's eyes recovered considerably faster than mine, plus she had Desmond. He was like the ultimate guide dog, though he'd probably take offense at me saying as much.

"Well, maybe the raid on the funeral home will turn up something vital and case-breaking," I said as we walked. "Or maybe the cops can run a sting for this Dr. Hadisty-Vogel-Basselet-Moyer or whatever he goes by next. But if not, I'm technically under contract with the

MCIB until this case concludes. If any clients call, can you cover them until the end of this case?"

"Of course," she said as she pushed open the Tongues for the Dead door to the familiar sound of chimes. "In the meantime, think you can help me with this missing-artifact case this afternoon?"

"Sure, if there's anything I can do while blind."

I met Briar at Central Precinct again the next morning. I'd had a text waiting for me when I woke telling me to meet her at eight. At least she hadn't shown up at the house this time. Considering I needed to pick up my car anyway, I'd already arranged to ride with Holly, so it worked out fine.

"Did you bring the tracking charm?" Briar asked as soon as I stepped into the conference room she was using as her remote office while on the case.

"Yeah, I take it the leads from yesterday didn't pan out?"

She lifted a hand and tilted it in a *so-so* kind of motion. "We managed to track down one of the flyers calling for volunteers. Contact was established and a questionnaire filled out, but now we are waiting for it to be reviewed."

"All the shades except Rosie said that the process took several days."

"Yeah." She nodded. "So that's out there. I don't really want this to drag out several days, though. Plus we have no idea what kind of criteria he has for accepting 'subjects.' There is always the chance our application will get bounced."

"What about the two ritual sites?"

The way Briar's lips curled into a repulsed sneer was answer enough. She picked up a tablet off the table and opened a digital photo album. "I don't think he'll use either again. Both sites were bleached and salted."

Bleach to erase DNA evidence and salt to erase magical evidence.

I scrolled through the photo album she'd handed me. There wasn't so much as a stray rune left on the floor. Aside from the fact that everything looked immaculately clean, I wouldn't have guessed anyone had been in either location in years.

The guy was thorough.

I handed the tablet back to her. "I'm guessing by the fact you know the place was salted, you've already had a sensitive walk the scene?"

She nodded. "The local ABMU has several on payroll. Nothing is left at either scene."

It made sense that the Anti–Black Magic Unit would employ their share of sensitives. The talent was uncommon but not truly rare. I was good but certainly not the best in the city. If none of the sensitives from the ABMU had picked up any residual magic, I was highly unlikely to find something they missed.

Briar walked over to a map of Nekros that had been tacked to a bulletin board. Over a dozen pins dotted the city. On the outskirts of the map were explanations for the pins and printed pictures of the known victims. The pins marked everything from the coffee shop where Annabelle saw the flyer to the museum where Rodger and I'd had our unfortunate encounter.

"So what next?" I asked as I examined the layout of the pins. I saw no pattern. The locations where the victims lived, where they found out about the study, where they died, and where their bodies eventually stopped moving were scattered all over the city.

"My partner is looking closer into the thefts the corpses have been committing to see if we can find out more about what the necromancer is after or what he might target next. The bank robberies, well, he's collecting money for something. Possibly a one-way ticket to a private island, but Derrick thinks he might be buying magical items as well as stealing them. He's identified the cup the shades described as an item sold on the black market a little over a week ago. It's a poisoner's goblet. Any liquid drunk from it becomes instantly deadly. Isn't that charming? In contrast, the tablet stolen from the museum is believed to be an ancient charm meant to prolong life. I'm not seeing the rhyme or reason in his actions, but Derrick will keep digging."

"And me?"

"You said you brought the tracking charm?" Briar asked, and once I nodded she continued, saying, "I made one. Having his body means we have as much material as one could possibly hope to use as a focus, but it only ever leads me to the corpse." She nodded to a small silver locket sitting in a petri dish on the table.

Her spell was definitely fancier than mine. I pulled out the cheap microsuede bag that held the tracking charm Rianna had made for me when this case first began. Cupping it in my fist, I felt the magic immediately make an insistent pull toward where Remy's body was a floor below us in the morgue. I waited, searching for the second trail I'd picked up two days ago.

Nothing.

I shook my head, and Briar sighed, her leather-clad shoulders slumping.

"Maybe it was a fluke, or maybe it was some sort of misspell, but just in case it wasn't, where did you first pick up the trail?"

I pointed to the northeastern quadrant of the city on the map. "I drove to the very edge of town, and it was pulling farther, out into the wilds."

Briar pursed her lips, studying her map. After a moment, she turned, striding toward the door.

"Come on, Craft," she said as she reached the threshold and I hadn't followed her. She didn't pause to wait for me.

I had to jog to catch up. "Where are we going?"

"There are no other leads, so we're going to check out the wilds."

That stopped me in my tracks, which caused me to fall behind again.

"You're kidding," I called at her back as I tried to catch up again. "For all anyone knows, if you don't use one of the passages in or out of the folded space holding Nekros, the wilds might go on forever. We can't hope to find anything out there."

"It's the closest thing we have to a clue right now. Unless you want to sit around hoping another walking corpse drops dead at your feet. Again."

No. I definitely didn't want more people to die just so we could learn more about our bad guy. But the wilds? As magic grew in the world, legends woke in the still-wild places in the world. They weren't the kind of places you decided to take a nice picnic lunch to relax. She was right, though; the charm having pointed that direction was one of the few unexplored leads we had left. And maybe the faint trail I'd found when I was out there was too weak to feel from the center of town. Maybe when we got closer the tracking charm would kick in again.

Into the wilds we go.

Chapter 13

⟡

We ran into our next problem before we even left the parking lot.

Logistics.

"This is not going to work," Briar said, staring at my mostly plastic convertible. "Does it even have a trunk?"

I rolled my eyes and hit the button to open the admittedly small trunk of my car. I'd pulled the little blue convertible beside Briar's rented Hummer, and it looked sleek, sporty, and really, really tiny beside the humongous SUV. The backseat was almost nonexistent, and the trunk space was limited, but it was the nicest car I'd ever owned, and I loved it. Also, the whole part about it being designed for fae with very little metal so driving around in it didn't make me sick was a big draw. But regardless of how much I loved my little car, it didn't carry around its own folded space, nor was the trunk bigger on the inside, so there was no way it was going to fit the two huge military-grade metal footlockers Briar hauled around.

"How much of that do you actually need?"

"All of it? None of it?" She shrugged. "Without knowing what we might find, it's hard to say. I like to be prepared."

I didn't comment on the fact she was basically a one-woman army with just what she carried on her person. I had no idea what could be in the crates that she didn't already have on her, but then the last time I saw her fight, she incinerated a graveyard full of ghouls without breaking a sweat. She was accustomed to wading into situations most normal people would run screaming from. I'd managed to toast one ghoul on that trip, only because Briar had given me several vials of a highly flammable potion, but I'd still ended up nearly eviscerated. Being prepared had likely kept her, and the people around her, alive more than once.

"I don't suppose you have a gun safe hidden in that minuscule trunk somewhere, at least?"

"I don't own a gun," I said, lifting my empty hands as if to prove the point.

Briar said a few choice words under her breath, then leaned into the back of the SUV and lifted a panel, pulling out yet another, albeit smaller, warded metal box and a flat black duffel bag. She rummaged through the larger crates, pulling out items.

A sawed-off shotgun went into the duffel bag. A tiny glass vial with a healing potion so potent I'd have believed it if she said it was made of unicorn tears went into the warded metal box. Priorities.

Weapons, potions, spelled disks and darts, all were

gathered and loaded into the bag or box. Several times she'd pick up a small case, evaluate the contents, and then put it back, deciding it wasn't important to carry on our reconnaissance trip. Watching her pack potions that would melt flesh or instantly cause desiccation made my stomach twist into several pinched knots. What did she think we'd find out there? I was feeling less than enthused about this trip. Once the duffel and box were filled to the point of bursting, Briar sealed the two footlockers and backed out of the SUV's trunk, the duffel slung over one shoulder and the metal box tucked under her arm.

"This will have to do," she said, moving both to my car.

"I think you forgot the kitchen sink." It was a feeble joke, more an attempt to cover my nerves than anything else. Thankfully, she didn't bother answering.

After slamming the trunk harder than my little car deserved, she moved around the left, as if she were headed to the driver's-side door. I all but dashed to the door, sliding behind the wheel before she had time to protest. It was my car. I was driving.

Briar grumbled under her breath as she climbed into the passenger seat. "Just so you know, I'm a horrible passenger."

She wasn't lying. Briar had opinions on everything from my speed—five over was still too slow—to which way would be the fastest route, and she seemed to feel obligated to share every one of these opinions. Or maybe she was trying to annoy me into letting her drive.

I stared straight ahead, not speaking as I followed the roads out of town. I pulled into the parking lot of the gas station where I'd turned around yesterday. Putting the car in park, I focused on the charm around my wrist. The distant pull of Remy's body was still distinct, tugging back toward the center of the city. No other trail appeared. Well, it had been a long shot anyway.

I shook my head, looking over at Briar, and she sighed. Then she leaned forward against the dash to peer hard through the windshield.

"So this is as far as you went yesterday?" she asked. At my nod, she said, "Well, nothing unusual here. We'll definitely have to go farther out. Any more specifics about direction?"

I tried to remember. The trail had been pulling deeper into the wilds. The road ahead of us was probably going close to the direction, but as soon as it curved . . . I glanced at the map in my GPS. There were very few roads past this point, but this one would take us into the wilds for a few miles before it turned to feed into the highway leading out of town.

I put the car in drive and Briar sank back into her seat. We drove in silence for several minutes. The forest grew denser as we drove, the trees encroaching on the shoulder of the road, as if the wilds were waiting in anticipation to reclaim the territory the street had cut from them.

"Slow down," Briar said, leaning forward to peer over the dash again. "There is a turnoff ahead. Take it."

I slowed, then stopped, not turning. "You mean that barely car-sized gap in the trees that is unpaved and overgrown?" I shook my head, shooting a dubious glare at the path, which wasn't defined enough to earn the name "dirt road." "This is not an off-roading vehicle."

"Drive it or hike it, Craft, but we are checking it out. There are fresh tire tracks going in that direction."

I narrowed my eyes, trying to force them to pick out the details of the tracks under the gloom of the forest canopy. I could make out the lighter dirt in the tire ruts, but a new or old trail? That was beyond me.

With a sigh, I turned the wheel and crept the car toward the dirt path.

"Okay, but if we get stuck, you're pushing," I grumbled under my breath.

Briar only smiled, her eyes scanning the forest as we slowly bumped and rolled down the dirt path. A few times the steering felt like it slipped a little in the sand, and the tree roots cutting across the path made my teeth knock together as my car rolled over them, but we didn't get stuck. The path narrowed, the trees growing so close I could have reached out a hand and brushed the bark.

"This is going to suck if we have to reverse out of here."

"Then let's hope there is a turnaround," Briar said right before we turned a shallow corner to discover an ancient-looking oak growing in the middle of the path. She sighed as I slammed on the brakes. "But of course, no. You're right, this is going to suck, but park first. I want to check out the area."

I did, frowning at the tree. "Where did the car go?"

Briar had been in the process of climbing out of the passenger seat, but at my words, she turned back to me. "What?"

"The path we followed. It's an overgrown mess, but the ruts we followed were mostly dirt and sand. That doesn't happen from a single car turning off the road once or even twice. This path has been used quite a bit, but why?"

"You're smarter than you look, Craft," Briar said, slamming the door as she stalked toward the tree. She circled it, glancing at the tire tracks that stopped in front of it and then at the forest closing in behind the large oak. "It's possible this is nothing more than a favorite hangout spot for some local teenagers. A place where they know that law enforcement or parents are unlikely to stumble over them doing something less than acceptable. Or—"

"The tree isn't real," I said, and Briar nodded.

"Also a possibility."

"No, I mean the tree isn't real," I said again, and Briar's head shot up, her gaze fixing on me.

I almost laughed. Being in the close confines of the car with Briar and her arsenal of spells, my ability to sense magic had gotten overloaded, desensitized. Now that she was farther away, my magic sense was starting to pick up individual spells again. Kind of like being in a room with a scented candle for a long time. Your nose gives out eventually, but if a breeze cuts through the room, stirring the air and momentarily displacing the scent, suddenly you become aware of the candle again. Briar had given me a little distance, and while I could still feel the maelstrom of spells surrounding her, as well as emanating from her stuff in my car trunk, there was also a distinct swell of magic encircling the tree.

"The tree is an illusion." A good one. The spell coalescing around the tree was tight and powerful.

Briar reached out, and her hand passed right through the bark. I'd half expected the illusion to be solid—I'd been around an awful lot of glamour recently—but this wasn't fae magic. This was a witch illusion spell, which meant there was no substance, just illusion.

Every witch could reach the magical plane and draw down the raw Aetheric energy stored there, but typically it took time, concentration, and a ritual. It was also typically only the witch's psyche that reached across, as he or she all but lost contact with his or her mortal body. It was possible to drag someone else's spell to the other plane, so that its magic could be studied and examined, even by nonsensitives, but again, it took time and ritual.

My planeweaving magic let me bypass all of that. I cracked my shields and the Aetheric plane snapped into focus around me, overlaying the mortal plane. Convenient at times, but also very dangerous. I examined the swirls of magic twining through the illusion. They were red and orange, twisted together with care and finesse. It was probably the most delicately spun spell I'd ever seen, and I'd examined a lot of magic. The red and orange threads spread beyond the tree, coating the trail and surrounding area as well, cloaking them in illusion. The entire spell was tied to a small focus at the base of the tree.

I closed my shields, cutting off the overlaid images of the different planes of reality. Looking was easy enough, as long as I didn't do it too long, but if I tried to interact with them, I risked dragging them all into mortal reality. We didn't need that. I stepped forward and, using my ability to sense magic to guide me, plunged my hand into the illusionary tree. The buzz of the tightly woven spell tingled along my skin, but there were no aggressive magics woven into the illusion, and in a matter of moments, my fingers closed on something hard that all but radiated magic. I pulled it up, out of the dirt, and the illusionary oak vanished, as did several smaller trees behind it and a large amount of fake undergrowth that had hidden several yards of the path.

Briar whistled. "Not bad, Craft."

I shrugged, examining the object in my hand. It was little more than a stick wrapped with vines and a few pieces of cloth. What looked like a small ceramic cup had been buried to the rim in the ground, and that was what I'd plucked the spelled stick from. I set it gingerly back into the cup, and the illusion sprang up around us again. Removing it made the illusion vanish as if I'd unplugged a battery.

"Nice," I said, genuinely impressed. "Whoever made this was very skilled. It probably needs to be recharged every so often, but otherwise, it's completely self-sustaining."

"They also want to hide something. Let's check it out," Briar said, climbing back into the car.

We drove for several minutes, the forest seeming to close tighter around us, until sunlight suddenly broke through the canopy and we pulled into a clearing. I stopped the car, giving my eyes a chance to adjust, and Briar took the opportunity to hop out of the vehicle again. She prowled around the clearing while I blinked in the bright light. The sun was high above us now. Between the time it took us to travel to the northeastern part of town and then this excursion into the wilds, we'd been out here awhile and morning was creeping toward noon.

I climbed out of the car slowly, watching Briar prowl around the clearing. After the thick cover of the woods, the clearing seemed too open, too exposed. It also looked really empty. The only things of any note in the entire clearing were the multiple tire tracks where vehicles had turned around. Someone used this road and clearing a lot. But why?

"Do you sense anything?" Briar asked, looking up from where she was examining tire tracks. "No one hides an unimportant clearing behind an illusion that strong."

I reached out with my senses, searching for magic. But it wasn't magic I found.

It was the chill of the grave that reached back.

I shivered, the grave essence calling to me, reaching icy claws through my sweater to prickle along my flesh. I lifted a hand, pointing in the direction I felt. "Something is dead in that direction." I let the smallest amount of the chill into my mind, so that I got a better sense of what manner of corpse was calling to me. "It's not human." I frowned. "I'm not even sure it's mammalian." Which was odd. While I could interact with the grave essence of other creatures, usually only mammals called to me, and only humanoids typically called this strongly.

Briar's lips pursed in thought. "Any reason to believe it's connected to this case?"

I shrugged. "No, but it's close and big. Really, really big. Actually, no. I mean yes, there is a big dead thing, but there are other dead things near it." Lots of dead things together? Never a good sign or natural, unless I was feeling something's den where it took its kills.

Briar turned in the direction I'd indicated and studied the woods on that side of the clearing. "I see the buzzards circling," she said, pointing above the tree line. "Well, we are here. Might as well check it out."

Several fae I'd talked to had mentioned that legends were waking in the wilds, and not all of those legendary creatures were nice. Wandering through a wild forest in search of dead things sounded like a bad idea to me, particularly when whatever had killed several very large animals all in one place could still be close by.

The thought must have been clear on my face.

"Do you have a weapon, Craft?"

I pulled the enchanted dagger I carried in my boot. It was fae-wrought and could cut through almost anything, and just touching the hilt let me feel the dagger's excitement about the possibility of being used. It was a good dagger, but it was small, and definitely not my top choice for fending off a large animal.

Briar frowned at the dagger and grumbled something under her breath about the idiocy of bringing a noncombatant civilian, then she said, "Stay behind me, Craft, and stay close."

Then she crossed the clearing and marched into the wild woods.

Chapter 14

You don't really notice the sounds of the woods until they stop. Distant birdsong, the buzz and chittering of insects, and the rhythmic sound of frogs had all blended into the backdrop of the forest as I followed Briar through the underbrush. But as the grave essence reaching for me thickened, growing more insistent as we drew closer to the source, an eerie silence fell around us.

Then a loud roar boomed through the trees.

Briar and I both froze. I didn't see her draw it—or where she drew it from—but Briar's crossbow was suddenly in her hand and up, swinging slowly side to side as she scanned the forest. Nothing moved. Not even the breeze in the leaves.

"Still think this was a good idea?" I hissed under my breath.

"Yes," she said, her whisper flat, determined. "How close are we to the corpses?"

"Close. Only fifty or so yards in front of us."

She nodded, starting forward again, but she moved slower than she had before, and she didn't lower her crossbow. I followed, my palm sweating where I gripped my dagger. I wanted to wipe my hand on my pants, but I didn't want to release the dagger long enough to do it.

We'd found the footpath we were following as soon as we'd left the clearing. Someone had traveled this way frequently. The clearing we'd left had clearly been the parking lot; whatever was ahead of us was the real attraction. I wasn't looking forward to discovering what that might be.

As we crept around trees and over underbrush, it became obvious we were approaching another clearing. Occasional growls issued from somewhere in the bright sunlight beyond the tree line, the sound of more than one very large thing moving around.

"Stop," I whispered, grabbing Briar's shoulder.

She half turned, lifting an eyebrow, but she stopped. I closed my eyes, trying to sift through all the different magics assaulting my senses. The grave essence was banging on my shields now, like a visitor who wouldn't leave but kept pounding on the door. The magics buzzing around Briar were a constant drone as well, but there was something else. Something new.

"The clearing is warded," I said in a hushed whisper.

"Keeping people out?" Briar asked.

I frowned. I could feel the ward, but there was too much assaulting my senses. I couldn't isolate it enough to dissect what it did. Which meant I needed to get farther from Briar . . . and closer to whatever was growling in the clearing.

I really didn't want to do that.

"Well?" Briar asked, sounding impatient.

"I'm not sure yet," I said between clenched teeth. "I'm having trouble separating it from all the magic you're carrying."

The smile she flashed me had a lot of teeth but wasn't exactly friendly. "Then you stay here and work on it. I'll run my own tests."

She pulled several charms as well as a spellchecker wand out of her pockets and crept forward. The farther she crept away, the easier it became to distinguish the signatures of her magics from the ward surrounding the clearing. I could have cracked my shields and looked at the actual magic, but with all the grave essence pouring out of the clearing, I didn't want to give it a single chink in my shields to try to bust through. It didn't help that my own wyrd ability was battering the inside of the shields, just as anxious to get out as the grave was to get in. So I focused on my ability to sense magic, feeling out the ward.

Wards were specialized magic. Recognizing that something was warded was easy, but figuring out exactly what a ward was designed to do . . . That was much trickier. Most spells were easy to distinguish, kind of like a rose is instantly identifiable and very different from a daisy. But wards were individual while also being only a slight variation from one to another. Figuring out exactly what a ward would do when tripped was about as simple as searching for one particular daisy in an acre of daisies. I was a decent sensitive, but I wasn't *that* good.

"It will definitely warn whoever cast it when someone crosses the perimeter," I said, creeping up to where Briar crouched just outside the edge of the ward. "But

I don't think crossing it will trigger any aggressive magical attacks." At least not by the ward. We still didn't know exactly what was beyond it. Through the brush I could make out several very large shapes moving in the clearing, but we couldn't get close enough to get a good look without crossing the ward.

Briar nodded, gazing down at the tools in her palm. "I'm picking up a lot of magic, but nothing is popping as malicious." She pocketed the charms. "So I guess it's time to go in there."

I blinked at her. "Did you not hear when I said the person who cast the ward will definitely know when we cross it? Because that part of the spell I can clearly sense."

"Which is perfect. I don't have to hunt someone who comes to me." Briar flashed another one of those toothy but not pleasant smiles, and then lifting her crossbow, she stepped into the ward.

I felt the sizzle of magic as the ward reacted to her presence, but whatever else the ward did, it didn't stop her from creeping forward to the edge of the clearing. I stared after her, unsure what to do. Briar made up my mind for me.

"Craft, get over here," she hissed in a loud whisper without ever turning away from whatever was in the clearing.

I sighed, tightened my grip on the dagger, and stepped into the ward. Briar hadn't even paused as she passed through it, but the magic in it tugged at me, forming not a solid wall, but certainly resistance that I had to push through. It felt like when I passed through a cemetery gate, which raised the question, was the ward meant to keep dead things inside, or soul collectors out?

I was neither. As a planeweaver, I was a nexus in which the planes merged, including the land of the dead and the crystal-like plane the collectors inhabited, so I could feel the resistance of the wards, but they didn't stop me. The sick feeling twisting in my gut squeezed tighter, though.

It took several moments for my eyes to adjust to the light, and once they did, I almost wished they hadn't. The clearing wasn't that large, only about the size of an Olympic swimming pool, but the creatures inside made it look even smaller.

There were four—no, five—creatures milling about the clearing. All were different sizes, different species. Most I couldn't have named. All were dead.

The largest was slightly bigger than a horse, and shaped similarly except that instead of hooves he had leathery splayed toes with massive talons at the ends of his legs and scales instead of fur. He also had two large buzzards sitting on his back, dipping their beaks into a massive wound in his side through which I could clearly see white rib bone. The creature whipped its head around, gnashing at the buzzards with needle-pointed teeth. They fluttered their wings, backing away, but the second the creature turned, the bolder vulture dipped his head into the wound again, dragging out a long gray string of intestines. I looked away, my gorge rising.

The smallest creature was about the size of a German shepherd, but it was covered with feathers and had a snout that ended in a beak the color of fresh blood. It dragged one of its back legs behind it as it prowled the edge of the clearing. For a moment, its cloudy eyes fell on the spot where Briar and I crouched, and I tensed, lifting my dagger. But its gaze slid on past us, and the creature kept walking.

Briar's charms. Okay, now I was thankful she kept them on more or less all the time, and that I could hide inside them as well.

The three creatures between the two extremes in size were more identifiable. One was a large black bear who'd lost so much fur and flesh on its face that skull was visible in several spots. The next was a gray wolf, who looked almost normal aside from clouded-over eyes. The last was built like a jungle cat with wings. Patches of fur still remained on parts of his body, but much of his flesh looked like a festering blister, glistening and raw. The wings had fared slightly better, though while most of the blue-tinged feathers were accounted for, they looked dirty and bent.

Bones and half-decayed carcasses littered the clearing, but those at least were still. True dead. Then there were the ghosts. So many ghosts. Not human ghosts, though. They were animal ghosts. From small mice and shrews to rabbits and even a few foxes, the ghosts scurried around the clearing, avoiding the walking dead creatures. I couldn't imagine why the ghosts weren't scattering, why they would gather in large groups in a clearing, until I considered the ward. It had felt like passing through a cemetery gate. In the same way, it must have kept the dead trapped in the clearing—both the walking dead and the ghosts.

Most of the walking dead ignored the ghosts, but as I watched, the largest dead creature's head shot downward, vicious teeth closing around the ghost of a small hare. The creature tilted its head back and swallowed the small ghost in a single movement.

Cold sweat slid down my neck. Ghosts stole energy from each other, that wasn't uncommon, but this? This was something else entirely.

"What are we looking at?" I whispered, my mouth dry, tongue too thick.

"Necromancy," Briar said, her lips curling in disgust. "This kind of walking dead I've dealt with before. Necromancers start off experimenting by raising animals before they move on to humans. Though they usually start smaller. I've never seen some of these monsters before."

Probably not all necromancers had access to magical creatures from the wilds. "That does explain the mice and shrew, I guess."

She cast a sideways glance at me. "You're seeing things I'm not."

I didn't answer or try to explain the dozens of ghosts because at that moment, the dead wolf swung his head in our direction, his ears twitching. He tilted his head back, his broad nose flaring as he sniffed the air. He howled, a warning cry, and the other animals stopped. Some turned to the wolf, but the large winged cat peered around the clearing. He took several steps in our direction and chuffed, letting the scents roll over his tongue.

Crap. Briar's spell hid us from sight, but it didn't seem to be doing a good job on any of the other senses. I glanced at her, my eyes wide. We'd seen what was in the clearing. It was a damn good time to retreat back out of the ward and call in the authorities.

Unfortunately, Briar was one of those authorities, and she didn't seem interested in backup. Both the wolf and the cat were stalking forward now. The bear's nose twitched, searching, and the huge beast's tongue flicked in the air, like a snake tasting scents. Its head swiveled toward us.

Crap. I shuffled back a step and a twig snapped under my boot. I cringed, holding my breath. It was too late. The dead things in the clearing might not know exactly where we were, but they were narrowing it down, and they didn't look friendly.

Briar watched the stalking winged cat and aimed her crossbow at the center of the beast's chest. I could feel the incendiary potion loaded in the steel-tipped dart. She wasn't playing around. That would almost certainly take down the beast. Walking dead or not, something about combusting and turning to ash tended to stop most things. The biggest problem was, as soon as she attacked, the camouflage spell hiding us would fail. So, while one beast would be a smudge on the wind, the other four would know exactly where we were hiding.

I glanced at my dagger. These creatures' bodies were decaying around them. Vultures were pulling the insides out of the largest beast, and it was just pissing him off. Poking holes in such a creature wouldn't stop it from attacking. I'd have to dismantle the deranged things, and by then, if I was close enough to deliver that many blows with my small dagger, the beasts would tear me to pieces. The dagger wasn't going to be much help. But surrounded by the dead, the dagger wasn't my only weapon.

I cracked my shields.

A cold wind tore through me, rustling the leaves of the trees all around me as the grave essence that had been battering me since we got close to this accursed clearing finally found a foothold and wormed into my psyche. I let it in, embracing the chill that warred with the living heat inside my body. Around me, a patina of decay coated the world, even as colorful strands of magic became visible. I could see the orange and red magic woven into the intricate ward surrounding the clearing. Similar strands of magic coated the beasts, binding their decaying bodies, and the soft glow of souls inside them.

The winged cat was racing forward now, straight toward us. The wolf and bear weren't far behind. A twang sounded, and Briar's dart flew. It landed in the center of the beast's forehead. There was a moment where the creature's legs straightened as it tried to stop its forward momentum, and then the fire engulfed him.

"What are you doing?" Briar hissed as she reloaded and took aim at the wolf.

"Helping."

They were all charging us now. A mix of teeth, claws, pointed beaks, and nightmare-inducing decaying flesh. The wolf was closest, but the strange feathered thing had overtaken the bear and was covering the distance toward us fast. Briar's crossbow twanged again, releasing another deadly shot filled with blue-white flame. The wolf fell, incinerated. I reached out with magic, my own living heat laced with ice from the grave, and wrapped it around the dog-sized feathered creature. The dead flesh offered no resistance, my magic quickly flooding the body and pushing out the soul without opposition. I'd never seen an animal soul before today, but a pale, glowing soul popped free of the creature, one that didn't match the body that fell prone and inert to the dirt.

I didn't have time to study or consider that fact. I

pulled the magic back, thrusting it into the huge, reptilian horselike creature. Again, the dead flesh gave easily under my magic, but this creature was bigger, so much bigger, and I poured magic into it, trying to fill it, to saturate it with so much grave chill there would be nowhere for the soul to cling.

Except there was no soul in this one.

No light. No fluttering warmth retreating from the grave. This creature was filled with the dark emptiness of the land of the dead, and it drank down my magic, eager for more.

I pulled back, drawing back as much magic as I could before it vanished forever into the darkness inside the dead beast. It kept charging, its taloned feet kicking up clouds of dust as it crossed the clearing, closing in on us. Briar's crossbow gave another twang as the cord released, sending a dart into the bear that was less than two yards in front of us. The heat of its body incinerating nearly knocked me backward, but Briar's bow swung to the giant reptile. It was the last beast standing.

"Capture that one. It's different from the others," I yelled, just as the crossbow twanged again.

Briar jerked the weapon up at the last moment, causing the shot to go wide. It passed within inches of the beast's head. The creature kept charging, picking up speed. It would be on top of us in moments.

Briar nocked a different bolt into her crossbow, cursing the entire time. She fired, taking the creature in the chest. I felt the knockout spell buzz in the air as the dart hit the creature in the chest and the vial of potion broke, but the beast didn't slow down.

"Move," Briar yelled as she rolled to the side.

I threw myself to the other side as the creature

crashed through the space we'd just occupied. I landed badly on one elbow but managed not to stab myself with my dagger or get trampled by the creature's talons.

Briar pulled something from the bandolier across her chest and hurled it at the creature. A net of magic formed over the beast, pinning it to the ground. The beast reared back, its large mouth splitting open as it released an ear-piercing screech.

I pressed my palms over my ears, trying to block out the sound. Something deep and instinctual urged me to run. Terror cut through my mind with the sound of the beast's scream. The sound promised that the beast would kill me. That I was small and soft and it would suck the marrow from my bones. I squeezed my eyes shut, clamping down on the terror spiking in my veins. The creature was caught. I was fine. But something inside me still reacted to the sound, and it was all I could do to keep from turning and fleeing.

The beast tore at the magic binding it, and it was gaining ground, moving toward Briar. She cursed and threw another potion at it. The ground reached up to lock around the beast's front legs. It bucked, screeching again. One leg broke free.

"Craft, I don't think we're taking this thing alive," Briar yelled to me between the creature's screeches.

"Obviously. It's already dead," I said, moving around toward its back. It ignored me. Apparently, I wasn't near the threat Briar was. "And we don't need it moving. Just not incinerated would be good. It's covered with magic. We might learn something."

The beast freed its other front leg from the trap of earth Briar had caught it in, and it charged. The magical net held, but the beast gained several feet, forcing

Briar to pull back. Her hand moved over her bandolier of potions, as if taking stock and not finding what she wanted. The creature lunged again, pushing on the net and gaining another foot of ground.

"No use, Craft. We're going to have to burn it."

"Wait," I yelled as she lifted her crossbow. "We could leave the clearing, wait for backup so it can be contained."

"I'm the person they send to take care of this shit." She sent a dart through its chest, aimed for where the heart should have been. I expected it to burst into flames, but she'd changed spells again. This one blasted a hole in its side. That didn't slow it down. It reared and then slammed its body forward again, forcing Briar to retreat as the magical net slipped more. "You want to study the magic. Do it quick, I'm burning it."

I'd been trying to decipher the spells on the creature, but my pulse was pounding in my ears, my heart thudding in my throat, and my brain was too frantic to make any sense of the magic I felt. We needed to neutralize its threat so there would be time to study the magic properly.

I darted toward the creature's back flank. Reaching through what was left of the magical net, I grabbed its knee and dropped the bubblelike shield that prevented me from touching the planes of reality I could see. The beast was already dead, already rotting, and it was nothing for me to push it further into the land of the dead. The real trick was to push only its knee and nothing more.

The flesh under my fingers withered, flaking away from my touch. The muscle was next. And then my fingers touched bone, which crumbled under the push of my magic. The whole thing took only a heartbeat. I was scrambling away before the beast could even whip its head around.

The creature tottered, the sudden loss of its leg in combination with its violent turn causing it to lose balance. It toppled, falling to the ground with a crash. Its surprise didn't last long though, and a moment later, it began scrambling up, using its three good legs. I needed to use its distraction. It was thrashing, trying to gain purchase with its one remaining back leg. I couldn't get close enough to touch its knee, but I could get its foot. I darted forward, pushing with my magic the moment I touched cold flesh. I had to pull back almost immediately or risk getting caught by one of its saberlike talons. But it was enough. I hadn't turned its bone to dust this time, but I'd pushed the decay far enough for the bones to turn brittle. The creature's ankle crumbled under him as he put pressure on it.

The beast collapsed again, the stubs that were left of its back legs moving but not able to help it stand. No blood poured from the lost limbs, but it screamed, clawing the ground with its front legs.

The creature screamed again. The sound still woke terror in me, but now the emotion warred with the revulsion I felt for what I'd just done. And pity. Yes, the beast had been trying to kill us, but this was not a clean death, and I pitied it even as its long talons dug into the earth, still trying to claw its way toward us.

Briar lowered her crossbow. The massive creature on the ground was no longer charging her but thrashing spasmodically without gaining purchase. She pulled a sword out of who-knew-where and stepped closer. Holding the weapon in two hands, she brought it down hard on the creature's long neck. The blade sizzled as it bit into flesh, but it sliced cleanly through bone, muscle, and tendons.

The creature's screeching cut off abruptly, its severed head rolling from its body, and the beast fell still, true dead at last.

I stumbled to the edge of the clearing as my stomach heaved. What was left of my breakfast returned, leaving my throat burning and my mouth tasting sour. I wiped the back of a shaking hand across my mouth. My adrenaline was dropping now, and I wasn't sure if I was more disgusted by what I'd seen or by what I'd done, but I had to stand back up. To turn around and face it again.

Taking a deep breath didn't help—the air was filled with the scent of rot, ash, and vomit. It was almost enough to force me over again, but I swallowed the sick feeling, refusing to continue to dry heave. Steeling my will, I turned around.

Briar looked up from where she was studying the corpse of the large reptilian beast when I walked over, but she made no comment on my weak stomach. I was glad for that. She hadn't released the magical net pinning the now-true-dead creature yet, and I was glad for that as well. She moved around the creature slowly, but as she reached what was left of its back legs, she stopped, staring.

"What exactly did you do?" she asked, staring between where the lower part of the left leg lay detached from the rotted stump above the knee.

I grimaced, looking away, but didn't answer. Instead I focused on reconstructing the bubblelike shield I used to keep my planeweaving abilities in check. I couldn't close all my shields—I'd expended too much magic, I'd be blind, but I didn't want to accidentally push or pull anything across the planes.

When it became clear I wasn't going to answer, Briar walked across the field toward the only other creature that had left a corpse. The buzzards had already gathered around it, and they spread their wings as she approached, trying to make themselves look bigger as they guarded their meal.

"How come you were able to drop this one from several yards away but couldn't stop that one?" she asked as she drove off the vultures.

"That one had a soul. The big one didn't," I said without thinking, and then immediately regretted the statement when she whirled around.

She crossed the area between us quickly. "Like the robbers in the bank had souls? So you can just reach in and jerk out souls whenever you want?"

Crap. "I—"

"Turn off the light and wind show, Craft," she said, pointing to my eyes.

"I can't."

"Why not?"

I glared at her. "Because my power damages my eyes, and if you'll remember, we tripped an alarm ward when we walked in here, and I don't want to be blind if whoever—or whatever—made these monstrosities shows up."

"Couldn't you just rip out his soul?"

"Only if he's already dead," I ground out between clenched teeth.

We stared at each other for a long time, and I could almost feel the scales in her head, weighing whether she should arrest me. I'd more or less admitted I had, in fact, been the reason the robbers had all collapsed. But you can't murder someone who is already dead.

"I have to call in a magical hazmat team. Don't go anywhere," she finally said, turning away from me.

I didn't plan to go anywhere. For one thing, I couldn't drive while peering across the planes. I had no idea how I was going to get my car out of these woods. Also, I wanted to check out the spells on the two beast bodies. None of the human corpses I'd encountered had been tied in spells. Of course, none had been visibly rotting either. That meant either we were dealing with two unrelated groups of walking dead—which didn't seem likely—or as Briar had said, these creatures were early experiments or progressions of the necromancer's process.

I knelt beside the enormous reptilian beast. I could barely stand to look at the stubs where his back legs had been. My gut twisted, threatening to rebel again, but I needed to examine the magic. It used the same orange and red energy I'd seen in the illusionary oak and the ward, but the intricate tangle of magic wasn't like anything I'd ever seen or felt before. It was powerful, and detailed, but I couldn't make sense of it. If I hadn't known that what I was examining was a dead thing that had been walking around, I wouldn't have guessed that was what the spell could do. Hell, I wouldn't have had any clue what I was feeling at all.

After fruitlessly tracing the magic with my mind, I stood. My legs ached from kneeling, and I'd been still so long that vultures had gathered around the beast. I startled them as I hobbled away and they squawked at my back. Briar was no longer on the phone—in fact, for a moment, I was afraid she was no longer in the clearing, but then I felt her distinct signature of spells near where we had first entered the clearing. She was here but hidden behind her look-away charms again. Which meant if the necromancer who could animate dead creatures returned, I'd be the only one visible. Great.

I considered heading over to where she was, to hide behind her spell as well, but once the hazmat team showed up, I'd likely not get another look at the bodies, and I wanted to compare the spells on the soulless beast with the one who'd had the wrong soul navigating it.

And speaking of souls, there were four new souls that had joined the army of animal ghosts in the clearing. Even with me straddling the chasm between the planes, the new animals looked weak, drained; like mere memories on the wind. I passed by the ghost of the winged jungle cat, and it looked up at me, its rounded ears pressing flat against its head.

"Nice kitty," I whispered, lifting my hands flat in front of me.

The ghost stalked forward. It looked insubstantial, even to me, but as I basically always existed on all the planes, more so when I had my shields open this far, it might still be possible for it to hurt me. I really didn't want to get mauled by a ghost after I'd just survived being attacked by corpses. I backed away slowly, never turning my back, but also not running. Smaller ghosts scattered around my feet as I moved, but all my attention was on the winged cat.

"Craft?" Briar called, the hint of concern clear in her voice.

I didn't answer or look over. Even with all the spells in her personal armory, it was unlikely she had anything that would be effective against a ghost. They just weren't something most people had to worry about.

I could have pulled the ghost's remaining energy out, draining everything that made the ghost still the animal it had been, and I would if I had to, but I'd already done horrible things today. I hadn't been sure before today that animals had enough ego to leave ghosts behind. Now that I knew they did, I didn't want to cannibalize a creature who had already been through so much.

So I kept backing up, moving slow, making soothing sounds as I crept away. The ghost stopped stalking forward as I felt the first buzz of the ward at my back. The ghost opened its mouth as if to let out a yowl, but if it made a sound, it was lost in the winds of the land of the dead. Its gaze moved beyond me, to the ward.

"You just want out, don't you, buddy," I said, still keeping my voice low, calm.

The ghost stared at me. I bent slowly, pulling the dagger I'd sheathed after the final creature had fallen. Then I half turned, not actually giving my back to the ghost, but turning enough that I could reach the ward.

"What are you doing?" Briar asked from a lot closer than I expected, and I jumped.

"I'm . . . uh . . . cutting a door in the ward."

"A door?"

I shrugged, dragging my dagger through the thick magic forming the ward. The dagger could cut about anything, including most spells. It didn't disappoint on the ward but sliced a clean line through the woven strands of orange and red energy.

"The ghosts are stuck," I said as way of explanation.

"Uh-huh," Briar said, lifting a skeptical eyebrow. "And how is that supposed to help? You can't cut magic."

This enchanted dagger could. Or maybe it was this dagger in a planeweaver's hand. I wasn't sure. I could have used a mentor in this whole planeweaving thing, but they were all dead or stuck in an inaccessible court in Faerie. So most of what I'd learned in the last few months since my planeweaving emerged was gained through trial and error—mostly error.

Door cut, I stepped to the side and looked at the ghost cat. It stared at me, eyes narrowed and ears flat. It didn't move. It didn't understand. Being dead didn't change that it was an animal with an animal's instincts and intelligence. There was also a good chance it couldn't see the force that held it in the clearing, it just knew there was a wall.

I frowned, looking at all the ghosts in the clearing. Hadn't they been through enough? I doubted they'd understood what was happening to them when they'd been stuffed into bodies that weren't theirs and then been forced to stay there as the foreign bodies rotted around them. Of course, that was assuming all were simple beasts. Most were. The small ones certainly. But the magical creatures? As they'd charged at us as soon as they realized we were in the field, I'd assumed that all were as much animals as they appeared. But maybe they weren't.

"Can any of you speak?" I asked, lifting my voice to be heard across the clearing.

Some of the ghost creatures looked at me. The wolf ghost growled. None answered.

Briar watched me as if I'd lost my mind. "Who are you talking to?"

"The ghosts." I waved a hand to indicate the ghosts she couldn't see. I could have expended energy to make them visible and more substantial, but that didn't seem wise. For one thing, these creatures had attacked us when they'd been inside bodies. And for another, I was already trembling, and not just from the adrenaline letdown anymore. I needed to close my shields soon. I'd be blind, but the longer I stayed in contact with other planes, the longer that blindness would last. I wanted to check out the other body first.

"Are the ghosts human?" Briar asked, her gaze searching for the invisible-to-her ghosts.

I shook my head. "The same creatures we fought as well as others. A lot of others. Small creatures. Probably early experiments, as you said."

I couldn't feel the age of ghosts, so I had no idea how long any had been dead. I could get a sense of some of the small bones in the field; though there were too many to examine each, the oldest I could feel was no more than two months old. In contrast, the two bodies of the beasts who had been walking were newer, no more than three weeks old. Strangely, the largest beast was the most recent of the two, even though it had been the most decayed out of any of the walking creatures. Possibly because it hadn't had a soul? I couldn't get anything from the ash left from the incinerated beasts.

As I considered that possibility, one of the circling birds overhead swooped down, into the woods, and through the door I'd cut in the ward. I'd thought all the birds were vultures, but this one was a raven. A very large raven.

It didn't fly to the two remaining corpses but to the ghost of the winged jungle cat. It landed on the ghost's back, its claws sliding into the insubstantial form. The ghost glowed, flashing bright, and then vanished. It had transitioned and moved on. The raven flew to the next ghost.

No, it wasn't a raven. It was a soul collector. An *animal* soul collector.

"Hello," I said, trying to get the large bird's attention.

"Now what are you talking to?" Briar asked. When I just waved her off without answering, she shook her head. "Sometimes I'm not sure if you aren't legitimately crazy."

I ignored her, making my way toward the raven collector. It looked at me a few times, cocking its head, but it kept flying from ghost to ghost. It had its work cut out for it, but it kept moving, swooping down to collect each soul, even the tiny mice. Once the clearing was free of ghosts, the raven turned and, without a wasted flap of its wings, it flew back through the door I'd cut and was gone.

Chapter 15

⇥━━➤ ◄━━⇤

It took nearly two hours for the magical hazmat team to arrive.

By then I'd compared the spells on both of the creatures who'd left behind corpses. The big one was covered in indecipherable spells I couldn't make sense of, but the smaller one, the one I'd ripped the soul out of, had minimal traces of magic, and what was left was too faint for me to get more than vague impressions. Briar was more than a little disappointed. After all, my specialty was the dead. But I dealt with shades, and occasionally ghosts. Despite the cheerily colored magical energy the necromancer used, whatever had happened to these creatures was very, *very* dark magic.

After I'd given up on detangling the spells, I released the grave and sat at the edge of the clearing, blind. Every time Briar made a noise I jumped, expecting the mysterious necromancer to appear. He still hadn't shown himself by the time hazmat showed up. Briar talked to the team for a while, but she was done hanging out in the clearing. Someone was going to have to stake out the area in case the necromancer did turn up, but Briar was delegating that to local law enforcement.

Once the scene had been turned over, Briar was ready to leave. Unfortunately, I was still more or less blind. A few shadows of shapes had reemerged in my sight, but it wasn't enough to get through a hike in the woods. I was too proud to ask Briar to guide me through—and I had serious doubts she would anyway—which meant opening my shields again. I wasn't actually using any magic this time, just looking, so it didn't do as much further damage as it could have, but I was still in no shape to drive the car when we reached it.

Which meant reluctantly handing my keys to Briar. And then sitting in the passenger seat of my car, more or less blind, feeling my newish-to-me car careening through the city. By the time she pulled into the parking lot of Central Precinct, I was clinging to the armrest and silently cursing my wyrd ability and my eyes.

I didn't bother following Briar inside. I was done for the day.

My eyes weren't as bad as they'd been the day before, but I was way below the visibility limit that I could legally drive with, so I called Rianna for the second day in a row. She was about ready to give up on her current case, but no new clients had stopped in, so she was still poking at the limp mess that was her search for her client's missing bottle.

It was early afternoon, and I should have gone back to the office, but I was so done with the day. I was hungry after losing my breakfast after the fight, and I was mentally, magically, and emotionally exhausted. I just wanted to go home. So that was where I had her take me.

"You've been really quiet," she said as we pulled into the driveway of Caleb's house. "Mulling over the case?"

"Something like that," I said, because I didn't want to talk about it. In truth, my brooding had only been tangentially connected to the case. I was thinking about the clearing, and watching that creature fall after I took out his legs because I felt that learning what magic had made him was more important than ending his suffering quickly. I didn't like what that said about me. And I was thinking about the look on that ghost's face when I'd pulled her out of Remy's body. His body was dead. She was dead. And I'd prevented people who were alive from being harmed or killed. Death had confirmed that more people would have died if I hadn't acted. But I was starting to question whether I'd done the right thing. Maybe there had been some other way to stop them.

I climbed out of the car before realizing Rianna wasn't following.

"You coming inside?" I asked, leaning down to squint at her through the still-open door. Desmond had already scrambled over the seats to take my place, so I mostly only saw a lot of black fur.

"No, I think I'll head back to the office and keep working on a spell to narrow down what area of the city this stupid bottle is in," she said from somewhere on the other side of Desmond. "The tracking charm actually picked up a lead for about an hour today, but I lost it before I got far. I'm going to keep watching it and try a few more things."

I nodded, wishing I could thank her. She was struggling with her own case and here she was playing chauffeur to me. It wasn't even like I'd been that great a friend lately. Everything was work and then home to the castle. I silently vowed that once this case was done, I'd have a girls' night out with Rianna, Holly, and Tamara. Also, tomorrow, if I ended up blind after wherever the case took me with Briar, I'd call a taxi. It didn't matter how much metal the vehicle contained.

I waved good-bye and headed inside. I glanced toward the stairs of my old apartment. It would be smart to set up my computer and do some more research. I'd had no luck looking for anything having to do with humans walking around after death, but the creatures in the clearing had been very different from the human corpses.

I didn't go upstairs. I was tired and hungry, and I didn't really want to be alone. I'd do it later. Instead I headed to the castle.

Unfortunately, it was the middle of the day, so the castle was empty as well.

I collected PC from my rooms and a sandwich from the kitchen, and then I headed to one of the gardens I hadn't explored yet. Usually I kept PC on a leash, but this particular garden was completely enclosed, so I let him run. Despite the fact that it was November, roses were in bloom all along the perfectly manicured path. They filled the air with a soft scent that seemed to swirl around me, making me think of sunshine and spring.

I stopped by one of the bushes to admire the flowers. Each deep red bloom was full and perfect, the petals velvety soft. Not one black or yellow mark marred the bush, which had to be magic in and of itself. My father had always had rosebushes around his estate when I was growing up, and his gardeners were forever battling black spot because of our humid southern weather.

PC ran up to me and dropped the ball he'd grabbed before we left my room. I tossed it and the dog scampered after it. I kept walking. He wasn't likely to bring it back until he got tired of playing on his own.

In the center of the garden was a small reflecting pool. I sat down at the edge so I could watch PC bark menacingly—if the yip of a six-pound dog could be considered menacing—at his ball and then lunge at it and toss it in the air before starting the ritual all over again. PC had just decided it was time to actually bring the ball back to me when I heard voices behind me. After the day I'd had, I jumped, twisting around so fast I nearly hurtled myself into the reflecting pool.

On the other side of the garden, Roy and Icelynne walked arm in arm. They noticed me about the same time I whirled around. Roy smiled, using an entire arm in his enthusiastic wave. Icelynne didn't smile. It wasn't that she didn't like me, or I her; I think she just hadn't figured out her place yet, and I confused her. Not intentionally, of course, but she was very stuck in her world views, and I didn't fit.

Icelynne began to curtsy but then caught herself halfway and seemed to get stuck, unsure how to proceed. She knew I didn't like it when she curtsied, but she'd been a very old fae at her death and had spent her entire life in the Faerie courts. Not being a very powerful fae, she'd survived those centuries by deferring to those who'd had more power or better position, and in most of the courts, the *Sleagh Maith* were the nobility. I hadn't grown up in Faerie, though, and I was just me.

"Hey, Roy, Icelynne," I said, trying to defuse the situation and free her from the awkward moment she'd gotten stuck in. "How are things?"

"Good evening, Lady," Icelynne replied, totally missing the lifeline I'd thrown her.

Roy hurried over, all but dragging the smaller ghost along with him. She stood only about four feet tall and couldn't keep up with Roy's much longer stride, so she eventually unfurled her wings, flying to keep up.

Roy didn't stop until he was right in front of me. "Hey, Al. So Icelynne and I have been talking and we thought it would be great if the castle had a winter garden."

"It's really nothing to bother Lady Alex with," Icelynne said, stepping back and visibly trying to reclaim her hand.

Roy, oblivious and ever eager, just frowned at her. "What are you talking about? Of course it is something we should talk to Alex about." He turned back to me. "Lynne's a frost sprite, but the castle seems to be caught in perpetual spring. She'd feel much more at home if there was a little more winter here. Just one garden would be fine."

Icelynne jerked her hand from Roy and held both out in front of her, palms facing me as if in surrender. "It's fine, really, Lady. The gardens are beautiful. We meant no disrespect."

It was my turn to frown at her. "Icelynne, it's okay, calm down." I almost told her to chill, but that would be too ironic. Besides, the little frost sprite likely wouldn't have understood. "I think it's a reasonable

request. We can ask the garden gnome if it's possible."
Or more likely Ms. B, who could talk to the elusive
gnome.

Icelynne blinked, her large inhuman eyes going first
wide in surprise, and then narrowing. "That is very kind,
Lady. What will I owe you for this boon?"

"It's not a boon, it's a courtesy. You're my guest
here." Not an intentionally invited one perhaps, but I
seemed to be collecting strays these days. She couldn't
return to Faerie—there was no land of the dead for her
to exist in there—and it wasn't like ghosts took up a
whole lot of space. "Guest" best described her role in
the castle. "That said, I don't know if it's possible for
the weather in just one garden to change, but I can ask."

"It's your domain, Lady. These grounds, this castle,
and everything are an extension of your will."

Riiiight. "Trust me, if this castle did what I wanted,
the banquet table would be filled with pizza once in a
while."

Icelynne cocked her head, her very alien features
pinched, searching, as if I'd mystified her again. Roy
smiled.

"Thanks, Al. You're the best," he blurted out, the
debt opening between us before I even processed his
careless thank-you. Then he hooked his arm through
Icelynne's again. "Well, we'll let you get back to whatever you were doing," he said, meaning what he actually
wanted was to get back to his alone time with the other
ghost.

I smiled and waved to them as they meandered back
the way they'd come. It wasn't until they'd rounded the
corner that I realized I'd never thrown the ball again
for PC. I looked around for the little dog and found

him pushing the small ball up to the base of a roughly carved statue half obscured by a rosebush. He took a few steps back, tail wagging as he waited. When the ball just sat at the little wood figure's feet, PC let out a demanding yip.

What is he—

The wooden figure suddenly flushed with color, the rough edges smoothing to soft flesh, and the now little man, who couldn't have been more than a foot tall, snatched up the ball and tossed it. PC turned, bounding after it.

"You're the garden gnome," I said, stating the obvious in my surprise.

The gnome turned. He looked like any lawn ornament of a gnome, right down to his friendly, rosy cheeks and a pointed hat almost as tall as he was. "And you're the mistress of the castle."

"I—" Well, yeah. I guess I was. "I'm Alex."

"They weren't wrong," he said, nodding in the direction Roy and Icelynne had gone.

"About the castle bending to my will? I'm not so sure— Wait. You can see ghosts?"

The little gnome shrugged. "Only when I'm wooden. But yes, you are the mistress of the castle. There was no spring here before. I must say, I'm enjoying it. So many things grow in spring."

"I didn't . . ." I started, but trailed off. He'd said all of that as a statement with very little wiggle room. While it was possible it was only his belief that I'd willed the castle to be caught in spring while fall hurtled toward winter just outside the door to this folded space, it might actually be true. And the other fae at the castle would probably know a lot more about it than I would.

Fae were extremely long-lived. Compared to most of the other people at this castle, I was very young. The fact that I'd grown up believing I was mortal didn't help. So I considered the weather here, and how I was always relieved to get out of the chilly November air and step into the folded space holding the castle. I was cold too often from the grave as it was; I didn't like cold weather on top of it.

"So if the grounds bend to my will . . . does that mean I can move the door leaving the folded space closer to the castle?" It would be a relief to not have to make that hike every time we needed to get to and from the other side.

The little gnome shook his head. "The castle and estate are yours. The folded space itself and the door are not."

"Oh." Well, darn. That would have been awesome. "But you can make a winter garden?"

"Yes, most definitely." The gnome perked back up. "You have to really want one. But yes, if you do, I can make something that will please the frost sprite's specter. Which garden would you like to freeze?"

I had no idea. I looked around. "Not this one. This one is perfect like it is."

The gnome bowed, both hands moving to his large hat to hold it on his head. "You honor me."

In my pocket, my phone began singing about how girls just want to have fun. Holly's new ringtone.

"You're the artist behind these gardens. I'll leave it to your discretion to decide which would look best frozen," I said to the gnome as I dug my phone out of my pocket. "I need to take this. Hello, Holly."

The gnome bowed again, and if I hadn't been on the

phone, I would have asked him to stop. Then, without another word, he turned and vanished into the hedge of roses. In my hand, the phone squawked, Holly's voice coming out broken and full of static. I glanced at the display. One bar.

"You're breaking up. I didn't get any of that," I told her, standing as if that would improve the signal.

"What? I can't understand you." She sounded like she was yelling into the phone, but while her voice was still a little garbled, at least I could make out her words.

"Better?" I asked, patting my hand on my thigh to get PC's attention as I headed for the entrance of the garden.

"Yeah. I take it you aren't somewhere you can turn on a TV?"

"Not if I'd need to do it in the next ten minutes."

Holly was silent for a moment and I glanced at the display again to make sure the call hadn't been dropped. The reception at the castle was horrid. No towers. Finally she spoke. "The broadcast is over now. I'll find a clip online and send you a link. You were on the news, and, Alex, it was bad."

True to her word, my phone buzzed with a link a few moments after I hung up with Holly. I didn't open it immediately but gathered PC and headed back into the castle. If it was bad, I wanted a little more privacy than the gardens offered. My growling stomach also demanded more food before bad news.

I passed through the kitchens on the way to my room. It was still too early for dinner, so the kitchen boasted fruit hanging in baskets and steaming baked goods that appeared to have just come out of the oven. In another hour, when the dining table filled with the night's meal, the kitchen wouldn't have so much as a crumb in it, forcing anyone who wanted food to present themselves for dinner.

I thought about what the gnome had said about the castle reacting to my will as I snagged a muffin the size of a small plate. Had I enforced the family dinner situation somehow? I certainly hadn't meant to, and sometimes it was annoying, but in truth, I did rather enjoy it. Maybe I had? If the castle was shaping itself for me, even here, at least half in the mortal realm, I would definitely have to pay better attention to my own thoughts and desires.

Back in my room, I set to work devouring the muffin as I clicked the link Holly had sent. It loaded slowly, the intermittent signal sluggish. I was about to give up and head back to Caleb's house when the video finally filled my phone screen. A pretty woman in her early thirties smiled out of the screen, addressing the camera directly as she finished a sentence pertaining to a report she must have been giving before the clip began. I vaguely recognized her as a reporter for one of the local stations, but the only news I watched with any regularity was Witch Watch. A small tag near the bottom of the screen identified her as Xandra Lundahl.

"In other news," Xandra said, still smiling directly at the camera, "the police are asking for help locating a person of interest in an ongoing investigation. Viewer discretion is advised as the footage you are about to see could be considered graphic."

The reporter vanished and a grainy black-and-white image appeared on the screen. It took me a moment to recognize the museum from the Magic Quarter, but as soon as I did, the muffin I'd eaten turned leaden in my guts. The angle was focused on the entryway, and as the museum's door opened, I wasn't surprised to see my own figure appear. I'd barely stepped inside when a middle-aged man barreled into me and we both froze, caught in the security spell. Lines appeared in the image, as if it had been recorded in analog and was being fast-forwarded. An effect added by the studio to indicate time, no doubt. People moved faster than life around the edges of the screen. I hadn't even noticed them at the time, and they were moving too fast to follow closely in this rendition. Then the lines disappeared and normal speed took over again. A crowd was gathered around the two frozen figures. A witch removed the spell, and the man in the video collapsed, clearly dead.

A buffering symbol popped up in the center of my phone screen and I cursed. The video Holly had sent me was only half finished. I paced as I waited for the phone to finish buffering, and fidgeted with the hem of my sweater until I noticed several strings fraying at the hemline. I didn't have the budget for new sweaters right now, so I forced myself still, willing the phone to load faster.

Finally the clip began playing again. A new image loaded on the screen. This time I recognized the location immediately. The bank. It was one of the security videos the police had shown me. This clip was shorter. Just a few seconds of the three robbers in the bank before all three simultaneously collapsed. Then Xandra was back on the screen.

"Police have confirmed that they do not yet know

the cause of death for these four people, but as you can see, this woman was present at both of these events." Small, superimposed boxes appeared on either side of the reporter, framing her red curls with two close-up images of me. The one from the museum in the Quarter was terrible quality, and the one in the bank caught me with glowing eyes and hair whipping around my face, but they were still very identifiably me.

Which proved to be a moot point a moment later as Xandra continued her report.

"The pictured woman is believed to be local grave witch Alex Craft." As she spoke, the two black-and-white security close-ups vanished, and the full-color headshot from my driver's license appeared. "Police ask anyone who has information about the where-abouts of Alex Craft to contact the number on the screen."

The camera panned out, revealing that Xandra sat at a table with several other reporters. The man to her left shuffled the papers in front of him and said, "This isn't the first time Alex Craft has ended up news in Nekros. Do the police suspect her of being involved in the deaths?"

Xandra turned, not completely toward the other reporter, but enough that it was clear she was address-ing him while still smiling into the camera. "Well, Chad, currently the police are only saying that NCPD and the MCIB wish to question Ms. Craft about the events that occurred. No one has currently been named as a suspect in the deaths."

The man nodded. "One has to question if magic was involved in the deaths. And if so, how? Has a new type of magic emerged? Something deadlier than we've seen before? And on that subject, the Humans First Party has made headlines again—"

The clip ended. The screen of my phone went blank as the video shrank.

I stared at the phone, too shocked to process what I'd just seen. Holly had warned me it was bad. I could have never guessed it would be this. Why would John have released those clips and statement? Not only had he questioned me about it already, but the shades' testimonies had cleared me. Plus he knew exactly where to find me. If he'd been looking for me, he would have called. Or shown up at my house or work. I wasn't hiding from the authorities. Hell, I'd been with Briar most of the day.

Briar.

Anger bled through my shock. The only thing that plastering those videos and my name over the media did was destroy my reputation. Oh, and let whoever had actually killed those people know who I was. That report wasn't John's style, but Briar? I wouldn't put it past Briar to try to stir up a reaction from the real killer by letting him know who had been breaking his toys. She'd just painted a target on my head.

Fuck.

I closed out of the browser app on my phone and pulled up the recent call list. The number Briar had called me from yesterday morning was second down on my incoming calls, and I tapped it. The first time the call failed. The second time, it rang three times before she picked up.

"What the hell is your problem?" I all but yelled into the phone.

"Craft, I take it you saw the afternoon news?"

"You just made me a target." Now I was yelling.

She'd also damaged my credibility and probably my business. I didn't add that yet. Right now I was more worried that the guy who ripped out souls so that other ghosts could navigate the bodies now knew who I was.

I could almost hear Briar's shrug through the phone as she said, "We had no leads. The clearing where we found those monstrosities is being watched, but since the necromancer responsible didn't show up immediately after we tripped his wards, it is unlikely he plans to show at all. But you've been breaking his puppets. The easiest way to flush someone out is to give them someone to blame."

The phone chirped, alerting me to another call coming in. I didn't recognize the number, so I sent it to voice mail before saying, "So you thought you'd just throw me to the wolves. Zombie wolves in this case. Are you insane?"

"What are you worried about, Craft? I'm on the case with you, so I'll likely be around if they come after you during the day, and you're sleeping with an FIB agent who looks more than capable of watching your back. Like I said earlier today, it's a lot easier to hunt someone who comes to you."

Great. Just great. I sank down in a chair and buried my head in my arms. Unfortunately, that didn't solve the problem.

"You could have at least asked," I muttered.

"But you wouldn't have said yes. This was easier. If you feel like you need extra protection, I can see if the NCPD can spare some extra bodies to watch your place, but for now I have to go. I'll see you in the morning."

She disconnected.

Chapter 16

I stared at the phone in my hands. Briar had just painted a bull's-eye on my back, but it was already done. What could I do now? Turn myself over to the police? They weren't actually looking for me, so that wasn't going to help. Unless I wanted to hide in my castle, I was just going to have to find the necromancer before he found me.

My phone buzzed and began playing "When you're a stranger." Another caller not saved to my contact list. I hadn't even had time yet to listen to the voice mail I'd received while on the phone with Briar. From experience, I knew I was probably about to get very popular. That happens when you make the news in a less than good way.

I didn't want to answer, but I did. Might as well get it over with.

"Alex Craft, it looks like you've stepped in it again,"

a vaguely familiar female voice said from the other side of the line.

I frowned. "Who is calling?"

"I'm hurt," the woman said, the words so overdramatic that I imagined her pressing a hand to her chest as if I'd actually wounded her by not recognizing her voice. "This is Lusa Duncan from Witch Watch. I just saw that hatchet job they did on you over at Channel Six. Why, they didn't even mention that those people you killed were robbing the bank at gunpoint. Promise me an exclusive at Witch Watch and I guarantee the coverage will be much less defamatory."

While she was speaking, the phone chirped letting me know that yet another call from a number I didn't recognize was coming in. *And so it begins.*

"Listen, Lusa. For starters, I didn't kill any of those people. And for another, I'm working with the authorities on this ongoing case, so I'm not free to offer exclusives or discuss it."

"Interesting . . . so the story was what, a ploy? I'm guessing the retraction will be interesting. Maybe I'm glad you didn't come to me."

And I'd said too much already. How had I forgotten that anything beyond "no comment" was too much when it came to reporters? It was time to end this call.

"I have to go. There is another call coming in."

"Wait, I—" Lusa started, but I said my good-bye over her and switched calls, prepared to tell whichever reporter was on this line that I had no comment on the current situation.

Except it wasn't a reporter.

"You were supposed to find him. Not *kill* him," a

distraught voice yelled through the line as soon as I answered.

Taylor. I probably should have anticipated my client seeing that broadcast. I was going to kill Briar.

"Taylor, calm down. I promise that I didn't kill Remy, and that wasn't actually him robbing the bank."

"Shut up. I never should have gone to you. I'm calling the police right now and telling them everything."

Great. Well, the police were probably about to get a lot of calls about me. I wondered if Briar had passed this plan by them before releasing a story full of half-truths and misdirections.

"Feel free to call them. I'm working with the authorities on this case." Which was more or less true. I was working under Briar, at least.

"Shut up, shut up, shut up. You're a liar and a murderer," Taylor said, her voice getting louder with every word until the final one broke into a sob.

The line went dead a moment later. She'd hung up.

Well, that definitely could have gone better.

I had to wonder what the police were telling people when they called. This was definitely not going to be good for business.

I shoved my phone in my pocket, and it immediately started ringing again, Jim Morrison's slightly creepy lyrics alerting me that it was yet another unknown number without even looking. I didn't answer. I was done with calls for a little while. I considered turning the phone off, or at least putting it on silent, but changed my mind. If someone I did want to talk to called, I wanted to be able to hear their ringtone. After all, it wasn't like most people could track me down at the castle if they needed me.

As if the universe wanted to immediately refute that thought, a loud knock sounded on my door.

I jumped, my hand flying to the dagger in my boot. Which was a rather ridiculous reaction. For one thing, if someone meant me harm, they wouldn't knock first. For another, the castle didn't get visitors, which meant it had to be someone who lived here. Despite that, my heart thudded in my ears as I cracked open the door.

Falin stood in the hall, his hand lifted as if poised to knock again. Small lines pinched at the edges of his eyes, betraying either agitation or worry, I couldn't tell, but I was guessing I was about to find out.

"Hi," I said, hoping my smile didn't look quite as feeble as it felt.

He didn't return the smile. "What is going on?"

I opened the door wider, revealing the empty room behind me. "What do you mean?" I asked with as much innocence as I could summon.

Falin was not fooled. He stepped into the room, scanning the interior, but the action seemed more habit. Most of his attention remained fixed on me.

"What were you thinking, volunteering for this farce? Do you understand how much trouble you've just created yourself?"

I grimaced. "I take it you've seen the news?"

His look was answer enough. He'd seen it.

"Well, in my defense, I didn't exactly volunteer. It was Briar's bright idea and I didn't find out until after the segment aired."

Falin stared at me, and then he shook his head. He sank down into one of the overstuffed chairs. "Only you," he said, running a hand through his hair. "You've put me in a terrible position."

"You? How does this have anything to do with you?" Me, yeah. I was in a bit of an ugly spot. But what did it have to do with him? "I've seen absolutely no connection to any fae or to Faerie in this case."

He frowned at me. "You. You're the connection, Alex. You're an independent in Winter's territory, and an asset the queen still plans to exploit if she can. My job is to protect her interests, which means I really should take you into custody right now and drag you to Faerie until things cool off in the mortal realm."

I gaped at him. He just sat there, studying me. When he didn't immediately follow through on those threats, I crossed the space and sank into one of the other chairs.

"So . . ." I started, but I'd had a few too many shocks in the last few minutes, and my brain wasn't coming up with anything clever to say.

Falin leaned back in his chair and ran his hand through his hair again. It was starting to look rather mussed. He still wore that same pinched expression, and I decided it was worry mixed with exhaustion. He was my friend. But he was also the head of the FIB and the queen's bloody hands. If she gave him a direct command, he couldn't disobey.

"How long before the queen is likely to hear about this?" I asked, because the silence was getting thick.

"I'm not sure. The situation in Faerie is . . . tumultuous. She's currently rather distracted by potential threats from other courts. She might not hear about what is happening here for a few days, if you're lucky."

So he wasn't going to act on his own. That was good.

"I'm surprised you're out here if it's that bad," I said, and he just looked at me. "Crap. You're not working in Nekros, are you? You go off fighting her duels and whatever other dirty work she has and then head back here for supper, don't you?"

And with the way the doors to Faerie worked, as long as he got the timing right, he could spend days at a time in Faerie doing whatever the queen needed while only a few hours passed in the mortal realm. No wonder he'd looked so exhausted most nights. I'd foolishly thought that the queen had forgotten to lift the proclamation that forced him to live in my home. That he was working with the FIB in Nekros and the queen hadn't questioned where he was living. But if he was in Faerie on court business regularly, she clearly was still sending him back each mortal night to keep an eye on her "asset." Me.

"Given the change in circumstance," he said, after another silence stretched a little too long again, "it might be prudent if I stay on your side of the door for the next few days."

"I'm guessing you don't mean in your office at FIB headquarters," I said, sinking lower into my chair. He shook his head and I sighed. "So you'll be what, my bodyguard? My keeper? My parole officer waiting for me to step over the line?"

"That's not fair."

"You're right, it's not." I pushed up out of the chair. "Because if it were Caleb, or Malik, or any other independent fae who had wound up on the news, you wouldn't be having this conversation."

He didn't stand when I did, which irritated me. It was hard to kick someone out who was still sitting.

Instead, he very calmly, but a little too quietly, said, "You're right. I wouldn't be having this conversation. I wouldn't be having it because I would have sent agents to pick him up and take him to Faerie. No questions asked. No options offered. But I try very hard to help you safeguard your freedom."

I faltered, my body already half turned so that I could storm to the door and tell him to leave. But he was right. I collapsed back into my seat, feeling like an ass. Falin usually pushed the limits of the queen's rules for me when he could. I knew that for a fact. He was here offering me help and protection instead of doing what would ensure the best interests of the queen like he was supposed to, and I was acting like a jerk.

"It's been a really long day," I said by way of apology.

He nodded, dismissing my outburst. Forgiven and forgotten without even a word. Yeah, I felt like even more of an ass.

"Are you planning to answer that phone?"

I glanced down, as if I could have seen the phone in my back pocket through my own hips. It had more or less been singing my generic ringtone the entire time Falin had been in the room.

When it was clear I wasn't going to answer him or the phone, Falin said, "Why not turn it off then?"

"I might miss something important. If Briar calls, I need to answer it or she might show up at the house again. Or Tamara could call with an emergency. I don't know. It's a cell phone. It feels wrong to have it off."

The look he gave me clearly said, *But it's okay to not answer it?*

"Maybe you should get a private personal line. One that doesn't come up in a simple Internet search of your name."

"You mean one of those pay-in-advance unlisted phones? What do they call those in movies, burner phones? Yeah, that would be good. Next time I plan to become unexpectedly infamous, I'll do that."

The phone started a new chorus of the song again. It really was getting annoying.

"So why did the MCIB investigator decide to throw you to the news wolves and make you the obvious target for whoever is animating corpses?"

I shook my head. "I was supposed to be her lead, and I didn't pan out, apparently. So she found another way."

"This sounds like a healthy working relationship."

"Right? Maybe she's crazy." I leaned back in the chair and let my head rest on the back until I was staring at the ceiling. "She's just going to love you joining the investigation. Not sure how I'll explain that."

"She's clearly already reached her own conclusions. I can play the concerned boyfriend."

I looked over at him and frowned. He shrugged, but there was the smallest teasing smile at the edge of his lips. That was way too dangerous of a topic to touch, so I let it drop.

We sat without speaking for a few minutes, the only sound the incessant singing of my phone. Finally, Falin stood and headed toward the door.

"Dinner should be laid out by now, are you coming down?"

The muffin I'd eaten earlier was still a leaden weight rolling around my twisting stomach. I knew I needed to eat. I'd been in enough shit-hitting-the-fan situations to know you grabbed food when it was available because you might be running for your life later and not have time. But I didn't feel up to it yet.

"You go ahead."

He paused, the door half open, and turned back to me. His expression was serious again, any hint of teasing or amusement gone. "You won't leave the castle without me tomorrow, right?"

I nodded, fishing the still-singing phone from my pocket and searching the settings. I'd read something once about a do-not-disturb feature that would only ring if particular numbers called . . .

"Alex," Falin said, still standing in the open door. "I'm serious. This hidden folded space is probably safe enough, but if you leave, I should be with you. If the situation gets too bad, I'll have no choice but to take you to Faerie. I know you want to avoid that."

I did. I held up my hands in mock surrender, but I was very serious when I said, "I won't leave without you." Then I thought about something else. "Do you not want me to go to the house alone either? I mean, the wards will warn us if anyone tries to break in." And would stop most people meaning us ill will, but I wasn't foolish enough to think wards were impossible to get around. They'd definitely be a deterrent, though.

"Hang out in an empty house alone on the same night your name gets splashed all over the news? Probably not the best plan."

Maybe true, but a totally sucky turn of events. I needed to go back to the house and spend some time on my computer now that my eyes had improved enough to focus on the screen.

"It's only been, what, an hour? The news didn't flash my address, so it would take a little while to figure out where I live. And that's even assuming the necromancer saw the broadcast."

Falin just frowned at me, the skepticism clear on his

face. I frowned back. Yes, the broadcast made me a target if the witch wanted revenge for losing his walking dead, but I doubted he'd come after me tonight.

The thoughts must have been clear on my face, because after a moment Falin sighed and offered me a compromise. "I have some work to do that would benefit from electricity and a reliable Internet signal as well. Let's go eat. After dinner we can both go to the house."

Which was probably the best I could hope for.

Dinner was awkward, to say the least. Holly and Caleb joined us soon after we reached the dining room. Once the topic of the news report had been discussed to death, it then became this awkward elephant in the room that continued to shadow the mood of dinner but that no one was actively talking about. I choked down as much of my food as I could, but my stomach felt knotted too tight to eat a full meal.

Falin and I left before Rianna and Desmond even made it to the table.

It was actually more comfortable once it was only Falin and me again, despite the fact that he was the one who could decide at any moment the danger had gotten too high and drag me to Faerie for my own protection. Maybe it was because he didn't waste time asking me how I thought this would affect Tongues for the Dead or what I would do if the necromancer tracked me down. He just walked with me back to the house and silently pulled out his laptop as I hooked up my own. He had my back, and for now, that was enough.

We worked in amiable silence for several hours. I

spent my time searching for information about the walking dead and necromancy. Most of it was useless fiction or folklore. I did find a couple of press releases from the MCIB, though most dealt with ghouls, which weren't the type of dead thing we had here. I found very little information on necromancy, as animating corpses was illegal, so what I could find that sounded legitimate was vague at best.

In the immediate aftermath of the Magical Awakening, grave magic had been viewed as no better than necromancy, but the key differences had eventually led to the legalization of grave magic while necromancy was condemned. The biggest deciding factor was likely that grave magic was a wyrd magic, and like any other wyrd magic, the users couldn't avoid using it. The magic wasn't learned, it wasn't a choice. It could be directed, but it still had to be used. So, the OMIH had taken the grave witches in, given us a strict legal and moral code to follow, and certified us to practice. Necromancy, on the other hand, was a purely witch magic. It had to be learned and practiced to have a chance at results. Teaching it was illegal, as was practicing on corpses—human or animal. Of course, being illegal didn't mean it never cropped up, but it did mean that no practical information on how it worked was available online. Not anywhere I knew how to get to anyway.

I poked around the Dead Club Forums a little, but again, I couldn't find anything that shed light on what we might be dealing with. Maybe Briar and the MCIB had some top-secret research banks that would provide more information than the general public could access? I dug out my phone, considering calling her, but a glance at the display told me I'd been online a lot longer than

I'd thought. It was late. Too late to call with anything short of an emergency, and even if she did answer, I shouldn't start a new line of research tonight. Who knew what tomorrow would hold? I needed sleep to let my body and my magic recover from the overuse I'd been asking of them the last few days.

"I'm heading back to the castle," I said, standing. Falin closed his laptop, turning, and I frowned at him. "You can keep working. I can make it back alone."

"I'm done anyway."

I shrugged. "Suit yourself."

We packed up and turned off the lights, heading back to the castle. Falin walked me all the way to my room and even opened the outer door for me.

"Door-to-door service? Don't you think this is a little bit of an overreaction?"

Falin only smiled. "I'll see you in the morning."

Then he turned and walked away. On the plus side, at least he hadn't insisted on standing watch while I slept. Shaking my head, I stepped into my room, shutting the door behind me by shoving it with my foot.

I'd just knelt to greet PC when I realized I wasn't alone.

I didn't scream, but it was a near thing. I did jump, but I knew the figure standing in the middle of the room, arms crossed over his chest. Knew him intimately.

"You startled me," I said, straightening and trying not to look flustered.

"Guilty conscience?" Death asked it with a smile, his voice light, but it still struck me as a real question.

"Long day."

He nodded toward the door. "What was that about?"

I set the laptop down on a small end table. "The case

I'm working got dangerous, so now I have a babysitter."
I shrugged like it wasn't a big deal, but the look on
Death's face was equal parts concern for me, and what
I guessed was distaste for Falin. Annoyance bubbled
up in me at his jealousy. After all, I had no idea where
he went or with whom, but I wasn't jealous. He visited
when he could, which usually wasn't often, and I
couldn't even contact him. Oh, but he had a freaking
tracking spell on me—a fact we mostly glossed over
and that I force-categorized under "a good thing" as it
allowed him to find me since I couldn't locate him. And
yet he was judging who was watching my back when
he wasn't around?

"Did you find out something new about the ghosts
navigating the bodies?" I asked, hearing the edge in my
own voice.

"I didn't come to talk about your case," he said, stepping toward me. The smoldering grin he shot me normally would have weakened my knees, but today I
wasn't feeling it.

"I'm tired," I said, stepping around the arms that
reached for me.

"What happened today? Are you okay?"

I whirled around to face him. "What, because I don't
want to have sex whenever you decide to come around,
something must be wrong?" If I had slapped him, he
couldn't have looked more surprised. Or hurt. I took a
deep breath. "That was uncalled for," I said, forcing my
features to soften, to convey the apology I wasn't saying.
"Like I said, it was a long day."

"Want to talk about it?" He stepped toward me
again, more tentatively, as if I were some delicate creature that might fall apart if he was too aggressive. I was

feeling rather fragile at the moment, so maybe he wasn't completely wrong.

I met him halfway, accepting the embrace and the chaste kiss he offered. But when I stepped back to gaze up into those worried hazel eyes, I said, "I actually don't want to talk about it right now. I'm honestly exhausted."

"Okay, but I'm here until I get called away again. May I hold you at least?"

I nodded. I was emotionally and physically over this day, but being held sounded nice. I led him to my bedroom and then quickly changed into the pajamas laid out on my nightstand.

True to his word, he held me, but less true to mine, I found myself talking.

"I saw animal ghosts today. And an animal soul collector. He looked like a giant raven." A yawn forced my jaw to crack open. Death didn't say anything, just stroked my hair with one hand as he held me close. I found myself telling him about the clearing, about what I'd seen. And about what I'd done. He was my closest friend. My confidant. It felt right to share with him my fears, my self-revulsion, and my concerns about Briar's little bait plan. He didn't interrupt but murmured soft, mostly nonsensical sounds of comfort. Listening, and letting me get it all out. I'd barely finished the story when he kissed me, his irises spinning with a kaleidoscope of colors.

"You have to go," I whispered.

He nodded and kissed me again.

"You should rest," he whispered. Then he was gone.

Chapter 17

─┄─═─◉─ ◉─═─┄─

I woke to the sound of sirens.

It was still dark outside my window, and I was alone in my bed aside from my dog. PC stood on the pillow beside my head, his ears pressed against his head as he whined about the sound. A light flashed on my dresser, and I scrambled out of bed, stumbling across the room to find the source of the light and sound.

The small glass orb Caleb had given me proved to be the source of both. Yesterday, when Briar had been at the door, the sphere had glowed a soft yellow. I was guessing flashing and blaring sirens were not indications of anything good.

In the hallway, I discovered I wasn't the only one who'd been startled awake by the ward alarms. It was like a small flash mob of people holding blinking orbs had formed in the castle foyer. The sound that had been obnoxious and startling in my room was deafening when combined with three other wailing spheres.

"You all had to bring them with you, didn't you?" Caleb yelled above the din. Out of Falin, Rianna, Holly, him, and me, Caleb was the only one who wasn't clutching a madly flashing glass ball. Of course, he and Holly shared a suite of rooms, so they probably only had the one between them.

Caleb walked over to each of us in turn, touching the spheres we held and muttering under his breath. Magic snapped in the air, and one by one, the orbs fell silent, though they kept flashing, the eerie red light bathing the gray stone of the castle.

"Does this mean someone attacked the wards on the house?" I asked, once only the hollow after-echo of the sirens remained.

Caleb shook his head. "An attack on the wards would get an alarm and orange flashing. Red means someone made it through."

We all turned in the direction of the castle door, as if we could see through it and over the distance of the folded space to the house beyond.

"So someone is in our house." Holly said it matter-of-factly, but there was a thinness in her voice that spoke of shocked fear. "We should call the police."

Obviously. Unfortunately, I hadn't thought to grab my phone. I glanced around. Caleb was in baggy sweatpants that clearly had no pockets. Holly only wore an oversize shirt that probably belonged to Caleb. Rianna had on a cute pajama set and was gripping her flashing orb in one hand and had the fingers of her other hand buried deep in Desmond's fur. Clearly no phone. By contrast, Falin was all but fully dressed in his jeans, white undershirt, and shoulder rig complete with gun. He had no shoes, but I would have bet money he had a phone on him. Probably a few hidden weapons as well.

"Falin?" I asked, looking at him.

Sure enough, he pulled a phone out of his back pocket. "I'll call my agents, and then I'll go check it out."

Holly crossed her arms over her chest. "I said police, not the FIB."

Falin paused, his thumb still poised over the call button. "Caleb is the homeowner. He is fae. Whoever broke in is probably after Alex, who is fae. This is clearly an FIB matter."

"Just call everyone," I said, exasperated.

Falin frowned at me, but nodded. Then he turned away to make his calls—hopefully to both police and FIB, though I didn't relish the idea of either going through the old house.

I should have been exhausted—I couldn't have gotten more than two hours of sleep—but I had too much nervous energy to stand still, so I ended up pacing the length of the foyer. Holly watched me walk one full circuit, then joined me, fidgeting with the side seam of her oversize shirt as she fell in step.

"What's the likelihood whoever broke in will find this folded space?" Rianna asked. In contrast to my and Holly's need to move, Rianna stood completely still, both her and the doglike fae at her side doing a good impression of statues.

"I imagine that depends on where they entered from," Falin said, hanging up his phone. "I'm going to go check it out."

"Shouldn't you wait for the cops?" Holly asked, and Falin gave her a look I couldn't quite interpret.

"He *is* the cops," Caleb said, crossing his arms over

his chest. "And he might as well be of some use since he lives here."

I stopped pacing to shoot him a dirty look. Caleb made no secret of his distrust of Falin, but usually he wasn't outright nasty to him. Of course, someone had just broken into his house, so he got a little leeway for stress.

I turned to Falin. "I'll go with you," I said, crossing the room.

"No," Falin and Caleb said simultaneously, and Holly said, "Not happening." If Rianna added her thoughts as well, I missed it under everyone else.

I frowned at the group collectively, though in truth, I didn't really want to go surprise someone who'd probably broken in to do me harm. But I also didn't want to wait for whoever it was to find the door to the folded space. If someone found their way in, they could hide in the area surrounding the castle for who knew how long. The castle had no wards on it like the house, or locks for that matter. I'd have to look into remedying both of those situations.

It was clear no one here was going to let me out of this castle, but I doubted I could keep Falin from going, so I simply said, "Be careful."

"I'll call when it's clear," he said, and then he was gone, hurrying out the door.

"I wonder what the burglar thought when they found the house empty?" Holly said, the titter in her voice that verged on amusement a clear sign of nerves.

I had serious doubts about burglary being the goal of the person who broke in, but I didn't say that. Instead I said, "I'm going to go get dressed. Caleb, will the orbs change when the person who broke in leaves?"

"It depends on how badly they damaged the wards on the way in."

So in other words, maybe. I nodded and headed back to my room. I dressed for the day, because despite the fact that it was only a little after four in the morning, I likely wasn't going to get any more sleep tonight. I left the orb behind. No reason to carry around a flashing crystal if it likely couldn't give me any more useful information.

When I returned to the foyer, it was empty. I slipped out of the front door unseen, but I didn't head to the house yet. The path was lit only with moonflowers, and I didn't want to go wandering in the mostly dark when I didn't know who else might be out there. Instead, I stepped back, turning to search the front face of the castle.

On a ledge not too much higher than the door perched a menacing-looking stone statue. The gargoyle was nearly three feet with a wingspan twice that, and looked like she'd been carved about to swoop down on anyone who dared trespass into the doorway. I'd never seen Fred move, but her current stance was way more aggressive than her typical pose. Either she was reacting to the tension inside, something more had happened, or something was going to—the gargoyle was a precog who sometimes seemed to have trouble telling the difference between present and future.

Other gargoyles dotted outcroppings all over the castle. Some appeared to be sleeping, but most were in aggressive poses, like Fred. When we'd all lived in Caleb's house, Fred was the only gargoyle I ever saw. She liked the taste of Caleb's magic, and the fact that I left cream out on the porch for her. I hadn't known at the time she was a *she* or that she was some sort of high priestess among her flock, so when she'd refused to tell me her name, I'd started calling her Fred. It amused her, so eventually the name stuck. When the castle had unfolded in the backyard, she'd moved her entire flock of gargoyles here. Maybe that was what she'd been waiting on the whole time.

"Hello, Fred," I said, waving up at her.

"There is an ill wind this morrow." The gargoyle's words weren't something I heard so much as felt in my mind. They were as hard and gravelly as her exterior, but not unkind.

"Someone broke into the old house. Can any of your gargoyles see the door to the house? Has anyone come through it?"

The gargoyle didn't move, but after a moment, I heard her again in my mind. *"Only the knight has passed that way, but we will remain vigilant."*

I nodded. The knight would be Falin, so we shouldn't have any unexpected visitors. Yet.

"Any warnings or advice you'd like to share?" I asked the gargoyle. Occasionally she shared hints that her precog abilities showed her. She gave them to me as puzzles, typically, but right now I'd take almost anything.

The gargoyle remained silent. I waited a moment. Finally her words rumbled through my mind. *"Look to yourself. What you seek is never far."*

Okay, I was wrong. I wouldn't take almost anything, because that sounded like it belonged in a fortune cookie or on a motivational poster. I'd try to keep it in mind, but I had to wonder if it was actually a warning for my future or just general advice. I nodded to acknowledge

I'd heard her, and then I glanced down at my phone. Falin had been gone at least ten minutes now. Had the police arrived yet? Had he encountered the person who broke in? Why hadn't he called?

I glanced out the open portcullis in the wall of the castle to where the door out of the folded space waited. I couldn't see anything in the darkness but the dim glow of flowers along the path. Though even if it had been day, I wouldn't have been able to spot the door.

While the door that led to the folded space was part of Caleb's house, which was in turn part of a larger neighborhood in the suburbs surrounding the Magic Quarter, on this side of the door, in the folded space, the door was just a frame and a door sprouting up from the ground in the center of an enormous field. Spotting it from a distance wasn't easy.

I glanced at the phone display again, counting the seconds. It had been too long. Shoving the phone in my pocket, I started down the path. I wouldn't walk through that door until Falin called me—well, as long as he called me soon—but I could be ready and waiting when he did.

I didn't consider the fact that as the door was in the center of a field that was more or less flat and empty as far as the eye could see, there was absolutely nowhere to hide. Good for spotting intruders, bad if you were trying not to be seen by them. By the time the phone finally rang, I was sitting behind the door as it was the only cover in the field.

"The house is clear," Falin said, and a breath I hadn't realized I'd been holding tumbled out of me. I sheathed my dagger as he continued, "Both the police and my agents are already here. You and the others can come back inside."

"Understood," I said, walking around to the other side of the door. I sent a text to the others, letting them know what he'd said, and then I walked into a crime scene that used to be my home.

Chapter 18

✦❖✦

It could have been worse.

I kept telling myself that, but it didn't help ease the violated feeling as I walked through my tiny one-room loft. The rest of the house had been left untouched, but the intruder had broken the wards and then kicked down my door. The sheets and pillowcases had been stripped off my bed and were missing. The police were speculating that the thief used them to store and carry everything else they stole, but despite the fact that all of my dresser drawers were lying empty on the floor, and all the cabinets and drawers in the bathroom were open and empty, nothing else was missing. Mostly because there had been nothing in those places to take.

The TV hadn't been touched, though it would have been a desperate thief who ventured to steal the old thing. The kitchen cabinets also appeared untouched, though Falin said the refrigerator had been open when he first walked in. Considering it had also been empty, nothing could have been stolen from the fridge. So as far as I could tell, the only thing missing was bedding.

And that worried me. As did the places the intruder had searched, because dresser drawers and the bathroom were where you'd normally find personal items. The kind of items one would use as a focus for a spell.

The sheets had been laundered and hadn't been slept on in a month, so they wouldn't make a particularly effective focus. All my clothes and toiletries had been moved to the castle, so there was nothing else personal in the loft. Ms. B and her brownie magic did the cleaning, so I knew that even if the intruder had time to check the drains in the shower, he wouldn't have found a single hair. All and all, aside from the broken doorframe, there was very little damage. It could have been worse.

The police didn't stay long. They dusted the door around the lock and a couple of the knobs on drawers the intruder might have touched, and then they left me with instructions to inventory everything stolen and turn the list in to the precinct later. That obviously wasn't happening.

The FIB left even before the police did. Falin had startled one of the intruders on her way out, but she'd jumped into the back of a waiting car and sped away. He'd gotten the tag number, as well as the make and model, so his agents were off searching for the vehicle. Holly and Rianna had remained in the castle, but Caleb was outside assessing the damage to the wards. So only an hour after I'd awoken to sirens, I was moving numbly through my old apartment, putting the spare set of sheets on the bed and trying to figure out the best way to clean fingerprint dust off wood.

Falin didn't press me to talk about it, or crowd me,

but picked up the scattered drawers, fitting them back into the dresser silently. I avoided looking at the door, which wouldn't stay shut so it hung open several inches, letting in a cold draft. But all too quickly the rest of the apartment was restored to the condition it had been in before the break-in, and all that was left was the broken door.

I stood in the middle of the room, staring at the splintered wood around the lock. One strip of the door-frame had broken off completely and lay dejected and mangled on the floor. I didn't live here anymore, not really, but I had for several years, and it hurt to think of someone I didn't know entering my space.

Falin stepped up beside me. "It's too early to call someone to fix it. In a few hours we should be able to find someone. With luck they'll be able to get to it today."

But what did we do with it in the meantime? We couldn't just leave the door hanging open. I might not sleep here, but I still spent time here occasionally.

"I guess we could seal it with tape in the meantime?" I finally said.

"Most people use wood, but yeah, duct tape would hold it." He gave me an odd look. It was torn between amusement and sympathy. Then his expression sobered. "I hate to mention it right now, but what kind of security do you have at your office?"

Crap. "Basic. The wards aren't even as good as here."

Would the people who broke in here really go to my office? They'd surely expected me to be asleep here, but when they hadn't found me, they'd searched for items they could use as a spell focus. There hadn't been

many. If they thought I was in hiding, my office would
be the next logical place to find personal items.

"Let's find some tape. I need to get to the office."

Dawn hadn't even arrived, and I was once again
watching police officers dust for prints. This time in the
Tongues for the Dead office. The window in the door
had been smashed and the door unlocked from the
inside. Glass littered the entryway, and shiny shards
spread like a trail deeper into the front lobby.

Ms. B's fastidiously tidy desk looked only slightly
disturbed. She would know better than I would if anything on it had been moved. Rianna's office didn't even
look like it had been opened, nor did the broom closet
Roy considered his office. Mine, though . . .

I'd only seen it from the doorway. The cops didn't
want me inside until they finished diffusing the nasty
ambush spell set to detonate just beyond my personal
office door. Falin had nearly set it off when we first
arrived and he wanted to ensure the building was clear.
I'd sensed it just in time, and had never been so glad I
was sensitive.

Now I sat on the small love seat in the lobby, staring,
but not really seeing the magic techs working on the
ambush trap, or the cops dusting the lock on the door.
With the escalation of an armed spell, the cops were
taking this much more seriously than the simple robbery
at the house. I'd texted Rianna. She and Ms. B would
head this way once sunrise passed. Now there was nothing to do except wait.

Falin had been talking to one of the officers working

on the spell, but now he walked over to stand beside the love seat where I was sitting. "You okay?"

I turned toward him, but my gaze was sluggish to follow. It felt like so many thoughts were buzzing in my brain that the commotion was too loud to follow any single one. I looked around the room, but my gaze kept getting caught on the little shards of glass ground into the carpet.

This wasn't just some missing bedding, and it couldn't be fixed by picking up a few empty drawers. A sharp tinge of magic snapped through the air, and someone yelped as the ambush spell reacted poorly to the tech's attempts to dispel it.

Someone had meant very deadly business.

Falin placed a hand on my shoulder, the touch tentative and light, as if he was prepared to draw back quickly. The contact grounded me, made the cacophony of warring thoughts tearing through my mind quiet a little, as I focused on the warmth of his fingers through my sweater. I reached up, placing my fingers over his, and his touch grew surer. We stayed like that, me sitting, him standing, both silent as the police worked.

I'd known as soon as I saw the news report that I'd be a target, I just hadn't expected it this soon. I'd expected more time to work on the case, to get ahead of the bad guy. Instead the day hadn't even properly begun yet, and it had already been a long and potentially dangerous one.

Briar walked through the front door as the techs unraveled the last of the spell in my office.

"Well, that escalated quickly," she said as she glanced around, her hands on her hips. Then she smiled.

She *smiled*.

My teeth clenched so tight my jaw popped. I wanted to jump up and throttle her. Or yell at the top of my lungs that this was not some game and nowhere in our contract had I signed up to be her disposable pawn.

"I should bring you up on charges," Falin said. His voice was that distant, scary tone, full of ice and danger, controlled, but with menace lurking below the surface, like an iceberg that could sink any unwary soul who ventured into it.

Briar cocked an eyebrow and rolled her shoulders back. "For what, exactly? There was nothing false in the information I provided the reporter. Alex is technically still a person of interest in this case. It was the videos that really condemned her, and that was all her, not me."

"But you leaked the videos," I said, my voice thin and a little shrill, but not screaming. I was proud it didn't come out a scream. No conversation goes productively after one party starts screaming. I'd get further sounding reasonable, even if right now I hoped to never hear Briar's name again. "And you gave them my name. Less than twelve hours later, both my home and work have been burgled, and a spell was set in my office that would have killed someone if I weren't a sensitive."

Briar glanced back at where the techs were cleaning up. "Yeah, but that means we got the necromancer's attention. That should prove useful. We just need a little better hook attached to our bait."

"Use yourself as bait. Oh, wait, you don't even walk down the street without a spell that makes you less noticeable. Fuck you, Briar."

And there went reasonable. Oh well, I didn't care. I was done. Briar could take her contract and shove it.

"I quit," I said, pushing out of the chair and storming past Briar.

"You're emotional right now, so I'm going to let you think about that one a little while longer," she called after me as I headed to my office.

The magic techs were done; I was clear to enter without dying as soon as I stepped through the door, but the crime scene techs still had work to do. They were going to let me do a visual survey, though, so they knew what to focus on.

The desk was the obvious target. The drawers hung open, papers and office supplies that had previously been stored there now tossed to the floor. The locked filing cabinet in the corner had been left alone, but the mini-fridge beside it hung open. Whoever had tossed this room hadn't been looking for information on my cases, they'd been searching for personal items. Which seemed like overkill, as the spell in the doorway had been deadly. The necromancer was clearly thorough.

"It looks like my coffee mug is missing. Maybe some pens?" I scanned over the loose papers scattered across the floor and desk, but the officer wouldn't let me move anything. "And . . . a picture of my dog." That realization made my already queasy, knotted stomach ache, like I'd been punched.

The cop looked up from his notepad. "So nothing of value? Computer? Electronics? Spell materials?"

I kept my focus on the desk so that I didn't glare at the cop. Didn't he realize the significance of what had been taken? Actually, I couldn't sense any magic on him, so he was likely a norm, maybe even a null. Without looking up, I shook my head.

"I don't keep any of that stuff here."

"Okay then, if you'll step out of the room, we'll let the crime scene guys in."

I nodded numbly and set my feet to follow the familiar walk out of my office that felt so very foreign today. I didn't stop in the lobby, where Falin and Briar were having what looked to be a very heated argument. I just kept walking until I was out the front door and on the sidewalk.

Dawn was beginning to paint colors across the horizon, and the glow from the windows behind me was too dim to light up more than small rectangles on the sidewalk. I walked to the edge of one of these islands of light and gazed out into the darkness beyond. There was no streetlight in our back alley road of the Magic Quarter, and to my eyes, the street might as well have been lost in a void for all I could see.

"I should take you to Faerie," Falin said, joining me on the sidewalk. "I don't suppose you'd agree to stay in the castle for a little while?"

I shook my head. "That won't help me find the necromancer. He spelled my office. What if I hadn't come in today and Ms. B had stepped in there first? Or Rianna? Or if I hadn't stopped you in time?" I wrapped my arms across my chest, hugging myself. Then I let my arms fall, my fists clenching. "The necromancer needs to be found quickly."

"I thought you quit?" Falin's voice was oddly dull, as if he was intentionally withholding emotion from the words.

"Yeah, that was dumb. Quitting the case isn't going to make him stop coming after me."

"Not bad, Craft. You came to that conclusion faster than I was expecting," Briar said from the doorway. "All quitting really does is remove the extra protection of me at your back, so I'm going to give you the chance to reconsider."

If looks could kill, my glare would have taken off several layers of her skin. She only grinned at me, waiting.

"You're a bitch, but yeah, I'm still on the job," I finally said, and I could all but feel Falin's disapproval.

"That's the spirit, Craft," Briar said. "Now ditch the suit." She nodded toward Falin. "We've got somewhere to go."

Chapter 19

The whole Alex-is-now-a-two-for-one-deal, the-FIB-agent-you've-been-arguing-with-will-be-joining-our-team talk went about as well as could be expected. In the end, Briar relented and she gave us an address where we should meet her next. After a tense start to a conversation in which Falin tried to encourage me to take a holiday in Faerie, and my subsequent poor reaction, we spent most of the drive in silence.

The address Briar gave us turned out to be for an all-night diner just outside the Magic Quarter. She already had a table when we arrived. There was no real surprise in the fact that the table was in a corner with a good view of the rest of the diner and the door, but what was surprising was that she wasn't alone at the table. A man sat in the chair beside her, his attention on a book in front of him. He looked up as we approached, closing the book with a soft snap.

"You must be Alex Craft," he said, offering a smile that looked genuine.

I nodded. "And would you be Briar's elusive partner?"

"One and the same," he said, his smile widening with amusement at the description. "Derrick Knight."

"Hopefully it will be nicer to meet you than it has been your partner," I said, holding out my hand, but Derrick drew his hands back, recoiling from my offered handshake.

"Derrick doesn't shake," Briar said, leaning back in her chair.

He lifted his hands in front of his chest, palms out in a supplicating manner. I noticed for the first time that Derrick wore gloves, not dissimilar from the gloves Falin wore to protect himself from iron. Was Derrick fae?

The thoughts must have been written all over my face because Derrick shook his head. "Touch clairvoyant," he said by way of explanation.

I blinked in surprise. Briar had said he was a premonition witch. If he was also touch clairvoyant, then he was doubly wyrd. That was almost unheard of. Wyrd abilities themselves were rare. But having two? And both with serious consequences. That had to be hell. I was even more impressed he was still sane. Or maybe he wasn't. After all, he was Briar's partner and I was starting to question my own sanity for working with her.

Derrick's attention moved over my shoulder, to the fae still standing a step behind me. Apparently Briar wasn't planning to do any introductions, so I turned, motioning to him.

"This is Falin Andrews."

Derrick nodded amicably, and Falin and I took our seats at the table. The waiter stopped by our table before any further conversation could occur. I hadn't had time to look over the menu, but it was breakfast time, so there were some obvious options every diner carried, like coffee and pancakes. Falin mimicked my order, Briar ordered a milkshake and onion rings, and Derrick ordered oatmeal with almond milk and fruit.

When the waiter returned with the two coffees and the milkshake, Derrick pulled a reusable water bottle out of his briefcase.

"I can get you a glass of water, sir," the waiter said, frowning at the bottle. When Derrick began to politely refuse, the waiter said, "I'm sorry, we don't allow outside beverages."

With a sigh, Derrick dug his wallet out of his pocket, flipped past his MCIB ID and badge to another card, and held it up for the waiter. I glanced over, trying to read the bold print from across the table. From what I could tell, it said something to the effect that the bearer of the card suffered a magical disability and might require special arrangements to avoid interacting with items that had come in skin contact with other people. The waiter's eyes widened.

"Sorry, sir. I didn't realize . . . I can ask if we have any sealed dishes."

"I'm fine," Derrick said, lifting his bottle.

The waiter nodded, still looking uncomfortable. Then he hurried off, muttering something about checking on the food. Once he was gone, Derrick took a moment to pull a set of silverware out of his briefcase, as well as a cloth napkin.

"Go ahead and ask," Derrick said without looking

up, and I realized that Falin and I were probably watching him a little too hard.

Heat crept to my cheeks. I of all people should know better than to stare at someone because they were wyrd. Touch clairvoyants were rare, but we'd had a few at my boarding school. I hadn't known any of them personally, but I'd seen them around school. They'd all tried as hard as possible to avoid touching other people or items recently touched by another person, as they didn't like getting flashes of others' lives unexpectedly.

I knew from my own wyrd abilities that the drawbacks often set a wyrd witch apart and it could be awkward. Sometimes I talked about it, sometimes I didn't want to. Of course, Derrick had offered.

"Aren't you worried about the food?" Falin asked.

Derrick shrugged. "There is a risk, but machines process most food, and food workers are required to wear gloves, so most food has minimal impressions." He turned to me. "Go ahead, you get one free question as well."

I frowned at him. "I doubt quizzing you about your wyrd ability is why Briar asked us here."

"Ten points for Craft," Briar said, saluting me with her milkshake. "We're here to strategize and try to pin down our next lead."

"And I wanted to give you something," Derrick said, opening his briefcase once again. He pulled out a silver charm on a thin black cord. He looked it over a moment, and then he held it out, letting it dangle over his gloved palm.

Falin scowled at the necklace in Derrick's hand. The silver charm looked like a cartoon fairy from before the Magical Awakening, complete with glass-jeweled butterfly wings. "Is that a joke?"

"No," I said, reaching out but stopping just short of touching the cord. "That's one of the most potent defense charms I've ever felt." I let my ability to sense magic wrap around the small charm. With Briar and her magical arsenal within arm's reach, it was hard to focus on the spells in the pendant, but I could sense a lot of protective magic packed into the tiny glass bobbles in the fairy's wings. "You're giving this to me? In exchange for what?"

"No catch."

The look on my face must have been more than a little suspicious because he laughed.

"You're too young to be that jaded. How about in exchange for putting up with Briar?"

Briar grunted but didn't put down her milkshake as she said, "I'm sitting right here, you know."

"You're going to need it," Derrick said, leaning forward to hold the charm closer to me.

When a premonition witch says you're going to need one of the most potent defensive charms you've ever felt, you don't second-guess the urgency. That doesn't mean you don't ask questions.

"Do we have a lead?" I asked as I accepted the charm, careful not to brush Derrick's gloved fingers as I took it.

He only shrugged.

Which didn't explain why I needed the charm. Briar had said he shared only what he had to about his premonitions. I guessed I should have been happy to have the warning and extra protection, but I was more than a little terrified that something was going to happen that I would need it.

"It will need to be personalized," he said, nodding to the charm.

I grimaced. Personalizing a charm wasn't hard, but the best way to do it was a type of blood magic. Many of the strongest protection spells used blood as a focus. As did the very strongest offensive spells. I flipped the little fairy over and saw the small well between her wings where the blood was meant to go.

If I needed a protection spell this strong, it was probably because of the items the necromancer had stolen to use as a focus. But he didn't have blood. It made sense to give the protection charm the best focus I could provide. Unfortunately, the only dagger I had on me liked to draw blood a little too much and I didn't want to give it access to mine.

I turned to Falin. "Do you have a knife that isn't enchanted?"

He hadn't stopped scowling since this bizarre conversation had begun, but he didn't argue, he just handed me one of his silver daggers. Pricking the side of my finger, I squeezed the smallest drop of blood onto the charm.

It was enough. I immediately felt its magic lock with mine. The protection spell that had been waiting idle, coiled inside the glass bobbles, expanded, crawling over my fingers where I touched the charm and then sliding up my arm, over my elbow, across my shoulder, and down my torso. It was an odd sensation, but not a bad one. Kind of like taking a dip in warm bathwater. Within moments, the spell had coated me in a thin layer of magical protection. It wouldn't completely deflect an offensive spell, and if I'd stepped into the ambush spell at my office wearing it, the charm couldn't have shielded me from all harm, but it felt strong enough that I probably would have walked away. I would have needed medical attention, but it wouldn't have killed me.

"This is amazingly done," I said, my voice sounding as awed as I felt as I clipped the charm onto my bracelet.

"I'm not so sure I like my partner giving other girls jewelry," Briar said, and while the words were light, playful, there was something in her dark eyes as she said them that made me think she meant the words more than she wanted to admit.

"Don't worry, I got you something too." Derrick held out his hand, where a tiny silver crossbow with a ruby-colored bolt dangled from another cord.

"Ooooh, what does it do?" Briar asked, accepting the charm.

"With any luck, it should keep the smell of decomposition out of your leathers," Derrick said as the food arrived, and the waiter almost dropped my plate of pancakes.

"Am I the only one getting increasingly worried about the things the precog is *not* telling us?" I asked. Because this case was sounding worse and worse.

"No," Falin said, and while there had been a hint of despairing amusement in my question, Falin's voice was anything but amused.

The waiter finished setting plates in front of us but didn't ask if we needed anything; he just hightailed it away from our table. He could have stuck around. The conversation petered out as we all tucked into our respective breakfast choices. I would have thought I'd be too preoccupied to eat by the fact that Briar would be covered in decomposition at some point soon and I needed a protection spell—which indicated a spell was going to hit it and I didn't know how much would make it through or what condition I'd be in afterward. Then the first bite of perfectly cooked fluffy pancakes hit my stomach and my body realized I'd skipped too many meals yesterday and hadn't had enough sleep. I barely tasted the second or following bites as I devoured them, and I'm not sure a single thought entered my head.

When everyone was done and the bills had been paid, I said, "So where to next? Do we have a lead or don't we?"

Derrick glanced at his watch. "We may have to order dessert first."

"Dessert isn't usually part of breakfast," I said, but as I spoke Falin's phone buzzed.

He took a glance at the display and excused himself to take the call outside.

Derrick lifted his gloved hands in a mock shrug. "Alas, it appears we will have to do dessert some other time."

I frowned at him. I wanted to tell him this wasn't a joke or a game, this was my livelihood going up in flames around me, but I held my tongue. Maybe he wasn't quite as sane as Briar touted.

Or, maybe he'd been stalling.

Briar pulled her phone from her pocket. I hadn't heard it ring or buzz, but she answered it saying, "This is Darque."

Falin rejoined us at the table as I pulled on my sweater.

"They found the getaway car the intruder at your

house used this morning," he said, scooping up my purse and handing it to me.

Briar looked up from her phone call. "A red hybrid sedan?" she asked, and then listed off a license plate number.

Falin nodded, looking skeptical.

"Small world," she said, shoving her phone back into her pocket. "That was Remy Hollens's car. The police are holding the scene for us. I guess we have our lead."

Derrick didn't accompany us to the scene but said he had some things to look into. As we had before, Falin and I drove separate from Briar, but this time we arrived together. I'm not sure what I was expecting, probably an abandoned car left somewhere obscure. What I was not expecting was to arrive at the scene of a multiple-car wreck.

The accident had traffic backed up for miles. Despite Briar and Falin both being told the best roads to take to reach the accident, we still hit terrible congestion as soon as we left the Magic Quarter and crossed over the Sionan River toward town. Even with official strobes for the vehicles, it took an agonizingly long time to reach the scene. The sun was well above the horizon by the time we arrived, offering me plenty of light to take in every terrible detail.

Three vehicles were involved in the accident: Remy's red sedan, an old pickup truck, and a small hatchback. From what I could gather, Remy's car had been driving erratically—based on the timeline, after fleeing my house. It merged into the pickup, which caused the car to spin out, hitting the hatchback. The red car then ricocheted into the concrete barricade nose first. The driver of the hatchback had been seriously injured and rushed to the hospital. The pickup driver had less severe injuries, though he still required transport to the hospital, but he'd been able to answer some questions before he'd been packed off in the back of an ambulance.

According to the officer who'd taken the man's statement, the man said that two women had been in the red car. After the vehicle had finally come to its violent stop, the passenger, who'd been ejected from the car at some point, had hobbled over to the car and tried to drag the driver out. That hadn't worked, as the driver's legs had been pinned. The passenger had then limped away, but the man swore she shouldn't have been able to. He said her body was twisted from the impact, and at least one bone in her arm had been jutting through the skin, one leg dragging behind her as she made her way off the highway. The other girl had yelled after her, begging her not to leave her until suddenly, she'd collapsed face forward into the steering wheel and not moved again.

The officer looked up from his notes. "The man had lost a decent amount of blood, and based on what he said, I'm assuming he had a head injury."

I glanced at Briar. After seeing the decaying creatures in the clearing still up and moving around, I wasn't so quick to discount the pickup driver's story.

Whatever Briar's thoughts were, she kept them to herself as she thanked the officer for his report. Then I followed her and Falin toward the scrap metal that had once been a car. I didn't want to go near it—I could feel the grave essence rolling out of the vehicle from a dozen yards away. As we approached, the reek of decay wafted out of the smashed vehicle. This was going to be bad.

Tow trucks were already loading up the hatchback and pickup, trying to clear more lanes of the interstate, but barricades had been erected around the smashed red car. It didn't appear that rescue workers had made any attempt to remove the woman's body from the driver's seat. Of course, one look at her would have been enough to see that she was beyond help. Putrefaction had set in strong, making her flesh dark and bloated. Foul liquid leaked from her slack mouth, and fluid-filled blisters had lifted on her exposed skin. As I stood there, a clump of hair fell from her head, taking flesh with it and making a wet sound as it hit the leather seat.

I turned away, breakfast rolling in my stomach, threatening to rebel. I wasn't going to lose my breakfast a second day in a row. I refused.

Neither Briar nor Falin had the same reaction. They stepped closer, examining the body. But I couldn't. I just couldn't. Not being able to see her anymore wasn't even enough, because I could still smell her, and I could feel the call of the grave reaching from her. It whispered the kind of secrets the grave always told me, like that she'd been young, maybe late teens or early twenties, and that she'd been dead for almost two weeks. That last part should have been a direct conflict with the fact that she'd clearly been driving the car only hours earlier, but walking corpses were no longer a shock in this case.

I knew better than to take a deep breath to try to calm my stomach—I'd made that mistake one too many times at crime scenes, I'd learned my lesson. It would *not* help with this much decomposition in the air. Instead I closed my eyes, gave myself a moment, and then walked past the barricade without turning back.

I started heading toward the car but then turned, heading in the direction where the pickup driver had said the passenger had limped away from the scene. Two lanes of traffic had opened again, but the drivers were all slowing down to rubberneck at what was left of the accident, so I had little trouble making it across the interstate. Two officers were on the shoulder of the interstate, taking pictures of what I assumed was the trail the woman had taken.

"Any luck finding the passenger?" I asked, approaching the closer of the two.

He looked up and gave me a quick once-over from feet to head before saying, "Miss, this is a crime scene. I'm going to have to ask you to move on."

"We've been invited to this scene," Falin said, stepping up behind me. I hadn't even heard him cross the street. He flashed his badge at the officer and said, "So what is the update on locating the passenger?"

The man let his camera drop to swing around his neck and straightened slightly at the sight of Falin's badge. "We've got an alert out to local hospitals, and we're sweeping the shoulder and the woods beyond, but the dogs can't get here for a few hours."

Falin nodded, an obvious dismissal, and the man took it, turning away and hurrying to go photograph evidence at a marker much farther away. When he was out of earshot, Falin turned to me.

"What are you doing? Why'd you head here?"

"I couldn't be any help back there." I jerked my head in the direction of the wreck without actually turning

to face it. "But I can help look for the passenger." I
didn't add that I would have gotten ill if I'd stayed by
the corpse any longer.

Falin scanned the tree line beyond the shoulder.
There was no obvious path where the passenger had
gone, and emergency vehicles had clearly pulled off
onto the shoulder before anyone realized there was a
missing injured party, so the ground was torn up with
tire tracks and footprints.

"How?" he asked after a moment.

"The driver was obviously another walking corpse.
Most likely the passenger was as well. I'm really good
at finding corpses." I tapped the spot beside my eye as
I cracked open my shields.

He watched me, his expression unchanged even
though I knew my eyes lit up as if they were backlit by
lanterns. Then I turned toward the woods, letting my
senses stretch. The corpse behind us called to me, but
I blocked it out as well as I could, looking for other
whispers of the grave.

There had been no ghost hanging around the car.
While it was possible the spells holding the ghost inside
the stolen body had broken after the crash, the witness
report sounded more like a soul collector had been on
the scene and collected the errant ghost. If that was true,
then it was possible the soul collector had gone after the
passenger as well. If not, well, she was probably still a
walking corpse and might be giving out enough grave
essence that I could feel her from a distance.

I closed my eyes, concentrating on the cold whispers
that grabbed at me. Most were lifting from small animals, the trails of essence thin and easy to ignore. One
to my left was stronger, pulling at my mind and my

magic. I turned, walking in that direction. Falin followed without a word.

I walked down the shoulder for several minutes, then turned into the woods. The feel of the grave was almost overwhelming now as it clawed at my shields. It was a woman, not much older than the driver from the wreck, but this one didn't feel like she'd been dead as long. We'd only passed the first few trees when I stopped abruptly, because we were almost on top of her. I looked around, letting my magic guide my gaze. Then I slammed my shields shut against the chill reaching for me.

"There," I said, pointing. I couldn't actually see a body yet, but it was there.

Falin walked forward slowly, careful not to trample through the heavy underbrush. I didn't follow. I'd already seen one body today. I knew it was there, I didn't need to see it. He stepped around a bush and stared at the ground.

"I'd wager this is her," he said, nodding to me.

"I'll go let those officers know," I said, turning back the way we'd come. We weren't even that far. I could still see the different-colored flashing lights from the emergency vehicles.

The officer I'd spoken to earlier was the first I ran across. He looked more than a little shocked when I told him I'd found the passenger's body. He radioed to someone over at the wreck site, and soon we had a small party headed to the second body. I left them as soon as they were close enough to spot Falin.

No one stopped me as I made my way back to where Falin's car was parked. I'd only noticed a hint of decomposition in the air when we first arrived, but now that I'd been close to the bodies, I couldn't seem to escape the smell. It was like the scent had crawled into my nose and taken up residence.

Tamara had arrived while I'd been in the woods. I could see her with Briar directing the team that was trying to extract the body without destroying it. They were having to cut the car apart to get to the driver's body, and the machines were deafening, even from a distance and with the top of Falin's convertible tightly sealed, but that was okay. I didn't really want to hear myself think right now. Nothing good was floating around my head.

I leaned the seat back and closed my eyes. Despite the hydraulic rescue tools loudly dismantling the red sedan, the press of gawking traffic, and the smell of decay, I fell asleep.

I was chased through my dreams by corpses. They herded me toward magical traps I sensed almost too late, and reached for me with hands full of rotting flesh that sloughed off when they managed to touch me.

At the sound of someone banging on the car window, I jolted awake to find Briar staring at me through the glass.

"You look a little green, Craft," she said when I opened the door.

"I don't do dead bodies."

She frowned at me. "You're a grave witch."

"Yeah, not by choice. I just try to make the best of it." I stepped out the car, rolling my shoulders to stretch my neck as I moved. "I'm good with shades and the magical part. Just not the blood and decay bits."

Briar shrugged with a sort of "whatever" expression,

and I gave a cautious look around. Tamara was supervising a body in its black bag being uploaded for transport back to the morgue. As I couldn't be sure how long I'd been asleep, I wasn't sure if it was the driver's or the passenger's body, but things were definitely wrapping up quickly at the scene. Falin was speaking to a small cluster of cops near where what was left of Remy's car was being loaded on a flatbed tow truck. Even the morning commute traffic had finally cleared, so only the occasional car passed on the open lanes of the interstate.

"The ME says she can't give us much information because of the advanced state of decay of the body," Briar said, nodding toward Tamara. "But she did say only the driver's lower legs were pinned, her rib cage and skull appear undamaged, and there isn't enough blood at the scene to indicate she bled out. She'll be able to tell us more post-autopsy, but right now, despite some obvious superficial damage from the crash, there is no obvious cause of death. Combined with the pickup driver's statement about the driver yelling for her friend and then suddenly just dropping dead, this looks a whole lot like the other bodies that collapsed, dead, and then rapidly decayed, but this time you have a rock-solid alibi."

"Lucky me."

Briar frowned at me. "Who else can pull souls out of bodies?"

I returned her frown. "Soul collectors?" I didn't add the *duh* at the end. I should have gotten points for that. With such a bad multivehicle accident, a collector must have been called to the scene by the possibility that one of the living accident victims might have died. The two walking corpses had probably been collected as soon as the collector noticed they were already dead.

Falin walked up. "I obviously missed something," he said, glancing from me to Briar. "Anyway, the scene is wrapping up. They need to get this clear. We should head out."

I couldn't have agreed more.

"Morgue's our next stop," Briar said, turning toward her hulking SUV.

Goody. More dead bodies.

Chapter 20

I once again stood in the center of a magical circle while flanked by corpses. There were no uniformed officers this time, so either I was no longer being treated as a suspect, or they couldn't find anyone else who could stomach being down in the morgue right now.

The morgue had decent air purifiers, but they were no match for the two putrid bodies from the wreck. Jenson looked positively green and had already excused himself once, returning paler and covered with sweat. Even John looked a little queasy, and he typically had the constitution of a stone. Falin hid his disgust better, only the smallest tightening of skin around his eyes and nose revealing that the smell had any effect on him. Briar was cool as a corpse, but she had so much magic on her, she likely had a charm that mitigated the scent. That was the only reason I was able to stand in the circle. When I'd first walked into the morgue, Tamara had slipped me a charm that knocked out my sense of smell. Usually I was kind of touchy about losing another sense, but in this case I was grateful. Tamara, having the same charm, was also unaffected by the smell, but she did preemptively pull a chair up to the outskirts of the circle this time so she could sit.

"Let's keep this short and to the point so we don't exhaust our grave witch," Briar said as I prepared. "I might need her after."

"I second the short bit," Jenson said, looking like he was about to lose anything still left inside his stomach onto his shoes.

"I'm going to begin." I nodded to John to turn on the camera and moved to unclasp my charm bracelet, but then hesitated. The bracelet contained the new protection spell Briar's partner had given me. Taking off the protection from a premonition witch seemed like a bad plan. Instead I tapped into the charms with the shields and drained the magic back into my ring, deactivating them. It was a lot slower than just taking the bracelet off, and it would suck when I had to reactivate them after the ritual, but at least I didn't lose the protection charm. As a side bonus, I also didn't lose Tamara's charm and suddenly get assaulted with the smell of decomposition.

Closing my eyes, I poured magic into the body to my right. I wasn't sure if she'd been the driver or the passenger, but I could tell she'd been dead slightly longer than the woman to my left. She was a few years older than the other woman as well. Neither body had been autopsied yet, or even removed from their black transport bags. It had been decided that a quick interview would be prudent. Then Tamara would begin her work.

The shade of a woman in her early twenties sat free

from the bag. Her dark hair had been pulled up high
in a ponytail on the top of her head, and she wore a
sports bra with tight spandex running shorts.

"What is your name?"

"Elisa Lambie."

Outside my circle, Briar and John pulled out notebooks and jotted down the name, but Tamara jumped
out of her chair at the name. I glanced back at her,
hoping the question in my expression was clear even
though my face would be lit by the eerie green glow of
my eyes. Tamara just shook her head, motioning me to
continue.

"How did you die, Elisa?"

"I was running with my training partner, Linda. It
was our normal path, but I'd had a headache all morning and I was considering turning back early. Then pain
exploded in my head. My vision got weird. I fell to the
ground. Linda started screaming. Someone loaded me
onto a gurney and into the back of an ambulance. They
kept shining lights into my eyes and asking my name,
if I could squeeze their hands. Then a man stuck his
hand into my chest and I . . ."

Died.

No one said anything for several heartbeats after
the shade fell silent. Finally Briar cleared her throat.

"Is it just me, or does it sound like she died in the
back of an ambulance?"

I nodded. "Or possibly at a hospital. Shades can be
a little fuzzy on time when they were barely conscious
surrounding their death, but it sounds like her soul was
collected normally."

"So how the hell did she end up in that car this
morning?"

I had no idea.

"Her body was stolen," Tamara said, her voice so soft, I wasn't sure I'd heard her at first. "I knew I recognized that name."

She marched off toward her office. I watched her go and then turned to John. He looked as confused as I felt. Tamara didn't immediately come running back out, so I turned back to the shade.

"Have you recently taken part in any studies involving ghosts or the dead?" I asked, because no one else had supplied any questions yet.

"No."

John flipped back a few pages in his notebook and asked, "In the last few weeks have you met anyone with the last name Hadisty, Vogel, Basselet, or Moyer, or anyone who claimed to hold a PhD in any witchcraft fields?"

I repeated the questions.

"No."

Well, we were striking out everywhere.

"What was the date of your last memory?" Falin asked, which I really should have thought to ask earlier.

"November fifth."

Over two weeks ago.

Tamara rushed back out of her office, a folder in her hands. "I was right. Elisa Lambie, suspected aneurysm," she said, reading from a sheet of paper in the file.

"You autopsied her?" Briar asked.

Tamara shook her head. "She arrived at the hospital unresponsive. She was admitted but died later that evening and was moved to the hospital morgue. Because she was young and described as healthy, she was slotted for autopsy, but when the body movers went to pick her up, the body couldn't be found. The hospital initially claimed it must have been a clerical error or a toe tag mixup, but after inventorying the cadavers, it turned out two bodies were unaccounted for: Elisa Lambie and Morgan McKenzie."

We all turned toward the body on the other gurney.

"Anyone have any more questions for Elisa?" I asked, and received a chorus of "No."

I released the shade. She couldn't help us. She'd never interacted with our necromancer, at least not while she was alive with her own soul in her body.

I turned to the second woman and let my magic fill her. The shade of a woman around my own age sat up from under the sheet. A shock of recognition jolted through me. I must have made some sound because Falin stepped up to the very edge of my circle, but thankfully he didn't actually touch it.

"What is it, Alex?"

"I know her, well, at the very least I've seen her." I stared at the shade. The nature of being a shade had washed out some of her skin tone, and she'd had her hair natural when she'd died while her mental image of herself as portrayed by her ghost had worn dozens of braids, but she was the same girl. I was positive. "Her ghost was piloting Remy's body."

"You're sure?" Briar asked.

I nodded. I'd only seen her for a moment, but she'd left an impression.

"What is your name?" I asked the shade.

"Angela Moore."

"And how did you die, Angela?"

"I had been at the library, studying late for an exam.

I live off campus, but only a few blocks away so I often walk home. Not many cars were on the road that night, so I noticed the one that slowed down as it passed me, but I didn't think much of it until it pulled over. I started walking faster. I thought I was being paranoid until I heard the footsteps right behind me. I started to run, but someone grabbed my backpack, pulling me backward. I tried to slip out of it, but something cold pressed against my neck, and then heat and pain charged through me. I blacked out. When I woke, I was gagged and blindfolded, but I could hear a man chanting. When he stopped, I felt him move close to me. He pressed a knife into my chest. It pierced my skin and kept sinking. It hurt so bad. He pulled the gag out of my mouth and pressed something to my lips and then . . ."

I glanced at Falin when she finished speaking. This was very different from the other shades we'd spoken to. There was a kidnapping instead of a ruse to make the victim come willingly. And he'd stabbed her. He hadn't physically harmed the others. Their autopsies had proven that fact.

"What day did this occur, Angela?" I asked.

"November ninth."

Ten days before Remy had died and Angela's ghost had wound up wearing his body. What had she said when she'd been trying to pull Remy's body back on after I'd forced her out? *He said if I did this, he'd put me back.* Had the necromancer promised her that he would return her own body if she robbed the bank?

Briar and John asked the shade several more questions, but she couldn't offer much information. She'd never seen her abductor, and it had been dark and she hadn't been paying much attention to the car when it passed, so all she could recall was that the headlights were very bright, like halogen bulbs.

When everyone ran out of questions, I released her, drawing my heat back. After the last few days, the magic in me that usually existed in a barely contained threat of overfilling was starting to run low. It was both impressive and terrifying. I reactivated my external shields, pushing magic back into the charms containing them until they buzzed around my psyche once more. With my external shields up, I closed the last slivers of my mental shields and darkness blanketed the world. The blindness was absolute, but this ritual had lasted a very short time despite there being two shades, so I hoped my vision would return quickly.

With my shields up, all that was left was to drop my circle. My hands were trembling, so I didn't lift one as I spindled the energy back out of the circle. As soon as the circle dropped, the warmth of another body crowded into my space. I backpedaled without thinking and bumped the gurney behind me. Only strong hands closing on my arms, steadying me, kept me from falling back against the body bag.

I recognized the touch immediately—Falin. It wasn't that his hands were that familiar, but he was the only person in the room whose body temperature was similar enough to my own that his touch wasn't physically painful.

"Steady," he said, his voice equal parts concern and amusement. "Should you sit down?"

I nodded. "Tamara's office." I lifted my hand to point in the general direction where I thought the door was located.

Falin put a hand at the base of my back and guided me toward the office. Once inside, he deposited me in a chair. It was all feeling very déjà vu.

"You're freezing," he said, and something fell around my shoulders.

His suit jacket. It wouldn't help much—the cold was coming from inside me, not outside—but it was still a sweet gesture.

"I was worse when I was here last," I said with a shrug, but I pulled the jacket tighter around me, huddling in the silk lining. While it might not offer much warmth, it did offer some comfort. "I can feel you hovering. I'm fine."

I was blind. And cold. But it was true that I was better off than I'd been the last time I sat in Tamara's office.

"What can I do to help?"

He knew my go-to answer: whiskey and a warm body against mine doing some squishy, sweaty activities. But that last part was out. And the former wasn't likely in Tamara's office. I shook my head. Only time was going to help.

"Coffee again?" a female voice asked from the darkness several yards to my right. Tamara must have entered during one of my particularly racking shivers because I sure hadn't heard her and she didn't exactly move stealthily these days. "This'll be the second time this week. I'm going to have to start charging you."

"I thought you said it was good the beans weren't going stale."

She made some noncommittal sounds as she went about fixing the coffee.

"Tamara, if you're going to be in here awhile, I need

to make a few calls," Falin said. Tamara must have waved him off because his voice grew farther away as he said, "I'll be back in a few, Alex."

"I don't need a babysitter," I muttered, but I heard the door shutting before I even finished.

"I can't say I get the relationship between you two," Tamara said, after the last echo of the door shutting faded away.

"What relationship? We're just friends."

Tamara made an *uh-huh* sound, and I frowned in the general direction her voice was coming from.

"I think that glare hit my file cabinet."

"I wasn't glaring."

"You so were. Oh look, you're doing it again."

"Ha ha," I said, but made an effort to relax the muscles in my face, forcing them to be more neutral.

I'd been hoping I'd at least be able to start making out shadows among the darkness at this point, but the blackness filling my eyes hadn't abated one bit. So, I sat in silence and listened to the sound of the coffee being made.

Tamara brought over a mug and handed it to me. I accepted it, lifting it to inhale deeply, but not a single scent of coffee ticked my nose. *The charm.* Damn, not being able to smell anything would likely ruin the delicious dark roast coffee, but considering I was still in the morgue, there was no way I was deactivating the charm.

The door swooshed open behind me.

"How are the eyes today, Craft?" Briar asked as she entered the room.

I shrugged. "Not great. I'm probably out for an hour or two. Not that we have any new leads unless you heard something back there that I didn't."

"You're not allowed to be out this time, Craft. For one thing, you're my bait and, like you said, we don't have any other leads. Bait is no good without the trap close by."

And of course, she was the trap.

"What do you mean, 'bait'?" Tamara asked, and she was getting that growly protective voice again.

I sighed. "I guess you haven't seen the news, huh?"

Her answer was drowned out by my phone singing. I dug it out of my purse, mostly to avoid having to re-hash the news report Briar had engineered.

"Why, Alex Craft, I didn't expect you to answer," Lusa Duncan said from the other end of the phone, and I groaned, already regretting answering.

"I'm a little busy right now," I told her, the operative word that made the sentence not a lie being *little*.

"I'm sure you are. Rumor has it you were just spot-ted heading into Central Precinct. Have you turned yourself over to the police?"

"Would I be answering the phone if I was in police custody?"

"A valid point." But she sounded skeptical.

I started to tell her I had to go when a thought oc-curred to me. "Lusa, you didn't report that I was in Central Precinct, did you?"

"I can neither confirm nor deny that you might have a sound bite airing in a few moments."

"Do not broadcast that," I said, hearing the smallest note of desperation in my voice and hating it.

"If you give me an exclusive I might be able to delay—"

I hung up on her.

"We have to go," I said, standing with my still half-full mug of coffee in one hand and my phone in the other. Which meant no hands on the purse that had been in my lap.

It fell to my feet, the contents making clinks and clunks as they spilled onto the floor. I swore, kneeling down, but without being able to see, my knee landed on my wallet and I had to straighten again. I couldn't see, my stuff was everywhere, and I couldn't even figure out where to put the cup of coffee I couldn't taste to enjoy.

I heard Tamara lower herself to the floor with a long exhale of breath, and I knelt again, not landing on anything, but still unsure what the hell to do with the items already in my hands.

I must have looked as frantic as I felt because Briar said, "Craft, calm down. What's going on?"

"Lusa is about to announce on the news that I'm here. That means the crazy necromancer you put on my scent, the one who already laid a *killing* trap for me, will know where I am. So I think it's time to leave."

"And go where, Craft? Sit behind your broken door and hope the nasty necromancer doesn't show up before you can see again? The wards on this building are better than at your house, plus, you know, the whole police force being here. Oh, and let's not discount that you're better off under my protection. Besides, you're the bait, remember? We *want* him to come after you."

I clenched my teeth, biting back the urge to tell her exactly where she could shove her protection, but she wasn't completely wrong. Granted, I was planning to go back to the castle, not the house, and with any luck, there was enough of Faerie at the castle that I'd get at least partial vision back immediately. Still, the wards had been breached once, and my front door was held together with duct tape. There wasn't a whole lot stopping someone from searching the house again, and maybe finding the door to the folded space this time.

"Al, why is your door broken? And what's this about a killing trap?" Tamara asked, concern lacing her voice.

Right. There was no avoiding the subject again.

"Briar decided to use me as bait to get the necromancer out in the open. He or some of his walking corpses broke into my house and my office." I left out the bit that personal items that could be used as a focus had been stolen.

From where she still knelt beside me, picking up the scattered items I couldn't see, Tamara reached over, her hands gripping my shoulders. "Are you okay? Of course you're okay, you're here. But you know what I mean. Geez, you're cold."

"Warmer than I was earlier," I said, lifting the mug to drain the last of the contents so I could put it down without spilling it.

She dropped her hands from my shoulders to take the mug, which was a relief. Tamara was one of my best friends, but I wasn't what people would call a hugger, especially when I was blind and feeling vulnerable.

I felt around for my purse and shoved my phone inside it. Then I tried to take a tactile inventory of the contents. As I felt around, I concluded that Tamara must have gathered nearly everything already. The wallet that was somewhere near my knee was missing, but I felt almost everything else. As I started to pull my hand free, my fingers brushed against something I couldn't identify. I tried to keep my purse fairly organized. With blindness as an occupational hazard that was bound to happen a few times a month, it was good to be able to grab exactly what I needed and know what anything was in an instant. This, though, was definitely not something I typically carried.

I pulled it free, letting my fingers feel what was obviously some type of microsuede fabric around Rianna's magical signature. *The tracking charm.* Holding it on my palm, I could feel the strong pull toward Remy's body a room away, but there was a second, faint tug leading off in another direction.

I was so surprised I almost dropped the charm.

"Uh, change of plans."

"Now what?" The annoyance in Briar's voice made me glad I couldn't see her expression.

As answer, I held out the small bag containing the tracking charm. She lifted it from my fingers, but she didn't speak immediately. Her boots were almost completely silent, only a soft shush of sound letting me know she was moving. The door opened, and I frowned.

"Did she just leave?"

"Yeah," Tamara said, but Briar was back a moment later.

"Okay, I give up. I followed it to Remy's body. There is no other trail."

"Are you sure? There was a second trail just two moments ago." I held out my hand for the charm. As soon as she plunked it onto my palm, the magic in the charm attuned to me and I felt the strong tug toward Remy's body and a faint one leading somewhere else. "It's there, faint but there."

The charm vanished from my hand so quickly that Briar must have snatched it.

"No. No, it's not. Do you feel a trail?"

"I—" I started, but Tamara touched my arm.

"She was talking to me." Her voice was soft, not reprimanding, just clueing me in to what must have been expressed through body language that I couldn't see. Louder, Tamara said, "I feel a well-constructed spell but only one trail."

I opened my mouth. Closed it.

"What about you?" Briar said.

Who? I could guess she didn't mean me, but I hadn't heard anyone else enter.

"One trail," Falin said, and I could almost hear the apology in his voice. He must have followed Briar back in after she'd followed the dominant trail to Remy's body, but that didn't explain why no one else could feel the second trail.

Falin placed the charm in my hand again. I still felt two trails. I didn't waste any more breath trying to convince anyone I could feel the second trail. Everyone in this room knew I was fae and couldn't lie; either they believed me or they didn't.

"Maybe I can feel the second trail because the charm was made by a grave witch and I am also a grave witch." Or maybe it was because I was a planeweaver, and even fully shielded, I was still a convergence point for realities. I would have loved to see if Rianna felt the trail when in touch with the land of the dead, but the trail had disappeared before, and there was no time to waste in tracking it.

"Get me to a vehicle, and I can tell you which way the charm is pulling."

Easy, right?

Chapter 21

It was *not* easy. It started difficult and steadily climbed toward nearly impossible. It had been hard enough following the charm when I'd been the driver and trying to look ahead for which roads would head in the direction the charm pulled. Now I had no idea where we were or what surrounded us; all I could say were less than helpful things like "We need to go more to my right. No, we turned too much. A little more in that direction" and point.

Falin, who was driving, was extremely patient with me, at least as far as I could hear. I couldn't see his expression or body language. By contrast, Briar, who was scrunched into the almost nonexistent back of Falin's sporty convertible, had a lot to say on everything from my less-than-precise directions and Falin's attempts to follow them to the seating arrangement. None of it was flattering and most of it involved profanity.

"We're close," I said after we'd been driving a little over half an hour. "Where are we?"

"University district," Falin said as he slowed the car.

That had not been what I was expecting. The trail we'd been following had been growing distinctly stronger for a while now. We were getting very close. I'd assumed we'd be headed to the wilds again, but the university district wasn't that far from downtown Nekros.

We drove a few more minutes. Navigating was even harder here than it had been in other areas of the city. There were just too many large green spaces or buildings connected by courtyards where vehicles couldn't travel.

"We should park and go on foot. We're close."

"How close?" Briar asked, still sounding petulant after being relegated to the backseat.

I tried to figure out any specifics from what I could feel in the pull of the charm, but "close" was about as accurate as I could get. "Walking distance," I said with a shrug.

"Are you going to be able to navigate on foot?" Falin asked as he pulled into a faculty and staff parking lot.

I shrugged again. My vision had finally started returning during the drive, but it left a lot to be desired. I had no peripheral vision and limited distance. I wasn't going to walk into a brick wall, but I might trip over a curb because I couldn't see the subtle hints of an elevation change. I also couldn't see color yet, so the world was all very flat gray tones.

I tied the nylon cord attached to the charm around my wrist and climbed out of the car. The lot Falin had parked in stood in the shadow of buildings in every direction. Some were dorms, others clearly contained classrooms or administrative buildings, but all were part of the university. Small brick-paved paths cut around the buildings, and we followed one of these to a green space separating even more buildings. I held my arm in front of me, following the steady tug of the tracking spell.

"Can we pick up the pace a little?" Briar griped as we walked down into a small tunnel that passed under the road.

"As I'm the only one who can feel the trail and I can only *kinda* see . . . No. No, we can't," I hissed between my teeth so that the group of college-aged girls walking the opposite direction in the short tunnel wouldn't hear.

We passed several more buildings and then had to navigate around a reflecting pool that seemed like it was as long as a football field before I finally hesitated in front of a building that had at least fifty steps to reach the front entrance. I cast a dubious glance at the stairs. From previous times I'd functioned at minimal sight, I knew that steps were funny things. Climbing them was part muscle memory and part depth perception. As I had about zero of the latter currently, climbing several flights of stairs was definitely less than an appealing prospect.

"What's the holdup, Craft?" Briar asked.

"I'm just trying to decide if he's inside the building or beyond it." But the frantic tugging of the charm suggested he was close. If he wasn't inside it, he had to be in the green space just behind it. That seemed less likely than finding him inside, so I took a cautious step toward the stairs. There were handrails, at least.

Falin's arm slid around my waist. I opened my mouth

to protest, but at the same moment I misjudged the rise of the steps and nearly stumbled. So I took the help for what it was and slowly but carefully climbed the stairs. When we finally reached the top, I was out of breath and had probably scuffed my boots something fierce, but the tug from the charm was so intense, Remy had to be just ahead of us.

"Come on," I said, shrugging away from Falin's arm and barging through one of the many glass-fronted doors.

I walked through the metal and spell detectors. A green light acknowledged that I carried active magic but nothing that set off alarms. Briar and Falin stopped before stepping into the detectors. Briar cursed and glanced around. Her look-away charms were top of the line, but with all her militarized magics and weapons, she'd set off both detectors and have every security guard on campus descend on us. There was a small amount of space between the door and the detectors, and she headed toward it. Falin handed her his gun as she moved. He stepped through the detectors without a blip—standard spell-detecting charms never looked for fae magic. Briar rejoined us a moment later, handing Falin back his weapon. No one had even noticed her moving around the scanners. Yeah, those were useful.

Past the detectors, we found ourselves in the university library. While there were books on this level, the front part of the room was dominated by the circulation desk, computer stations, and artfully arranged small sitting areas. We wove through these, following the tug of the charm. It led us deep into the building. Rows and rows of shelves surrounded us, and while there were a decent number of people in the front part of the library, as we got deeper into the stacks, it got very quiet. We passed one girl sitting at a desk set up at the end of one of the long shelves, but after that, there were just books, books, and more books.

The tugging grew stronger and stronger and then suddenly began to lessen. I stopped, turned, and backed up. It grew stronger again. I looked around. We were in the middle of a very long aisle of books. An aisle empty of any other people. I peered through one of the shelves, looking over the books to see if there was anyone in the next aisle over. No one on either side.

"Let me guess," Briar said, her arms crossed over her chest. "The trail ends here. Where there is no one. So it is a weird fluke and not a real trail."

I frowned, not yet ready to admit defeat. My eyes had not recovered from the last time I used my grave magic, but I cracked my shields anyway, letting the other planes of reality superimpose themselves over the world around me.

It was possible that Remy's ghost was here, but deep in the land of the dead, deeper than I could typically see without spanning the chasm between the living and the dead. Around me, the books appeared to wither and flake away, and I was careful not to touch anything. The thin bubblelike shield I'd built around my psyche to contain my planeweaving abilities was active, but I didn't want to risk pulling anything over into the land of the dead and making what I was seeing a reality. I searched, letting my psyche stretch further. Around me, the books appeared to crumble to dust and drift away in the wind; the shelves they sat on rusted and rotted into collapsed husks. In the darkness just outside my field of vision, shadowed forms lurked. Not Remy. Not even ghosts. Things that had never been alive but could scent my shimmering life energy.

I drew back, pulling away from the land of the dead and slamming my shields closed. I hadn't found Remy, but I didn't dare send my psyche any farther across without a circle in place. Besides, I doubted the charm could have tracked his soul as far across the chasm as I went, let alone farther. Which meant Briar was right. It was a wild-goose — or in this case, ghost — chase.

I brushed back several curls that had been tossed into my face by the chilled grave wind, and the charm tugged harder. I glanced at where it was attached to the arm that was now at face height, and then I extended my arm over my head. The charm gave a slightly harder tug. I lowered my arm and the tug calmed ever so slightly.

I'm an idiot.

"Upstairs," I said, bustling down the aisle.

The world was slightly more shadowy after my quick look through the planes, but considering I was already functioning in an odd grayscale, it was hardly noticeable. I was expecting to find a staircase but was pleasantly surprised when Falin pointed to an elevator set in the far wall of the building. There were several options of basement and subbasement levels, but only one floor above the main level. Falin hit the button and the doors gave an earsplitting creak as they closed. The elevator lurched, dropping several inches. We all grabbed for the rail before it stopped and started its slow journey upward with what sounded like straining gears.

"Craft, after all the shit I've lived through, if I die in a freak elevator accident, I'm coming back to haunt your ass."

"I already have two ghosts haunting me. Position's filled." I made the words sound flippant, even though I was still gripping the railing.

Briar smiled, but she was the first out of the elevator when the doors opened again.

I led the way, following the tug of the charm. This level of the building was more of a mezzanine than an entirely new story. The front was a balcony that looked down over the many lounges and study nooks on the main level. The back appeared to be administrative offices. The center, through which we were following the charm, appeared to be some sort of rare book collection.

We passed an illuminated scroll under glass, the yellowed paper looking like it was close to falling apart. Display cases and glass-topped pedestals were scattered through the space, holding more ancient, weathered books and scrolls. In the center of the space were bookshelves, but very different from the ones we saw on the main level. These bookshelves were fixed with heavy Plexiglas panels that kept anyone from touching the books. There didn't appear to be any scrolls on the shelves at a casual glance, and the books themselves looked much less ancient. Some still sported the telltale signs of age in cracked and split leather bindings, but others looked much newer. I assumed that this was a rare book section that authorized faculty and the occasional graduate student were granted access to. Security cameras hung from the ceiling in plain view as a deterrent. Heavy wards surrounded the texts on pedestals, but only the locks on the Plexiglas secured the books on the shelves. Apparently they were accessed frequently enough or by such a diverse number of people that warding hadn't been practical.

We walked past the first two aisles of sealed shelves. When we rounded the third, the charm on my wrist jumped, trying to pull me down the aisle.

A woman maybe twenty-two years old knelt in front of one of the shelves. She had long black hair that had been pulled back in a ponytail so messy it looked like a drunk who'd never touched a hair tie before had pulled it back for her. The Plexiglas in front of her was slid to the side, and she appeared to be sliding something inside a backpack that rested at her feet.

She was also a corpse. I had to crack my shields to be sure—she was the best corpse I'd seen the necromancer create yet, barely any grave essence rose from her, but she was still dead.

"Hey, Remy," I said, forcing as much bubbly cheer into my voice as I could muster.

The girl's head shot up as one of her hands moved to clamp her bag closed, hiding whatever was inside. The other slipped inside her big coat, reaching for something underneath.

"Oh, hi. I, uh, was just browsing. Uh, do I know you?" Her voice was high, the words spit out fast in a nervous tangle.

Falin stepped in front of me. "Are you going to use the weapon you have under your coat?" he asked, nodding to her.

"I, uh . . ." She backed up a step. "I'm late for class. I have to go."

"Remy, wait," I said as she started to turn. Behind

me, I felt one of Briar's tranquilizer charms prime for action. I held up a hand, trying to stall her. People tended to cooperate better if you didn't start your introductions by shooting them. I'd rather try talking to Remy first.

The girl flipped back around. A gun emerged from under the big coat, and she lifted it, pointing it at us with a shaking hand. "Don't try to stop me. I'm desperate and—" she said, but cut off suddenly, her dark eyes going from squinted nervousness to rounded shock. "What did you call me?"

"Remy. Remy Hollens," I said, staying very still. Both because I didn't want to get shot, and because I didn't want to escalate anything to the point Briar thought she had no choice but to take Remy down.

"How do you know who I am?" the body that contained the soul of Remy asked, the arm holding the gun slowly lowering until the barrel was pointed safely at the ground.

I gave a sigh of relief. First because I was no longer in danger of getting shot and also because I'd been right about this being Remy. It seemed a given as the charm had led us here and the body was dead, but in this case, I wasn't taking anything for granted.

"Taylor hired me to look for you," I said as explanation. Taylor had also fired me, but that was beside the point.

"Yeah, but . . . How did you know it was *me*?" He glanced pointedly down at his very female body that looked nothing like the picture Taylor had supplied me.

I turned to Briar and Falin because that was a rather complicated subject. While it had been a good assumption, even if I'd opened my shields, I couldn't have made out the image of his ghost while it was inside a body, just the general glow of a soul that didn't quite fit inside a body correctly.

"What did he have you steal?" Falin asked, nodding at the book bag Remy held.

Remy clutched the bag, pulling it against his chest and then nearly dropping it, surprise flashing across the body's pretty face. I was guessing it was the boobs he hadn't anticipated smashing when he hugged the bag. That would probably take getting used to.

"What do you know about him?" Remy asked, glancing between Falin and me.

I realized that he never once glanced at Briar on my other side. She was hiding behind her charms again, but she hadn't plugged him with any kind of knockout spell yet, so whatever. As long as she was hanging back, I'd assume she approved of my line of questioning, and of me choosing what to reveal.

"I know that you signed up for a study with a man named Hadisty and wound up in another body."

Remy scoffed under his breath. "Hadisty." He shook his head. "You know that's not his real name, right?"

I nodded and Falin said, "We know a couple of names he goes by, but we doubt we know his real name."

"I might not either, but his friend called him 'Gauhter' and I think that's probably real." Remy glanced at the watch on his wrist and cursed. He tucked the gun back under his coat. "I have to go. Tell Taylor I'm okay, and I'll be home soon. Don't tell her about me looking like this. I don't want her to ever know."

But he wouldn't be home soon.

"What did he have you steal, Remy?" I asked, taking a step forward.

Remy slung the backpack over one shoulder and turned to walk the other way. I couldn't hear her, but I knew that Briar would be lifting her crossbow, preparing to take him down. He couldn't be allowed to leave. Could we arrest him for being dead?

"Wait," I called after him.

He just shook his head. "I can't. I have to get back. You don't understand."

"He said he'd put you back in your body if you do this," I guessed, based on Angela's ghost's words.

"Yeah, exactly. So you understand how important this is."

"He can't put you back," I called after him.

Remy stopped. "He put me here. He can put me back," he said, and there was something a little desperate in his voice, something that rang of radical conviction. He *had* to believe he'd get his body back.

And I had to disillusion him.

"Your body is dead."

He shook his head. "No. No, I saw it walking around recently."

"It's in the city morgue," Falin said, and Remy recoiled, his lips pulling back from his teeth in an expression that was too primal to rightly name but definitely included fear and anger.

"You're a liar." He spat the words at both of us.

Falin pulled his wallet from his pocket and flipped it open to flash his badge. "I'm Falin Andrews with the FIB. The body of Remy Hollens has been positively identified and is currently in the city morgue."

Remy hadn't asked us who we were, which shouldn't have surprised me considering he'd barely been paying enough attention to describe his own death, but that meant Falin's action created quite a response. The anger on his face drained away, leaving only the horrified shock. He sank to his knees, hands slack by his sides, his gaze a million miles away but directed at the carpet.

"Well done, Craft," Briar said without a trace of sarcasm in her voice.

"That wasn't well done. We just destroyed him," I hissed in reply.

"Yeah, but I didn't have to shoot him."

True. Though letting her tranquilize him might have been kinder. He would have had to find out about his body at some point, though.

"So, I'm like this forever now?" Remy whispered after several minutes, and I cringed.

Eventually I'd have to tell him that the body he was wearing was dead as well. Not yet, though. That would be too many blows for anyone to handle.

Footsteps sounded out of sight but somewhere close. Briar, who was closest to the bookshelf, discreetly closed the open Plexiglas.

A security guard turned the corner around the bookshelf. His pace was quick, not casual, so this wasn't him on rounds. We'd drawn someone's attention.

"You kids doing okay over here?" Friendly words for a man who was studying us with a suspicious frown. He also wasn't old enough to call us kids, but I let that slide as we were on a college campus.

"Just having a conversation," Falin said with a smile.

The guard turned to study him, his eyes narrowing as he took in Falin's appearance. Maybe Falin could pass for a postdoctoral student, but he sure couldn't pass for the typical undergraduate. That said, the university was pretty diverse.

The guard's gaze eventually moved off Falin and fell on Remy's still-kneeling form.

"Miss, you okay?"

Remy didn't move, he didn't even breathe, though I'm not sure he was aware of that fact. His gaze was still distant, unfocused on the carpet. Of course, he probably didn't even realize the guard's "miss" was addressed to him.

"Remy," I coaxed, kneeling down beside him, close, but not close enough to touch. My grave magic might be exhausted and behaving, but he was still a corpse. He lifted his head, but he didn't seem to see anything. I looked back up at the guard. "He just got some bad news about the death of someone very close."

Confusion flickered over the guard's features, and I realized I'd used a pronoun he probably hadn't been expecting. Female body. Male ghost. Pronouns were a little tricky.

The guard let it pass without comment. Just nodded and said, "Maybe this isn't the best place for such a conversation. Sorry for your loss."

Then after one more searching glance that encompassed us all, except Briar, he turned, waved to someone watching from one of the cameras, and walked away. No one spoke as we listened to his footsteps grow more distant. This close to Remy, I could feel more than just the magic in the backpack he carried, but also another charm I hadn't sensed earlier. It was subtle, and illegal. It kept the wearer from showing up on cameras. I recognized it only because I'd used one before. Briar's news stunt wasn't the first time I'd ended up on the wrong end of a reporter's story. It did explain how Remy got the book into his bag without the guard showing up earlier. Or why none showed up when he pulled a gun on us. But we probably did need to move on before the guard realized the number of people he spoke to didn't match up with the number on the screen.

"Taylor will never accept me like this," Remy whispered, but he wasn't really talking to us, his voice distant and introspective. "What am I supposed to do now?"

The body he was wearing was petite and I had to slouch to get down to eye level with him. I would have liked to reassure him that Taylor would love him regardless of what body he wore, but I could only imagine the shock his high school sweetheart would experience when she learned her football-star boyfriend was now her girlfriend. Maybe, under different circumstances, she could have learned to accept the changes, but she was never going to get the chance. This body was already dead. There was really only one thing he could do.

"You help us find the necromancer who did this to you so we can stop him from doing it to anyone else."

"But that doesn't help me. I was saving for a ring . . ." There was so much pain in his voice, it broke my heart even though his shade had already given away that particular secret.

"No, it doesn't directly help you, but it can give you closure. And revenge."

Revenge tended to be a great motivator. An empty, soul-destroying motivator that rarely left the one seeking it satisfied, but it certainly inspired action.

Remy's eyes narrowed, his gaze snapping into focus. "What can I do?"

Briar stepped closer, dropping her look-away spell. "What did he have you steal, and where are you taking it?"

Chapter 22

"**N**o way," Remy said, shaking his head. "I'm not going back there. My real body is already dead. I'm not risking this one by leading you to the guy who killed me."

We'd moved our conversation to a narrow table in the far corner of the room, hoping we didn't attract the attention of the guards again now that we were farther from the books. Remy had handed over his bag to me, and the book was still inside, but I wasn't sure what to do with it.

"I thought you said you wanted revenge?" Briar said, crossing her arms over her chest.

"I want to live more. Even if it will be"—he glanced down—"a very odd adjustment."

Briar and Falin both glanced at me, Briar thrusting her chin slightly, one eyebrow raised in a clear demand. I could guess for what. I sighed.

"That's not really an option," I said, trying to keep

my voice gentle because if I'd devastated him before, I was truly about to shatter him now.

"Why, because I stole some old book? It hasn't even left the library yet, so not stolen. You've got nothing on me."

"That's not it. The body you're in right now. It's already dead."

"You're crazy," he said, staring at me. He looked to Falin and Briar, waiting for them to refute my statement. Briar gave him what I supposed was meant to be a sympathetic look but mostly just made her look constipated. Falin offered him a solemn nod. Remy shook his head violently. "You're all absolutely crazy."

How were you supposed to convince someone they were dead? I'd had to clue in the occasional ghost, but the whole not-having-a-body-anymore thing helped. Remy was up walking and talking, even if he wasn't in his own body.

"You're dealing with a very stressful time right now. How fast is your pulse racing?" I asked him.

"What the fuck does that have to do with anything?" He stood as he yelled the question, his hands balled in fists at his sides.

"Just check, okay?"

He gave me a disgusted look. Then, determined to prove his living status, he lifted two fingers to his throat and pressed them where his pulse point should be. He waited, concern etching around his eyes. He moved his fingers over just slightly. Then again, and again. He lifted his wrist, searching there. Then he shoved a hand down his shirt, pressing it against where his heart should have been pounding. If he were alive.

The horror in his face was absolute. Frantic eyes

begging me that it couldn't be true. But I couldn't take it back, couldn't rescind the information now that he'd acknowledged it. So I had to continue.

"You probably didn't notice, but you aren't breathing either."

"That's not true. I have to breathe to talk," he said, drawing an intentionally large breath.

"True. So don't say anything, just hold your breath until you get the urge to breathe."

He crossed his arms over his chest and did a little twist with his shoulders, marking the seconds with his body movements. After nearly a minute the smug movements began to slow down. Another minute, and he sank back into his chair, looking freshly stunned.

"You don't blink either," Briar added. "It's freaky."

I shot her a glance over where Remy had just buried his head under his arms on the table. He was breathing now, fast and jagged, like he was close to a panic attack. I doubted he could actually have a panic attack without a beating heart, but his mind was still reeling, so I gave him a minute. Eventually he sat up. He wiped at his eyes, but they were dry. Apparently he couldn't cry either, not even for his own death.

"So, what does that mean for me? Is this body going to rot around me?"

"Not initially," I said, and here was where I could get into some trouble with the collectors, but he deserved to know. "Your soul is what is powering that body. The longer you are in it, the weaker you will get, until the you that is looking out through those borrowed eyes, that remembers you are Remy, will cease to exist." Or at least, that was what I'd gathered from my conversation with Death.

"Oh, great." He laughed, the sound harsh, verging on despair. "So what are my options here? I'm dead so I can't die again, but what am I if I don't have this body?"

"A ghost, if you stay. Or you let one of the soul collectors send you on."

"Send me where?"

I shrugged. "I don't know for sure, but to answer your options question, you have the option to stay as you are, existing in this half-life for a few days, maybe weeks, or you can avoid destroying your soul by not draining away your energy to fuel a dead body."

"Those options are crap."

I couldn't disagree with that.

"Before Craft goes and talks you out of your body," Briar said, leaning forward, "we still need to catch the necromancer who did this. Our best bet is catching him when you give him the book."

"Well, it sounds like I've got nothing to lose," he said, his shoulders slumping, as if he could sag into himself. He sighed, taking a deep breath, and looked up at me. "We better hurry, I'm supposed to meet him in fifteen minutes."

We were considerably farther than fifteen minutes from where Remy was supposed to drop off the stolen book. He'd driven to the library in a car that had belonged to the girl whose body he wore, so Briar went with Remy while Falin and I followed. It was a considerably better seating arrangement than the drive to the library.

Against my better judgment, we'd gone through with stealing the irreplaceable rare book Remy had been sent to take. Briar said that she'd take responsibility for us borrowing the book and would see it returned. There were probably official channels she should have gone through, but those would have taken time, and Remy was on a strict deadline he was already running late for.

I'd been sure the alarms would go off as we walked out of the library, or we'd get caught in a security ward, but between the fact that the backpack Remy had been given had some hard-core wards built into it and contained several other charms to facilitate this theft, which was how Remy got the book off the shelf in the first place, and the fact that Briar carried it out the same way she'd walked in, no one had blinked as we walked out of the library. Judging by the amount of magic embedded in the bag, Gauhter was not playing around or sparing any expense. Which meant this book had to be important.

But why?

I'd held on to the bag and book during the drive to try to figure that out. The book Gauhter had Remy steal was the journal of an alchemist who'd died hundreds of years before the Magical Awakening. There had been a lot of magic in the world before science and technology first began crowding it out, but magic had long been in heavy decline by the author's lifetime. During his time, there had been a lot of incorrect assumptions about how the world worked and superstitions that weren't magic at all. Alchemy was a gray area of history. It was considered a magical science, but whether any of it actually worked was a highly debated topic. Many scholars had studied the old texts and illuminations since the Magical Awakening, and some of the things alchemists strove to achieve could be done with magic these days, but the processes and recipes that had survived seemed rather ludicrous. As Falin drove, I flipped through the journal's pages, occasionally stopping to scan a hand-scrawled block of text or carefully drawn image.

"You should be wearing gloves and using tools. That book is probably four hundred years old," Falin said, glancing at where I was poring over the pages.

"Remy had it shoved in a backpack," I said as I flipped another page. "It's seen worse."

Falin didn't argue, but his lips compressed into a thin line of disapproval. I consented to digging out my gloves. I had them on me anyway, though they made turning the pages significantly more difficult.

From what I could gather from my quick skimming, the book was a journal chronicling the alchemist's experiments. His main areas of alchemical interests were the creation of an immortality elixir and engineering homunculi. Neither were unusual alchemical goals for his time, but there was no proof any alchemist had ever succeeded with either goal.

During the author's lifetime, magic would have been thin. If this alchemist had been studying ancient texts, what had worked in ancient times wouldn't have created any results for him. Alchemists of his era ended up using a very strange pseudochemistry approach to magic, which was evident in how he logged his experiments. I turned the page to discover a carefully illustrated account of one homunculus attempt that involved slowly heating a chicken egg in a mix of urine, semen, and silver nitrate at a precise temperature for two weeks. *Case in point.*

So what did Gauhter expect to find?

I flipped to the end of the book, but the last third seemed to be blank. Either the writer had given up before he ran out of paper, or he'd succeeded and stopped having to track his experiments. I thumbed back, looking for the last journaled page. When I finally found it, the page didn't contain any words but was a line drawing of a woman heavy with child standing on a moon with stars in her hands. While it may have been some sort of alchemical imagery—my limited knowledge of alchemy came from history class back in school and a recent brush with a fae alchemist distilling glamour—but the image seemed very out of place in the book. I laid two gloved fingers on the page and let my ability to sense magic stretch.

It took a moment. The spell on the page was so old and so unlike any kind of magic I'd ever felt before that I almost missed it, but it was there. I couldn't have proven the alchemist was the one who placed the spell on the page, but the magic was definitely old. A whole lot older than seventy years, so someone put it on the page before the Magical Awakening. I tried to untangle the traces of information I could feel buzzing through the page, but the magic was too foreign to gather a hint of what it might do.

I flipped back a few more pages and found more enchanted illustrations. When I finally found more text, it was clear several pages had been torn from the book between the last journal entry and the first full-page illustration. I glanced over that last entry. It was more of the same as the first part of the journal except that this one ended midsentence before the formula was listed. So had the alchemist torn out the pages to hide his results, or had someone else? And were the odd illustrations clues to his final experiment, meaningless ways to help mask whatever the spells on the page hid, or part of the spells themselves? I glanced over the handful of illustrations, but they were bizarre: men in beakers, the sun and moon in each other's landscape, and so forth. They looked vaguely alchemical, so they might have had deeper meaning. Or they might have been nonsense.

I closed the cracking cover and called Briar. When she answered I said, "I don't think we can risk handing over this book."

"We're not going to let the necromancer keep it," Briar said, as if nothing could possibly go wrong. Taking the chance of allowing Gauhter to slip away with whatever information he was searching for between the covers of the book sounded like a really bad idea to me.

"I'm not sure if he's after eternal life or the ability to create a homunculus, but there is something hidden behind really old magic in this book. If he knows how to activate the spells, he could very well get whatever it is he's after." I explained what I'd found in the book. I couldn't show her the images, as she was in the car ahead of me, but I told her about the spells and gave her a brief summary of what the images depicted.

I didn't realize that she had me on speakerphone until Remy said, "Wanting eternal life I get, but what is a 'homunculus'?"

"It means 'little man,'" Briar said, and since she had

me on speaker, I put her on speaker as well so that Falin could hear more than my side of the conversation. Briar went on, "It was said to have been a perfect copy of the alchemist who created it, except small."

"So a magical clone?" Remy asked.

Briar made a sound that made me think it had accompanied a shrug. "Sort of. But it lacked a soul because it was never technically born. Or that's what is theorized. There's little to no evidence that anyone was ever successful in creating one. Craft, I want to see those images before we turn this book over."

"I'm still against turning the book over." I looked at Falin. "If we had another book to use as a base, do you think you could glamour it to look similar to this one?"

Falin glanced away from the road for barely a moment, evaluating. "It would depend on how deep an inspection you wanted it to pass. Just the cover? Sure. Believable contents? No. Not unless I had several hours to work on it, and then it would still revert to normal at sunset."

We didn't have a few hours. I directed my next question at my phone again.

"Remy. The place you're supposed to deliver the book, have you been there before? What did you see before you were in this body? You said the necromancer's friend called him Gauhter; what did this friend look like? Who else did you see there?"

"Man, I just finished answering similar questions from her," he said, and he could only mean Briar. There were more reasons why she'd wanted to be the one to ride with Remy than escaping Falin's cramped backseat. He let out a long sigh, which had to be intentional considering what we'd recently discussed about his breathing needs. "The other guy I saw was maybe a little younger than Gauhter, I don't know."

Right, Mister Observant, I forgot.

"I think I . . . died"—he paused, struggling over the word "died" before continuing—"somewhere else. He kept me in a bottle before putting me in this body, and the bottle was in a bag most of the time. When it wasn't, it was still hard to see. The bottle had this weird, gold lacelike thing covering most of it."

I went cold, not even daring to breathe. "You mean like a gold filigree?"

"He's shrugging with a dumb look on his face," Briar said, and I heard Remy make some sort of exclamation of dismay in the background.

"Were there gems inlaid in the glass? Sapphires? Rubies? Emeralds?" I asked.

"Maybe," he said. "I think my bottle had some stone. Blue maybe?"

"Alex, why does it sound like you've heard of these bottles before?" Falin asked, his grip tight on the steering wheel.

"Because I have," I said. "I'll call you back in a minute."

I disconnected before Briar could reply and hit the speed dial for Rianna. It went to voice mail.

I started to leave a quick message for her to call me back, but then I hesitated. This was too important to put off or risk me missing her call when she returned mine.

"Stop working your case on the missing artifact," I said, unsure how much I should leave on a recording. "I think the necromancer I'm chasing probably has it. Gather all your notes on the case and the original con-

tract and e-mail them to me when you can, okay? Just
whatever you do, don't track the bottle." I sagged in my
seat. "Geez. I don't think your client gave you enough
information. That bottle? I think it's been being used
to store souls."

Chapter 23

As soon as I disconnected, I tried Rianna's number a second time, just in case. It went to voice mail again. If she was in the middle of a ritual, she wouldn't have taken her phone in the circle with her. I just hoped she'd listen to her voice mail before she went chasing any leads.

Falin was staring at me as best he could out of the corner of his eye, not fully taking his attention from the road. I sighed and filled him in on the case Rianna had been working.

"And she was sure he was fae?" he asked when I finished.

I shrugged. "Desmond thought so."

Falin pulled his phone from his pocket one-handed and dialed one of the numbers on his favorites list without ever slowing the car—he couldn't have. Briar was the one driving Remy's car, and we'd have lost them if

Falin so much as blinked too long. The woman liked her gas pedal.

"I need you to see if we were brought a case about a missing artifact a few weeks ago. The item was a bottle." He described the bottle to someone I could only guess was one of his FIB agents on the other side of the line and then paused a moment before saying, "Call me back as soon as you know." Then he hung up.

I was about to dial Briar back when she turned off into the rest stop just outside town. Falin followed, pulling in beside her to park. We were a few miles outside the northeastern part of the city, only a dozen or so miles from where Briar and I had discovered the dead creatures. It wasn't a particularly grand rest stop. It was perfunctory at best. There were a couple of covered picnic tables, a small building with bathrooms, and some vending machines. I think the city planners added it just because the last stop on the interstate had been a while, and when the city was still new, it made Nekros seem more official, but it was rarely used. It was faster to go around the folded space containing Nekros than to go through it, so anyone using this highway had somewhere they were headed in the city and could probably wait for a bathroom.

"We'll have to walk from here," Remy said, shouting to us from over the top of his car.

I climbed out of the car. It wasn't like I'd expected Gauhter to have his circle drawn in the middle of the men's bathroom, but aside from the rest stop and the wilds, there was theoretically nothing out here. I glanced around. There were a surprising number of cars parked in this lot, but no other people.

"Do you think all of these cars belong to Gauhter's

victims?" I asked, counting cars. There were nearly half a dozen besides ours.

Falin frowned. "Surely not all of them." But he took his phone out of his pocket and began photographing license plates. "I'll have an agent run these through the system."

We followed Remy past the building and picnic shelters, into the woods behind the rest stop. He stopped just past the tree line and dug a small disc out of his coat pocket. It appeared to be just a clear glass disc until he set it in his palm. A small red arrow appeared in the disk, pointing deeper into the woods.

"This way," he said, leading us in the direction the arrow pointed.

He had to consult the charmed disc several times as we navigated through the woods, making sure we continued on the right path. At times I was sure it was the arrow that turned, not us or the terrain, but a guidance charm that led the user on an indirect path so they'd have a hard time finding their way would be quite the spell. I itched to get a better look at it, but I was pulling up the rear of the group, far from where Remy led the way. Navigating through the woods under a thick canopy that cast the ground in gray shadows would have been a challenge for me on a good day. Today was not a good day. I kept tripping over roots I couldn't differentiate from the rest of the forest floor and getting tangled in vines that snagged my boots.

"Can you possibly make *more* noise?" Briar asked, sounding disgusted with me. She slipped silently through the woods, her footing sure and steady.

I hated her a little.

Falin was just as silent—a graceful predator in a suit.

Remy at least made a little noise as he tromped along, but not nearly as much as me.

I was concentrating so hard on my footing, I almost missed the feeling of magic ahead of us.

"Stop," I yelled, hurrying to catch up and nearly landing on my face when I tripped over a fallen branch.

Briar and Falin froze, but Remy took a couple more steps before turning.

"What's wrong, Craft?" Briar asked. At the same time Falin said, "Alex?"

"We're about to cross a ward," I said, trying to catch my breath. Not that anyone else was breathing hard.

"Someone cast a ward in the middle of the forest?" Briar asked, glancing around.

I understood her confusion. Wards were typically placed on boundary points: doorways, fences, even small objects like boxes and bags, something that had a clear transition from one place to another, inside from outside. The magic stuck to those physical representations of transition best. A line or circle scratched or painted onto the ground could offer a temporary place for a ward to grab hold, but it wouldn't last long. Creating a ward that held in a mixed terrain like a forest would be hard.

I narrowed my eyes and scanned the trees ahead of us where I could feel the spell. While it appeared like the trees kept going forever, it was marginally brighter just ahead of us. I could feel an illusion spell mixed in with the wards, and I would have put money on the fact that we were moments from stumbling through that illusion and likely into a clearing. The openness of a clearing compared to the woods around it would be an acceptable transition point.

"What does the ward do?" Falin asked, moving to stand beside me and casting his gaze to match mine as I stared at what I was now positive was an illusion of more forest.

"There is an illusion in the same spot, but I think the ward is just an alarm. It won't stop us, but Gauhter will know how many people crossed it, and maybe if we are normals, witches, or fae." I bit my lip, trying to search down anything else I could discern about the ward. When this was all over, I was going to have to spend some time with Caleb and learn a little more about the intricacies of wards. "It might detect weapons and carried spells too. I can't tell. But it definitely will destroy any chance of surprise."

Briar cursed under her breath.

"Are we aborting this mission?" Remy asked from up ahead. "Because I have no issue turning around and walking right back out of here."

"Don't give up so easy. No one is leaving," Briar said. "Besides, you wouldn't have your charm. I bet you couldn't find your way back out."

Remy scowled at her, and Falin smiled, looking down at me. "Come now, even a blind goblin could follow the trail Alex left on the way here."

"Ha ha," I said, but I didn't mind the teasing. Besides, he was probably right. "So seriously, though, what's the plan?"

"I'm assuming you're taking us to a structure," Falin said, looking over to Remy. "How far are we from it?"

Remy shook his head. "I'm . . . not exactly sure where we are. I've never been here before. I was told to drive to the rest stop, park, and then follow where the arrow pointed."

"So, when we pass that ward, we might be right out-side the designated meeting place," Falin said, rubbing a thumb and finger along his jaw as he thought aloud. "Or this could be a distant-perimeter ward and you might follow that charm for another half hour of hiking."

"I hope not," Remy grumbled under his breath. Everyone ignored him.

"You're right." Briar nodded to Falin. Then she pulled her crossbow and checked its configuration. "We will have no idea what is across that illusion until we've already set off the ward. We can rush the place, hoping speed is enough to catch Gauhter unaware, but if that is a distant-perimeter ward, we'll have lost all element of surprise and Gauhter will likely be gone. If he's even there in the first place. Option two is to send Remy and the book over alone. He can communicate back to us what the terrain and walk is like, and how many people are on the other side."

"Both those options suck," Remy said, crossing his arms over his chest.

"Out of those options, I vote we rush the place," I said, though a raid wasn't something I exactly had experience with. "There is less chance of Gauhter ending up with the book if we rush the place than if we send Remy alone."

Falin shook his head. "But there is a higher chance of Gauhter slipping through our fingers or casualties if we run into something unexpected. I vote we send Remy to do some reconnaissance."

Briar evaluated her crossbow for a moment, checking the resistance of the string. She was a kick-ass-now, ask-questions-later type, and I had no doubt she'd side with me. But after a moment she looked at Falin and nodded. "I agree. We need more information. There would be nothing suspicious about Remy walking over that ward alone."

I wasn't exactly outvoted, as Remy had yet to voice an opinion beyond the general suckiness of both options. Everyone turned to look at him.

"How would I communicate with you if I go in alone? I'm guessing you don't have a police wire randomly on your persons out here in the woods."

"And magic might be sensed by the ward," I said, wishing I could give a definite yes or no on that, but "maybe" was as good as I could get.

Falin and Briar glanced at each other, some sort of private communication going on between them that Remy and I weren't invited to.

"I have a hands-free device for my cell phone," Briar said, pulling a small earpiece with microphone from one of her pockets.

Falin nodded. "I can hide that. I doubt the ward detects or dispels glamour."

Briar dialed my number on her phone before handing both phone and hands-free earpiece to Remy. "Craft, keep that line open. Remy, I want these back, so don't lose them."

"Right," he said, stuffing the phone in his pocket.

Once the hands-free set was secure in his ear, Falin cupped his hand over the side of Remy's face. It looked oddly like Falin was caressing Remy's face, and as that face was currently that of a pretty young woman, it was awkward to watch. I turned away.

While Falin worked on the glamour, Briar said, "When you cross the ward, just act normal. If no one is watching, mutter to yourself about what you see. If there are people, well, if they are that close, they might be watching now, but assuming they aren't, do what you can to let us know what you see."

"Oh, that makes me feel so safe. Here is a phone, go walk into a trap."

Briar ignored him. "Your safe word is 'apples.' If things go wrong or you don't think you can get back out, say it and we will come get you."

As he was already dead, I wondered how quickly we as the cavalry would actually rush in if he reported overwhelming odds. When I glanced at Remy, Falin had finished and stepped back. He'd done a good job; there was no sign of the earpiece.

I lifted my own phone. "Testing, testing."

"I hear you loud and clear," Remy said, and I gave a thumbs-up that I could hear him as well before switching to speakerphone. Remy turned, lifting the glass disc with the glowing arrow pointed at the illusionary woods ahead. Falin handed Remy the backpack, and then the ghost piloting a corpse gave us a small salute. "Off I go."

Chapter 24

There was nothing to do but wait as Remy vanished behind the illusion.

"Crap, guys. It's a freaking clearing on this side. With a shack in the middle."

"Not so subtle, Remy. You should probably act natural in case people can see you from that shack," Briar said. She still had her crossbow in her hands, ready to charge forward past the illusion if she needed.

"Natural? I'm walking around in a dead girl's body. Natural isn't on the table," he said, but his voice barely carried through my phone this time, so at least he was whispering.

"I guess I'm supposed to knock," he said, and we heard a soft thudding as he did just that. It had only been a minute or two since he crossed the ward, so the clearing was small, the shack close to the tree line.

"You're late," a gravelly voice said, and I glanced at Briar and Falin. Could this be the infamous Gauhter?

Remy answered that question for me a heart-beat later. "Who are you? And who is she? Where is Gauhter?"

"Gauhter's busy. He sent us to pick up his package. Did you get the book?"

So no, this was not Gauhter. Our necromancer was MIA. I sagged as disappointment weighed me down, but then I forced myself to straighten again. Remy could need help soon. There were still two unknown potential threats across those wards.

"I have the book, but I'm not giving it to anyone but Gauhter," Remy said, his voice sounding petulant but determined.

"You are giving it to us. Gauhter has a new job for you." This was a new voice. The unknown female in the shack.

"He told me if I brought him this book, he'd return my body." Considering Remy knew he wasn't getting his body, it was a pretty stellar performance.

Falin looked at Briar. "Gauhter's not going to show. We should get Remy out and detain these two, see what we can find out."

She nodded. "Agreed." Then into my phone she said, "Remy, keep stalling, we're about to raid the shack. When you hear us enter, hit the floor."

Remy was smart enough not to answer.

The male voice on the other side of the line said, "And you'll get your body back soon. Gauhter just needs you to run another little errand for him."

Briar moved to just outside the ward, ready to rush it. I began to follow, and Falin caught my shoulder, stopping me.

"You stay here," he said.

I cocked an eyebrow. Not that I was about to complain about *not* having to raid a bad guy's shack. I did feel a little put out that he didn't think I could pull my weight in this investigation, though.

Falin must have taken my expression as a preamble to an argument because he said, "You're half blind and your idea of a fighting style is trusting your movements to the guidance of a dagger that likes blood and isn't picky where it draws it. Just sit this one out, okay?"

"We need to move. Craft, stay," Briar said, and then she charged across the ward. Falin followed her a moment later.

I didn't.

"What the hell was that?" the man's voice said over my phone as soon as Briar passed the ward.

"Someone is here. Two someones and one is carrying a crap-ton of magic," the woman said. "We should get out of here."

And then chaos exploded over the phone. It was hard to follow what was happening through the choppy bangs, yells, and crashes that crackled over the line. The line went silent a moment later. At first I thought the call had been dropped, but it was just that the fight was over that quick.

"Did you see the woman?" Falin's voice asked, sounding distant and muffled through the phone.

There were some shuffling sounds, and then Briar's voice came through the phone loud and clear, like she'd just reclaimed her hands-free set. "Craft, did anyone come your way?"

I opened my mouth to say no, but then I felt the

magic coming straight toward me, fast. I couldn't see anything move through the ward, but I could feel the spells surrounding the figure.

I drew the dagger from my boot. It buzzed in excitement, happy to be drawn and happier that I might use it.

"Stop," I yelled, extending the dagger in front of me.

The knot of magic cloaking the figure didn't stop. It turned, making an arc around my location. *Damn.*

I didn't have any offensive magics. I should have made Briar leave me one of her potions, but I hadn't, so unless I was willing to chase the figure down and stab her, I didn't know how to stop her.

I cracked my shields, reaching with my grave magic. But the magic-cloaked figure wasn't dead—which was a surprise in and of itself. What was even more of a surprise was that when I opened my shields and the Aetheric plane snapped into focus, showing the otherwise gray world with an overwhelming amount of color, the invisibility spell suddenly snapped into focus as well. It coated her form, creating a perfect glowing layer over her skin.

She glanced over her shoulder, and a jolt of recognition jolted through me. I knew her face, I'd seen it recently. But where? I didn't have time to think about it. I gave chase, but if it had been hard to navigate the terrain at a walk when I'd simply lacked depth perception and color, it was nigh impossible trying to do it with those same issues combined with the fact that now I couldn't see some of the fallen debris because it appeared rotted in the land of the dead. The second time I tripped, I ended up on my knees, my palms the only thing keeping my face out of the dirt. The dagger skittered out of my hand, and I scrambled after it.

Falin was suddenly by my side. He held out a hand, dragging me back to my feet.

"Did you see her?" he asked as soon as I was upright.

I nodded, lifting the hand clutching my dagger to point ahead of me, though while I could feel her, there was too much Aetheric energy clogging the space between us for me to still see the outline her spell created. "She has an invisibility charm. Best one I've ever felt."

He scanned the area where I'd pointed, but only shook his head. "Let's head back to the shack. At least we caught one of them."

"I just had it," Remy said as Falin and I walked into the shack. He knelt down on his hands and knees, looking under the table where I guessed he must have hid when the raid occurred.

"Just had what?" I asked, but my attention was on the body sprawled in the middle of the floor. The stranger looked dead. He *felt* dead. "Is he dead?"

Briar pursed her lips and toed the body with one of her black biker boots. "I'm not sure. I mean, I'm guessing he started out dead, so yes. But will he wake up when I counterspell the sleepytime and immobility spells I hit him with? I honestly don't know."

I considered opening my shields and looking to see if the soul was still inside, but it wasn't *outside* the man, and the body was in good shape for how long dead it felt, so I gambled that it was still inside.

"Do we call the police?" I asked, taking in the broken door, turned-over chairs, and seemingly dead body. This would be fun to explain.

"Yeah, we'll need them to come process everything,

see if we can identify any prints in this room, maybe find Gauhter's real name, those of his accomplices, and possibly more victims. Speaking of which, I take it you didn't catch the woman?"

Falin shook his head. "She had an invisibility spell."

"And an oddity for this case: She wasn't dead," I added.

Briar cursed under her breath and pulled out her phone. "I'll send GPS coordinates to the locals. Hopefully at least one officer is close by who can take custody of this scene. I want to question this guy, if we can wake him."

"It's gone," Remy said, scooting out from where he'd squeezed himself under the dilapidated bed frame in the corner of the room.

"What's gone?"

"The backpack," he said, clenching his hands by his sides.

A cold stone dropped into my stomach, weighing down my guts with dread. "And the book?"

Remy nodded. "It was inside."

Fuck. The woman must have taken it. That meant Gauhter would soon have the alchemist's journal and whatever was hidden in those magical illustrations. I didn't know what secrets the spelled pages contained, but the fact that Gauhter wanted them worried me. His magic was strong and evolving, and left a lot of dead bodies in its wake.

Chapter 25

⟶══⊙ ⊙══⟵

"This has to be the oddest thing that has ever happened in my morgue," Tamara said with a shake of her head as Remy climbed up onto one of the gurneys.

"It's really cold," he said, sitting on the gurney and staring dubiously at the shiny metal surface.

Tamara laughed. "Really? I've never had a customer complain before."

I let that one go. "Remy, you should lie down."

"Don't I need to sign a release or something? Maybe some sort of lost-and-found form?"

John, who was here as a witness, shook his head, but he didn't say anything.

"Briar recorded your witness statement on the drive here. Do you need more time to think this over? You burn your own soul's energy while you are in that body, but I don't think a few hours would make much difference," I said, keeping my voice pleasant, calm. He'd decided he wanted to do this, but I wasn't going to force it if he needed more time. He was about to save his soul but lose even the semblance of the life he'd been clinging to inside his stolen body. It was a hard decision.

"Maybe I should see Taylor first. Just in case," Remy said, starting to slide off the gurney. "There are so many things I never got to say."

"Kid, do you really want her last memory of you being this?" Briar asked from across the morgue where she was leaning against the wall. She had the tact of a charging rhino. "We need to get this over with. I want to interview the walking corpse upstairs."

I shot a glare over my shoulder at her but forced my features to soften again before I turned back to Remy. "You'll actually be much more recognizable once you're a ghost, but you won't be able to interact with the mortal world in the same way you do inside a body. I will try my best to ensure that you talk to her once this case is over."

Remy stopped sliding off the gurney and sighed, his shoulders dropping with the movement. Then he twisted, pulling his legs up, and lay down.

Tamara snorted under her breath. "I wish all corpses were so agreeable."

I shot her a look that was part amusement but mostly asked her to stop mumbling jokes loud enough for Remy to hear. I knew it was her way of dealing with a situation that made her uncomfortable—after all, most corpses didn't walk in and pick out their own gurney—but she wasn't helping. She gave me a shrug, the movement jerky with nerves.

"I'm ready," Remy said, and closed his eyes, looking for all the world like any other inanimate corpse.

I nodded to Tamara, who stepped closer to the gurney.

"Before Alex begins, I'm going to do a very quick sweep for spells, okay?" Tamara asked as she lifted her hands, palms flat, several inches above Remy's still form.

He didn't open his eyes as he nodded his consent.

She moved her hands slowly through the air over his body, working from head to feet. Once she reached the bottom of the gurney, she shook her head, biting her plump bottom lip as she looked up at me. "I almost sense something. Like there is a spell I can't quite wrap my senses around, but nothing blatant. Nothing that screams magic."

Which was what I'd suspected because that was all I could pick up as well, at least with my shields closed, but while I might have been a skilled sensitive, Tamara was quite possibly the strongest in Nekros. There had been a chance she would have sensed something I couldn't. She stepped back, and I took her place by the edge of the gurney.

I opened my shields, reaching for my grave magic. It took a moment to gather enough to be usable—I'd really been burning through it quick the last few days. I reached out with the magic, slipping it into the corpse on the gurney. The magic easily crept through the dead skin and sank deep, trying to fill all the space. I kept the trickle slow, trying not to oust Remy's soul before I could feel around a bit. His soul was so loosely connected to the body, I almost ejected it by accident before I managed to stop the slow dribble of power.

I opened my eyes, my magic whipping around me. The body Remy was wearing hadn't been dead long, maybe ten hours at most, so the decay I could see in my gravesight wasn't as horrible as it could have been. Beneath the rotting flesh, Remy's soul glowed a brilliant yellow, almost vibrating as it tried to cringe away from where my magic filled the body around it. Death had told me the spell was on the souls. I searched for it, and even gazing across several planes of existence, I nearly missed the seven small clumps of magic sewn into the soul at Remy's chakra points. They loosely secured the soul to the shell. I mentally reached for the magical suture in the center of Remy's forehead. The spell was the tightly constructed magic I'd come to expect in this case, and while I could feel the familiar signature of power, untangling how the spell worked was beyond me.

On the gurney, Remy's features had formed into a sharp grimace, and his soul writhed, jerking against the spell I was examining as my focus brought my own grave-chilled magic closer. I pushed with my magic, giving his soul the smallest shove. The magic binding him to the body snapped and his soul popped free of the dead body it had been trapped inside.

Remy shimmered for a moment, and then he solidified, the ghost looking exactly like Taylor's picture of him.

"Whoa," he said, running his hand over the football jersey he wore. "That was different . . ." He looked down at the body he'd vacated and his mouth twisted into a frown as he stared at the now-truly-lifeless body. "So that's her? Man, why didn't you tell me what a mess I'd made of her hair? I bet she would have been upset to know her body was walking around looking such a mess. I should have taken more care." He glanced at me. "When you find out who she was, you'll let me know, right? It seems wrong to not even know her name."

I nodded and then motioned that the morgue attendant could cover the corpse. The inevitable rapid decay was not evident yet, but I guessed it would be soon.

"Is it done?" Briar asked, pushing off the wall.

Remy walked toward her. "What, you can't tell?"

She never glanced his way.

I nodded to Briar, and John ran a hand down his mustache.

"The paperwork on this is going to be a nightmare," he said, turning to leave.

"Tell me about it," Tamara groused as she followed the gurney into the cold room.

Remy gaped between the two retreating figures. He had his back to Briar and didn't notice her walking until her shoulder passed through him. He screamed, staring at the spot where, for a brief moment, they'd occupied the same space on different planes. I had it on good authority that it didn't actually hurt ghosts when people walked through them, but it did feel odd.

"They can't see you, Remy," I said.

He whirled around. "Why can't they see me?"

"Like I said earlier, you can't interact with the mortal world the same way without a body. Did you ever see a ghost when you were alive? Most people can't."

His mouth fell open, as if he was going to say something, but no words came out. He looked around and seemed to see his surroundings for the first time. I'd closed my shields already, but I could guess what he saw—a wasted and rotted version of the mortal world.

"This sucks," he finally said. "Put me back."

I shook my head, the movement small, sympathetic. "I can't."

"I take it Remy's ghost stuck around," Briar said, and I nodded to her.

"As long as he avoids collectors, he can remain in the land of the dead as long as his energy lasts. Now that he's not burning it fueling a dead body, that could be a very long time." I said it more for his benefit than hers.

He stared at me, his expression torn between incredulous and angry. "You took me out and can't put me back? This sucks. What good is being stuck in purgatory forever if Taylor can't even hear me?"

"I told you that I would help you talk to her."

Briar, who could only hear my half of the conversation, glanced at her watch. "Can you wrap this up, Craft? I'd like to go question our guest and see if we can't get a line on Gauhter."

"Yes," Remy said, crossing his arms over his chest. "Let's go find Gauhter. He at least can put me back in a body."

I didn't think that was likely to happen, but I didn't argue with the ghost. I let Briar lead the way back out of the morgue as we went to deal with yet another dead body.

I once again sat in an uncomfortable chair in one of Central Precinct's interrogation rooms. At least this time I sat on the interviewer side, not the interviewee. An empty chair sat to my right, waiting for Briar once she doused the theoretically sleeping dead guy with an antidote for the potion her foam dart had showered him with earlier. Remy was in the observation room, sulking. John and Jenson were also in the observation room, despite this being their case. I wasn't sure exactly how they'd lost out to Falin, but the fae stood at my back, looking intimidating.

He'd spent the time I'd been in the morgue on the phone with one of his agents who'd been running down license plates. Most of the plates in the lot hadn't matched the make and model car they were registered to, but it at least gave us a starting point and a partial list of names. Two of those names we recognized: Annabelle McNabb and Rodger Bartlett. We weren't sure yet if we had plates that matched the body Remy had temporarily resided in, or the sleeping corpse in front of me, but Falin's agent was working on pulling driver's license photos that corresponded to registrations. She'd send us a file with them to review soon. Until then, the best way to find out more information was to question the corpse in front of me.

As I sat in the chair, I let my senses stretch to the corpse across the table. It was coated in a thin sheen of magic that was easily recognizable as the cocktail Briar had used to knock him out. Under that, I could sense a preservation spell, the kind you'd put on food to keep it from rotting. That was interesting. I hadn't sensed such a spell on any of the other walking corpses. Of course, by the feel of him, this corpse was older than any of the humans I'd encountered while they'd still been inhabited by souls. Not quite as long dead as the two victims from the car wreck, but older than Rodger, the corpse I'd been able to feel on the street. Rodger hadn't had a preservation spell on him. I wasn't sure about the two girls, as they'd been collected before we found their bodies, but this fit with the evolution we'd seen in the necromancer's magic. I definitely would have felt this corpse from a distance, while the newer victims, like Remy, had been caught at the moment of death, keeping the grave essence rising from them to a minimum.

Briar dripped two drops of the liquid from a small bottle on the corpse's forehead. Then she capped the bottle and retreated back around to our side of the table, sliding smoothly into her chair.

"How long before we know if it works?" Falin asked.

"If it works on the walking dead? It shouldn't take—"

Her last word cut off as the corpse's eyes flew open and he tried to jump to his feet. His hands were hand-cuffed behind the chair with a chain leading to a loop bolted into the ground, so that didn't go so well for him. He got his feet under him, but his top half didn't follow and he crashed back into the chair. As the chair was also bolted to the ground, it didn't budge. If he'd needed to breathe, he would have been sputtering, but as he didn't, he just looked stunned. His gaze finally landed on us on the other side of the table, and his eyes narrowed.

"Who the hell are you?"

"We were actually going to ask you the same question," Briar said, leaning back in her chair with a casualness she couldn't possibly feel.

The guy looked around the room, assessing. Then his gaze returned to us, studying first Briar in her biker leathers, me with my grave-wind-tossed hair and my coat on despite being indoors, and then finally his gaze moved to Falin in khakis, his jacket off so his shoulder holster stood out in stark contrast to his white oxford shirt. Falin at least looked like a detective type.

"What is this? Where am I?" the corpse asked Falin. Apparently Briar and I had been dismissed. One glance at Briar made me think this guy would probably regret that action.

"You're in an interrogation room at Central Precinct," she said.

The top of his lip curled into a sneer. "You can't keep me here. I've done nothing illegal. Am I under arrest? I haven't been read my rights."

Briar gave a bark of a laugh, the sound loud and abrupt enough to make the guy actually look at her. She leaned forward, making herself impossible to ignore.

"You," she said, moving into his personal space, "don't have any rights. You are a corpse."

The guy looked like he was trying to swallow something that wouldn't go down. Then he pursed his lips and lifted his chin in a stubborn tilt as he met Briar's gaze. "You're trying to scare me, but it won't work. I'm a pre-law major. There is no precedent for stripping me of my rights just because I'm . . . uh, 'mortally challenged.' That's discrimination. Either charge me with something or let me go."

The revelation about him being a pre-law major surprised me. Of course, maybe I was judging him too much by the corpse he was wearing. He was a big guy, easily six seven and wide with muscle. He had a skull tattooed on the top of his shaved head, and more tattoos peeking out of the collar and sleeves of his shirt. When Briar had been handcuffing him, I'd noticed he even had words on his knuckles, though I hadn't been able to tell what they spelled. He was a tough guy with a big voice who filled a lot of space . . . but that was just the shell. We had no idea who the soul inside was.

Briar cocked an eyebrow. "Actually, my directive as an MCIB investigator includes terminating any zombie, ghoul, or shambling dead monster I encounter, as well as determining the potential threat of any animated inanimate creation or magical constructs that could pose a threat to the human or witch populace. I'm pretty sure it would be within my legal scope to forgo this interview and make sure you are true dead and no threat, but as you are capable of speaking, I thought I'd give you a chance to do so." The smile that spread over her face as she spoke was wolfish, showing too many teeth. It knocked the cocky defiance right off the corpse's broad face. She pressed her advantage. "And if you really want criminal charges, how about we charge you with possession of stolen property—which would be that body you're wearing. Or would what you've done be more like kidnapping and murder?"

The man's eyes widened, the whites showing all the way around his dark irises. "I'm the victim here."

"Really? You're not acting like a victim. In fact, when we found you, you were in the process of coercing a murder victim to perform crimes for you." She was stretching it a bit, but by the way the man's frantic eyes scanned the room as if he'd magically find some way to escape, she was making an impact.

The man looked to me and then glanced at Falin, the expression on his broad face a clear plea for help. We both remained silent, offering him no assistance. The corpse turned back to Briar.

"I'm the victim here," he repeated.

Briar leaned forward. "Then you should be happy we liberated you from Gauhter and be anxious to tell us everything you know about him and his operation."

The man stared at her for a long moment, not saying anything, his mouth a thin line as he considered her. Finally he said, "Of course. What do you want to know?"

I fought the urge to turn and look at Falin's expression, to see if he felt that the corpse's quick flip toward helpfulness was too abrupt and insincere. Personally, I wasn't buying it, but I schooled my features blank and continued silently studying the corpse.

"What's your name?" Briar asked, picking up her pen and pulling her pad of paper closer.

"Bruiser."

I managed to swallow my laugh but couldn't hold back my disbelieving, "Really?"

That earned me the smallest twitch of a frown from Briar and a glare from the corpse. I'd already started interrupting, I might as well continue.

"Your mama looked at you after birth and thought, this adorable newborn looks like a Bruiser?" I asked.

The corpse cringed, looking away from me.

"Your *real* name," Briar said.

His answer was mumbled too quiet to hear the first time. It took some prompting to get him to speak up, but he finally sighed and cleared his throat.

"Tiffany. Tiffany Bates."

Or, I guess, *her* throat. I blinked, readjusting pronouns in my head, and evaluating differently why she randomly kept staring at Falin.

"Just so there is no misunderstanding, with a name like Tiffany, you mean that your real body was female before your soul got shoved into that one?" Briar asked.

Tiffany nodded, the movement sharp, like it was almost a cringe.

"Gauhter really likes throwing souls into opposite-gendered bodies, doesn't he?" Briar muttered as she jotted Tiffany's name on her notepad. It was more an observation than a directed question. Despite that, Tiffany shrugged, lifting her huge shoulders as much as she could with her hands cuffed behind her.

"It motivates people. You put an old guy in a young man's body and he might decide he hit the fountain of youth. But you start screwing with people's basic identity, like whether they are male or female, and they get desperate to get back in their own bodies. Gauhter could guarantee good behavior by ransoming a person's own body."

We'd technically already gathered some of that from Remy, but the fact Gauhter intentionally made the souls he stole more uncomfortable than he had to fanned a new flame of anger in me.

"So that's why you were working for him? Because he's holding your body ransom?" Briar asked.

"Yeah," Tiffany said, but her gaze hit the table.

Briar glanced at something in her palm. She placed the small disc she'd been cupping onto the table. It was glowing an angry red.

"Do you know what this is?" Briar asked, and when Tiffany shook her head, Briar continued, "It's a lie detector charm. Guess what color it turns when you lie to me? If you're thinking red, you'd be right. So you're not working for Gauhter because he's holding your body ransom. Want to try that again?"

Tiffany glared at the little charm. It was green again, now that Briar had been the last one to speak.

"I," Tiffany started, and then cut off, frowning. It took her a moment to speak again, and when she did, her voice was barely a whisper, as if she couldn't admit what she was saying too loud. "I like this body. I don't really want my old one back."

"So then why work for Gauhter?" Briar asked. "Why not run away and live out your life as Bruiser?"

"Because I *want* to keep this body, and sometimes it needs a little . . . tweaking."

I stared at her. "But it's not your body. Don't you think the person it belonged to would rather you weren't walking around in it?"

Tiffany's frown deepened, but she didn't turn toward me. Instead she kept her gaze locked on the table as she shrugged, the movement stunted. "Gauhter never actually returned any of the bodies. I was just making the best out of a bad situation. People respect me in this body. No one whistles when I walk by, or tries to grab my ass. Instead they duck their heads and get out of my way."

"They fear you," I said.

She shrugged again. "But I feel safe in this skin. I can intimidate whoever I need. I can walk down the sidewalk without worrying about who else is on the street. I can—"

"Pee standing up?" Briar offered.

"Probably not," I said. "That body is dead, I doubt she pees."

Tiffany looked up long enough to shoot us both a glare.

"Hmmm. True," Briar said, as if she hadn't noticed the change in our interviewee. "But we are getting off topic. Do you know the name of the person whose corpse you're wearing?"

Tiffany shook her head, but she didn't look concerned about not knowing the name of the man whose body she wore. From what she'd said, I could guess she'd been a victim long before Gauhter found her, but her admission that she'd been willing to work with Gauhter in order to keep a murdered body made me feel far less sympathetic toward her than I normally would have. Hopefully we'd be able to identify the body by other means, like fingerprints or a missing-person file.

"Did you know many of the other people who had their bodies switched?" Briar asked.

"Yeah, most."

"Two girls, their bodies at least, with Gauhter's history no telling who was inside. They were found in and around a car belonging to a boy named Remy." Briar described what the two girls from this morning's wreck had looked like before their swapped souls had been collected. "Did you know them?"

Tiffany nodded. "Only by first names. James and Becky. They're dead?"

They'd been dead before the car crash, but now they weren't walking around anymore. At Briar's nod, Tiffany sagged. She might have been working with Gauhter, but she was clearly sad to hear about the passing of her companions.

"I knew it was bad news when they didn't check in. The newer bodies don't seem to have an issue, but the older ones, our reflexes aren't always right. Driving a car is . . . hard." She stared at the table, falling into a long silence.

"Tell us about Gauhter," Briar prompted.

Tiffany grimaced. "That's a really broad question."

"Okay, tell us where to find him," Briar said, impatience making her voice sharp.

Tiffany shrugged again.

I could practically hear Briar's teeth grinding. "You were picking up a book for Gauhter when we found you. Where were you supposed to take it?"

Another shrug, but there was a hint of the cockiness that had been present when the interview first started. She was playing us.

I wasn't the only one who noticed.

"Okay, this is getting us nowhere." Briar turned to face me. "Craft, remove Tiffany from that body."

I blinked at her, too stunned to reply.

"You can't do that," Tiffany sputtered, trying again to stand, to fight her cuffs.

"I can't. She can." Briar nodded at me.

Tiffany scanned my face again, and her jaw fell open. True fear showed in her eyes. "You're the lady on the news."

"Yeah."

"You'll be a lot more cooperative outside that body," Briar said, invading Tiffany's personal space again. "So unless you want to lose that tank of a corpse you're wearing, I suggest you pony up some real answers."

"I can't tell you what I don't know," Tiffany said, her tone a panicked whine, which sounded odd in the deep male tones.

"Then you better give us something useful," Briar said, tapping her fingers on the tabletop, the staccato beat impossibly loud as Tiffany looked between the two of us.

I was fairly certain Briar was using me as an idle

threat, but I wasn't sure what she'd do if Tiffany called her bluff. While Tiffany's body was dead, and it was true that I'd pulled ghosts out in self-defense and by accident in previous encounters, I wasn't comfortable ejecting Tiffany from her body just because she wasn't cooperating. That definitely felt like a moral gray area.

Tiffany looked from Briar to me. She didn't bother looking to Falin. He'd been a silent shadow behind me, making it clear he wasn't going to help her. An incredulous look passed over her features and she glanced down at the lie detector charm still sitting on the table. It hadn't changed colors when she'd spoken last, which was apparently a good reason to repeat herself.

"I can't tell you what I don't know." Tiffany gave what might have been intended as an apologetic smile. It came off smug. She was going to call Briar's bluff.

This was going to suck.

Briar turned to me again. "Alex?"

Crap.

"Can I speak with you a moment?" I asked Briar, which made her scowl at me.

"Just a moment," she told Tiffany, and then she stood, motioning Falin and me to the corner of the room. As she turned, she snatched the lie detector from the table.

As soon as all three of us had reached the corner, Briar activated a privacy bubble. "What's the problem, Craft?"

"For starters, we never discussed me popping her out of that body, and for another, I think it's a terrible idea."

"I'm with Alex on this," Falin said, nodding. "This interview will be much more difficult if most of us can't see or hear the person we are interrogating."

"Well, obviously we wouldn't want Tiffany out of the body permanently. We just need to scare her into co-operating."

I frowned at her. "Briar, I can't put her back. If I were to eject her—and that's a big *if* because with her being neither a threat nor willing, that feels a lot like, well, I guess it can't be murder as she's already dead, but assault at the very least—so *if* I were to eject her, she's out for good."

"Okay, okay. Keep her inside her stolen body, which, by the way, makes ejecting her a way of reclaiming stolen property. Maybe even recovery of a kidnapped person."

"Definitely a gray area," Falin said, and I nodded.

"How good an actress are you, Craft? Because I'm about to look very stern and I need to you to walk out of this corner looking resigned to get her out of that body."

"But we just said—" I started.

Briar cut me off. "I said acting, Craft. It's a bluff, but it has to be a good one, so do the creepy wind-from-nowhere and possessed-glowing-eye thing."

So push the bluff to the furthest possible point. I glanced at Falin.

"What do you think?"

He didn't speak as he considered it. After a moment he said, "This interview turned to threats quick, and she already called your bluff once. If she does it again, you're out of cards."

"But you've been hanging back," Briar said, a small smile spreading over her face. "Are you waiting to play good cop?"

He answered with a small twitch of his eyebrow. Briar turned back to me.

"Time to look duly cowed, Craft. Let's do this."

She dropped the privacy bubble and we headed back to the table. It wasn't hard to look like I was about to do something I didn't want to do.

"Last chance," Briar said as she slipped back into her chair.

Tiffany looked from Briar to me. Her eyes were wide, the whites shiny in the bright lighting of the interrogation room, but she remained silent.

"Okay, do it, Craft."

I opened my shields, letting my psyche straddle the chasm between the living and the dead. A frigid wind ripped through the room, tossing my curls and catching the notepad Briar still had sitting on the table, making the pages flip noisily. Tiffany stared at me, the horror written in her open mouth, bunched brow, and staring eyes. She looked away, as if not looking into my glowing gaze could stop my power. It couldn't, but as this was meant to be a bluff, looking away could lessen the intimidation.

I reached out and placed two fingers in the center of her forehead. It wasn't necessary, and if I hadn't spent the last few days exhausting my grave magic, it would have put me in danger of losing control, but the magic in me was sated so it behaved nicely. I let the smallest touch of the grave curl out from my fingers, spreading the chill of the dead over the broad forehead my skin touched. Not much; I knew from the previous walking corpses I'd encountered that the soul was not firmly attached to the body the way it would be in its own.

As I let the magic unravel, I searched for the spell binding Tiffany to her shell. It was easier to find than the one on Remy had been. The magical sutures were larger, sloppier, and in different spots. The spell tied her to the body at the head, heart, hands, and feet, and it looked like the spell had been reinforced in several places at least once. Tiffany had said she'd needed Gauhter for magical tweaking. More evidence that his ritual was evolving—but what was his end goal? A seamless soul swap? Why?

As the chill of my magic settled through her, her soul recoiled and Tiffany jerked, trying to get away from my touch. She bucked in the seat, ripping at where the cuffs bound her.

"I'll talk, I'll talk. What do you want to know? Please stop. Please."

I started to pull back, but Briar slammed her palm down on the table, the sound booming through the small room. "You had your chance. Now we'll question your ghost when you can't lie or avoid our questions. Craft, keep going."

That wasn't the least bit true, and Briar knew it. Which was probably why she'd hidden the lie-detecting charm.

"Let her go. She said she'd talk," Falin said, from behind me. *Good cop coming into play.*

I didn't hesitate or wait for Briar to push, but sat back, closing my shields. The wind immediately stopped, and Tiffany sagged in her chair.

"Thank you," she said, gazing at Falin like he was her savior.

"You're welcome. I expect you to answer the investigator's questions honestly and in full for my intervention." As soon as the words left his mouth, I could all but feel the electric charge in the air as the price he'd set for her debt wrapped around her.

Clever fae.

Tiffany nodded enthusiastically, likely not even realizing the binding her own words of gratitude had tied
around her. It had been well played. Very well played.

A wolfish smile spread across Briar's face as the realization of what Falin had just pulled occurred to her.
She gave him a quick nod of approval, and then she
straightened the notepad that had gotten tossed about
in the grave wind and looked at Tiffany. "Let's try this
again, shall we? Where were you supposed to take the
book?"

"I'm not sure. Honest! Rachael had those details."

"Rachael?" Briar asked, but I gasped. She turned to
look at me, a dark eyebrow lifting.

"Rachael Saunders," I said, the name jarring a memory of where I'd seen the face before. She'd looked
different in my office than when I'd seen her outlined
in a brilliant coating of magic in the woods, but now
that I'd put it together, I could have kicked myself for
not recognizing her earlier.

Tiffany frowned at me. "I only know her as Rachael.
They don't trust us. Not even me despite the fact that
I agreed to help in exchange for keeping this body."

Briar glanced at the charm concealed in her palm.
It glowed a cheery green. Tiffany was telling the truth.

"Do you have any idea where Rachael might have
planned to meet Gauhter?"

Tiffany shrugged.

Briar frowned at her. "Use your words."

"Gauhter has a lot of different places he uses," Tiffany said, and then looked surprised that she'd spoken.

Welcome to the binding compulsion of repaying a

debt to the fae. I almost felt sorry for her. Except that she seemed content to work with a bad guy and hide his secrets.

"Where are these places?" Briar asked.

Tiffany started to shrug, but then her mouth opened as if she couldn't keep the words back. "Some I think he rents. Some he just squats in for a few days at a time. He doesn't seem to stay in the same place for long. Though I heard them mention 'the cemetery' several times over the last week or so. Rachael mentioned it earlier today, so maybe that's where we were supposed to take the book, but they've never taken me to a cemetery before." The confusion on her face knotted to anger as she spoke, but she couldn't stop herself from answering Briar's questions.

It didn't surprise me that Gauhter had never taken her to the cemetery before. She was still a corpse. She would get stuck if she ever passed the gates.

"Which cemetery?" Briar asked.

If Tiffany answered, I didn't hear her. A tingling feeling crawled over my flesh, like a spider creeping up my arm, except the feeling was everywhere. Then it intensified, no longer a tingling, but a burn, like I'd spontaneously caught fire.

I pushed away from the table, trying to stand, but tripped backward over my chair. I landed on my ass, all the air rushing out. Lack of air was the only reason I didn't scream. I was on fire. I was burning.

Except there were no flames.

There was smoke. Though it wasn't coming from stinging flesh but from my charm bracelet. *The charm Derrick gave me.*

This was the spell he'd given it to me to protect against. Gauhter had finally used my personal items as a focus to send his attack.

"What the hell, Craft?" Briar said, staring down at where I was trying to get my legs under me.

"Spell. Fire," I managed to get out.

Falin knelt beside me. He grabbed my shoulders, and I felt cold pour down his hands, into my skin. It wasn't the chill of the grave, but the cold of snow, of winter.

It didn't help. The fire kept trying to burn through the protection charm. Any second now it would make it, and I'd burn from the inside out.

I opened my shields. It was foolish, it gave the spell another way inside, but I didn't know what else to do. I wanted to see what was attacking me.

Aetheric energy washed over the world. The spell attacking me consisted of a tight network of red and orange magic spun into an angry net draped over me. Derrick's charm was a thin coating of green energy holding the aggressive spell at bay, but I could see that green light dimming, growing weaker.

I could barely breathe. The air seemed superheated as I tried to draw it into my lungs around the spell. I was going to ignite. Die.

I dropped the bubble that kept me from touching other planes. Raking my hand over my arm, I sank my fingers into the red and orange energy and tugged. A handful of malicious magic pulled free. I flung it away from me. It hit the tiled floor and sizzled, bursting into a small flame that immediately burned itself out in a puff of black smoke.

I grabbed at where the burning spell was trying to smother me and pulled off another handful. Then another. My fingers felt like they were blistering. Small smudges of ash circled me. But my face was clear, no longer burning. And my arms. My chest.

At some point I realized it wasn't just my hands pulling the spell free. Death knelt beside me, pulling the spell apart with his fingers. I must have been in true danger because the spell Death had tied to my life force only called him when I was in mortal peril.

My hands were burning, the skin angry, red. My fingernails were blackened at the tips. But we'd pulled apart enough of the spell that the rest dissolved, unable to sustain itself. As the burning along my body dissipated, I collapsed forward onto my hands and knees. I lowered my head to the cool tile floor, sucking down air that was no longer threatening to boil my lungs.

I realized it was snowing. Falin had conjured or glamoured snow in the interrogation room. I wasn't sure which. It probably hadn't helped, but it had been a nice effort and the cool flakes felt good as they touched the bare skin of my face.

Death ran a hand through my hair, murmuring soothing words in a language I didn't know. He placed a cool hand on the back of my neck. It felt good against my still-too-hot flesh.

Death. Death was here. In the room with a walking corpse. As if my thoughts had drawn attention to her, I felt Death's hand still. His gaze locked on Tiffany, his hazel eyes narrowing.

"Leave her. We're still questioning her," I whispered, the words almost lost against the tile where my cheek still rested.

Death heard me anyway. He glanced down at me, regret in his eyes, but shook his head. "I can't."

My head shot up. "Circle Tiffany."

The words came out hoarse. Falin and Briar only looked at me.

"Get Tiffany in a circle," I said, looking directly at Briar. "Now."

She didn't question me but vaulted over the interrogation table to land beside the massive body that held the ghost we didn't want collected. She placed her hand to the ground by Tiffany's feet, and magic snapped through the air. She hadn't drawn a circle, but one crackled into place around her and Tiffany. It was impressive. I couldn't have done it.

Death scowled, the look one of the most serious I'd ever seen on his face. "Alex, what have you done?"

"Protected my lead," I said around shaky breaths.

"That's a dead body. That soul can't stay in there." He rose to his feet effortlessly, taking a step forward.

"You're right. But we need more time. The guy who just sent a killing spell after me? She's our best bet for finding him. Please, we just need more time."

Death looked away from me. "You'll find another lead."

"That's the second spell he's sent for me today. I don't think I'll survive a third." The naked plea in my voice was clear even to my own ears, and I imagined I was a sad sight, slightly singed and still on my knees surrounded by melting snow and charred tiles. I didn't care. I needed him to understand why this was so important. This wasn't just me asking as his girlfriend for him to bend the rules and reveal secrets like his name because the secrets hurt. There were lives at stake. More than just mine.

Death hesitated. Then he squeezed his eyes shut. My chest constricted as I realized he wasn't going to give us time to question Tiffany. He was bound by rules and duties, and even if he'd just disregarded both by helping me destroy a killing spell, he still had to follow most of those rules.

To hell with that. He chose to break the rules all the time. Our entire relationship was against the rules. I wasn't asking him to forget about Tiffany's soul forever. I needed an hour. And he wouldn't give me that. Gauhter's spell had failed, and once the necromancer realized I'd survived, he was likely to send another wave. Next time it could kill me. And I likely wouldn't be the only victim if we didn't find him today. Gauhter's experimentation was accelerating. How many more would die if we didn't locate him soon? But Death wouldn't even delay an hour on a soul that had been walking around in a dead body for more than a week already. That stung.

"I can't, Alex. Now that I've seen her. I can't leave her here." He didn't say he was sorry about that fact, though I could hear the regret in his voice. "I'll keep an eye on you. If he sends another spell . . . I will be there. But I have to take this soul now."

He started forward.

Briar was kneeling on the ground inside the barrier, drawing a true circle. I didn't know how strong the one she'd spontaneously erected was, but circles needed something physical to cling to. One created without something to cement it would be weak, prone to shattering if hit with too much. I doubted it would keep Death out long.

I had to stall him.

I jumped to my feet and grabbed his arm. I almost screamed as my blistered fingers touched him, but I didn't let go.

He turned and frowned at me. I couldn't hold him back physically, I knew that. I wasn't strong enough, especially when my fingers barely agreed to move in their damaged state. Death looked at my hand on his bicep. We were precariously close to a line. We both knew it. The only question was, what would be one step too many?

Death shrugged away from me. Pain shot through my hand as his arm jerked from my fingers. One of the newly formed blisters tore open, oozing hot liquid.

I didn't reach for him again. It wouldn't have done any good. I could at least let Briar see he was approaching, let her know where the threat was. She had to be almost done with her circle. It wasn't that big a circle.

I reached out with my magic and pulled Death into mortal reality. Once I would have had to be touching him to do it. I no longer needed that. I pulled, and everyone in the room could see him.

Falin stepped into Death's path, his daggers appearing in his hands. "Leave the witness be."

Death stared at him. "Get out of my way."

Falin didn't move. Behind him, a second, stronger circle snapped to life around Briar and Tiffany. Death's gaze moved past Falin to the much stronger circle, and his scowl deepened.

He turned and looked at me. He didn't say anything. He didn't need to. The line had been crossed. A trust betrayed.

He vanished.

No one moved. I held my breath, waiting for Death

to pop back into the room. He didn't. After a moment, Falin sheathed his daggers. I dragged myself over to Briar's chair—mine was still on the floor—and sank into it. I wanted to draw my knees to my chest. To cry. I didn't do either. I just put my hands on the table, palms up, and stared at my blistered fingers without seeing them.

Falin moved around the room. He picked up the fallen chair and sat down facing me. He took my burned hands in his and pressed cooling magic into my skin. John walked into the room, dropped a first-aid kit on the table, and then walked back out without a word. Falin didn't question it. He opened the kit and examined the contents before choosing a tube and rubbing the ointment on my blistered flesh. Once I was a sticky mess, he bound my hands with gauze saturated in a healing spell.

As Falin worked, Briar continued to question Tiffany from inside the circle. I caught enough to know that the shaken corpse was cooperating. Death might not have worn black robes or carried a scythe, but Tiffany had clearly recognized him for what he was. An end. One we'd prevented, at least temporarily. I didn't listen to most of what was said. Briar would fill me in later. I'd bought her time, and she'd use it.

I was stuck inside my own head, shaking from the adrenaline drop after escaping the spell, but dwelling on what had happened after. Had I done the right thing? The look in Death's eyes . . . I wanted to explain, but what could I say that I hadn't already? Tiffany sure as hell better give us the best lead in the world.

"Hey, Craft, think it's okay if we come out of the circle now?"

I looked up. I had no idea how much time had passed. Falin had long ago finished binding my hands.

I nodded. "Yeah. But you should move Tiffany somewhere secure. She needs to be inside a circle if you don't want another collector coming for her." Or in a graveyard or behind the type of ward Gauhter could make, though I had no idea how he'd accomplished it.

"We could drop her body down at the morgue like we did Remy."

I was too tired, emotionally and physically, to glare at her. I just shook my head warily. "If she doesn't agree to leave the body, I'm not forcing her out." I'd done too many things I wasn't proud of recently. I wasn't tacking on another.

Briar shrugged and unchained Tiffany's cuffs from the floor. "I guess you get a cell with a circle. Let's go."

Chapter 26

Twenty minutes later we were sitting in the conference room that had been transformed into Briar's temporary command center. Briar had updated the map with all the different locations Tiffany had provided. Officers had been dispatched to each, with orders to call if they found anything out of the ordinary. Falin's agents had created a cursory list of driver's license images to match the registrations from the cars in the rest stop lot. It was still incomplete, but we'd visually matched Tiffany's body to one, and the ghost I'd seen in Rodger's body to another. Past victims didn't narrow down where Gauhter might be now, so the list was currently being put on the back burner to be examined when we didn't have so many physical locations to search. Some FIB agents were also following up on the stolen bottle. The theft had been reported over two months ago — which fit with the age of some of the animals I'd seen in Gauhter's clearing of experiments.

Investigating the theft had apparently never been prioritized or followed up on before, so Falin had his agents reexamining the case with instructions to call if they found anything.

Now we were poring over the map evaluating which cemetery Gauhter might be using. Well, Briar, Falin, John, and Jenson were. I was sitting in a chair hugging my bandaged hands to my chest. It was only four, but I was so done with this day. The day wasn't done with me, though. I had to find Gauhter before he realized his spell hadn't killed me. Which meant narrowing down his most likely hideout.

Tiffany had provided us with the locations of safe houses she and the other corpses used, as well as a couple more ritual sites, but none were places Gauhter or the Saunderses did more than pass through. If the officers found more walking corpses, we'd question them. Or maybe they'd find a giant clue pointing us to Gauhter's actual base of operations, but I wasn't holding my breath. Right now, narrowing down which cemetery Rachael Saunders had planned to take the alchemy book to was our best lead.

"It can't be one in the center of the city. They are too public. Someone would have noticed," Falin said.

"True," Briar agreed, moving to mark the inner-city cemeteries off her list.

"Remember the tree? And the shack? He's excellent at illusion magic," I said, my voice sounding oddly hollow even to my own ears. "Or, *they*, I guess."

"Craft, we're supposed to be eliminating possibilities. And what do you mean by 'they'?"

I frowned, forcing my focus out of my head and onto Briar. "The magic. I've noticed since the first time I saw it that it is super dense and intricate. Almost amazingly so. I thought at first he was just that good, but when Rachael ran from the shack today, the magic she wrapped herself in was exactly the same shade. All the spells Remy carried were the same as well. As were both the fire spell that attacked me and the trap laid in my office. No matter how powerful the witch, that's a lot of magic to move around and cast in a short amount of time. Some of it could have been pre-cast, waiting in charms, but not all of it. I think Gauhter and the Saunderses are joining their magics to do these castings."

Briar's brow bunched as she considered it. "That would be exceedingly rare. Most magic won't meld."

"That's because most witches commune with only one or two colors of Aetheric energy. If a witch who uses one color releases it to someone who uses different strands"—I lifted my bandaged hands in a shrug—"they don't meld. I mean, it still works, but the finished spellwork comes out patchy, weak. The merged magic is still bigger and can be cast faster, but the spells aren't particularly good. But if you have a group of witches with harmonious magics, and they are capable of putting their egos aside and releasing it to one skilled witch . . ." I shook my head. "The spellwork I've seen is impressive." And I'd seen more than most. Several electives on Aetheric theory in school guaranteed that. Unfortunately, they hadn't improved my own poor spellcasting ability much.

"Are we sure Rue Saunders isn't Gauhter? We know Gauhter is fond of aliases," Falin said, frowning at the possibility I'd laid out.

Briar was the one who shook her head. "I saw him. He doesn't match the description of Gauhter."

"So these were clients of yours, Alex?" John asked.

"Do you know what they would want that would encourage them to work with a necromancer?"

"Their daughter," Briar and I said in unison.

The men in the room gave various looks of confusion, and I sighed.

"They wanted me to find their daughter's ghost, which was an odd request. Gauhter must have promised to put her ghost in a new body." And the couple I'd seen in my office were probably desperate enough to jump at that chance. A witch giving their magic to someone else took trust or desperation; it was hard on the body and on the mind. But for the promise of having a child returned? I could see a parent jumping on the possibility.

I pulled out my phone and brought up a browser, but pecking out letters on the touch screen was impossible with my hands covered in gauze.

"What are you doing?" Briar asked.

I thrust the phone toward Falin. "Pull up the Nekros City newspaper."

He tried to take the phone from my gauze-bound hand, but I didn't give it up, so he settled for pecking out words with his pointer fingers while I held the phone. When it loaded I said, "Pull up the obits and type in 'Katie'—no, that has to be a nickname. Try different spellings for 'Catharine Saunders.'"

It took him several searches, but finally he nodded and I pulled the phone back.

"Kathryn Saunders, age six, passed into the arms of angels on November first." I scrolled down the page, scanning over the obligatory list of people she was survived by and the gushing report of her character typical of any obituary listing. "Here we go, it says a viewing was held on November fourth at noon followed by a graveside service at *South Cemetery*." I looked up. "That's where we should look."

Briar nodded, but John's mustache pulled downward with his frown. "It's as good a lead as any, but I don't think we should focus solely on that cemetery." John turned to the map. "This cemetery is the closest to the northeast wilds where the bulk of Gauhter's activity has been. It is also a very viable option. But it could be any of them. We should send teams to systematically search all the cemeteries in and around the city."

"Sure," Briar said, already on her feet. "But you still have men at the rest stop and shack. And you sent more to the locations Tiffany gave us. Manpower is running pretty thin. Craft is right, Gauhter tends to use illusions, which means each team is going to need a sensitive or to do a sweep by hand with a spell detector. It's going to take time to search all the cemeteries. We have our own sensitive." Briar nodded to me. "So we should join the search, and I think Craft's lead is the most likely."

"Then I'll take a team to the cemetery in the northeast," John said.

Briar headed for the door. "Get your men organized and briefed. We will head out now since South is one of the farthest cemeteries. If anyone finds anything that seems to point to the necromancer's presence, I'm their first call. Craft, Andrews, you two coming?"

And we were off to look for a necromancer, in a cemetery. Where else?

Rianna hadn't called me back yet, so I called her again as Falin drove toward South Cemetery. Voice mail, again. I dialed the Tongues for the Dead office next. Considering the damage the office had taken, I wasn't sure anyone would be there, so I was pleasantly surprised when Ms. B's gruff voice answered.

"Tongues for the Dead, where the grave holds no secrets."

Well, it was better than the line she'd been using the last time I'd called. I decided not to mention it. "Hey, Ms. B, it's Alex. Is Rianna in the office? She's not answering her cell."

"No. She ran off to chase a lead before lunch. It's getting late. She's probably back at the castle by now. Reception is iffy there. Is there something you need?"

"True," I said, but it wasn't like Rianna to not return calls. "I wanted to ask her about the case she's working. It appears to be tied into mine. Do you think you could scan the contract her client signed and e-mail it to me? It probably won't lead to anything as he was the victim of theft, not our bad guy, but you never know."

Ms. B grunted. "Sure. It might take me a minute to locate. Rianna's filing system leaves even more to be desired than yours."

"Great," I said as way of thanks, ignoring the insult tacked on the end. Ms. B was a brownie; anything short of perfect organization was a mess to her. Then another thought occurred to me. "Also, the clients I saw but didn't accept a few days ago, Rue and Rachael Saunders. Do we have any information on them from when they booked the appointment?"

I heard the sound of her tapping something on her keyboard, one keystroke at a time. We'd been looking for a keyboard that she could learn to type on, but they didn't make many options for someone slightly smaller than your average toddler.

"Looks like all we got was a phone number," she said after a few moments. "Will that help?"

"Can't hurt," I said, and she read it off to me. As I couldn't exactly take notes with my hands heavily bandaged, I called the number out to Briar as Ms. B read it to me. She punched it into her own phone before repeating it back to me.

"Anything else?" Ms. B asked, her gruff tone making it sound like my call was inconveniencing her. I didn't take it to heart.

"That's it. I'll see you back at the castle tonight." I exchanged my good-byes and then twisted in the seat so I could see Briar. "So can we trace the Saunderses' phone or anything now that we have their number? Get a GPS fix or something?"

Briar frowned at me. "I sent it to Derrick; we'll see what he can gather for us. It might take some time, though."

I nodded, admittedly disappointed. Then I had nothing to do but wait impatiently for Derrick to get back to us, the e-mail from Ms. B to arrive, or to reach the cemetery. Or you know, Gauhter to send another spell after me.

The overcast day made the approaching dusk seem to arrive early, so that by the time we reached the gates of South Cemetery, the world was caught in an oppressive gray gloom. My eyes had mostly recovered from the abuse I'd put them through this morning, but as night approached, my normal night blindness set in, making me feel vulnerable. I didn't like being here this late. Half of me hoped we didn't find anything, even though I knew time was at a premium. Maybe I could sleep in a magic circle tonight . . . and stay there for the foreseeable future. That wouldn't work, and I knew it. Besides, my circles were too weak. Had I been inside one this afternoon, it would have crumbled under the assault of the spell Gauhter had sent. And as that spell had failed, I would bet the next one would be even stronger.

So I followed Briar and Falin into the cemetery.

South Cemetery was the oldest in Nekros, older than the city itself, and judging by some of the bodies I'd sensed here in the past, older than when the space had unfolded after the Magical Awakening. Though it was a large, beautifully maintained cemetery full of statues and ornate mausoleums, it wasn't a cemetery I particularly liked. Not anymore, at least. The last time I'd been here hadn't been for a job, but when I'd been kidnapped by skimmers who wanted me to tear a hole into the Aetheric for them. I'd escaped that night by pouring energy into the dozens of ghosts haunting the cemetery and using their sudden appearance as a diversion. Tonight, as we walked among the hulking mausoleums and granite angels, the cemetery was oddly quiet. Too quiet.

"Where are the ghosts?" I asked, stopping and looking around.

Briar and Falin turned, giving me twin quizzical looks.

"Last time I was here, you couldn't enter without at least a few of the dozens of ghosts following you around. I haven't seen one since we arrived." And I'd left the ghosts in this cemetery with a major power boost, so they should have been abundant and obvious.

Briar shrugged, looking unconcerned. Falin scanned the cemetery, but even if the ghosts had been present, he wouldn't have been able to see them.

"You picking up any spells, Craft?" Briar asked as she started walking again.

I shook my head. We were headed for the largest mausoleums on the grounds, which would be the easiest to conduct rituals inside. So far, I hadn't felt a hint of anything. I knew that at least one of the mausoleums had a secret underground bunker beneath it, but we'd already passed the crypt Bell and his flunkies had held me in, and I hadn't felt anything there either.

Briar paused, pulling her phone from her pocket. She answered, but almost immediately pulled the phone away from her ear and hit a button on the screen. "All right, Derrick, you're on speaker. What's the warning?"

"Are Alex and Falin with you?" Derrick asked from the other side of the phone.

I stepped closer so I could hear better, and Falin said, "We're here."

"Good," Derrick said, and I heard relief in his voice. "Whatever you do, the three of you do not split up, okay?"

I glanced at my companions. Don't split up. Well, it wasn't like I was planning to wander off on my own in the growing dark.

"Got it," Briar said. "Anything on that phone number?"

There was a pause, like he'd been about to say something else and her question had derailed him. "It was a prepaid line, untraceable. It's off at the moment. Nothing useful."

"Well, that sucks," I muttered.

"Alex." Derrick took a breath. Even through the phone it sounded heavy and strained, either like he was about to say something he wasn't sure he wanted to, or like whatever had happened before he made the call had frightened him. Either possibility was scary considering he'd clearly called because he'd just had a premonition. "Alex, you must hurry. Do not let sunset beat you."

The phone clicked as he disconnected before I could ask any questions. Briar tucked the phone back into her pocket, but I was still frowning at the spot where the phone had been.

"What happens at sunset?" I asked.

Briar shrugged. "You know as much as I do, Craft."

"I think I hate your partner. Why can't he give us more guidance than that?"

She gave me an annoyed look, and I got the feeling the subject of her partner was off-limits. "He does what he can. We stick together and we finish this before sunset. Now come on, we are burning what passes for daylight."

She was right; if we had to find the necromancer and his cronies before sunset, we didn't have much time left. The gloom made it feel later, but we had about forty-five minutes before the true moment of sunset.

We finished our search of the graveyard within fifteen minutes. We hadn't found any magic, and more alarming in my opinion, we hadn't found any ghosts. We had found dozens of disturbed graves, including little Katie's. I'd let my senses stretch. Each disturbed grave we found had been empty, no trace of the body that should have been inside. Our necromancer had been here, surely, but where was he now?

"It would have been helpful if Derrick had told us if we were at least looking in the right place," I grumbled as we walked back toward the entrance.

I was more than a little concerned about what would happen at sunset. Would that be when Gauhter would attack me with the next spell? As a fae, I'd be at my weakest at sunset, and the charm Derrick had given me had been exhausted by Gauhter's spell, so it would offer no more protection.

"Is that a light?" Falin asked, pointing somewhere in the back of the cemetery.

I turned, trying to pick out anything in the growing darkness, but I couldn't see a light. Briar on the other hand, spotted it.

"Let's check it out," she said, leading us in that direction.

There was a small growth of trees beyond the final gravestones and statues, and we walked through them, emerging on the other side to find a simple but old house. As Falin had said, there were lights shining through the windows.

"I think it must be the caretaker's home," Briar said as we approached the side of the house.

I shivered. "We're still inside the cemetery grounds." I lived with ghosts, but I wouldn't want to live locked inside cemetery gates with ghosts who couldn't leave and often weren't terribly happy about that fact.

Not that I'd seen a single ghost since we arrived.

It was likely that the occupant of the small house was the graveyard caretaker, but then, why hadn't he or she reported the disturbed graves? We were looking for a necromancer; a report like that would have been flagged. Just in case, we kept to the shadows as we scoped out the building.

There was a covered carport in the back of the property, about fifty yards from the house, and we ducked into it. Four cars were inside, two covered with tarps. The closest to us looked vaguely familiar. Falin pulled out his phone, scrolling through the pictures he'd taken at the rest stop earlier today. Sure enough, this car was one from that lot. The one that had been missing by the time the crime scene techs arrived.

"So Rachael is here." Equal parts excitement and terror pounded through me, making my heartbeat loud in my ears. We were close now. But that also meant they were close.

"Can you sense anything?" Briar asked me.

I let my senses stretch. We were too far from the house to get specifics, but in the distance I could feel the slightest tingle of familiar magic.

"Definitely the necromancer's magic. We should call the police."

Briar put in the call, giving a brief summary of our location and what we suspected we'd found. When she disconnected she glanced at her watch. "Twenty-five minutes until sunset."

Crap. The cops would never make it in time. Derrick had said we needed this finished before sunset.

Briar pulled her crossbow from whatever magic space she stored it in on her back. "We're going in."

Falin crossed his arms over his chest. "Alex is injured and a noncombatant."

"We can't split up," Briar said.

"And we can't wait," I finished for her, because those

were the warnings from Derrick. I didn't know what would happen if we ignored his warnings, but I was guessing it was worse than what would happen if we took his advice. Of course, everyone dying and the bad guys getting away was a worse scenario than only two out of three of us dying while stopping the necromancer, so there were degrees of better scenarios and sometimes they still sucked.

Before anyone had time to say more, the back door of the house opened, spilling light onto the lawn. A small figure, a child by the shape of her, stood silhouetted in the doorframe, peering out into the growing darkness.

We ducked into the cover of the carport as she hopped down the steps. The girl was barefoot and wore only a simple frilled dress despite the cold. Briar lifted her crossbow. Falin grabbed the shaft in one hand, forcing it to point to the ground.

"It's a child," he hissed.

"That's no child," I whispered. She was still at least forty yards away, but my skin felt like it wanted to crawl away rather than stay anywhere near the wrongness oozing off her.

She was a corpse, but it was more than that. The grave essence lifting from her was darker, almost sticky as it brushed my mind. She was something so much worse than any of the walking corpses we'd encountered.

I opened my shields a crack, hating how the inky darkness tried to slide in through the holes. It was too thick, my cracks too narrow and carefully made to let it in, but that didn't stop it from trying. I wanted to get a look at the small corpse skipping across the lawn.

"Cut the light show, Craft."

"In a moment." I focused on the girl. In my grave-sight, she was rotted and bloated, the curls that looked perfectly arranged in the mortal realm instead stringy, clumps missing from her exposed scalp. But that wasn't surprising. It was what was under her rotted body that shocked me.

Or really what wasn't under the decaying flesh. There was no soul. There was just a darkness that whispered of long-dead things and the wastes of the land of the dead. Whatever was inside that child, it had never been a person. Like the creature Briar and I had fought in the clearing, she was filled with something that didn't belong in the mortal realm.

"Katie, come back inside," Rachael yelled, appearing in the doorway her dead daughter had recently passed through.

The little girl stopped and turned, looking back at her mother. "But I'm hungry, Mama."

"You've had enough for today. Come back inside."

Katie didn't listen. She turned back toward the patch of woods that separated the house from the graveyard proper, resuming her skipping progress.

Rachael rushed out of the house. "Kathryn Lane Saunders, get back in the house this minute."

"But, Mama . . . I'm soooo hungry," the little girl said without stopping.

Her mother hurried across the lawn after her. "I'll see if Mr. Gauhter will give you one of his bottled ones. Just come back in the house."

A jolt of revulsion clawed my guts. One of Gauhter's bottled ones? We knew what Gauhter kept in bottles. Souls. I suddenly realized why there had been no ghosts in the graveyard.

Whatever was inside that little girl had *eaten* them.

"I guess they found their daughter," Briar said softly.

I shook my head. "She may call Rachael Mama, but there is no little girl under that skin."

Rachael had reached the middle of the yard now, but the little girl was already disappearing into the trees. Briar lifted her crossbow. Falin didn't try to stop her this time. There was a soft *ping* of the cord releasing, and then Rachael collapsed, doused in Briar's signature combination of an immobilizer, a sleeping spell, and a draught that could temporarily block a witch's ability to channel Aetheric energy. Rachael wouldn't be going anywhere or doing any magic for at least twelve hours without Briar's counterspell potion.

Briar swung her crossbow toward the woods, but the little girl had already disappeared. I could see the need to track the soul-eating corpse in Briar's eyes as she peered at the trees. I thought for sure the child would realize her mother was no longer following her and run back, raising the alarm when she saw her in a crumpled heap in the middle of lawn, but Katie didn't return. She was off to hunt ghosts. I hoped if any were left that they were hiding well.

"She can't leave the cemetery," I whispered. "The gates keep everything dead inside. We should focus on finding Gauhter."

Briar nodded, lowering her crossbow, and glanced at where Rachael was sprawled in the middle of the lawn. "One down, two to go." She moved to the front of the carport and nodded to the house across the lawn. "What spells are on the home?"

I shook my head. "It's too far. I can't tell anything specific from here."

"Then I guess we'll have to get closer. Come on."

We crept across the lawn, passing only a few feet from Rachael's unconscious form. The door to the house was open, light spilling into the yard, but I couldn't see anything beyond it. I could feel the wards on the house, though. I could have stopped there and told Briar what she wanted to know about the house, but there was no cover in the center of the yard. We couldn't tarry. Rachael's soul-eating daughter could return at any moment, or one of the men might wonder why Rachael hadn't returned yet. And, of course, sunset crept closer by the second. We had to hurry.

When we reached the house, Briar tucked herself into a shadow and all but disappeared. Falin also seemed to fade into the darkness, which had to be a glamour because unlike Briar with her dark clothing and hair, Falin had shocking platinum-blond hair that should have glowed in the dark. Instead he blended with the shadows clutching the house like he wasn't even there. I wished I could have done the same, but the best I could do was follow them as deep into the shadows as I could and squat with my back to the house, hiding behind the porch, and hope not to be spotted.

"The wards are both alarm and barrier," I said as I let my senses trace the magic I could feel pooling in the doorway. There was something sharp to it, potentially dangerous. "They might also be booby-trapped against intruders."

Briar cursed. "Well then, we can't sneak in, or just bust through them. We will have to disable them." She began pulling pouches from her pockets and then stopped, turning to me. "Craft, the other day you said you cut a door into a ward. Did it work?"

I didn't like where this was going, but I nodded. She gave me an evaluating look. "Think you could cut through this one?"

"Without triggering it?" I trailed my senses across the ward again. While strong, it was thin, no more than an inch thick. The fae dagger probably wouldn't trigger the ward; it was almost undetectable to witch magic. I moved to retrieve the dagger but then hesitated. My hands were still bound in gauze. *This is going to suck.* I held out my hands to Falin. "Unwrap me."

He didn't look pleased about the plan, but he didn't argue. When he finished, I studied my unbound hands, flexing my fingers. It hurt, but not as bad as I expected. The healing spells in the gauze had done a good job, and the blisters were already flat, the fluid gone. *Not bad.* I took the gauze from Falin and shoved it in my pocket—it was covered in my DNA and no way was I leaving it lying around when there was a necromancer sending killing spells after me. Then I knelt and pulled the dagger from my boot.

The hilt bit into the healing flesh on my fingers and palm, but I forced my hand to grip it and hold firm. I crept up the steps, stopping just outside the threshold of the open door. The ward buzzed along my skin. This was going to hurt so bad if I was wrong. *Here goes nothing.*

I plunged the dagger into the ward and waited. Nothing happened. No spells reached out to engulf me, no alarms sounded, and no necromancers rushed out of the house at me. So far, so good. I dragged the blade down the doorframe, mere centimeters from the wood. I followed the full outline of the doorway and floor, until the ward, no longer attached to anything, dissolved in the door opening. The threshold was bared.

I crouched by the edge of the porch. I couldn't see anything in the shadows, but I knew Briar and Falin were there. "Done."

A moment later, both joined me on the porch.

I stepped aside so Briar could take the lead. I thought Falin would go next, but he fell in behind me, covering my back. He had his gun drawn, pointed toward the ground, while Briar had her crossbow loaded with more of her nonlethal, triple-threat darts. I gripped my dagger, barely feeling the pain through the adrenaline pumping through my veins.

"Okay," Briar said, lifting the crossbow. "Seventeen minutes until sunset. Let's do this."

Chapter 27

The first room we entered was a small living room. Toys were scattered across the floor, most mangled beyond recognition. A child-sized plate of food sat untouched on the coffee table beside a cup filled with juice, also untouched. The living room opened to a small kitchen, the open floor plan making it easy to see that both rooms were empty. Briar pushed open a door to reveal a small bathroom, also empty. There was only one other door besides what had to be the front door. Briar pulled it open, sweeping her crossbow in both directions, but there were only stairs, no people.

The small house was a split-level, with stairs going both up and down. Briar glanced at me, a question in her cocked eyebrow. I let my senses stretch.

"There is magic in both directions. But there are dead things below us. A lot of dead things. Maybe buried in the basement. Maybe walking. I can't tell."

Briar nodded, and then she lifted a hand to indicate

we'd search the upstairs first. Her steps were soundless as she walked up the steps, as were Falin's behind me. I felt loud by contrast, every scuff of my boots seeming to echo in the narrow stairwell. When we reached the floor above, we found a small hallway with three doors.

The first door revealed a room with two beds, one larger and unmade, the other smaller and covered with a pink ruffled comforter and a filmy pink canopy. The Saunderses' room, but wherever Rue Saunders was, he wasn't here. The next door revealed another bathroom. I grabbed Briar's arm before she could open the third door.

Ward, I mouthed silently. Then I frowned, because the ward wasn't an alarm or a booby trap, but that strange configuration I'd felt in the clearing. The one that kept soul collectors out. Which was overkill, as we were inside a cemetery anyway, and soul collectors couldn't enter. I nodded, motioning that it was okay to cross the ward, and Briar pushed the door open softly, her crossbow at the ready.

This room wasn't empty, but its occupant also wasn't a threat, and Briar lowered her weapon a hair. At first I thought the woman in the bed was old, but as I looked at her, I realized she was probably only in her forties, illness having aged her. Magic surrounded the bed in heavy layers, tied through both artifacts and medical machines. The tablet that had been stolen from the museum hung above her head, heavy lines of magic connecting it to her. A basin of dark liquid saturated in magic had tubes trailing from it, leading to one of the bags connected to her IV pole. Runes were scrawled on the floor around the bed, as well as other arcane languages I couldn't recognize but could feel the power lifting from.

The woman was alive, but she shouldn't have been. The mix-match of machines and magic connected to her were keeping her heart beating, her lungs breathing, but the soul inside her was dim, tired. A chair sat beside her bed, close enough that a person sitting in it could talk to her, hold her hand. A pillow and blanket sat crumpled on the chair, as if whoever used it regularly slept in it, keeping vigil. A single silver-framed photo sat on the arm of the chair, showing the woman as she must have looked when she was healthier, wearing a wedding dress and smiling as she stood arm in arm with a man I guessed was a young Gauhter. We backed out of the room soundlessly, though she was beyond disturbing.

Once the door closed, we looked at each other.

"Well," Falin whispered as we crept down the stairs. "You surmised that the Saunderses are part of this because they wanted their daughter back. I think we just found Gauhter's motivation." He nodded back toward the dying woman's room.

I thought about the items Gauhter had stolen, the evolution of his ritual, of the fact that the earlier bodies felt very dead but the new ones had gotten increasingly better preserved—at least while a soul was still inside them. He'd been creating better and better vessels for the souls, probably in preparation of moving her to a new body once he perfected his ritual. He was trying to save his wife.

And in the process, he'd murdered at least half a dozen people.

We descended all the way to the basement level. The stairs ended at a door, which was closed. The moisture in the air thickened as we reached the bottom of the stairs. The smell of mold, mildew, and rot permeated the air.

Briar glanced at me before reaching for the door-knob.

"No wards. But a lot of magic. And a lot of dead things." I shivered, the grave essence tracing over my flesh like a pair of frigid hands. It was the same dark, inky essence I'd felt coming from the soul-eating child. Which meant the dead things I felt weren't buried but were walking around. And animated with things that had never been meant to exist in this plane.

"Thirteen minutes," Briar whispered, then shoved open the door.

Chapter 28

I was expecting darkness, but as the door crashed open, light from a dozen lamps flooded out, blinding me momentarily. Briar didn't have the same issue. I heard the *ping* of her crossbow release before I even had time to blink. It pinged again as I squinted into the room, which was actually rather dim, I realized, as my eyes adjusted.

The two foam darts, though they'd been perfectly aimed, hung in midair several feet from their intended targets. The potions in the darts, which were designed to splatter the target, were instead dripping down the invisible barrier of the magic circle the darts were caught in. Two stunned male faces stared at us from several feet behind the suspended darts. A dark cauldron stood between them, and beside it, bound to a chair, sagged the form of a woman. Her back was to us so all I could see was the slump of her shoulders and her red curls caught in a dingy cloth that must have been used to gag her.

"Who the hell are you?" Rue Saunders yelled, taking a step toward the edge of the circle.

The other man, presumably Gauhter, caught his arm.

"We are at a delicate transition. We must finish." He turned back to the cauldron, consulting the book he held in his hand. A book that looked a hell of a lot like the alchemist's journal. In the cauldron, something moved, lifting what looked like a half-formed arm, the skin translucent and clinging to bones that didn't appear quite sturdy enough.

A homunculus.

We rushed into the room. The men were behind a circle, but circles could be overloaded. The process had already started, sparks of magic breaking in lightning flashes around where the potion had spilled on the barrier. Briar shot the circle again, this time with a steel-tipped incendiary round. Fire crawled over the circle, sending more flashes of light through it, but the barrier held.

"FIB," Falin called out. "I suggest you drop the circle and surrender." He lifted his gun and aimed at Saunders. "There is no magic in these bullets, and your circle won't stop them."

As he spoke, I was still staring at the woman in the chair. She looked just like . . . "Rianna?"

Her head jerked up at the sound of her name, and she twisted, the one green eye I could see wide with terror, the other swollen shut. Blood dripped from her nose onto the gag. I hadn't noticed what looked like another shadow in the back of the circle before, but now I could make out Desmond's hulking furry shape at the edge of the corner. His paws and muzzle were bound with duct tape. A dark pool of blood had gathered around him.

"That's Rianna," I yelled, running toward the circle. I wasn't sure what I would do when I reached it, throw everything I had into it most likely, but I had to get to her. Derrick had said I had to beat the sunset. Now I knew why. Rianna would die if she wasn't in Faerie at sunset.

Gauhter lifted his hand and made a swatting motion in the air. Magic crackled. Not a spell initiating, but magic breaking.

"He just collapsed a circle," I yelled, turning in the direction from which the discharge of magic had originated. Briar and Falin followed my lead.

All the lights were in the part of the basement where Gauhter and Saunders were working. The rest was lost in shadow, including the area where I'd felt a circle collapse. A part of the basement where I could feel the dead waiting.

As the containing circle broke, the smell of decomposition intensified a dozenfold, spreading like a choking miasma through the underground area. Bile rose in my throat, but I didn't dare flinch or turn away. I couldn't see what was coming, but I could feel it.

Briar clearly had the opposite issue.

"Fucking zombies," she yelled, lifting her crossbow and releasing two shots back to back. "Why can't I ever encounter a necromancer without fucking zombies."

Two bodies exploded into flames as her shots hit. The light from the fire provided enough illumination that I could finally see what I'd only felt before. I almost wished it hadn't.

The dead heading for us weren't corpses with their time stopped like the ones piloted by the ghosts, or even well preserved like the soul-eating child outside. These were rotting corpses, mad with hunger. They ran toward us, scrambling over each other. Some dragged themselves, their legs too decayed to carry them. All stared at us with cloudy or missing eyes, emanating hunger because we had something they wanted. Our living souls.

Briar lit up two more. They kept moving several steps, even once already on fire. They didn't burn as well as ghouls—too juicy. But after a couple of steps, the incendiary rounds did their job, and the zombies fell.

Falin fired repeatedly, but body shots did nothing, and it took too many head shots to stop one. He emptied his magazine and only dropped three of the corpses. With a curse in the musiclike language of the fae, he holstered the gun and drew two daggers as long as my forearm. I had my dagger in my hand as well, but I wasn't keen on getting close enough to use it. I backed away as the zombies charged nearer. Briar incinerated another, but they just kept coming.

"Any truth to the fact that a zombie bite makes you a zombie?" Falin asked, as he made a wide slash with the dagger, decapitating the zombie closest to him.

"Myth." Briar kicked a zombie, knocking it back so she had time to reload her crossbow. "But flesh-eating bacteria tends to breed in their mouths."

Falin slashed out with the dagger, and another zombie fell, viscera flying. "I'll keep that in mind."

Zombies burst into flame or fell headless, but more took their place. They pressed in closer, too close for Briar to keep incinerating them without catching fire herself. She pulled a short sword from her back and kicked at the dead bodies, trying to open enough space that she could swing it. Falin was facing similar issues. Two slipped around Briar, headed for me. I considered the dagger in my hand. It was eager to be used, but even it knew it wasn't up for this fight.

I threw open my shields. The zombies paused. I felt the moment they all turned, sensing me as something new. Different. Roy once told me that when I straddled the chasm between the living and the dead I lit up like a sun in the land of the dead. These zombies had never seen a sun before.

They forgot about Briar and Falin, shambling and scurrying toward me. Now that my shields were open, I could feel each of them individually. There were still nearly three dozen up and walking.

The first one reached me. I thrust out my hand and pushed. Not with muscles or grave magic, I pushed with the part of me that touched different realities. I shoved the corpse into the land of the dead. It crumpled into ash and blew away in the wind whirling around me. I did the same to a second. A third. A zombie charged into the space where I'd disintegrated the first, and its skin fell away, followed by muscles. It dropped to the ground, only inanimate bone before I even had time to touch it. I wasn't just pushing the zombies into the land of the dead, I was pushing the reality around me. I didn't have time to think about it or try to fix it. I had to keep moving, keep pushing. Flames burst from near Briar; she'd used the distraction to get enough space to use incendiary spells again. Falin was a pale blur of movement to my side, zombies falling at his feet. And I just kept pushing the corpses into the land of the dead, accelerating decay.

It seemed to go on forever, but when the last zombie fell, sunset had not yet hit. I glanced down at my watch, but it was gone. As were the sleeves of my coat and my sweater. Small decayed bits of fabric still clung to my shoulders, but my arms were bare aside from my charm bracelet, which was badly tarnished, several of my charms made of less permanent material missing, presumably rotted away. I'd deal with it later.

"Time?" I asked, turning back to the circle where Saunders and Gauhter stood, their heads pressed together as they conjured magic.

"Four minutes until sunset," Briar called back.

I hadn't closed my shields, so I could see the magic swirling around the two men. It whirled in a tightly woven ball, growing larger and larger and feeding down into the cauldron between them. Gauhter was the one weaving it, Saunders freely surrendering his magic to the other man. Another tendril of the magic was tied to Rianna, draining energy from her life force into the homunculus. The shimmering ball of orange and red magic sank to the thing moving in the cauldron. If it reached the homunculus . . . Rianna would die. Her soul might move to the homunculus, but her body, her real body, would die. I had no doubt.

"Shoot Gauhter," I yelled.

Out of an MCIB investigator, an FIB agent, and a private investigator, I was the least authorized to make that command, but Falin didn't question it and Briar didn't contradict it. Falin pulled his Glock, slammed a fresh magazine in place, and pulled the trigger.

The shot took Gauhter in the chest. There was a

moment when the report of the gun was still echoing in the basement, where Gauhter looked stunned, his mouth falling open and his eyes going wide. Then the book he'd been holding slipped from his fingers. He looked down and pressed a hand to the growing red stain on his shirt.

The magic he'd been working with churned, incomplete. I saw the energy start to unravel, growing unstable.

"Rianna, get down," I yelled.

She was still bound to the chair, so there weren't many options for where she could go. She kicked her feet, and the chair teetered before crashing to the side. Even through the gag I heard her scream of pain. It was better than the alternative.

A heartbeat later the unstable spell exploded. Gauhter and Saunders were flung backward, a magical ricochet bouncing through the circle. Fire crawled up both men where the spell struck. Saunders hit the ground. He rolled, screaming, trying to extinguish himself. Gauhter slammed into his own circle. It shattered with a discordant snap of magic, and he screamed as the backlash tore through him. Then he fell silent, still on fire, but not dead yet. I would have felt it if he'd died.

The blast also knocked over the cauldron. It rolled, spilling liquid that glittered in the weak lights and dumping a body onto the ground. It was almost fully formed, though skeletally thin and shimmering with the liquid it had been grown in. Red curls were plastered to a face that looked far too much like Rianna.

I took only a heartbeat to see it roll to a stop, falling still and lifeless, but not dead as it had never been alive. Then I rushed to the real Rianna, ignoring the two burning necromancers—they could fend for themselves.

I didn't have time to be delicate, but pushed the rope binding Rianna into the land of the dead. I pulled her free of the chair as soon as the coarse knots had deteriorated enough to release her.

"We have to get you out of here," I said as I dragged her to her feet. One of her arms hung funny; it had broken when the chair landed on it in the fall.

"And go where, Al?" she asked, rushing to Desmond as soon as she got her legs under her. "There's what, two minutes until sunset? I can't reach Faerie that fast."

No. No, that wasn't acceptable. Why would Derrick have warned me I needed to beat sunset only to have me find Rianna in time to watch her wither and die?

Rianna fell to her knees beside Desmond. He was hurt. Bad. But Desmond was fae. As long as he survived his injures, he would heal. Rianna would die if we didn't get her to Faerie.

Rianna sank her good hand into the fur around Desmond's ear, careful not touch the large bleeding wound on the back of his skull. At her touch, his eyes opened, and he whined around the tape sealing his muzzle.

"We have to get this off you," she said, trying to gently peel back the tape, but her broken arm wasn't doing what she wanted and she couldn't do it one-handed.

"No, we have to go to Faerie, Rianna," I said. The big, doglike fae made a sound deep in his chest that I took as agreement.

Rianna shook her head, looking defeated, but resigned. "There is no time, Al. It's okay. I'm okay with it." She tried to smile at me, but her lips trembled, refusing to hold. "Hey, I found the missing bottle." She laughed, the sound more hysterical and desperate than anything that could pass as humor.

"When I defeated Coleman, you ripped a hole into Faerie. Can't you—"

"No. That was part of Coleman's spell. I can't rip through reality and space like that normally."

Reality. She couldn't rip through reality, but I could. And I could weave it together too, theoretically.

I just needed enough of Faerie to work with.

I looked around. We were minutes from sunset, from the time between when Faerie's influence was thinnest. But it was never gone. Not fully.

So where were the threads of Faerie? The shadow court tied into every shadow, and there were plenty here. The nightmare realm drew power from nightmares. I glanced at the fallen zombies, at least those rotted bodies that hadn't turned to ash. They were definitely the things of nightmares. Belief. Belief was the greatest source of power Faerie had. And there were mortals here. I pulled off the chameleon charm that hid my telltale *Sleagh Maith* glow, letting my true self show.

I couldn't exactly see the threads of Faerie, but I could feel them. They were too thin, too sparse. They couldn't sustain a changeling. Where else could I find the magic of Faerie? Enough to create Faerie where it wasn't?

Fred's words came back to me. *"Look to yourself. What you seek is never far."* Her advice may have sounded like it belonged in a fortune cookie, but . . . I was a true-blooded fae, which meant the magic of Faerie ran through my blood. And through Desmond's and Falin's.

"Desmond, I need your blood," I said, kneeling to dip my hands in the dark puddle around his head.

He didn't growl, so I took that as consent since I

didn't have time to secure anything better. The blood from his wound had stopped flowing some time ago, and the puddle surrounding him was already cooling, congealing. I swiped it across the cement floor, drawing a circle around Rianna. The cooling blood didn't go far, so it was a small circle.

"Al, what are you doing?" she asked, her voice shaking. Even if she'd accepted death as inevitable, she was terrified of it.

I didn't answer but sliced a gash across my palm with my dagger as I yelled, "Falin, I need you."

Falin had Saunders on his stomach, his hands cuffed behind his back. The man was no longer on fire, which was more than he deserved. Falin dropped him as soon as I called and rushed over.

"What—?"

"Add your blood to the circle," I said as I let my own blood dribble over the circle I'd drawn with Desmond's.

Blood magic was dangerous. Illegal. But Falin didn't question me. I'd asked for his help, and he offered it, cutting his palm in the same way I had.

I'd done true blood magic only once before, and it had been only my blood then. Now, with blood from all three of us in the circle I'd drawn, I could feel the three different, potent magics we each possessed. And I could feel the common thread that tied us all together. The thread that was Faerie.

I still couldn't see it. I was used to magic being visual to me, but this wasn't. I could feel it, though, so I closed my eyes. I reached down, lifting the dainty threads of Faerie magic from the blood with my fingers. Then I reached out, gathering everything around me that felt like Faerie, and began knotting them together, piece by piece, strand by strand, like a fishing net. I worked by feel, looping, threading, knotting. As I worked, the strands grew thinner, Faerie magic drawing out of the world, but it caught between my knots, held.

"Duck," I commanded Rianna. I heard the sound of her clothes moving and felt the air shift slightly, but I didn't dare open my eyes and see the emptiness I'd been working with—I didn't want to disbelieve my net of Faerie away.

I tossed the net over her head, pulling it down.

"Get as low as you can," I said, and she must have listened, because I was able to pull the net down to meet the circle of blood and tie the points down.

Then all that was left to do was wait.

We didn't have to wait long. I finished only moments before sunset. Usually I wasn't very aware of sunset. I might feel slightly tired, but it wasn't devastating. This time it hit like a punch to the gut.

The breath rushed out of me and my head spun. I could feel the draw of energy and magic being pulled from my blood to maintain the net of Faerie. The others must have been feeling the same. I heard Falin collapse to his knees beside me, and Desmond whined. I bowed my head, tucking it between my knees as vertigo made the world lurch despite the fact that I was perfectly still. But I didn't open my eyes.

I tried to count heartbeats but couldn't seem to get over three. I wasn't sure how many times I counted to three and then stopped, feeling ill and wondering what number I'd left off on.

Finally the world calmed. I could breathe again. I waited for the vertigo to return, but it was gone. Sunset had come and passed. Faerie magic was reentering the world now that night had arrived. I lifted my head and cautiously opened my eyes, afraid I'd see one of my best friends aged several hundred years inside a bloody circle.

Silent tears ran down Rianna's still young, still-living face. She jumped free of the circle and threw her one good arm around my shoulders, nearly dragging both of us to the ground.

"You did it," she whispered. "You actually did it."

Despite my exhaustion, a smile I couldn't have contained if I'd wanted to claimed my face, and I hugged her back fiercely.

When she finally pulled away, I swayed and pressed a hand against my head. "I don't think I want to do that particular trick again anytime soon, so let's make sure you make it back to Faerie from now on?"

She beamed, studying my face. "But you did more than just save me. Al, you *wove* reality. Normally you just shove it around. You actually wove it together."

I hadn't thought of it that way.

On the other side of the circle Desmond gave out another whine, and Rianna's eyes widened before she whirled around to run to her four-legged companion. I turned to Falin. He'd picked himself off the ground, but he looked shaken. His glamour had snapped, letting the natural glow of his skin show, but it wasn't as strong as it should have been. His soul inside his exhausted body still glowed strong and healthy, though, so I hoped I hadn't done any of us permanent harm.

"You don't look so hot," I told him when he offered me a hand up.

He gave me a pointed look. "You should talk."

Yeah, I bet I was frightful in my half-decayed clothes, grave wind still blowing my hair every which way, not to mention the power drain of what I'd done.

"I should say th—" I started, but Falin pressed his fingers to my lips, stopping me.

"Do not offer me any boon she could use against you." He didn't have to say who *she* was. At the end of the day, he was always the queen's tool.

"You didn't have to do what you did."

"I know." He lifted my hand to his mouth and pressed a quick kiss to my knuckles. "One day I'll ask you for a boon with no debt. Grant it to me."

He said the words like a requested oath, but they held no binding power. I nodded anyway. He turned my hand over and winced.

"We'll need to rebind this."

I frowned at my hand. I thought at first that the blood was from where I'd cut my palm, or perhaps Desmond, but no, it was actively flowing from the shredded skin of my fingers. Touching reality had cost me some flesh.

"Well, I guess that wraps this up," Briar said, climbing to her feet from where she'd been tending to Gauhter's wounds.

He was alive, and apparently would stay that way.

"And I guess I know why Derrick gave me my charm," she said, making a face at the viscera splattered over her jacket and pants. Yeah, without a charm preventing the smell of decay from sinking in, that would never come out.

She leaned down and picked up a bag near Gauhter's workbench. Opening it, she whistled slowly. "I thought your client lost one bottle. There are three in here." One by one, she lifted three ornate bottles out of the bag. One was empty, two were not. "Now for a harder question. What do we do with these?"

"We should release the souls outside the cemetery gate. They'll get stuck if we release them inside," I said, frowning at the bottles. "Then we should smash them." I turned and gave an apologetic nod to Rianna. "I don't think you're getting paid for this case. Those bottles should not continue to exist. Your client is not getting them back."

"Whether or not to smash them will be up to my bosses," Briar said, placing the bottles carefully back into the bag.

"I think it will be up to the FIB." Falin crossed his arms over his chest. "They are stolen fae artifacts."

They stared at each other, stubborn sets to their jaws. Above us, heavy boots crashed on the floor and I heard an officer yell, "Police, we're coming in."

The cavalry had arrived.

Chapter 29

<figure>❦</figure>

It took three days for my sight to return this time. I'd really pushed it not just gazing across planes but shoving zombies through them. It did return, though, to something at least akin to my normal. My hands were a completely different matter.

A week later, they were still a mangled mess and no amount of magic-laced gauze or applied healing charms seemed to speed their recovery. Rianna, in contrast, was on the mend, her no-longer-broken arm already out of a cast. Even Desmond was back to his grumpy self.

Gauhter and both adult Saunderses had been taken into custody. I'd lost track of how many magical artifacts were pulled out of the groundskeeper's house. Some had been reported stolen, but some appeared to have been purchased legally. I guess now we knew what he was doing with the cash from the bank robberies. Gauhter's wife had been transported to the local ICU.

I hadn't heard if she'd survived being relocated, but now that she was no longer behind wards blocking soul collectors from reaching her, I didn't expect she'd be among the living long.

Katie had been tracked down and laid back to rest, as I was calling it. She hadn't really been alive and the thing inside her wasn't human. Without a constant supply of souls to consume, she would have quickly degenerated into the same hungry, rotting dead we'd fought in the basement, so it was a kindness to put her down quickly.

Over four dozen graves had been disturbed in South Cemetery. Less than a quarter of the bodies had been recovered and were waiting to be identified and reinterred. There was no accurate count of how many had been incinerated or deteriorated. At least the bad guys hadn't ended up ashes this time—maybe that would improve John's opinion of me again. But I wasn't holding my breath.

Once my sight had returned, I'd helped Remy and Taylor find their closure. It was sappy and there were a lot of tears and a good bit of human-on-ghost kissing, which was awkward for me, but they were teenagers. In the end, I'd had to cut the session off or they would have tried to go on like that forever. Remy had stayed behind even after Taylor couldn't see or hear him anymore, though she'd kept talking to him, trusting he was there. I wasn't sure where he was now. He could have been found by a collector, or he could still be haunting her. She'd never know the difference. It was sweet and sad at the same time.

Channel Six had retracted their story on me, with Xandra running a short sound clip on how there'd been a miscommunication and I'd actually been working for the police, not a suspect. It hadn't helped Tongues for the Dead. We hadn't had a client call since the story ran. With me pretty much out because of my eyes and hands, Rianna recovering from her own injuries, and the front door needing to be replaced, we'd decided that the firm would close for a holiday. It wasn't going to be a great month, but I'd made more in three days working with Briar than I would have from half a dozen other clients, so we'd make it. We'd open back up in a few weeks, and hopefully by then the smoke would have cleared and we'd get some new clients.

In the meantime, I'd had way too much free time while being unable to actually do anything because of my hands. I'd spent some of it carefully studying the threads of reality in the castle. I only spent a few hours spread over each day doing it, to try to reduce the damage to my eyes, but I needed to learn more about my plane-weaving abilities and what I could do. So far, there hadn't been any huge breakthroughs, but I hadn't given up.

"Alex," a voice said from the center of my previously empty room.

I jumped at the sound, nearly dropping the novel I'd been reading. I looked up at Death's familiar outline, a relieved smile rising to my lips.

It never made it all the way there.

I took one look at his expression, so solemn, so serious, and the smile died before it ever had a chance to reach my mouth. I closed the book, setting it carefully on the coffee table. The bindings on my hands made it difficult, but I dragged it out longer than strictly necessary, avoiding looking back up. When I finally did, Death still stood there, with that same sad expression.

I stood, taking a deep breath. "You came to say good-bye?"

He nodded.

Something in my chest shattered, the jagged edges piercing deep inside me as they fell. My throat was burning, and I tried to swallow the heat back down, knowing that otherwise it would keep heading up, toward my eyes, and I wasn't going to cry. I wasn't.

"I didn't want to just vanish," Death finally said.

It was my turn to nod. And then we both stood there for several heart-wrenching moments, not saying anything. Finally I couldn't take it anymore and I looked away. I walked over to the castle window, gazing out at the magnificent gardens below without seeing them.

"So," I finally said, not even sure if he was still there. "I'll never see you again?"

I felt him fill the space behind me. He placed a hand on my shoulder and leaned his chin on the top of my head. It was friendly, intimate without being sexual. But it was still too much.

I stepped away. He nodded, as if that had been the right thing to do, like maybe he'd regretted touching me as soon as he'd done it but didn't know how to pull away.

"I'll always come when you're in danger. I won't let you disappear into the darkness. That hasn't changed." He looked down at his hands and sighed. It was obvious it took effort for him to look back up, to meet my eyes again. "But this, what we have. Had. It can't continue. Not right now."

"You were my friend before you were my lover," I said, and the world was getting a little hazy, so I knew I was losing my fight against the tears.

He looked at me, and there was true anguish in his face. He shook his head. "I can't be here and watch your heart move on to someone new. Not yet. Maybe not ever."

I didn't promise I would wait for him. I didn't beg him to reconsider. I just nodded.

"So that's that then," I said, hating the throatiness of my voice.

He nodded. He stepped forward like he would kiss me, and part of me wanted him to more than anything in the world. The smart part of me was glad when he vanished instead.

And like that, my oldest and closest friend wasn't anymore.

A knock sounded on my door. Rianna pushed it open without waiting for me to answer.

"Hey, Al, I'm heading down to dinner, want to join?" She paused, frowning at me where I was standing in the center of the room, still staring at the spot where Death had been. "You okay? Did something happen?"

I turned to her and forced the tears back down. "Yeah. Dinner sounds good. I'll be down soon."

I forced a smile I didn't feel. Yet. This castle was full of friends. A family I'd accidentally built around myself. I might not feel the smile yet. And I would grieve the end of this first real relationship. But the smile would be real again. Eventually.

First though, I'd test the garden gnome's theory that the castle bent to my will. Because I wanted ice cream. And cake. And chocolate. Lots of chocolate.

Chocolate could fix anything.

Ready to find
your next great read?

Let us help.

Visit prh.com/nextread